VIOLENT

Book One: Violet's Tales

E. N. Chanting

©2024 E.N. Chanting

Editing and Formatting by J. Tylee Ertel

Cover Design by Ampersand Book Covers

ISBN: 979-8-9893509-7-1 paperback

ISBN: 979-8-9893509-8-8 eBook

CONTENTS

SONG LIST

Shout- Disturbed
Royals- Otep
The Devil's Bleeding Crown- Volbeat
Cemetery- Aviva
The Violence- Asking Alexandria
Sweet But Psycho- Ava Max
Bury a Friend- Billie Eilish
Bulletproof- Five Finger Death Punch
Flaws- Bastille
They're Coming to Take Me Away- Butcher Babies
Mz. Hyde- Halestorm
Coming Undone- Korn
Crazy Train- Ozzy Osbourne
Psycho- Puddle of Mud
Mayhem- Halestorm
Monsters- Ruelle
Pretty, Pretty, Please- P!nk

Dedicated to all of the lost, the broken, and survivors of abuse who wish for a hero to slay the monsters.

FOREWORD

If you haven't read Origin of Violet, her becoming Violet story, please sign-up for my newsletter and receive it free here: https://www.enchantingauthor.com

Violet started out happy, she loved her mother and the man who acted like her father. But her parents betrayed her trust, her love, her innocence, and now, she's out for payback. At just twelve, Violet embarks on a violent path to remove all the monsters from her world. She's good at it and she likes it, slicing into her prey satisfies her dark soul. If you've ever harmed a little girl with long blonde curls and eyes black as coal, you may want to run. F*ck it, that won't help you! If she wants revenge, you're already dead. Fasten your seatbelts, VioleNt is a dark horror RH romance in a duet and a half. Neither volume ends in a cliffhanger, but there may be hangings. Note the trigger warnings and only continue if you feel safe.
Yours truly,
E.N. Chanting, Author

CHAPTER ONE

Someone carried me to my room and put me in bed. I don't remember who. My room is dark and I'm alone. My mom and dad's faces float in my mind. They cannot be dead. They wouldn't leave me. They love me and I love them. This just can't be real; I must be having a nightmare. When I wake, mom will be cooking breakfast while dad reads her funny stories from the internet. I'm going to keep my eyes closed until I wake up safely in my room with mom and dad downstairs. I'm being childish, and I don't care. I want my parents! With my eyes closed I eventually drift off.

I'm awake now. The sun shines brightly through my windows. Oh, thank God everything's fine, I'm safe in my room. Dread fills my stomach. No! It can't be true. Mom and dad kissed me goodbye in the morning just yesterday. They said they love me. They were only going to work! It's not possible to think that they're never coming home.

Oh no! I rush to the toilet just in time as vomit spews from my twisted gut, tears flood my eyes. Plopping onto the floor I sob. I vomited a few more times, then brush my teeth, crying the whole time. I flop onto my bed and hug my pillow while my tears soak it.

The misery I feel consumes my complete being, head, heart, and soul. It manifests in a physical ache that I'm unable to pinpoint. I hiccup between sobs. I've never cried this hard in my life. I never cared about anyone this much. I won't ever make this mistake again. Giving someone your heart means it can be broken. Mine is permanently out of service. I feel my blood leak away as my veins fill with something thicker, darker, and ice cold.

I don't respond when someone knocks on my door. I'm lost in my head... plotting. A plan of action is forming, and it eases my pain. My door opens slowly.

Uncle Randy sticks his head through the threshold, "Hey sweetheart, how're you holding up?"

"I'm fine," I respond in a robotic voice.

"Okay. Why don't you come down and have some breakfast?"

"No thanks."

"Violet, I'm sorry, but I must insist. I need to evaluate how you're really doing. I need to get some food into you in case you need some medication."

My eyes see him for the first time. He looks awful, pale, and shaky. His hair and clothes are disheveled, and dark bags rest beneath his eyes. His face is covered in a five o'clock shadow from yesterday and his eyeballs are bloodshot. I feel a pang of guilt for giving him a hard time. So much for closing off my heart. Apparently, it doesn't apply to people I already love.

"Okay, I'll try to eat." He gives me a weak smile. I force myself to smile back in response and I follow him downstairs.

Krewe is in the kitchen. He looks up when we enter, sympathy showing on every corner of his face. Ugh! I can't deal with pity right now. I force another smile, this one's a little easier to manage.

"Good morning, Violet."

"Morning, Krewe." I don't meet his eyes. I don't want to see the charity.

Uncle Randy asks, "What can I fix you? I found cereal, granola, fruit, and bread. I can make toast."

"Just some yogurt and granola. I'm not feeling up to anything more. Is there coffee?"

"Yeah, I'll make you a coffee. Can you choose your own yogurt and granola?" I nod.

Pulling open the fridge I take out a strawberry yogurt, grab a packet of granola, and a spoon. Then I sat next to Krewe, my lawyer and friend, on a barstool at the kitchen island. Uncle Randy sets a mug in front of me, and the brew in it smells amazing. My stomach growls and I hope that means breakfast will soothe my tummy trouble. Dammit, that's what mom always called it. *Tummy trouble.*

I'm not going down that rabbit hole. I take a deep breath and calm my thoughts, open my yogurt, and dump the granola on top. I stir everything together until it's a satisfying pink color and it looks perfect.

I take a bite, chew, and swallow. My stomach doesn't revolt, and the sky doesn't fall. I take another bite, reevaluating after each one, until I scrape the bottom. A small burp escapes, surprising me, but the relief is acceptable. I guess I'm going to act like a robot now. It seems to be the only way I can make myself function somewhat like a person.

Taking a sip of my coffee I look at Uncle Randy. He's busy scrutinizing me. I see his concerned psychiatrist face is in full control.

I'm going to humor him since it's what will help him get through this. He's not just Uncle Randy because that's how I feel about him. Mom and dad were like his siblings and best friends. He needs something to focus on to help him cope with his loss too. I've been in therapy for a long time. I know all the tricks and tips. I'll let him take care of me to help him...us...get through this.

"Can I ask you a question?" I asked.

"Violet, please, ask me anything. If I don't know the answer, I'll find out. I won't hide anything from you either. So, shoot." Uncle Randy has always been honest with me. It's what I like most about him.

"I honestly didn't hear a word the police said last night. I heard the word accident, and nothing else."

"Okay, what do you want to know?"

"What happened to them?" My eyes feel glassy and my chin wobbles. Uncle Randy clears his throat.

"Ahem, hmm, they were in a car accident. There was a wrong way driver without any lights on. It was raining and they had poor visibility. Without his lights on, they didn't stand a chance." Anger pushes him to ball up his hands, trying to control his emotions.

"The guy was drunk. They took his blood alcohol level, and it was point three-one-oh. Highest I've heard in a while," pipes up Krewe.

"Is he still at the hospital?" Uncle Randy asks.

"What!?! The guy who hit them is alive, how do you know?"

"Yeah, sorry Violet. I read the police reports. He has a crushed sternum, a broken collar bone, a concussion, and a leg that's broken in three places. It happens all the time with drunks. The theory is that they're so relaxed, the impact on their bodies is lessened, so they aren't injured as easily as a sober person." Krewe shrugs at me.

"You know, Uncle Randy, I think you may be right. Maybe I do need some medication. Hearing about this is upsetting me. I feel angry and depressed. Why shouldn't I go join them in heaven, I don't want to be alone?" I stare at him, he knows I'm not suicidal, but he won't take a chance and not evaluate me, which fits my needs perfectly.

"All right Violet. I'll need to take you over to the hospital so we can do some bloodwork and a quick physical before you start a new medication. Will that be, okay?"

"Yeah, of course. I'm going to take a shower and get dressed then we can go. Thank you, Uncle Randy. Thank you, Krewe." I give them each a hug. Uncle Randy cries. I have to escape before I do too.

Once I'm ready to go, I hunt down Uncle Randy. He's in the kitchen leaning over the sink, looking out the window. His phone is pressed to his ear. My mouth snaps closed. I stop and backing up I quietly take a seat at the island behind him.

"Joyce, I don't believe that's up to you. Well...no, I don't know anything about their will." He looks tense and mad, and I can't even see his face.

"Look, until we see their attorney, I don't think we need to discuss any of this. What? Absolutely not! No Joyce, I assure you there'll be no will that names you as Violet's guardian... Fine, yes, fine. Goodbye."

"You're going to break your phone squeezing it like that," I say. Uncle Randy jumps. "Oh! How'd you do that? I didn't hear you come in."

"Of course not, you were on the phone," I laughed.

"How much of that did you hear?"

"Enough to know *Grandmother* is going to be trouble."

"That's putting it nicely. She actually wants custody of you since you're only seventeen. I need to find out from Krewe if you go back to emancipated status or back to childhood or become a ward of the state? I've no idea how any of it works."

"I'm ready to go, whenever you're ready," I grin.

"Give me a couple minutes. I'll be right back." He takes off down the hall, and I can't even look towards my parents' room. It's always been a safe haven for me, but without them, I'm afraid the sorrow will erase all my good memories in that room.

When we get to the hospital, we go straight to Uncle Randy's office in the Psych wing. I'll never forget meeting him for the first time. Dr. Randall Nercy always barged into my room as he knocked. He admitted me for evaluation after a particularly traumatic event. Turned out to be the best thing for me. I made such good friends here. I still can't believe how long I stayed in the ward. It seems like someone else's life.

Uncle Randy gives orders to run the tests on me and the nurses jump into action. Before I know it, he has all my blood sent off to the lab. We're going to hang out while they run my blood STAT. He's going to check on some patients while we wait. I can *feel free to use his computer,*' blah, blah, blah.

As soon as he leaves the room, I switch to the hospital data server. I find one Mr. Raymond Hartley, aged forty-three, assigned to room four-twelve-A, with a concussion, broken sternum, collar bone, and leg. I scribble a quick note.

U.R. -

I went to the cafeteria. Text me when you need me.

Thanks-

V

I know I should text him, but I'd rather have a head start. I make my way to the Baker Wing. The elevator lets me off on the fourth floor. I walk with purpose. Since I know where I'm going it's easy to act like I belong. Taking a quick glance around I take note of where everyone is and what they're doing. I duck into room four-twelve and check bed 'A' and 'B'. There's a sleeping man in bed 'A', the other one is empty. I close the door behind me as I step up to his bed. His leg isn't in a cast yet since the swelling needs to go down. I smirk. That makes it easy. I check the room and find a package of hospital socks in the closet.

I unwrap them and stand next to his head on the side furthest from the door. I stare at his slack face, most certainly drug induced. I reach out and punch his broken leg right in the knee. His head jolts as his mouth opens wide. I shove socks into his open maw before he can scream. His eyes shift to me, fear on his face. I've missed this. I smile wide at the terrified man.

"Hi, ya, Ray. How're you feeling? Oh right, you can't talk, can ya? Let me take a stab at a guess. You're terrified you're gonna choke on those socks, right? You're wishing someone would come in here because your leg hurts like a bitch. Huh? No that's okay, don't answer. You're wondering if I escaped from the psych ward. Believe it or not, I'm not an escapee today. But I am crazy and I'm going to hurt you. I want to *kill* you. But I'm going to make a deal with you."

His eyes get wider. He's trying to get free from where my hand holds the socks in his mouth. I smile brightly and shake my head slowly.

"Ah, ah, ah, Ray-man, you need to listen close, I'm offering you a deal remember?" His head pulls slightly up and down as he tries to nod.

"Good boy Ray-mo. So, here's what's gonna happen... you're going to plead guilty and refuse any and all advice against it. You got that?" I stare at him intently, hoping he sees how deadly serious I am.

"You're also going to give up driving, forever. Do you know why Ray-meo? Because you killed people. You're done. You'll take your punishment and you'll never put anyone in danger again. You feel me? Do you get what I'm saying, Ray-bird? You wanna know why, don't you? I'm sure you're wondering why. Because Ray-lo, I'm going to be watching you. I see that excites you, because your eyes are huge." I smile at his pain. This is fun.

"I'm going to make sure you never hurt anyone again. I'm going to make sure you pay your debt to society. I'm going to personally remove your head if you don't do as I say. You can understand that right? I mean Ray-dar, you killed two people, and you have to go to prison for that, right? I see you understand. Now, do as I say, and you won't have to see me again. But Ray-ban, my man, if you fuck up and drive, or do something to keep you from prison, you'll be seeing me... up close, and personal. You get it. I know you do. So be good." I slapped his cheek a few times. I released his face and quietly exit. Then I go straight to the cafeteria.

Waltzing in like I own the place I purchase a vitamin water and take a seat in a quiet corner. I sip my drink and play a game on my phone. It's an hour before Uncle Randy shows up, and we leave.

"Uncle Randy?"

"Yeah?"

"What's going to happen now?"

"Um... we'll speak to the attorney with Krewe and figure out the legal stuff. Then I'll probably move into your guest room, at least until you're eighteen. Whether you're emancipated or not, your parents would never forgive me if I left you there alone. I'll do everything I can to honor their wishes."

"Me too. I want to honor them. But I mean what happens now, like tomorrow? I've never been to a funeral. I'm lost on what to do next." I wasn't looking forward to this part.

"Oh. Yeah, we're having a funeral, but it's not tomorrow. Your parents left specific instructions and pre-planned everything; it's all arranged. We don't need to do anything. It's going to be the day after tomorrow. The attorney also wants to do a reading of the will, as per their instructions."

"When do we have to do that?"

"Krewe is working with their estate attorney to arrange the reading. I think it'll be tomorrow. He's going to represent you. If you want, we can call him, and you can ask him any questions."

"I'm okay seeing him tomorrow. I don't have questions now but after they read the will, I might have some. Don't you hate how everything just keeps going? I feel like everyone should stop and acknowledge my parents. All of their favorite shops and restaurants should be closed in mourning. Don't you think that would be better? I know it's a good distraction having things to do, but I don't need more. I need a moment where the whole world is silent. Does that make sense?"

"Of course. No matter what, your feelings are your feelings. They don't have to make sense. Although... I know exactly what you mean. It's like my world has stopped spinning, so why is the earth still spinning?"

"Yes. That's it, exactly. Is there a pill for it? I mean feeling this way?"

"I did prescribe two medications for you. One for anxiety and one for depression. I want to start you on the anxiety med first."

"Okay. You're the doctor," I genuinely smile at him. He's the only adult I have left who's like family. He loves me, and I love him. I hope he'll always love me, no matter what. Do uncles give unconditional love?

CHAPTER TWO

My knees bounce under the table. Uncle Randy's on my left, Krewe on my right. I'm between the two people on Earth who want to protect me the most. Krewe's been my attorney since I was twelve. He's not family, like Uncle Randy, but he's the next best thing, a friend.

We're at a conference table in the law offices of De La Hoya, Sanchez, and Cruz. Cesar Cruz is seated across from us. His nose holds up reading glasses and is laughably close to a packet of legal papers. My *grandmother* sits at the end of the table. Her hair is perfectly coifed, face pulled into a caricature of a woman from too many cosmetic procedures. Her brown leather Louis Vuitton bag sits on her linen covered lap. Her perfect red nails tap on the smooth wood top of the table. She's never possessed any patience as long as I've known her.

Mr. Cruz clears his throat and I jump. My eyes shift to him. He's a nice-looking older gentleman, like an aged movie star. His gray hair is slicked back, and he has a strong jaw and a quick smile. His warm brown eyes look at me kindly, and without pity. I appreciate that he's the only person I've seen in two days without pity in his eyes.

"Okay, Miss Henley, I'm ready to begin. Do you have any questions first?"

"No, sir. But please, call me Violet," I grin at him, it's an attempt to show him I'm okay. Of course, I'm not.

"Certainly, Violet, you may call me Cesar."

He looks at Grandmother, "Mrs. Morgan, are you ready to begin?"

"I was ready when I got here, *twenty minutes ago.* Get to it already Cesar." Her equally red lips form a thin line when she purses them at Cesar. It looks like someone has slashed a bloody gash across her face, I smirk. It suits her. I might need to help her with some new style choices, my smirk widens into an evil grin.

"Yes, well, ahem! I'll skip over the introduction. I don't believe there is any dispute over the authenticity of the will?" He glances at grandmother and then Krewe. Neither speak up.

He continues, "In the event of both parents passing away simultaneously, we grant custody of our daughter, Violet Andrea Henley, to our closest friend, Dr. Randall Nercy. He will assist Violet with her finances and property. She will be in control of her inheritance. Violet will make her own decisions and may attend the college of her choice. Dr. Nercy will only assist and advise Violet. Should Dr. Nercy not wish to accept this responsibility, or be unable to accept, custody and advisement will fall to her attorney, Krewe Krowley, Esq. Only until age eighteen. Once Violet reaches the age of majority, she will be solely in control of all assets."

"Wait, does that mean they left everything to a child? A child who isn't even their blood? That's outrageous! I demand that you prove this is what they wanted," Grandmother shouts. Her face is red now, giving her lips a run for their money.

"I assure you, Mrs. Morgan, this is exactly what they wanted. They completed these documents after they adopted Violet, with two witnesses and the will has been certified by the court. You may contest the will, as is your right, but all that will do is tie up a large amount of funds for no reason, and the outcome will remain the same."

"Well! You'll be hearing from my attorney!" She stomps out of the room. Good riddance!

"I apologize, Violet. If your grandmother follows through with her threat, you'll be required to stop spending any monies that don't maintain the property or provide for your direct care. Such as food and electricity. I'm afraid, it may delay your ability to attend college."

My mouth falls open. That selfish bitch is going to interfere with my future just to get her hands on a few bucks.

"Violet, don't worry, I'll pay for school. When your finances get straightened out, you can repay me if you feel you must. But it won't be necessary," Uncle Randy speaks up.

"I'll file for emergency funds for school. I'll also serve her with a cease-and-desist letter. Is there a No Contest Clause in the will, Cesar?" Krewe questions.

"There is, and it's specifically aimed at Mrs. Morgan. They expected trouble from her. However, that won't stop her from filing and freezing up Violet's funds. It completely removes her from inheriting anything if she loses. If she had stayed, she would've found out they left the beach house to her. Mr. and Mrs. Henley believed Violet didn't like that property, so they didn't want her to be stuck selling it. They decided to pacify Mrs. Morgan with it. They hoped it would protect Violet from Mrs. Morgan doing exactly what she's threatened."

"Ugh! That woman... she makes me angry like no one else," Uncle Randy grumbles.

"Don't worry Randy, I'll get it stopped."

"Thanks, Krewe. Uncle Randy, I don't want to take money from you. But I'll take your help with everything else. I don't have a clue how to take care of a house or pay people to do it."

"Do you want me to finish the will, Violet? Or shall I summarize?"

"Thank you, Cesar, but a summary will be fine. I assume you're going to give a copy to Krewe?"

"Yes, absolutely. The will lists all of the assets and accounts as well as property. As I said, the beach house is meant to go to Mrs. Morgan, unless she contests the will and loses, in which case she'll get nothing. You own the house you're currently living in, four apartment buildings, one restaurant, and multiple bank accounts. There are four safe deposit boxes. I have the keys and instructions here. I also have a court certified authorization for you to deliver to each bank, so they'll allow you into the boxes. Please call me if you have any difficulty. Do you wish to know the sum of the accounts?"

"You know what? I'm feeling a little overwhelmed. I'm sure Krewe can explain everything to me later. If you don't need me, I'd like to go."

"I just need you to sign a few papers, and you as well Dr. Nercy."

He presses a button on a little box on the table. The door opens a moment later and a young man walks in holding a stamp and a notebook. He hovers next to Krewe. He has dark hair and looks a little bit tense.

"This is my notary, Frank Chalmers. Frank, this is Violet, Dr. Nercy, and Krewe Krowley, her attorney," he points towards each of us as he names us.

"Pleasure to meet you. Dr. Nercy, and Violet, I'll need to see your identification."

I fish out my driver's license, and Uncle Randy does the same. I handed it to Mr. Chalmers. Krewe hops out of his chair and moves to a seat a few spaces down. Frank sits next to me in Krewe's vacated seat. Cesar hands over some complicated looking documents, and they have tabs where each of us needs to sign. Uncle Randy starts signing the line next to his name, then he hands me each page to sign. I handed them off to Frank. He stamps each one and signs them and logs each one in his notebook. We have an assembly line going.

"The papers you're signing just acknowledge you've been informed of what the will says. You accept responsibility for Violet, Dr. Nercy, and for you Violet the ownership of everything is officially changed. Once these affidavits are filed all of the titles of ownership will be in your name, Violet, with Dr. Nercy having a trustee role. I'll have copies for you Krewe.

"Violet, I wanted to say that your parents were lovely people and they loved you very much. They came to me as soon as they took you into foster care. When they adopted you, they reconfirmed that you would be provided for and cared for to the best of their ability. Whenever their wealth increased, they would check with me and make sure everything would be yours if anything were to happen. I know it's little consolation, and you must miss them very much. However, I hope you know they loved you more than anything in the world, and they never wanted you to be in this situation. They also had the utmost faith in Dr. Nercy. I believe he'll always look out for your best interests. If you need anything at all or if you have any questions, please contact me any time. Krewe will be on top of this situation with your grandmother, try not to be stressed about her."

"Thank you, Cesar. You've been very kind, and I appreciate your words. I agree that I'm in good hands with Uncle Randy and Krewe." I offer the room a small smile. Uncle Randy puts his arm over my shoulders and gives me a squeeze.

After we sign everything and thank Cesar and Frank, we say goodbye. Krewe stays behind to wait for the signed copies of everything. We went home and I took some anxiety medication and head to my room. It was only a few hours, but it exhausted me. The emotions and grandmother are a lot. I just need some peace and quiet, and maybe a nap.

The funeral is tomorrow, and I've picked out a plain black dress. It's a sheath of silk. It's sleeveless and hangs straight. I like it because it has pockets. I think everything should have pockets. Feeling unsafe for the first time in probably five years, I secure my pocketknife under my pillow and coil on my bed to try to take a nap.

Sometime later, my phone chimes. I resurface not sure if I actually slept or not. It's a text message from my best friend, Harmony.

Harm: Hi babe, how're u holding up?

Me: I'm okay, resting.

Harm: I think Max wants to see u but he's afraid to bother u while ur dealing with all of this.

Me: I'm not up for company today. Please tell him I'm sorry. I just need to be alone right now.

Harm: I get it. He'll understand. Boy loves u!

Me: I know. Thanks Harm, I'll see you tomorrow at the church, okay?

Harm: of course! Mike probably gone to drive me and Max.

*Harm: *going*

Me: good. See you tomorrow. Goodnight

Harm: Goodnight doll

I'll never get back to sleep. I gather some pajamas and take a shower. I missed lunch and my stomach is protesting out loud, I head to the kitchen and raid the fridge. I love Uncle Randy so much. He left me a sandwich covered in plastic wrap, with a note:

V- This sandwich is for you. Wheat bread, no mustard. I remembered. I had to run home and take care of a few things. I'm bringing more clothes and other items so I can stay in the guest room long term.

Call me if you need anything. I should be back before 6 p.m.

XO- UR

Taking a huge bite out of my sandwich, I dug through the pantry looking for some chips. I find salt and vinegar, Dad's favorite. Why do the simplest tasks keep leading me to the most painful memories? The ache in my chest flares. I never knew grief could be so physical. A breath leaves me as a sigh.

I carry my dad's chips to my sandwich on the island, get a root beer from the fridge, and reclaim my seat. Opening the chip bag, I take a deep sniff. The pungent scent smells wonderful. I can see dad sitting next to me with a handful of chips. He's teasing Mom and we're all laughing. It hurts so much worse when I remember the happy times. The pang of loss once again renewed, unfurls in my gut like the leathery wings of a bat at sunset. They stretch and flutter across my insides. My eyes flutter as well, blinking back at the liquid pooling there.

I'm missing our dog too. He's been gone for over a year, our sweet, Copper. He was the best dog for hugging. He loved to snuggle in for a good long hug. Mom and dad decided not to adopt another pet since I was leaving for college in a year. They aren't...I mean *weren't*, home enough to have a new dog. But I assumed they would probably adopt a pet of some furry variety once I left for school. They would be having empty nest feelings, and I could see them getting a fur baby to fill the void. I wish Copper was here, but I'm glad he doesn't have to suffer through their loss with me.

When I finish my sandwich, I'm still hungry. I dig out the chocolate ice cream. Thankfully it's my favorite and no-one else's. I found the biggest metal spoon we have and go into the den. Squeezing the buttons on the remote as I plop onto the sofa, I search for something mind numbing on TV. Perfect, some random reality show is already in full swing. I shovel ice cream into my mouth until I scrape the bottom of the cardboard container, as I watch the mindless scripted reality show and brood.

I had my second dose of anxiety medication before we went to the lawyer's office and another when I got home. It hasn't started helping yet; that will take weeks. I have a sleeping pill prescription that I hate, but since the funeral isn't until the afternoon, I'll risk it tonight. It sucks because I know I'll feel like a zombie the next day, but motionless and dreamless rest sounds perfect. Nothing will soothe my aching soul better than a night of deep sleep.

Uncle Randy makes a bunch of noise when he arrives. He drags in a wheeled suitcase, has a duffle slung over his chest, and arms full of straps to various bags and satchels. I know one of them contains his laptop, I don't have a clue about the rest.

"Is there anything left at your house?" I ask.

"Don't be a smartass Violet," he chuckles.

"Is there more outside?"

"No, this is everything. I ordered groceries, I didn't have time to shop. They should be here any minute. If you would keep an eye out for the delivery, and let them in, that would be great, thank you. I'm going to put all this stuff away."

"Yeah, I got it." He drags his suitcase down the hall as the doorbell rings.

"That's them, I've got it under control," I announce to his back. He grunts a response. I sprint to the door and fling it open expectantly.

An older man stares at me, his hands filled with grocery bags as he asks, "Where you want 'em Miss?"

"Follow me, you can put them on the kitchen island."

He walks silently behind me. Not solely for lack of talking, but his movements and footsteps are silent, it's weird. I almost expect to turn around and find the kitchen empty. He's there when I walk to the other side of the island. Something about him has my hair standing on end. I wave my arm at the island, as if I'm displaying a game show prize. While he places the bags on the smooth granite, I scrutinize him closely. He has tattoos peeking from the cuffs of his shirt. His small brown eyes are intelligent, cataloguing the room. He lifts his eyes to mine and dissects me. It feels like a physical touch, I don't like it, and I don't like him.

"Is that everything?"

"No, Miss, one more trip," he nods respectfully which is at odds with all of my instincts.

I follow him to the door and watch as he collects six more bags from the trunk of his nondescript, dark, sedan. It looks like the majority of cars on the road. The tint on the windows is darker than is legal, and that might get him noticed by law enforcement, but usually it's a secondary citation. I studied so much and had in-depth chats with Krewe about what to do and not to do to avoid tickets when I was getting my driver's license. Unfortunately, my brain is clogged with too much useless road knowledge.

He notices me watching him and rather than show any embarrassment, he smirks. He noiselessly passes me and makes his way back to the kitchen. He's likely in his early sixties, his hair is streaked with gray, and he looks sturdy. After he places the bags next to the others, he eyes the room and me. His observation slows on my body, and I've had enough.

"Okay! Thank you, this way," I announce, and my game show arms reappear. I wave him towards the door. I want him out of my house.

As he crosses the threshold, he gives me a two-finger salute and completes his visit with a nod. I make note of his license plate when he drives away. Something about him is not sitting right with me.

Chapter Three

My feet are sweating in my shoes. I feel so uncomfortable seated between Uncle Randy and Grandmother. My parent's coffins are in front of me. I can't picture them lifeless, without laughter animating their eyes. They loved me so much, more than I deserved. I counted on that love. I knew they would do anything for me, be there when I needed support, hold me when I was scared or lonely. I think I've reached the angry phase of grief. I want to rip the arms and legs off the asshole who hit them. Maybe I should've just killed him.

Grandmother pokes me in the ribs with her elbow, again. Talk about someone I'd like to injure. I swear if she pokes me one more time, she's going to get a punch in the throat. I've had it with her. *Please, God, if you can hear me, I know I'm not your favorite person, but please don't let her poke me anymore. I don't want to kill her in church, with witnesses.*

"Violet, sit up straight! You're embarrassing me slouched over like that. What's wrong with you? You have to behave appropriately in public. Honestly, I don't know what my daughter was thinking," she whisper-shouts at me.

My hands clench into fists. She's on my last nerve. Uncle Randy grasps my hand and gives me the barest shake of his head. He can still read my mind. He knows I'm thinking about hurting Grandmother. I smirk at him. He gives my hand a soft squeeze. He lays it gently on my knee and pats it once. He does this without turning his head towards me at all.

Thank you, God, for letting me keep Uncle Randy. Please don't ever take him from me. My stomach twists at the thought. I've been avoiding tears but thinking of losing Uncle Randy has me blinking rapidly, and tears pool in my eyes anyways.

I listen to the Reverend. "Though we cannot know why our Lord has called home our brother and sister, we must turn to Him and accept His guidance, and blessings. At this time, if there is anyone who would like to say a few words, please come forward." Grandmother shifts like she's going to stand up. Uncle Randy beats her to it, and he moves up to the podium. The Reverend relinquishes his post. Uncle Randy clears his throat. He smiles at me then looks down and a solemn look overtakes his kind face.

"I'm not sure where to start. I've known Xander and Emmy for many years. Xander and I met when we started college and when Emmy came into the picture, she fit right in. They were like my brother and sister, my family. When I met Violet, I knew she would benefit from knowing Xander and Emmy. I had no way of knowing how quickly they would fall in love with her. I was pleasantly surprised when Violet loved them back." I could feel Grandmother shift in agitation when he mentioned me.

"One of the best days of my life was the day they became parents, by adopting Violet. I never prepared myself for this tragic possibility. I don't know why this happened to them, and us...

but Violet, I do know how much your parents love you. You're their whole world. They didn't make any decisions without your well-being at the forefront of their minds. You're their daughter in every way that counts. I promised them that I'd always be here for you Violet, that I'd take care of you. I'm going to take care of you, and I'll always be here for you. Yes, I wish to honor your parents, Violet, you're an amazing young woman. I'll do everything in my power to protect you and guide you into the successful life I know lies ahead for you. Thank you."

Tears overflow my eyes. I sniffle and when Uncle Randy comes back to his seat, I engulf him in my arms and crush him with all my strength. He hugs me back and I feel his tears drip onto my cheek. We must be quite the sight; Grandmother is probably disgusted.

"I love you Uncle Randy. Thank you, for everything."

"I love you too, Violet. You are, for all intents and purposes, my kid now. I'll always be here for you. I don't care if I get married or have some biological kids, you'll always be my first kid. I want to give you everything I can to help you achieve the life you should've always had; a good life."

"You're the best, Uncle Randy. Thank you."

"Oh please! That's enough already. You're embarrassing our family and the memory of my daughter with your disgusting display. It's bad enough everyone knows you two are shacking up together, do you have to declare your love in public?" Grandmother officially pushed the boundaries.

"What the fuck is wrong with you?" I shouted.

"Violet, calm down, I'll deal with Joyce, just sit down, please." Uncle Randy steps between me and Grandmother. He watches me stiffly sit back into my seat. I narrow my eyes to the hateful shrew.

Seriously? What the fuck is she saying? That I have some kind of sexual relationship with my uncle, my doctor? He's twice my age, granted he's very nice looking, but he's like a father to me. A real father, who gives me unconditional love, not just a guy who pays the bills. He's a wonderful person who saw something in me, despite my tendency for violence. He recommended his very best friends meet me and possibly foster me. He couldn't have known how well we'd get along and they'd adopt me.

Why? Why'd they have to die? Ugh, I just keep going around in circles. One minute, I'm remembering their love for me, and how much fun we had together, then it's right back into a pit of grief that seems bottomless and without escape. Harmony hands me a tissue over my shoulder. I give her a grateful, watery smile.

She smiles back, nodding in understanding. She hates Grandmother too. She brought Mike, her boyfriend, and Max, who's mine, I think. I haven't really spoken to him since my parents died. He tried to help when it first happened, but I mostly ignored him. I wasn't able to form words through my despair. He's watching me, his face is neutral. I know he loves me. He's been a great friend and a fine boyfriend. I've been the difficult and overly high maintenance one half of our relationship. I don't see a light at the end of the tunnel for my emotional issues. I'm going to have to let him go. I can't keep him trapped with me when I'm not emotionally available and may never be. I sigh sadly. He frowns, and I think he can read my mind too.

"Joyce, you need to sit your ass back in your seat and close your mouth. If you say one more lie to upset Violet, I'll have you removed," Uncle Randy growls at Grandmother. Her face pales and she snaps her lips together, her nose is scrunched in disgust.

I chuckled silently, *way to go Uncle Randy!* I focus back on the Reverend. I'm ready for this to be over.

CHAPTER FOUR

After the service everyone gathers at my house.

My empty, *lonely* house.

"How're you holding up?" Max asks me. He looks nervous.

"I've been better." I shuffle my feet, feeling bad about this, but it's unavoidable. "Listen, Max, I don't think I can be in a relationship right now. I'll always love you. You've been so kind and patient with me. But I'm a mess. I don't know what's happening with school, I'm emotionally locked in a box, I'm numb... and I can't be the other half of a couple right now. I don't know what's going to happen or where I'm going. I can't leave you hanging in the wind while I figure it out. I love you too much for that. Please understand."

"Well shit, Violet. You aren't really giving me any say in this are you? I love you, and I want to help you get through this. I understand that you're hurt, angry, and confused. But please, I'm begging you, don't push me away." He reaches out to take my hand, I pull it away and his face falls.

"It's not just about losing my parents. I'm struggling in an internal battle with my demons. I don't know if I'll ever be capable of intimacy, physical or otherwise. Max, I can't drag you through my mess. You're one of the best people I've ever known. I've loved being your girlfriend, but I just can't do it anymore. I'm sorry." I flee from the room rushing up the stairs and close myself in my room.

I fall onto my bed with tears pouring from my eyes, and it feels like my heart is being ripped from my body once again. I cuddled with the stuffed horse Max gave me for graduation. I stifle my sobs with its fuzzy purple fabric as I drool and cry into its soft side. I let myself cry for a long time, and when I run out of tears, my face is tight from them drying on my skin. My throat is scratchy, my nose is stuffy, and I feel like I've been run over by a truck. I steel my heart, wrap it in chains closed with a sturdy lock, then I bury it in the deepest part of me, vowing to never let anyone touch it again.

When I emerge from my bed, with its soft purple covers, I'm a new version of Violet. There's no longer a shred of the happy child I was just a few days ago. I'm hard, cold, and unfeeling now. I'll never allow my heart to be broken again. I'm ready to fight. I'm on a new mission in my life. All of the monsters are going to pay, and I'm personally going to collect.

I change into yoga pants and a sports bra, then I spend the next two hours punching and kicking everything in our home gym. Uncle Randy sticks his head in when he sees me working hard, and he leaves with a grim look on his face. I don't want to hurt him, he's my only family now, but nothing will change my mind.

Dripping with sweat, I turn off the music, and The Pretty Reckless fades away. I grab a towel and wipe my face and neck, then I chug my water bottle. While I was working all of my muscles, I was plotting with my biggest one. With plans forming in my head, I'm ready to move forward. I ran up the stairs and take a shower.

I collect some boxes and fill them with my childhood memories. I pack up everything, including the beautiful purple linens my mother bought for me. I ditch my bright clothing, opting to keep only the dark items. They match my eyes, and now my heart. Going back to work is difficult and I decided to put in my notice. I can't be kind to strangers and provide them with friendly service. I was going to quit when school started anyway, and my boss is understanding.

Access to my inheritance is limited by my grandmother. She filed every injunction she could think of, and it infuriated my uncle and my attorney. I don't care, they can sell everything and give her all the money. The greedy bitch can have it. I still want to go to school because my parents really wanted me to have a college education. I don't want to smite their memory and skip it, but my priorities and plans have changed. I'm still going to study computer science. I want to learn anything and everything that will help me hunt down monsters. But I no longer care about any type of altruism or helping anyone. The monsters will find justice in my hands, not mercy. If paying for their crimes helps their victims, I'm good with that.

I thought I might need to take Uncle Randy up on his tuition offer, but the judge is allowing me the funds for school. Nobody knows about the money my parents left me in cash. I found it in the safe in dad's home office. He and mom showed me how to access it years ago. I'm going to use the cash for the things I need to complete my plan. They wanted me to have it for whatever I needed if anything ever happened to them. Honestly, I think they worried grandmother would be a big problem if they died before she did. They knew her well.

I registered for the school here in town, Henry Plant University. I graduated with what equates to an AA degree from high school, so I'm going to be starting college in what is essentially my junior year. I've already finished all of the required courses, and I can jump right into my concentration. It's a pretty small school, the class sizes are small, and the campus is as well. I like it. All of my friends are going to Tallahassee or out of state. I'm sure Max will do great and with a large campus full of coeds. I know he'll forget about me in no time.

Harmony and Mike are in their senior year of college, and they'll probably get married soon and live happily ever after. I'm happy for them, but we aren't quite as close as we once were. They're a couple years older than me and further along in life as a result. I'll never have another a friend like Harmony, and she'll always be my best friend, but I need to keep my distance for her safety. I'll be her friend for life. I'll never disappear from her world completely.

Colby's still my hacking buddy. He's inside the psych unit more often than not and his condition has only gotten worse as time goes on. He lives in the pool house on his parent's property when he's released. They don't know what to make of him. I think they're afraid of him. They let him do whatever he wants, which is usually eat pizza and play video games. They have more money than God as the saying goes, and he doesn't need to ever work a day in his life. Although, he has designed a few video games that he sold and can probably support himself with the profits. We never talk about money. I don't care about it. We play video games and compete against each other to hack the un-hackable.

We also combine forces to fuck with bad guys, and the monsters of the world. He loves to steal their money and donate it to charities. I just want them to burn. I like to expose their disgusting activities. You'd be shocked to learn how many pedophiles are supposedly upstanding businessmen who're married with families. It's disgusting. I like to plaster their dastardly deeds all over their work servers or their wife's accounts. I share with the feds anonymously too. I don't always watch how things play out for them, but I've seen a few get sentenced to long visits in the state penitentiary. It's a good feeling, but nothing feels as good as hands on revenge.

Colby goes by RobNdaHood, as his handle online, and mine's VioleNt1. There are some people beginning to notice our efforts, so we have to be extremely careful and cover our tracks. Honestly, I'm not worried, I don't do anything illegal... online. I have lots of very violent, illegal activities planned in person, though. I'm going to begin setting my plans into action.

The first thing I need to do is move into my own place. I can't live with Uncle Randy while I embark on my revenge. It won't be safe for him. He plans to move back into his own place when I leave for college anyway. I want to sell this house or give it to my bitch grandmother. I want to live alone, and I want to be able to come and go without anyone watching.

My parents prepared me for life on my own. They taught me how to make good financial decisions, how to invest wisely, and how to care for a home and myself. I think I forgot that when they first died, and I was faced with our family home without them. I just didn't want to be there without my parents, and it was overwhelming.

Now I feel ready for my own domain. I need a fairly large space that'll offer privacy if I need to bring anyone home to suffer my vengeance long term. From the house I'm only bringing a few family photos, my dark clothing, computer, books, a few pots, pans, dishes, and the cash they hid for me.

My mother has, dammit, had some beautiful jewelry, but I have no interest in any of it. Uncle Randy can have it or sell it. I'll keep my parent's wedding bands, nothing more. They didn't collect things or have any particularly meaningful memorabilia. But there's a motorcycle in the garage and my SUV that I want to keep. There's some MMA equipment I'll take and some hiking and hunting gear. My parents never killed any animals. They enjoyed the quiet nature you can observe while waiting for the game to cross your sights. They also enjoyed target practice. I'll keep their bows, arrows, rifles, nine-millimeter pistols, and hunting knives. I can foresee many uses for hunting items.

I need to tell Uncle Randy that I'm moving out and going to HPU. He's going to be disappointed. I hope he can understand my reasons. Not that I'm going to tell him all of them.

Chapter Five

"Why did you decide to stay here if you wanted to move out?" Uncle Randy asked.

"I broke things off with Max. I decided I don't want to go to State with him and my other friends. I want to stay in town and attend HPU, for several reasons. It's less expensive and it has a great computer program. I don't want to be away from you, and it's just what I want to do. Maybe be close to my parent's memories, you know?"

"Okay. But then why move out? Why not stay here, with me, and the memories?"

"You already made arrangements to move back to your place. You can't have your life disrupted by staying in this house with me. I don't want to stay in this house without my parents. The memories here are too painful. I'm sorry if I'm not making a lot of sense, I just know this is what's right for me. I'll be in town. We can have weekly dinners if you want. I'll be able to see you for therapy if I need to. Please support me on this Uncle Randy, I need you to be on my side." Tears begin to fill my eyes; his face falls as he rushes to hug me. We stand there, holding onto each other, silently crying. He's going to cave. I can tell by his hug. I hope he stays cool when he finds out I spent this morning online finding a place.

He sniffles and says, "Okay Violet, I understand. You can move into your own place, and I'll move back into mine. I'm going to hold you to weekly dinners at a minimum. You also have to promise you'll tell me if you have any trouble with anything. I'm helping you move, and I want to make sure your place is safe. All right?"

"Deal. I found a place already. I put a deposit on it to hold it. It's a great place, close to campus and shops where I can get a job. It's not the best area, but it's not bad. I'll put in a security system with cameras and everything."

"I should've known... you always were very mature. After the lessons your parents taught you, I'm not surprised you've got everything planned out and taken care of already. Where is it?"

"It's a warehouse loft type place off Broadway and Second. I can pull right inside the building, so you won't have to worry about me coming home late. There's a twenty-four-hour store on the corner and it's not far from the fire station. I'll even be able to walk to school if I need to, since it's only about a half mile from campus."

"I see you've looked into all the amenities that'll make me feel better about this. Let's have some breakfast and talk about this some more. I'll have Krewe check over the lease for you. I'll help you get the security system installed before you move in. We should probably make a list of things you're going to need. A vacuum cleaner for instance, and linens, dishes... that kind of stuff. There's no reason you can't take what you need from here." I don't tell him I plan to buy it.

"Good point. I didn't think about a vacuum cleaner. What do you want for breakfast? I can make French toast." I grabbed a pan from the cupboard.

"That sounds perfect." We spend the rest of the morning going over all the things I'll need and collecting what's available in the house. It'll probably take a few trips to move me, something I didn't anticipate initially. I'm glad Uncle Randy's on board. He's always been supportive.

When we have everything loaded into my new place, I feel accomplished. Just one last trip to pick up the motorcycle. All of my childhood stuff will remain in boxes, but I have plenty of room for it here. I have a gym area where my MMA gear will live, and some gym equipment I ended up taking from the house. There's only one bedroom and a bathroom. The rest of the apartment is an open area with my desk in one spot and there's a kitchen along the wall. The rest is my living room, though I have no plans to use it.

I picked up a small table and chairs for the kitchen. Uncle Randy wants to get me a sofa or take one from the house, but I don't need it. I'll be in my computer chair if I'm doing anything other than cooking or eating. The warehouse side has a huge open area where I'll park, and the gym is in the corner. There are a few rooms off the open area that are beneath the apartment, and I'll use them for storage until I need one for some other activities.

The apartment only has one window facing the outside, it's in the bedroom. The other windows overlook the warehouse. Vaultech came to install the security system. I have exterior cameras facing each direction including three in the alley. Two point at the exit and entrances to the alley and the third is pointed at the garage style overhead door. There's also a regular sized entry next to the big one. It has a reinforced steel door with a serious locking mechanism. It has a peephole and a doorbell camera. There're two interior cameras covering the open warehouse area, and another covers the stairs to the apartment. There's also a heavy-duty door in the apartment with another doorbell camera and a peephole. Nobody'll be able to sneak up on me. I teased Uncle Randy that he'll never be able to try to have a surprise inspection at my place.

He's driving me back to the house and we'll say our good-byes there. I'll never live in my parents' home again. I'm not sad about it, all of the memories will live forever in my head. We talked about listing it for sale but with Grandmother's lawsuit, it may be problematic. For now, I'm just going to hold onto it. We hired some services to maintain it, lawn, interior cleaning, and a maintenance contract service for any necessary repairs.

I walk the bike outside and close the garage behind me. Uncle Randy watches me and I can't tell what he's thinking at this moment. I smile at him and get closer for a hug.

He places his hands on my shoulders and says, "I'm proud of you Violet. You're smart and brave after all you've been through., You're still here and ready to fight through whatever gets thrown at you. You're an amazing woman. I know you'll do incredible things. All right, give me a hug."

I chuckle, as he has no clue what incredible things I'll do. I love this guy, and in all honesty, he's the only family I have left. My birthday is rapidly approaching, and I'll be a legal adult. I could've fought for my emancipation, but being so close to eighteen I didn't see any reason for it. He'll be my uncle forever as long as I'm concerned. I return his squeeze and smile.

He kisses the top of my head, "You'll text when you get there?"

"Promise."

"You'll call me if anything happens, or you get scared?"

"I will."

"You need any money? Or anything else?"

"I need my most favorite uncle to remember he already stuffed my refrigerator with groceries, that he's checked over every inch of my place and made sure it's safe, and that I'm just about an adult and I'll be fine," I beam at him with my brightest grin.

"Okay, okay, point taken. Please don't forget to text or I'll be at your door. I love you, young lady. Make me proud."

"I love you too. Bye, Uncle Randy."

"Bye, sweetheart."

Chapter Six

A half hour later, after I put the bike to bed, then I message my uncle as promised.

Me: I'm safe. Bike in the warehouse, all doors locked, alarm engaged.

Uncle Randy: Thank you. Have a good night. I'm here if you need me.

Me: I know, love you!

Uncle Randy: love you too.

Once I've pacified my protective uncle, I put the sheets on my bed and put away my clothes and toiletries. By the time I'm finished my stomach is growling. I slap together a sandwich and begin hooking up my computer components. I paid the Vaultech guys extra to install dedicated fiber cabling for me. My set up will be completely protected from prying eyes. I'm going to have Colby test it and see how long it takes him to get in. I've been writing my own security protocols for a couple years. I can be virtually untraceable, and with a bouncing VPN, it'll look like I'm all over the world every thirty seconds. Colby will find any holes and then we'll work together to plug them.

Once everything is connected and loaded, I take a shower and get ready for bed. Once I crawl under the covers, I realize I'm having zero anxiety about being alone. I think about my plans for tomorrow and before I know it, the sun is shining through my only window.

I wake up feeling rested and I'm ready to begin working on my plans. The first thing is to launch my program. It's going to scour the dark web for specific monsters, the ones I owe some serious payback to. If I catch any unknowns on my web, I'll deal with them swiftly. The monsters I know are going to suffer slowly for as long as they live. Which may not be all that long.

After I get my *Comet* program launched, I get dressed and ready to head out for my errands. I have to take the SUV so I can carry everything I need. The first stop is at my new school to purchase my books and sign any last-minute paperwork.

When I return with my new books, a few black clothes, and the custom holsters and knife sheaths I ordered from a craftsman, I take a walk to the twenty-four-hour market. I'm looking to get a feel for my new neighborhood. I figure a market like this sees the worst of my small corner of town.

A bell jingles as I cross the threshold. The clerk is a middle-aged man with disheveled greasy dark hair and sweaty looking skin. He looks me over and returns to whatever he's doing behind the wall of glass. I walk all of the aisles and check out the products on every shelf. I feel slightly hormonal, so I choose a chocolate bar with something crunchy inside. I also picked up a tech magazine, it has an article about the dark web. Seems ironic that I'm buying a paper magazine about the web written by a bunch of computer geeks.

I noticed a slushy machine and it gives me a flashback to a memory of my mom. We attended an MMA match in a hot gym, and afterwards we stopped for slushies. I had grape and she had blue raspberry. Feeling the ache in my chest from losing her, I fill a cup with the frozen blue treat. I bring my items to the front and watch the clerk cautiously.

Before he finishes my transaction, the bell rings again and again. Three men enter, they look to be in their early to mid twenties and are dressed in the fluorescent vests of construction workers. One of them drops something and it slides across the floor and comes to a stop against my scuffed army boot. When I look down, I see it's his phone.

His cheeks turn pink as he apologizes to me, "Sorry about that."

"No worries," my lips curving into the smallest grin.

He bends and collects his phone. He continues to offer me his embarrassed smile. I turned my attention back to my business with the cashier. After I collect my change, pocket it, my candy, and scoop up my cold cup.

"Hey gorgeous, where're you off to?" The clumsy guy's older dark-haired friend asks as I walk towards the door.

I ignore him and push open the door to escape. I pass a large cabbed pickup truck on my way down the sidewalk. A man in the driver's seat watches me. When I get to the corner of the store's walkway he whistles. I ignore it assuming it has nothing to do with me. I hear a metal door squeak open and the driver steps in front of me, blocking my path. I roll my eyes and look at his face. He's a nice-looking guy, probably around twenty-two or so. I stare into his eyes, daring him to say something to me. He swallows and takes me up on my challenge.

"Where ya headed pretty girl?"

"Why?"

"Why? Lots of reasons," he smiles like he's made a profound declaration.

"Like what?" I goad.

"Well, for one, I don't want you to leave. I'm not done looking at you with your beautiful hair and smokin' hot body."

"Too bad," I respond and shift to move past him.

"Aw, come on. Talk to me! Do you live around here?"

"That's none of your business." Again, I move to walk past him.

"Do you need a ride?"

"No."

"Could I get your number?"

"No."

"Please. You gotta gimme something."

"Actually, I don't." Becoming exasperated, I roll my eyes again.

"Fair enough. How 'bout you just tell me your name?"

"No. I have to go." This time I push past him and continue walking.

"You're killing me pretty girl. *Hi.* I'm Jackson, what's your name?" He follows me, keeping next to me as I ignore him. I look where I'm going and not at him. He turns so he's walking backwards in front of me.

"How about I guess your name? If I guess right, will you tell me?"

"No."

"Vanessa? Tiffany? Oh, I know, Brittany!" He walks into a sign and smacks his head, "Ow!" I let out a small chuckle and try to cover it up with a cough. But I'm not having any luck keeping the smile off my face.

"I saw that. You smiled, granted it took me walking into a post, but I'll take it." He gives me a huge grin.

"Look, I'm sorry you weren't looking where you're going and walked into a sign. But I'm not interested; please quit bugging me."

"Wow. You really know how to wound a guy."

"You've no idea. Now, if you'll please excuse me, I need to go." I'm polite, but firm. I walk around him and continue on my way. Barely two steps later, someone grabs my arm and spins me around. Without any forethought, I react by punching them.

He grabs the left side of his very red face and stares at me with his mouth hanging open. My own eyes are wide, and my mouth also falls open. It's not the good-looking guy who was talking to me, it's the darkhaired construction worker I ignored from inside the shop.

"You fucking bitch! What the *fuck* is wrong with you?"

Regaining my composure, I reply, "Lots of things. Hasn't anyone ever taught you not to sneak up on someone and grab them?"

"You better fucking apologize right fucking now, you cunt!"

"Look, I don't want to hurt you. So just run along and leave me the hell alone."

He starts laughing; a menacing sound, "You're going to hurt *me?* That's rich." He looks back at his three friends all staring in shock. The cute one who lost his phone inside looks embarrassed. The other good-looking one, Jackson, looks dumbfounded. The third one has no emotion at all beyond shock.

"Come on Dave, leave her alone. We gotta get back to work," Jackson says.

Dave doesn't listen to his friend, and he gets right up in my face. I really hate that name. Every Dave I've ever met was an asshole.

His finger pokes my chest with each word as he says, "Fuck no! This bitch is going to apologize or she's going to be sorry. I'm waiting, you stuck up whore."

I look at his finger, poked into my chest, then back at his angry face. "Remove your finger, or you'll be the one who's sorry."

Before anyone can do anything to stop him, his hand grabs my throat, knocking the frozen treat from my hand. His face twists into a snarling sneer as he applies pressure to my delicate trachea. Feeling that my life is threatened, I react on instinct alone. My hands come up and break his hold on me, and my fist meets his nose in a hard punch causing his honker to burst with a gush of blood. My foot meets his balls next, and he doubles over with a woosh of breath leaving his lungs. Then I smash my entwined fists onto his trapezius muscle at the base of his neck, causing him to collapse on the ground, face first.

His buddies are stunned silent with their jaws flapping in the wind. I turn on my heels and resume my journey. After just a moment I hear heavy footsteps running towards me from behind. I spin, ready to knock out the next asshole who touches me. It's Jackson, the good-looking one.

He raises his hands in the air in surrender, with a pleading look on his face, he says, "Holy shit, you're incredible! I'm so sorry Dave is such an asshole, and I'm sorry for what he said and what he did. He deserved exactly what he got. You're...you're an amazingly beautiful badass!"

"May I go now?"

"Yeah, of course. I really am very sorry. Please don't think the rest of us are like him."

"Okay. Goodbye, Jackson."

"Yeah, okay, goodbye...?"

"Violet."

Chapter Seven

I'm careful to make sure they aren't following me, and when I approach my warehouse they're nowhere in sight. Out of the corner of my eye I spot a movement in the alley. It seems to be a big rat. I close in for a closer look and watch as a tiny gray kitten makes its way from one trash can to another, dodging quickly between them for shelter. When it crawls under a piece of newspaper, I pick it up. The little ball of fur begins to screech out in distress. I look into its tiny green eyes and see the fear. I search for any more of them or their mother.

"Aww, you poor baby. Are you alone? You'll never make it out here by yourself. At least not until you're bigger. You look too much like a snack right now."

Meow, meow, meow.

"I get it. It's no fun being alone... an orphan. Want to come inside?

I don't have any kitty food, but I've got some milk and a can of tuna. How's that sound?"

Meeeow!

"All right, come on then."

I open the door and disarm the alarm, resetting it to occupied mode once we're inside. I carry my new little friend to the kitchen and place him on the floor at my feet. I dig out the tuna from the cupboard and locate the can opener. He just stares at me. When I place a small scoop of tuna on a plate in front of him, he makes a dive for it. He stands on the plate and begins inhaling the improvised kitty snack. His body begins to vibrate with loud purrs as he gobbles it down.

"Wow, you were hungry huh? I'm going to pour you a very small helping of milk. We don't want to upset your little tummy." I find a shallow cereal bowl, and then grab a second. I fill one with water, and a couple tablespoons of milk goes into the other. As I watch him devour everything, it occurs to me that what goes in will need to come out.

I enter my bedroom and find a shoe box. I take out my shoes and then fill the box with torn pieces of the magazine I just bought. I save the dark web article, but the rest gets shredded and put in the box. It'll have to do for now. When he's full I show him the box. He immediately digs in it and then uses it for its intended purpose.

"You're such a good kitty!" I praise.

"We need a name for you. Hmm, you're an orphan just like me. I don't know if you're a boy or a girl. I may need to look up how to figure that out. I don't even know how old you are cutie." I scratch his ears, and he rubs against me. It's comical; he's so incredibly small.

After a quick search and an uncomfortable examination for both of us, I'm able to determine he's a male. In order to give him a good name, I decided to choose an orphan in literature. I mean, what else would I do? I write my four favorites on pieces of paper.

I crumple them each into a ball and toss the four of them in front of my new roommate. He chases after one of the four and knocks it around for a minute.

"Okay, let's see what you chose." I open his selection and read it out loud.

"Tom Sawyer, good choice. Sawyer it is," I smile at him, and he watches me. He wants his makeshift toy back. I crumpled it back into a ball and toss it back to him. He happily swats at it and rolls it around. He attacks it with his whole body. Man, he's cute.

"All right Sawyer, I've got some things to do. You be good and don't chew up any of my stuff."

I get my computer online and then order some cat supplies. Who knew such a tiny creature needed so much stuff. My research brings me to the conclusion he must be about six weeks old. I order some age-appropriate food and vitamins, a litter box with litter, a cat tree, some toys, two dishes, and a bed. He should be set once it arrives in the morning. I love overnight delivery.

While I'm looking for a local vet for Sawyer, an alert pops up on my screen. It's a notification from my *Comet* program. It's located someone who meets my search criteria. I minimize my veterinarian search and maximize the monster search box.

Subject: Sardon, David Raymond

DOB: 08/13/1976

ID: FL DL S028-399-76-802-4

Location: 4811 N. Meyer Street, Mystic Cross, FL 42480

Criminal History: Possession 2, Domestic Battery 3, Sexual Assault 3, Sexual Battery Minor 3, FTA-bench warrant, DWLSR, Fleeing to Elude, False Imprisonment, Possession 3

Status: Parole, Registered Sex Offender

Release: 06/06/2024, COND.

As I look over his information, I realize two things. First, he's out, which means I can get to him now that's he's not being protected by steel bars and armed guards. Second, he had to be accessing the dark web for my program to capture him. Some people never learn, and he's definitely stupid and evil.

I copy his address and paste it into a map app. It's only about eleven miles from here. I can swing by there tomorrow while I'm running errands and check it out. Just because this is his registered address, it doesn't necessarily mean he's actually living there. A lot of criminals claim they're staying with a relative to meet parole conditions when in reality, they're back with their drug using friends, the victim of their domestic crimes, or fellow pedophiles. I'll need to see if I can get a visual of him.

The next step is to trace how he's accessing the web. I know for certain he's not allowed on there while he's on parole. I search the IP address he used. After a few seconds the IP registration information comes up.

"Oooh, Davie, you're a very bad boy, aren't you? I don't think you're allowed to be hanging out with Jimbo, now, are you? Hmmm, your dumbasses are going to make this easier than I thought." Sawyer begins rubbing on my leg and meowing at me. I scoop him up and place him on my chest. His nails are like needles as he clutches me in his tiny claws. Once he curls up, he eases his grip and begins to purr.

"You're a good boy, Sawyer. You nap while I work. You won't believe it, little man. The jackass that just got out has led me to the jackass I've been searching for, how about that?"

Raow!

"Exactly." I save everything I need to make my plan a reality. I book a vet appointment for Sawyer, then I move to the kitchen area and make a sandwich.

I share a bite with him. "You can't have any more or your tummy will get sick and make me so sad." He watches me with his head tilted like he's taking in every word.

I spent the rest of the day unpacking boxes and finding a place to keep everything. When I'm finished, I turn on some music after locking Sawyer in my bedroom. I like it loud, and I don't want to hurt his ears. I begin my work out by warming up on the treadmill. Next, I begin punching a hanging speed bag. I add front and side kicks, then move on to roundhouse kicks. I jump and flip on the mat, then I climb the wall using the various colored handles I installed like those on a rock wall. I need to sharpen my parkour skills. I move around the space climbing and swinging on everything I can. Lastly, I work with some of my blades. A sword I keep on my spine, some butterfly knives, and my throwing blades hit the target on the board I set up for that purpose.

Working on my fighting skills brings up painful memories of my mom and me spending endless hours training. I have no more tears. My grief has been honed into a sharp point of anger and vengeance; its tip more deadly than any of my blades.

Satisfied with my workout, I turn off my music after *A Warrior's Call* ends. It's a favorite in my workout playlist. I hit the shower and once I'm dressed in fresh clothes, I'm ready for a meal. I roast a chicken breast with some vegetables and brown rice. It's good and I feel like a grownup.

Sawyer is happy with his portion. His full belly makes him sleepy, and he curls up in my lap while I work on my plan. As I'm mapping my target location, a chat request pops up from Colby.

RobNdaHood- Hey VioleNt1, how's the new place coming along?

VioleNt1-It's good, how're you?

RobNdaHood-Crazy as a loon and happy as a clam in my lair. Any hits on Comet?

VioleNt1-How do you always know?

RobNdaHood-Haven't you learned yet? Crazy people and children tap into their psychic abilities much easier than anyone else. Fill me in.

VioleNt1-Don't you already know with your crazy psychic abilities?

RobNdaHood-Ok I walked right into that one. Spill!

I tell him everything I've got. I have no secrets from Colby. He's one of a kind and I trust him implicitly. Then I expand on how things are going in my new place. He's especially excited about Sawyer; he loves cats. His parents won't let him have any pets on their property because he's often in treatment and they don't want to have to babysit for his animals. I feel bad for him on that front, he needs somebody to love. A cat would be ideal for Colby. They're independent enough not to need constant attention, but they're affectionate enough to let you feel the love.

When I share about my experience at the market, he laughs hysterically. He's quick to tell people about his skilled bodyguard, meaning *me.* I would absolutely kill for him, but I wouldn't call me a bodyguard by any means. Tired of typing with him, I call him on speaker, he continues the conversation without acknowledging the change.

"You know why that happens to you, right?"

"Are you trying to say I provoke aggressive men?"

"Nah, I'm saying you're too pretty and all that blonde hair is too flashy. You can't help but attract attention from everyone, especially aggressive men."

"So, you *are* saying it's somehow my fault. You sound like my birth mother!"

"Low blow! I hope you don't hate me like her."

"Of course not, but never victim shame anyone, it's unacceptable dude."

"I miss you! You're such fun, when're you gonna visit me again?"

"Soon, will you be home next weekend?"

"As far as I know, but I have no control over the voices in my head. That's funny! You better laugh."

"Always, you crack me up man. When you say my blonde hair is too flashy, are you serious?"

"Sorry, that got to you. I was only joking. But you're very pretty and it's very hard for dudes to keep their eyes off you. Don't you remember when you first got to the ward? Every guy in there suddenly needed something down your hall. It's only gotten worse since then because you're prettier than ever. Sorry to break it to you."

My stomach hurts like someone kicked me. I never really think about how I look. I dress for comfort and ease of movement to kick ass. I never want to attract anyone, especially men who want something from me. Maybe if I go see Enrique, I can lessen my allure and keep the assholes away.

After I finish chatting with Colby, I make an appointment on-line with Enrique at the salon. I still see him because every year I donate ten inches of my hair to Locks of Love. It became an annual tradition for me and mom. We would get our hair done, shop, and have lunch. Enrique has been my hairstylist since that first donation, I see him three to four times a year.

I spend a few more hours planning and plotting before I get tired and take Sawyer to bed. He decides the best place to sleep is on my throat. It's not easy falling asleep with a hot furry body on your trachea. Eventually exhaustion wins.

The next morning all of Sawyer's goodies arrive and he immediately christens the new litter box. He really seems to enjoy digging in the litter and knocks some out of the box. After I clean up his mess, I make a shopping list for my plan.

I'm excited to shop at the home improvement store. Where else can you buy zip-ties, rope, tarps, duct tape, shovels, wire, batteries, tools, and plants? Oh, and some sound proofing for one of the spare rooms. Just in case I want to play loud music there.

Definitely not to mute any screams from monsters getting what they deserve.

I ordered a lock picking kit along with Sawyer's things. I spend a half hour watching YouTube videos on how to use them. Then I spent an hour practicing. I'm making good progress when it's time to leave for my hair appointment. To keep him safe, I close Sawyer in the bathroom with a bowl of water and dry food. I put his favorite toy in there too. He gives me the saddest face when I say goodbye.

"I'll be back buddy, just be careful and don't get hurt, okay?"

I closed the toilet lid, removed the trash can, and there's nothing else he can get into... I hope. After I set the alarm, I drive off in my SUV, again, I need it to carry my purchases.

When Enrique sees me, he lets out a squeal of delight. "Aaah-hh! Violet! It's so good to see you. How are you doing my dear-est?"

"I'm okay. How are you? Anyone new and exciting in your life?"

"Don't try to avoid it, get over here and let me give you a hug. I read about your parents in the news. Are you doing all right?" He envelopes me in a tight hug and plants a wet kiss on my cheek.

"I'm taking it one day at a time. It sucks, but I'm getting by."

"I'm so sorry, dear heart. Your mom was one of the good ones. I'm sure she's got her angel wings and is watching over you."

"I hope she isn't watching too closely." He releases me and bursts out laughing.

"I hear that!" He high-fives me.

"Okay, have a seat and tell me what we're doing today."

"I want to donate all of my hair. You can style it however you want. I just want short and easy." Shock makes his eyes pop and his mouth flop open. He's frozen.

"Are you okay?" I ask.

"Are you serious? You want all of your hair cut off? Like, all of it?"

"Yep."

"Girl! I'm going to make it super-hot. I can't believe you're willing to part with all of it. It's going to be a blessing for some lucky child or two."

"I'm glad. I just want a big change. New life, new hair, you know?"

"I feel you, just leave it to me. I'm going to braid it, then I'll scalp you and style my heart out. Cool?"

"Go for it."

"You won't believe the date I had last night. I show up looking totally hot and this guy is wearing a bowling shirt! I mean a freaking *bowling shirt*, for real. I told him right away it wasn't going to work out, but then he flexes, and these cut muscles pop in his arms, and chest...I thought I was going to pass out. Holy shit was he hot under that stupid shirt..." As I listen to Enrique's love life story, I watch as he braids my long hair for the last time. I thought I would feel something when he cut it off. All I felt was relief.

After two hours of Enrique's stories, he finally spins me around to check out my new look.

"Wow! I don't even recognize myself. It looks great. How hard is it going to be to style at home?"

"You'll be able to towel dry it, run your fingers through it, and that's all you need to do."

"I can't believe it. Thanks Enrique, I love it."

"I love you. This is going to help so much. You're the best. You'll have to see me every six to eight weeks or so if you want to keep it this length. Okay?" He waves the braid of my former hair around. Good riddance.

After I'm done with him, I take care of my shopping. Finally heading home once my car is loaded with the murderer's DIY kit. Uncle Randy is coming over for dinner. I have to make sure everything I purchased is hidden out of sight. When he knocks on the door, I take one last glance around to make sure I didn't miss anything.

"Holy cow! What happened to your hair? It's all gone!"

"Do you like it?"

"No! You look like a grown up! Where's my little girl Violet? You're not allowed to grow up so fast." I stick my tongue out at him like a brat.

"There she is! Okay, I like it as long as you're not as mature as your hairstyle. It looks amazing. I love the blue streak at the front. What made you cut it all off?"

"I was just ready for a change, a fresh start. You know... new place, new school, new me."

"I didn't even recognize you until you said something. Seriously, you look good. I'm happy to see you haven't burned the place down yet. I brought your favorite Chinese from Who Song's, sesame chicken." He grins like a mad man.

"Thanks. I'm starved, let's eat." Sawyer likes him right away and purrs every time he pets him. He watches our every move, or he might be watching the chicken in my chopsticks.

I had a great evening with my uncle. It's nice to spend time with family, even if they aren't blood related. He's actually better than my blood relatives. He loves how I set everything up in the place. He looks at my knife board for an extra-long moment, but he doesn't say anything.

"Joyce is still being a bitch. She's doubling down on everything and we're eventually going to have to face her in court. If she contacts you, don't speak to her, no matter what excuse she gives you."

"Why would she contact me? She hates me."

"Maybe so, but you're the beneficiary for the bulk of the estate. She may be plotting something, who knows. Just don't engage with her unless Krewe is with you, okay?"

"Okay."

"Do you need anything? Groceries? Advice? Books?"

"Just a hug. I'm tired, but I'll see you Sunday at your house, right?"

He hugs me. "Yeah, come before four and we'll watch the game. Please call me if you need anything, or just to talk. I'll always listen without judgement, no matter what. I love you, kiddo."

"I love you too. Thanks for coming."

"My pleasure. Sawyer, take care of her okay, buddy?" He lifts his head at his name then plops back down. He's worn out too. Its hard work being a kitten... too many toys to conquer.

"Lock up after I leave. Bye."

"I will, bye."

I love him, but I'm relieved he's gone. Once I'm sure he's left the area, I put Sawyer in his bed in the bathroom and wheel my motorcycle out the overhead door. I set the alarm and took off like a bat out of hell. Nothing's better than the wind in your face and empty miles of asphalt ahead. I take a drive around all the places I regularly visit. Then I aim for the hideout of my quarry.

When I drive past, I can see the flickering light from a TV flashing in the large front window. The house is a squat structure, and I think it was yellow at one time. Now it's a faded, dirty, pale color that seems to be peeling from the plaster. The roof looks dark and moldy. The small amount of vegetation in the dirt lawn is overgrown and being choked by weeds. Some vines have climbed the shutters of a small window next to the bigger one. There's a rusted old sedan in the driveway missing all four wheels and lifted on cement blocks. A tarp takes the place of a hood.

Behind it there's a minivan that's seen better days but looks operable. It's a dark color, maybe blue, and has dark window tint. Its back window has a family of stick figures depicting a father, mother, three children, a baby, and a dog rounds out the image. I know for a fact there's no family living here. There never has been a child in this home since the current owner purchased it, unless they were brought here against their will.

I circle around the block and find a spot to park. On foot I approach the house and check out the back yard. There's no fence from the front to back yard. The exterior perimeter of the yard is fenced by the neighbor's fences and covered in foliage forming a sufficient barrier from prying eyes. The back of the house sports a collapsing covered patio with ripped screens and filled with junk. There's a path through the mowers, weights, trash bags, and other debris to the back door. The back of the house still has the ancient jalousie windows that were likely installed when the house was built in nineteen-sixty-nine.

The interior probably still has lead paint covering its walls based on the level of upkeep visible outside. There's a large half dead tree reaching its bare branches into the sky like a skeleton begging for answers from above. What a depressing place, it reeks of misery and despair. The far side of the house has a broken garage door barely hanging on and six trash cans overflowing with beer cans. It stinks of rot.

I make my way to the sidewalk and stand in a shadow, observing the building that contains two of my childhood nightmares. An evil grin curls my lips like the coyote when he thinks he's finally going to catch the roadrunner. I won't fail like Wyle E. Coyote. My roadrunners won't be able to run from me and I won't be relying on Acme to foil their attempts.

Satisfied with my expedition, I walk back to my bike and head home. When I get the bike safely tucked in for the night, Sawyer's thrilled to see me and we snuggle under the covers. He quickly falls asleep on my throat, while I go over every detail of my plan in my head, again and again.

CHAPTER EIGHT

Having survived an entire week on my own I celebrate by applying for a job. Mostly I just need something to occupy my time while I wait for school to begin. I can't spend all of my days obsessing over my plans, the income won't be unwelcome either. I turned in an application at the bar and grill closest to my home. Close enough to walk if necessary. It's a criterion I set for myself.

My experience and common sense, mixed with a good recommendation from my former employer lands me the job. I start tomorrow and they're willing to work with my school schedule once the semester begins. I didn't tell them I'm not eighteen yet and they didn't ask. They're a family-owned business and they pay cash under the table. My hourly rate plus tips isn't too shabby.

Uncle Randy is surprised when I tell him about my new job, he says he's proud of me not taking the lazy route. Having a job will be a great excuse when my plans interfere with visiting him. Colby claims he's going to visit me sometime when I'm working. We'll see if he follows through.

My first shift is filled with training. I need to learn the menu and how to ring up orders on the register. It's all fairly simple. The menu is just a few bar items, burgers and chicken wings; that type of stuff. There are more drinks to learn than food items.

The waitress training me is at least fifteen years my senior. She's nice enough, just a little rough around the edges. She has a sleeve of tattoos on one arm and piercings in her lip, nose, and eyebrow. She speaks with a cigarette roughened voice, and she also seems to have a drinking problem. Her addictions have aged her appearance. My dad used to say, *'They look like a horse who was ridden hard and put away wet.'* His saying comes to mind when I work with Danielle.

By day two, I'm fully trained on the POS system, and I learned the menu on my own time overnight. My boss, Javier, is impressed and he schedules me for solo shifts over the next few days. Danielle thanks me profusely, since her youngest child needs to visit the doctor and with me taking those shifts, she's permitted to schedule the appointment.

On day three, while I'm waiting on tables and taking orders, a male voice calls out, "Violet?"

Seated at the bar is none other than Jackson, the good-looking one from the market incident. Great. I signal him to give me a minute and I finish taking the order for an older couple. Once I get it entered, I approach Jackson.

"Hi, what can I get for you?"

"I knew it was you. What happened to your hair? Sorry, that came out wrong, it looks good. I'm just shocked to see it cut off."

"I wanted a change. Did you want to order something?"

"Yeah, I'll take a cheeseburger with fries, and a coke. When did you start working here?"

"A few days ago. Do you want lettuce, tomato, and onion on that?"

"Sure. It's nice to see you. Thanks."

"I'll be back with your drink in a minute." I take his menu and leave to enter his order. After I bring his coke, I get busy with other customers. Every time I glance in his direction, he's watching me. When his food is up, I take a bottle of ketchup with his plate and deliver everything to him.

He smiles at me, after I set his plate in front of him, I ask, "Do you need anything else?"

"Yes."

"Would you like to tell me what it is?" I question.

"I really need your number so I can call you for a date."

"Sorry, that's not possible. Let me know if you need anything food related," I state firmly and walk away. I keep busy checking on the other customers, refilling drinks, and taking and delivering orders. When I notice his glass is two thirds empty, I bring him a fresh cup of soda. He thanks me and I'm able to continue working without him questioning me further.

It gets busy and I don't notice him leave. He left cash with the check on the bar. He gave me a fifty percent tip; that's not okay. He's not going to buy my affection and I'm kinda pissed. But it's too busy to worry about it for long. I'm making good money working here. The tips are great, and the people are pretty friendly. I'm glad I decided to apply here.

When I get home, I give Sawyer a small piece of grilled chicken I saved for him from work. He's doing well coping with my schedule. I think he'll be fine when I start school. I'm off tomorrow. Tonight is the night I'm going after Dave and Jimbo. I've got everything planned down to the smallest detail. Colby is going to monitor the dark web for their activity and watch a camera feed from me, just in case. I have a backpack filled with everything I need. I'm an expert with my lock picking kit now. This is going to work perfectly.

I shower and dress all in black. I load up my various sheaths with my favorite blades. I put Sawyer in the bathroom to keep him safe. Colby has strict instructions on what to do with Sawyer if anything happens to me. I attached my backpack and leave my place. When I leave my bike and start on foot to the house, I start my video feed.

Colby sends a thumbs up to my phone, he's able to see the feed. I make my way to the back of the house, staying in the shadows. I pick my way through the garbage strewn across the patio. The small path to the door is big enough for me to navigate. The monsters are playing on the dark web, doing disgusting things with horrible images.

I expertly pick the lock, spraying the hinges and knob with WD-40 to prevent any squeaks and alerting them to my presence. The door gives way silently and I enter a dingy kitchen. It smells like mold and stale beer with a hint of rotting food. The sink is piled high with dirty dishes and every surface is covered with trash. Mostly beer cans litter the table and old food containers are scattered on the counter tops. I move with purpose and without a sound. I can hear them laughing in another room.

The dining area is attached to the kitchen, and I stick close to the wall so no-one can sneak up behind me. Making my way slowly to the room I hear voices funneling from, I remove my backpack. I take out some zip ties and put them in my pocket, then reshoulder my pack. Since there are two of them, I may need to subdue one completely and cuff him before they realize I'm here. That way it will only be necessary to fight one at a time.

"I'm gonna piss, you want another beer?" one of them says. If memory serves, it's Jimbo. I press myself into a corner by a closet holding perfectly still.

"Yeah. Hurry up, they're almost ready to start."

"I know! I'm going, don't nag me dickhead."

A large body exits the room, he turns into the rest room further down the narrow hallway. I enter the room, it's a bedroom with a twin mattress on the floor. A laptop computer sits atop a wooden TV tray, there are two folding chairs set in front of it. One chair is occupied. On the screen is a blurred image with a countdown timer. I recognize Dave even from behind, the memory of him makes my skin crawl. He's fatter, grayer, and missing more hair, but it's definitely him. Anger floods my veins and without hesitation I whip my favorite sword from the scabbard on my spine. Despite my careful plan, my emotions take over. I use all of my strength to slash through the air and into his neck. It's an extremely sharp blade, but it's not capable of removing his head in one blow at this angle.

He makes a startled yelp and falls to the ground with a crash as his metal chair tumbles with him. Blood squirts in a dark stream from the wound. My sword stuck when it hit his cervical vertebra. I pull it back sliding it from his spine. I carefully wipe it on his shirt, removing the gore from my pristine blade. I spin, ready for Jimbo to enter. With Dave incapacitated, I'm not worried about him attacking me from behind. He's making strangled gurgling sounds while he flops around on the floor. The hideous, seventies remnant of filthy orange shag carpeting helps muffle some of the sound and definitely soaks up the river of blood cresting from the fatal wound.

Jimbo charges into the room with a baseball bat raised and ready to attack. I can't help chuckling at how ridiculous he looks. He's old and dirty. He's had a rough life, and he looks awful, wrinkled, and decrepit. Not that he was ever nice to look at, but this is almost pitiful.

"Wow, are you planning to hit me with that bat?"

"Who the fuck're you?"

"You don't remember me? Aww that hurts my feelings," I smile brightly at his pale pink face.

"Tell me who the fuck you are, and we'll find out if I remember."

"Does the name Jerry ring a bell? How about a little girl with long blonde curls and dark scared eyes? Does that jog your memory?"

"Violet?"

"Ding-ding! We have a winner! What do you have for him Bob?"

"What the fuck did you do to Dave?" he asks, finally noticing his friend's convulsing body, in its final throes of ebbing life.

"Nothing he didn't have coming. I have something for you too. Do you recall the first time you touched me?"

His eyes get glassy as he recalls torturing a little girl for his own pleasure, "Mmhm, you cried so beautifully. Your sobs made my dick so hard."

I swallow my revulsion, "Do you remember what you said to me?"

He rubs his erection through his pants, and I want to vomit. Anger flares hot in my chest, but now I can protect that scared little girl. I'm going to protect her along with all of the other children this monster has harmed. He won't ever touch another child again.

"Yeah, I promised if you were a good girl that it wouldn't hurt."

"But you lied, didn't you Jimbo?"

"Uh, I guess, but you weren't a good girl. You scratched the fuck out of my face. I still have a scar right here." He points to the white line beneath his left eye. I tried to claw his eyes out, but I wasn't strong enough. He held me down and did what he wanted to eight-year-old Violet.

"Do you know how many scars I have? They're not all visible either. You're a disgusting child molester Jimbo and I'm here to get revenge."

He laughs, "How do you expect to do that? You're still a tiny little thing, but a little old for my tastes. You're no match for me! I can still take anything I want from you."

"You think so?" I sheath my sword and subtly slide two throwing knives from my waist.

"I know so!" He charges at me with his bat held high to strike. I throw my blades, and they hit with pinpoint accuracy. One goes into his shoulder knocking the bat from his grasp. The other lodges in his groin, just south of his little bat. I smile with satisfaction. He screams like a little girl, ironically, and grabs his shriveled member, trying to feel if it's still in one piece. He falls to his knees sobbing and pleading. Nobody's coming to help him.

"How ya doin' there, Jimbo? Still think you can hurt me. I've got news for you, asshole. You're never going to hurt another child. You're going straight to hell tonight and I'm going to deliver you... personally."

"Please! No! Please! I-I-I'll do whatever you want! Please!"

"I begged you to stop hurting me. You know what you did? You laughed. You kept hurting me and laughing about it. Why would I spare you?"

"P-please...I'm begging you. I'll do anything, please!"

"Oh Jimbo, tsk, tsk, I might be inclined to give you a chance if you're a good boy. How about you take out your tiny little dick and cut it off with that knife in your leg. If you're a good boy and do what I ask, I'll let you live. Go on, unzip..."

He starts crying uncontrollably, "Please, please, no, anything but that. Please, I promise I won't touch another kid ever again. Please."

"No. It's the only way. If you cut it off, I'll walk out this door and leave you be. Go on now... I'm not going to wait all night. You have ten seconds to unzip. Nine, eight, seven..."

"Okay! Okay!" He unzips his pants and opens the button. His pants fall to his thighs where the blade keeps them from going any further.

"Three, two, one. Times up!" I lean towards him, and he screams. He pulls the blade from his thigh and with a horrible, blood curdling yell, he severs his flaccid dick. He faints and falls to the ground. Honestly, I'm shocked he did it. Fear is a powerful motivator. I retrieve my blade from the ground and snap smelling salts under his nose. He jolts awake and begins sobbing. I'm surprised he's conscious with all the blood gushing from his thigh and the bloody nub that used to be his filthy pecker.

"Please. Help me. I'm dying. I did what you said, you promised," he begs as his tears and blood flow freely.

"Here's the thing Jimbo, I said I would leave. I didn't say I would help you."

"Please, you promised to let me live."

"Yeah, I did. But just like you, I lied." I lean over him and twist the blade into his shoulder. I make sure to sever his arteries. Blood spurts in time to his heartbeat. I leave him there while I rinse my blades in the bathroom sink. Then I spray the liquid from the bottle in my bag on Dave, then Jimbo. He squeals like a pig being tortured. I step into the hallway and light a match. Then I light the whole match book and toss it into the room. Flames burst to life instantly. Both men are ablaze in fire, and I'm mesmerized as they burn. The smell of burning hair and flesh doesn't even faze me. It's something I've wanted to see for a very long time. I shake myself back to the present and get out of there.

I quickly make my way back to my bike. I rode down the street to have a final glimpse of my handiwork. The roof is fully engulfed, flames rise above it, and I'm satisfied. My heart sings with joy as I bask in the glow of the bright flames. I drive home with a smile on my face.

Chapter Nine

W hen I turn off the bike, parked inside my warehouse, my phone rings.

"Hi Colby. How's everything?"

"That was awesome! You're my hero! But you need to turn off the video before you change."

"Yeah, turning it off now. Any fire reports yet?"

"Oh yeah, they're trying to put it out. It went up like dry tinder, and there's nothing but a concrete block shell left and half of that collapsed. There won't be anything but ashes left. You locked the door on your way out, not that there'll be a door left, but they'll never even know you were there. You did so great! How do you feel?"

"Good. Relieved. Satisfied. Like I have a lot more work to do. Those two were idiots and easy. Tracking down the others is going to be more difficult. They're smarter and take care not to get caught. I need something extreme to get them. I've had this idea floating around for a while."

"Are you going to share this amazing idea or what?" I explained my plan to Colby, who constantly gasped in awe.

"I'm blown away. You're a genius."

"We'll need to flesh out the details and think on it a while. I'm gonna shower and hit the hay. We'll talk more tomorrow, yeah?"

"All right. Sweet dreams Wonder Girl!"

"You too, Boy Blunder!"

I take a long hot shower and scrub the smoke from my short hair and skin. Sawyer is thrilled to curl up on my throat for the night. I may need to stop letting him do that, eventually he's going to be too big to sleep there without strangling me.

I fall asleep quickly, but it's anything but restful. I toss and turn with nightmares about my tragic past, only now the monsters are like zombies with bloody wounds and burnt skin. They chase me and pop out of every dark corner, every time I think I'm safe, another scarred hand with bones protruding grasps my hair or my throat.

I jolt awake and something is pressing on my esophagus, in the dark fearing it's a zombie claw, I swipe at the imaginary fingers of doom.

Meeeeow! Sawyer loudly protests as I shove him off of me.

"Oh no! I'm so sorry baby boy, I was having a bad dream. Come here, let's go get a drink." I scoop him up and carry him close to my heart into the kitchen. I pour him a tiny helping of milk and warm it for a few seconds in the microwave. I put a hot chocolate k-cup into the coffee maker for myself. When both of our warm drinks are ready, I let him drink his on the table. I pull my legs up underneath me and sip the chocolatey goodness.

Now that my head is clear, I can make sense of my dream. My past collided with my present in a twisted way. I may need to complete some sort of cool down after a hunt in the future to avoid having nightmares next time. Since I'm awake, I begin analyzing my plan to lure in the next round of monsters. I can't guarantee it'll snare the right monsters, but it'll definitely capture monsters that need to be stopped. I think I'm okay with that.

Using a pad of paper I keep on the table; I make a few notes. I need to get a mani-pedi, purchase a bikini, get a sparkly anklet, get my legs waxed, purchase a large piece of fabric, and a cute, girly chair. Oh! I need a wig too. I can set everything up in one of the extra warehouse rooms. I think this is going to work great. I check the time. It's four and I don't think I'm going back to sleep. Sawyer has no such difficulty; he's curled on my lap out like a light.

I scoop him up again and place him in his kitty bed that he only uses for naps. I sit at my desk and get to work making appointments and ordering things I need. I'll need to pick up the fabric in person, and the bikini too. Once I check off everything I can on my list, I start looking at the websites I need to use to attract the monsters.

I've never looked at *ITZYuu* before and I think most things on there are consensual, but it might be a good way to get a buzz going about my plan. I make an account and start looking at the types of things the fans like. Oh yeah, this is going to work really well. I'm only seventeen so I can't legally post anything sexually explicit. I won't, but what I have planned doesn't involve any sex or naked sexual body parts.

When the sun comes up, I do my work out. Then I carefully clean all of my blades and sheaths with alcohol, sharpen the blades, and polish them with mineral oil. Mom taught me to maintain my blades, so they'll always work the way I expect. Dad gave me my first set of throwing knives and they're safely stored with my treasured possessions. The ones I use for hunting aren't sentimentally valuable.

I've got the day off and as soon as the stores are open, I'm there to pick out a cute bikini. I find a purple one with white daisies on the front. The flowers line the front of the waist and what I guess would be the collar of the top. I like how well it covers me and I don't want to show off my assets. Then, I head over to grab fabric. I've never purchased fabric before. I watch a few ladies get a length of fabric cut at a counter in the middle of the store. I check out the bolts of fabric neatly displayed by color, and after watching surreptitiously for a little while, I determine how it works. I calculate the need to purchase nine yards of a double folded, shimmering amethyst fabric and bring it to the counter to get cut.

Next, I browse a jewelry counter until I find the perfect sparkling anklet. It's sterling silver with small cut pieces in the chain that catch the light. I visit the furniture section of the same girlie shop. There's a fuzzy magenta chair that screams girl's room. I get the chair and a fluffy heart shaped rug in a shade of orchid that compliments the fuzz on the chair.

After I load everything into my SUV, I'm right on time for my waxing and mani-pedi appointments at the salon. As luck would have it, they sell wigs in the shop, as well as hair pieces and extensions. I pick out a long wig, with curling blonde locks that end in a pretty shade of violet curls. It's perfect. I spent a lot of money today, but it's an investment for the greater good. I'm excited to get home and set up my special room.

Being cautious not to nick my newly purple nails, I carefully unload everything and carry it to my new themed room. I tack up the fabric against the wall to cover the unmistakable warehouse appearance. I position my fuzzy chair on the rug at an angle. I looked around and realize I didn't get any lighting. It's dim and dark even with the yellowed fluorescent fixture glowing from above. Sawyer is busy sniffing my new purchases, so I leave him to collect odors to his tiny heart's desire.

Finding a few different social media circle lights attached to posts withstands I order three for overnight delivery. I've heard they make you look amazing. I'm curious to see what they can do. I don't plan to show my face online, but I can try it when I'm not live. My stomach growls and I decide it's a great time for lunch, then maybe a nap. My limited sleep is catching up with me. After I share a turkey sandwich with my shadow, I curl up on my bed with him. As I lie there waiting for sleep to find me, my phone rings.

"Hi Harmony, what's new?"

"Violet! Hey! I miss you, just wondering how the new place is going."

"It's pretty good. I'm moved in, I found a kitten who's now my roommate, and I got a job."

"Holy shit! You've been busy. Tell me about the job, then the kitty."

"I'm working at Mystic Cross Cantina, it's a bar and grill. I'm waiting tables, it pays well, and the staff is cool."

"That's fantastic Vi, now fill me in on the kitty."

"I found him in the alley behind my place. He was only about six weeks old; he's growing fast though. He eats a lot. He's a grayish color with bright green eyes. He's adorable, I'll send you a video. What's up with you and Mike?"

"We're good. We renewed our lease for the apartment, so we don't have to move. He's away right now, on that study abroad program this week and next, in Spain. We saw Max last weekend, and he misses you." Crap. I don't want to hear about Max unless he's doing great. I told Colby not to tell me anything, but I guess I didn't tell Harmony. Awkward.

"That's great Harm, but I don't really want to hear about him unless he's doing great and happy. Okay?"

"Yeah. Okay. You know I've got your back, I'll let Mike know. How're you doing? Any run-ins with your evil grandmother?"

"I haven't even thought about her, as she means nothing to me. I'm doing fine without my parents' money. She can pull whatever she wants, since it won't change my life at all. If I need money, Uncle Randy will lend me whatever I need. But I'm fine. My job can support me without even trying. I make great tips, and my place and school are very affordable. How are you and Mike doing when he's in town?"

"We're so good. Believe it or not, his mom likes me! She says my sass reminds her of when she was younger, and Mike needs a sassy woman to keep him in line. I don't agree, but I'm so excited she likes me. I'm not gonna disagree out loud. My parents still think I can do better, and they refuse to get past his exterior. I hate their racist asses more than ever, but they're paying for school and the apartment, so I don't say that out loud either. Sometimes families suck. Oh, fuck! I'm sorry Violet, that was so insensitive of me."

"It's okay, don't freak out. I'm doing all right, and trust me, I know how much families can suck. Did you decide if you're changing your major yet?"

"No. I'm still debating. Nursing and business both have their merits, but I'm leaning towards nursing. I think about that wretched nurse Tiffany at the ward, it makes me want to be the kind nurse for all the kids, so they don't have to deal with anyone like her. Is that lame?"

"Of course not, it's great. You would make a wonderful pediatric nurse with your experience. I think you should go for it. Sounds like it's where your heart lies. Sorry, but I need to get a nap. I didn't sleep well last night. I'll call you soon, please give Mike a hug for me when he gets back and tell him, *Hola!*"

"I will sweetie. I almost forgot to tell you, I'm still the same weight, my anniversary is coming, and I haven't lost an ounce."

"I never doubted you, happy anniversary! You're my hero. Love you babes."

"Love you too... later babes!" I close my eyes with a smile on my lips. Sawyer climbs onto my chest and digs into my neck. No bad dreams, just a long restful sleep takes me under.

I woke up two hours later and decided to see what's happening online. I look over my new *ITZYuu* account and see that I have dozens of messages. Half of them from the site itself, with welcomes and tips, the others are from people wanting to connect with me. I haven't posted a single word or image. What is wrong with people? Unfortunately, I can't kill them all. Some days I sure would like too though.

Sawyer is asleep on my desk; he was playing with my mouse a minute ago. My phone chirps with a text alert and I see Colby's name on my screen.

RobNdaHood: How are you today? Any issues?

Me: Nope. I got a lot done for phase two.

RobNdaHood: Great! I have news, they finished their investigation. They think the dumbasses were drinking moonshine and accidentally started the fire. It's being called a careless accident. The report also covers the fact they weren't allowed to be together or on the internet. I get the distinct feeling they think the creeps got what they deserved, and the investigators are happy to close it out quickly, possibly without investigating as much as they should. The property owner will get a check, you're home free, end of story.

Me: That's good news. On to the next.

RobNdaHood: When you're on live streaming I'm going to mirror your activities, and I can back trace everyone who participates. I wish my brain could work as well as yours. I think we're going to be surprised by how successfully this plan works.

Me: I hope so. There's a couple I'd like to find, and I'm sure we're gonna find some new ones that'll put them to shame.

RobNdaHood: I agree. Are we starting tomorrow as planned?

Me: Yeah, as soon as I get back from work, we'll get started. I should be home around seven and I'll need a shower, so like seven thirty?

RobNdaHood: Works for me, see you then. Get some rest.

Me: Yes boss. Love ya!

RobNdaHood: I return an appropriate amount of affection.

I chuckled and woke Sawyer. I'm done looking at screens. I need some workout time. I dress in my workout clothes and connect my phone to the speakers. I blast my workout playlist and scare poor Sawyer. He took off to hide in the carpeted box on his cat tree.

I strike the bag in time to *Shout by Disturbed*. I worked hard, covering all the equipment, my blades, and parkour. I'm getting pretty good at getting to the second level without placing a foot on the stair treads. I jump down from the second level as well. I need to be prepared for anything. When you're hunting monsters, you need to have monster skills.

After a shower, I feed a noisy boy and myself. When I'm ready for bed I decide to give Uncle Randy a call just to check in. He appreciates it when I check in without him leaving messages first. Plus, I worry about him being alone. He swears he goes on dates he just hasn't found anyone worth introducing me to. It makes me sad since he's a wonderful guy. He deserves a great woman who loves him for something other than his title or money. Maybe I should sign him up on a dating site.

"Violet! Hi, how are you?" Uncle Randy chimes.

"I'm good. I'm still alive, eating three meals a day, and I haven't burned my place down. Things are going well. How about you?"

"Same old same old. Work is busy, which is good to keep my mind occupied. I'm thinking about asking someone to join us to eat on Sunday. Would that be, okay?"

"Krewe is always welcome, of course it's okay."

"Not Krewe. It's a woman... I met her at the hospital, and she's new to the area. I've been helping her get her bearings at work. Her name is Stephanie St. James. What do you think?"

"Really? That's fantastic! Yes, invite her. Is she a nurse? Or a doctor? Tell me more."

"She's the new head of radiology. She's my age, and she moved here from Seattle. She's never been married, no kids. She focused on her career, like me. I think you'll like her, but if not, just tell me."

"She sounds wonderful. Is she pretty? Tall or short? What does she like to do?"

"Oh boy, you're not going to go easy on me, are you? I'm not proposing marriage, just inviting her to have a meal, you know. Yes, she's pretty. She's shorter than me. She likes to go hiking, rock climbing, and kayaking, and she wants to learn more watersports since she's in Florida now. We might try paddle boarding and sail boating. Does that cover everything?"

"I'm so excited for you. I can't wait to meet her. Did you tell her about me?"

"Yeah. She knows a little, I told her about your parents passing and me technically being your guardian. I didn't tell her any history or about your grandmother, or that you were adopted. I figure you can share what you're comfortable with whenever you're ready. Is that all right?"

"If we like her, I'm okay with sharing whatever you want. What time do you want me to come since we're having a guest? Does she like sports?"

"Actually, she does like football and hockey. You can still come before four and we'll watch the game. I'll give her the same option. Okay?"

"Sounds perfect. I'll see you Sunday. I'm looking forward to meeting her."

"I'm glad. I'll see you Sunday. Love you."

"Love you too. Bye."

"Bye."

My face hurts from smiling so hard. I'm so excited he met someone. I hope she's nice. I can't contain my excitement or my curiosity. I log into my laptop and begin researching. It doesn't take long to find all kinds of information about Dr. Stephanie St. James, formerly of Seattle and Tacoma.

Seems she moved here to become the head of radiology as a promotion. She was in the radiology department at Washington State Medical Center. Now she's in charge of radiology at our little Mystic Cross Medical Center. That's such a big move, I wonder why she chose to go across the country to such a small hospital.

I dig deeper, and soon find her parents have retired to a town further south a couple hours from here. That's a good reason, but I have a feeling there's more to it. I keep going and discover a scandal. Her boss was fired and went to prison because he got caught molesting vulnerable patients. She was a whistle blower in the case and testified against him in the trial. Looks like they offered her his position and she chose to leave. Her letter rejecting their offer explains how she believes there's a system in place making it difficult to protect the patients, and report wrongdoing especially by those in higher positions. She wants to work in a place where patient care and safety is the priority. I like her.

I may have hacked into her personnel file. I may have also read some patient letters complimenting her care and kindness. I might have also read some recommendations from supervisors and professors over the years singing her praises. I feel a little guilty for being so nosey and stop there. I justify it in my mind because I'm looking out for my one and only remaining parent. I can't lose him. I hope she likes me. Now I'm nervous about meeting her, she's obviously wonderful, but if she doesn't like me, it will probably be my fault.

I scoop Sawyer from the floor, he gets sleepy and just falls where he's standing and is asleep that fast. He was playing with my purple toes and bam, asleep on my foot. He stretches in my hands; I hold him to my face and snuggle on him. I'm trying a new idea. I make a hole in the pillow next to me, then I put him in the hole to sleep. He opens his eyes and looks at me, closes them and is back asleep immediately. Whew, maybe this'll work.

CHAPTER TEN

It didn't work. I wake up with a hot ball of fluff pressed into my neck. Maybe if I put his bed on my bed, I can convince him to sleep in it. I'll try tonight. I collect my delivery of lights and set them up in my theme room. I need a name for it, I know, Bait and Slice Inn! I shoot off a text to Colby, he'll appreciate my humor. He gets back to me immediately.

RobNdaHood: Love it!

I arrive at work at ten-fifteen, my shift starts at ten-thirty. We open at eleven, our food is equally suitable for lunch or dinner, so the menu is the same all day. Once in a while they put something on special with discount pricing, it'll be on the board if there's anything on special that day. Danielle says it's rare they have any special deals. When I came in today, it said Fifty Cent Wings, on the board. I make a mental note to push the special. Javier tells me he has a bunch of wings about to spoil so he has to sell them before they're no good. I'm not gonna have any wings.

As usual the place is hopping from when we open the door. People are ordering dozens of wings; they love it when Javier orders too many. When I reach the end of the bar taking orders, I look up to acknowledge the last customer on the end. Oh boy, it's Jackson.

"Hi, what can I get for you?"

"Hello, Violet."

"Hello, Jackson. What would you like to eat?"

"I think I'll try a dozen wings, with barbecue, steak fries, and I'm on my lunch break, so root beer?"

"Got it. I'll be right back with your drink."

"Thank you." When I return with his soda, he gives me a strange look with his head tilted. I look down to see if I spilled something on myself, then I wipe my face.

"What?" I ask.

"You obviously don't want to go out with me. I can respect that. The thing is, I like you and I want to get to know you. Are you willing to work on a friendship?"

"How do you propose we do that?" I ask.

"I was thinking we each get to ask three questions, we have to answer, but the questions can't be about, sex, family, religion, or politics. If the question is too personal for the person answering, they get one pass for every three questions. What do you think?"

"Does that count as one of the questions?"

He laughs, "Man you're tough. No, nothing counts until we agree and officially begin."

I laughed too. I was just teasing him. I think it over, and I don't see any harm in making a new friend. If we exchange questions while I'm working there's plenty of people around and regardless, and I can protect myself. I nod.

"Okay, I agree. One more rule though," I wait.

"What is it?" he queries.

"We can add more rules if it becomes necessary. Do you agree?"

"Yeah, that's fair. So, are we ready to begin?"

"Sure, as long as you keep in mind I still have to work. Go ahead."

"How old are you?"

"Pass." He smiles. Uh oh, did he know I would pass on that so he can ask two hard questions?

"Why won't you go out with me?"

I surprise him when I don't flinch, "I just broke up with someone a few weeks ago. I'm not up for dating anyone else right now." I don't add that I'm grieving my parents and I'm a child abuse survivor who's never had consensual sex. A survivor who's terrified she can't ever enjoy sex and will ruin any loving relationship when she freaks out about her past. I can feel perspiration building on my face, neck, and hands.

I rush off and help a few customers while I think about what to ask him. I decided turnabout is fair play. After I bring some meals out and refill some drinks, I return to Jackson. I smile and wait for him to speak. I can be incredibly patient; it's why I think I'd make a great sniper, plus you know, the killing.

"Stop teasing and ask your question."

"How old are you?" I ask, curious if he'll answer.

"Turned twenty-one a couple months ago." I'll be eighteen in a couple months, we're not that far off. Friendship range for certain.

Obviously, anyone can be friends, but I find having similar interests helps. I don't know how I stay friends with Harmony, since we are almost complete polar opposites.

"Cool. Are you going to ask another question?" I asked him.

"I think you should go again. I'm down to one and you have two, so ask your next question for me."

"I'm not prepared. Give me a minute, I'll be right back."

I fill up a fresh cup of root beer for him and collect his order from the window. I've got it, maybe he'll pass. I drop off his food and I can see a couple of my customers need my attention.

"Why don't you eat your wings while they're hot and I'll be back in a few minutes. Duty calls."

"Okay. Thanks." After I cash out a couple tables, take an order, and deliver some food and refills, I return to Jackson.

"Have you ever cheated on someone you were dating?"

"Oh, that's a good question. No. But..."

"No buts! It's a yes or no question," I tease.

"I didn't cheat, but I was casually seeing two girls, not exclusive in any way with either of them, and one chick saw me out with the other and flipped. She accused me of cheating and made a huge scene at a restaurant. It was so embarrassing, we ended up leaving. The one who flipped then decided because I was cheating in her crazy ass mind, that it would be fun to trash me online and key my truck. I had to take her to court for damages. Does that answer your question well enough?"

"Geez! That sucks. Sorry, that happened to you. I don't understand why she would agree to a casual non-exclusive arrangement if she wanted to be exclusive. That sounds really dumb."

"Well, obviously she was just bat crap crazy. No way to make sense of what a crazy person does."

"That's definitely true." I gave him a mischievous grin. Little does he know; I'm well acquainted with crazy.

"Your turn," I push.

"Do you have any hobbies you participate in regularly?" he asks.

"Oh. Hmm, I train in MMA regularly. I don't compete or anything, but it's my favorite workout. Does that count?"

"Sure. That explains what you did to Dave. How long have you been practicing?"

"Nope, you're out of questions. You'll have to save that one for next time."

"Can we make a rule to allow one follow-up question?" he asks with a pleading face. Sawyer makes that same face when he wants more food.

"Okay, as long as it's a direct follow up for the original question. Nothing that requires a new topic, deal?"

"Deal. So will you answer my follow-up question?" He gives me the kitten eyes again, this isn't good.

"Since I was thirteen."

"That explains so much. There's a guy waving his check at you."

I jolt, "Oh. I'll be back," I rush off to take care of the customer. After a ridiculous number of apologies, the man accepts finally. I helped a few more customers before returning to Jackson for my last question.

"I've got an easy one. What do you do for work?"

"I'm a boring contractor."

"I'm sure it's not boring. Please, elaborate."

He chuckles, then tells me, "No, really, I'm a boring contractor. I use equipment to dig precise holes under or through things." I burst out in hysterical laughter. For some reason I find this to be the funniest thing I've heard in a long time. He laughs because I'm laughing, and we must look like we've lost our minds. My eyes water from laughing so hard and I dab at them with a napkin.

"Shoot, I'm sorry I don't know why that tickled me so much. How long have you been doing that type of work?"

"My cousin, Austin, the other younger guy, you probably saw him the first time we met, he's been working for this company with a friend from school and told me about the work. It sounded interesting to me, I was already working for a GC, but I wasn't happy. I interviewed with the owner and signed on as an apprentice. It was three years ago, right after I graduated."

"You like it?"

"Nope, you're out of questions. You'll have to ask that next time," his grin is triumphant.

I acquiesce, "Okay, you got me. But I could argue it's a follow up question, if I didn't need to get back to work. Six people just got seated in my section."

"Sorry, I have to get back to work too. This was fun. I'll see you next time, Violet."

"It was. Bye, Jackson."

I watch him walk out the door, then I take the orders for the six new guests. My work shift continues to be a non-stop rush of hungry patrons. I don't mind when its busy, time goes by more quickly. My esteemed co-worker aka Danielle runs around complaining about her feet and her ex for my entire afternoon. When the clock strikes six, I'm more than ready to punch out and head home.

I'm excited to begin working on my other job, or maybe it's a hobby. How do you classify revenge killing? My blades are thirsty for more vile blood, and I can't wait to quench them. The images of blood fleeing the monsters in the world keeps a smile on my face as I shower and prepare for my first night on the job.

CHAPTER ELEVEN

After my shower, I dress in my costume and wig. I bring my laptop and set everything up in the Bait and Slice Inn. I'm a little excited to be doing this. I'm also curious to see if it works like I think it will. Once I check to make sure the image angle is right, I sign into the website and start making my first live stream.

Almost instantly people start joining. Colby is watching from his terminal at his pool house. He's signed into the live stream and is directly monitoring my stream; he can kill it instantly if it becomes necessary. My face is not on screen, only from my neck down is shown. My new swimsuit and wig contrast with the bright colors against my smooth skin. I lower the frame to focus in on my feet. I point my toes and turn them to the side and back again.

Requests begin popping up on screen. Rub your feet together. Turn them to the left. Curl your toes. Rub your foot up your calf. I accommodate the requests. I don't allow sound, just a stream of music. The requests ask me to try on some sexy shoes. I slide my feet into a pair of heels, and I stroll in front of the camera.

I pretend to accidentally aim the camera up my legs for a moment and the watchers go wild. Holy shit! There's eighty-four thousand watching my live stream. How's that even possible? I give Colby a face showing my disbelief. He's probably having a field day. He loves the chase, just like I love the hunt. My fingers twitch for my blades thinking about the sickos watching me right now.

Reaching down I clasp an ankle bracelet with little hearts, onto my right leg. It's so sweet, for jewelry. After a few more turns, as planned, Colby tells them I'm tired and I need my beauty sleep. I'll be back tomorrow, with a big surprise, and to make sure they're signed up and to make their donation to my college fund. Sweet dreams and some other crap they'll believe. He says it from my account, so they'll think it's from me. I sit and tilt my knees so I can place my feet beneath the chair, crossing them at the ankles. I leave it to be the final image as my livestream closes for the night.

"Great job Vi! Did you see how many perps were watching? I've got so many traces running and my modified Comet Program, thank you by the way. I'll be up all night following the really bad ones. I love it. We need to make a tantalizing ad video. Whatcha got?"

"I know you think I've got nothin', but I've got somethin'. Give me two minutes, be right back." I rush upstairs and collect some panties from my dresser, two pairs of heels from my closet, and I give Sawyer a treat on my way. I made it back in less than the two minutes I requested. I begin pulling the panties over my swimsuit. I pull each one on over the others. Six pair should be plenty, I place the heels at enticing angles and instruct Colby.

"Film me, dude. Zoom into my thighs, nothing higher. Then follow each pair until I kick it off. Got that?"

"Yes, ma'am. Signal when you're set."

Quickly, I place myself on my fuzzy rug right behind the high heels. I slide the outer pair of panties down a bit, so they won't get caught on each other. Then I signal for the start. When I see the light on my screen flash, I begin to slide the panties down, careful to get nothing more than my hands in the frame. As soon as they're low enough to fall, I let them. Then with pointed toes, I kick them off. The next pair is ready. I drop my panties over and over until they're all kicked off screen in a pile. On the last pair, I accidentally, allow my long blonde curls, with the violet ends, to fall into the frame right beside my hands. I let them dangle for a few seconds, then quickly whip them out of the shot. Hopefully, it'll seem like an oversight. Within seconds Colby has the teaser set to music, in slow motion, and slower where needed. He posts it before I can even approve of it out loud.

"You're taking advantage of your knowledge of my brain, you know that, right? Why didn't you let me decide if I liked it before you posted it?"

"Did you like it?"

"Well, yeah," I give in.

"Anything wrong with it?"

"No, but..."

"Ah! In other words, it was fine, and I saved this thirty second conversation which would've ended with the same result. Right?"

"Ugh! Love you Rob-N, but sometimes you freak me out. Are we ready for tomorrow?"

"Of course, the clones are multiplying. By morning Comet will have used all of their terminals against each other, and I'll have terabytes of data. I told you how fast the clones worked on that gang test. Caught over two-hundred and I was able to lift a hundred-twenty-five-K for foster kids. It was a brilliant idea I had to mix Roger Rabbit with Comet to get where we are, huh?"

"Seriously? Your idea?" I grill him.

"Fine, our idea. But you're not allowed to stop us from making millions selling it."

"Okaaay. Why would I stop you? If we sell it, we can get access to more monsters and have millions more to donate. Selling the public commercial version will do our best work."

"Oh. I thought maybe you wouldn't let this one go since it's your best work ever. My bad."

"I take it all back, you don't know me at all," I chuckle. He totally knows me; I've just already decided it makes sense. We can get our program into the places we need it to go and make a ton of money to donate in the process. What's not to love about this plan?

"All right. I'm going to get a shower. I'll see you at the same place, same time, tomorrow. Night Rob-N. Thank you."

"Okay. Hasta manana!"

After I'm dressed, I have some strawberries while I watch the screen on my laptop. Comet is working hard, the design I made for a screen saver flashes as it goes round and round. Sawyer mewls at me I close the top, scoop him up and take him to bed.

Two hours later I'm still tossing and turning. It's not that I'm baiting the monsters, it's the way I'm doing it. Dressing like a young girl, dressing as me when I was a young, abused, girl. Memories are swirling in my head, and I really want to catch one specific monster who was always a little scarier than the others. I want him with his neck beneath my blade. Finally, I decided I'm going after him this weekend. Sleep overtakes me the minute I choose.

I start my morning with a workout, my playlist blasts across the warehouse, sweat drips down my face, and the heavy bag swings with my strikes. Sawyer doesn't care for my music choices usually, but for some reason the heavy metal cranking at full blast doesn't bother him. He's perched on the weight bench watching me with his tail flicking in time to the beat. I quit after three reps and started my stretches. When I squat down onto the floor for more stretching, he joins me and pushes his way into each pose.

"I give up! You're impossible you little troublemaker," I chuckle as I hold him close and scratch his tiny chin.

After I shower and get dressed, I ride my bike to work. I want to do some recon when I finish. I park it in a space where I can watch it from inside while I wait on customers. I carry my helmet and backpack inside and ask Javier if I can store them in his tiny office. He nods his reply while he flips some burgers on the grill. He's a man of few words, my favorite kind.

Once I check my section and see there's already one group seated there, I head over to take their orders. Just like that I settle into the flow of work and before I know it, a few hours have passed. I don't always take a meal break, but for some reason I'm starving today. When Javier offers me a burger, I accept. I don't care that it's one he made incorrectly and was going to toss out, I like mustard and mayo, but the pickles I could live without. Luckily, they come off easily enough. I lean against the wall and stuff my face.

"Hey Violet, there's a guy asking for you," Danielle says on her way by.

"Mmmhmm?"

"Can't understand you with your mouth full, it's that guy who comes and talks to you sometimes, the really handsome one. Want me to help him?"

"Will you get his drink? I'll be right out," I say stuffing the last chunk of burger into my mouth.

"My pleasure, he's hot!"

"Mmmhanks." Chewing as fast as I can, I take a drink from my water bottle and then catch my breath. I'm not a fast eater,

I'm getting faster since I started working here, but I'd much rather graze all day. I wipe my mouth and hope I don't have anything in my teeth. There's no staff powder room, if I need a mirror or a toilet, so I'm stuck in the well-used customer restroom.

I make my way out to Jackson and another guy at a table in my section. When I get closer, the guy looks somewhat familiar. Jackson smiles when he sees me. He is pretty to look at. I sigh. The other guy looks at me and tilts his head, and he looks perplexed. My haircut might be throwing him off.

"Hello, Jackson. Are you guys ready to order?"

"Hello, Violet. This is my cousin, Austin."

"Hi, Cousin Austin. Are you ready to order?"

Austin smiles at me then smirks at his cousin before saying, "Hi, mystery woman Violet. I am ready to order. I'd like a burger, no cheese, no condiments, all the vegetables and a side of fries, please."

"Jackson?"

"I'll have the fried chicken, with fries and honey mustard. I'd also like to ask my first question for today, after you put our order in," he offers me a cheesy grin.

"I'll be right back," I shake my head as I aim for the kitchen. Danielle passes me with their drinks and winks at me on her way. I don't know what she thinks, but she's very mistaken. I take a minute to turn in the ticket. I glance at my only other table and they're still picking at mostly empty plates, but their drink refills are still good. Unable to procrastinate any longer, I return to the booth where Jackson and Austin sit.

"Okay. Shoot."

He grins at me again before taking a deep breath and asking, "Where do you work out?"

"That's your question? I was expecting something... more."

"It's something I've been wondering. I figured I may as well ask it as a question. So?"

"At home." It's my turn to grin, then I remember I haven't checked my teeth and close my lips.

Austin perks up, "Do I get a question?"

"It's not really fair for both of you to gang up on me." I give him a suspicious glare.

"Aw, it's not fair to let Jackson ask all the questions, he's obviously a dumbass," Austin pleads. I can't help chuckling, he's pretty funny and also not hurting my eyes.

"Okay, you can play. Have Jackson explain the rules I'll be right back."

I check in with my slow table and they're finally ready to cash out. I take care of their check and to-go boxes. Then I fill up some fresh drinks for my other table and pick up their food at the window. I carry everything over and give the guys their meal. When I take the tray back to the bar, I collect my water bottle. We've hit the weird lull that happens sometimes around three. It's too early for dinner and too late for lunch.

I lean on the bar and sip my water. Danielle has two tables left from the rush we had for lunch. Both are older couples who look fairly tame, but Danielle keeps rolling her eyes every time she walks away from their tables. Maybe she's just having an off day. I replace my bottle and return to the guy's table.

Austin speaks first. "I've got my question. Why did you cut your hair? It looks great, I'm just curious."

"I needed a change."

"Why?"

"Now who's the dumbass? That's another question, you only get three and it's her turn," Jackson explains.

"Thank you. My question for you is, how old are you?" I direct at Austin.

"Twenty-three, in two weeks," Austin grins at me with his answer. "Okay, Jackson, where were you born?" I ask my question.

"Mississippi. Down on the Gulf in Pascagoula, but I grew up in Florida," he answers me with a smile.

"Ooh! I've got my next question!" Austin exclaims.

"Geez dude, chill." Jackson chastises him.

I bravely raise an eyebrow, "Well?"

"What are you doing after work?" His grin widens into a smile that would make the Grinch jealous.

"Oh. Umm, I have plans," I mumble.

"Is that allowed? She didn't really answer the question," Austin grills Jackson.

"Hmm, that was a bit of a non-answer. I don't know if I'm able to judge. I guess I have to since I'm the outside party here. Okay…Violet has to either give a real answer or use her pass. What's it gunna be?"

"I'm working on a personal project, and I need to do some things to progress it along. So, I'll be out in the community working on my special project," I stared into Austin's eyes willing him to accept my answer. He looks to Jackson; I join him waiting for judgement from our self-appointed mediator.

"That's an answer, my turn. Austin, did you take a twenty out of my wallet?" Jackson asks.

"Wait…what? You can't ask me a question, only Violet can ask me. Right Violet?" Austin questions.

"No. If you're playing, it's fair game. Everyone gets three questions, including. You." I widen my eyes to emphasize my comments, and he catches on, I can tell by the mischief in his eye he's going to use it to his advantage.

"No, I took a ten and two fives, and I left you a twenty."

"You did?" Jackson asks with a look of confusion.

Austin jumps on that, "You can't ask another question it's her turn and learn how to count, dude. How embarrassing," Austin chuckles and his face looks triumphant. There's a dynamic at play here I'm unfamiliar with.

Before they lose me further, I ask my question, "Jackson, do you have any pets?"

"My dog stayed at my mom's when I moved out. I don't have any at my home, just my former dog. My apartment wouldn't accept dogs and my mom would've been lonely if I took her, and Cola would've been miserable alone at my place all the time. I made the best choice for both of them."

"Austin, same question."

"No pets, I'm not home enough but I'd like to get a dog or a cat, eventually."

"It's my turn, right?" Austin asks, we nod at him and grin at each other. "Okay, Jackson. Did you sleep with Sarah Markowitz at Terry Parker's party?"

"I told you no sex questions. But I'll answer, and never admit I said this to anyone else. Yeah, in the back of her father's car." Austin busts out laughing. I look between them like I'm watching a tennis match.

"I knew it!! Ryan and Corey wouldn't believe me, but I knew it! Ha! I can't wait to rub their faces in that shit." Austin continues his excited giggling, and I laugh because he's laughing. Then Jackson starts laughing and we're having way too much fun at work. Javier is probably going to yell at me any minute.

As Austin's chuckles subside, he clears his throat and asks me his next question, "Violet, how many boyfriends have you had?"

They both freeze when I say, "One." I can't tell if they're surprised, I answered or by my answer. Jackson knows I recently broke up with someone, so I can see the dots connecting on his forehead.

"Just one? How's that possible? Sorry, I know I can't ask another question. I just, I'm having a hard time believing you've only had one boyfriend. Maybe we're defining it differently? I mean guys you've gone out on dates with, kissed goodnight, you know like dating them."

"My answer sticks," I say possibly too serious for the moment.

Jackson clears his throat and when Austin looks his way, they conduct a silent conversation. Austin's eyes dart my way, then he looks down, not holding my eyes. I look at Jackson for answers. He gives me a sweet grin and clears his throat again.

"Violet, do you have any pets?" I give Jackson a friendly smile, thankful for his easy question.

"I do, a sweet gray kitten I found in the alley. His name is Sawyer, and he has green eyes." They're both grinning, they must like cats. The bell on the door jingles and reminds me I'm supposed to be working. I rush to greet the family of four and seat them in Danielle's section. She must be outside smoking. I collect their drink orders. I signaled the guys to give me a minute and go through the kitchen to find Danielle. She's outside the back door puffing on a Marlboro and talking on the phone. I whistle to get her attention; I hold up four fingers then point to myself and mime drinking from a cup. She nods and returns to her call; it reminds me of the guy's silent conversation. Grabbing a tray, I squeeze behind the bar and fill up the drinks for Danielle's table. I turn in their food order and return to the guys. Now that there's other customers I can't keep standing around.

"We gotta finish quick, I've got to get back to work. It's my turn. Umm, Austin, have you ever cheated on a girl?" I couldn't think of anything else. He seems surprised by my question.

"No." I nod and look at Jackson.

"Jackson, what's your favorite style of music?"

"I like alternative, local bands, indie artists, heavy metal, country, seventies, eighties, and rock."

"Wow. That was specific. Okay, whose turn, is it?"

"I think we might be out of questions. But I have another if you're willing," Austin posits. His eyes are focused with concentration, his jaw a little tight, he seems serious. I decided to let him go ahead and nod my acceptance. I think my willingness to keep chatting with strangers is a leftover habit from group sessions when I was an in-patient at the psych ward.

"Okay. Would you be willing to hang out with us sometime? Outside of your place of employment, you know, like friends who hang out after work and shoot the shit."

Both men watch me closely, no doubt trying to guess my response. I look between them and hope I'm not making a mistake. I can always change my number if things go south. I shrug a little and their faces tense up.

"Sure. Maybe we should exchange numbers so we can plan something," I casually reply. Both of them have really wide eyes and lips open in rings of surprise. I smile at their shock; I've always liked shocking people.

Jackson recovers first, "Great. Tell me your number..." he fumbles with his black device until he perches ready to type the digits. I tell him the numbers and he sends me a text. Then Austin sends one, and just like that I have two new numbers in my phone which only had five a moment ago.

"Got both your texts. We can set up something after the weekend. I've got to get back to work. See ya."

"Goodbye, Violet," Jackson says with a smirk.

"Bye, Violet. I look forward to talking to you again," Austin adds. I give them a wave and check on my other table. Out of my peripheral view I see the guy's place money with the check and leave. I collect their bill after I finish with the family. They left me a huge tip, calculating in my head they left me a forty-six percent tip. I'll have to ask them to quit that.

Finally, I placed my helmet on my head and say my internal goodbye to Mystic Cove Cantina. I thought six o'clock couldn't come fast enough. The purr of my matte black bike warms my heart, flooding me with happy memories of my dad. I smile as I turn right out of the lot and point towards the far side of town where the most fearsome monster of them all lives.

The huge metal gate looms over me as I look up the slope to the enormous two-story house where light glows warmly from several lower windows. The gate won't keep me out, it doesn't faze me at all. My eyes scan the landscape in search of an alarm company sign. Bingo! Why do people think it makes them safer? It just makes my job easier if I know what alarm system is installed. I can see video cameras. I'm sure they're the good ones. I sigh, how can such evil live in a beautiful place like this?

My memory flares to life and begins the reel of this monster hurting me. I try to fight it off, but it doesn't work until I begin plotting his demise. I have such lovely plans; he's going to be my first capture. His suffering needs to last a long time. I turn away from the pretty estate and let my imagination get creative with his upcoming time in custody, while I return home on autopilot. When I realize my garage door is right up ahead, I snap out of my quickly spiraling plot. It's like the saying, don't go grocery shopping when you're hungry. Well, don't plot to hunt a monster when his reel is playing on repeat. Just like what would happen in either fabled scenario, I've got some weird shit filling my head.

CHAPTER TWELVE

S howered and properly costumed, I smile at the camera even though they can see above my knee. I read the messages and try to correctly execute their requests.

Colby speaks like a carnival barker, "Alllll righty folks! It's time for your final bids, remember, this is one hundred percent virgin skin. Annnnd don't forget! You choose the design! Your mark will be the first thing to mar that smooth young canvas! Come on folks, this is a one-time only auction to own a piece of this body forever. You choose her first tattoo! We're down to the final two minutes. Get your final bids in now!"

I try to make my feet as exciting as possible during the bidding. I want to do whatever it takes to catch these animals. I tune back into Colby, and I'm surprised at how quickly those two minutes passed.

"That's five, four, three, two, one!!! We have our winner, the winner message is going out now, just follow the instructions. Thanks for visiting, have a great night."

In his regular, non-carnival barker and not technically altered, voice, Colby says, "You're clear."

I let out a deep breath, relaxing tension I didn't notice a moment ago. I stretch and try to loosen all of my muscles that became inexplicably tight in the last couple minutes.

I wonder out loud, "How did that go? Did we get a lot of them? How much was the winner?"

"Really well, yeah a good amount, eighty-seven thousand."

"Holy fuck! Are you serious? That's insane! Some jackass paid eighty. Seven. Thousand. Dollars to tattoo me? These people are sicker than I thought, maybe Uncle Randy needs to start doing outreach to these wackos."

"Wow, so quick to call them crazy. Remember who you're talking to," Colby reminds me.

"Sorry, I don't mean crazy like you and me, I mean sickos that want to do hurtful things to kids. How many bidders were there?"

"Three-hundred-twelve of those, forty-six are relatively local. I mean within a few hours' drive from here. It was overwhelmingly a US audience and skewed to our time zone. It makes sense since we had it in the evening in our time zone so people who share it were the most likely to attend. You got several requests to allow them to attend the tattooing in person, including from the winner."

"Really? That's very interesting, I may decide to do that if he checks out as a target. I'm tired. I'm going to bed, talk tomorrow?"

"You got it, VioleNt1. Night."

"Thanks, sweet dreams."

Finished with this particular plan, I collect the shoes, panties, and other props to return them to their rightful place. When I get upstairs Sawyer follows me around until I fill his dish. I wash my face and get dressed in my PJ's, by the time I crawl into bed Sawyer is waiting for me. He's at the foot of my bed licking his belly with his leg stuck up in the air at an obscene angle. I leave him to it.

I curl up in my covers and start figuring out a schedule for my plan to capture the worst monster of them all. I want to do it tomorrow, but it's too soon, I need to make sure every detail is just right. I have to meet Uncle Randy's girlfriend this weekend and I don't know enough about the monster's daily routine to grab him at the right time. But it's going to be soon, because I need him in captivity, suffering.

I'm nervous as I pull up to Uncle Randy's place. I haven't been here in a while, and it looks the same as always. He used to have an apartment when I first met him, but he bought a house a few years later. I don't know if he planned to find a wife or just wanted to make the investment of property ownership. It's a cute place, it has a World War II bungalow feel. It's a pale blue with dark blue shutters and doors. It even has an adorable white picket fence around the back yard. I thought he would get a dog with such a nice space, but he has no furry roommates.

When I raise my hand to knock on the perry-winkle door, a silver SUV pulls into the driveway, the sun reflects off the windshield so I can't see the sole occupant. As I watch, a tallish, slender, bespectacled woman emerges from the driver's side and quickly moves to the rising tailgate. In a flash she's aiming towards me, her arms loaded with plastic food containers.

I snap out of my stupor and rush to help her with her parcels. She startles when I reach for her, then her face breaks into a friendly smile, causing my own lips to curl in return.

"Well, hello! You must be Violet; Randy always talks about you as if you're a little girl. I know you're almost eighteen, but I can't help seeing you as much younger. I'm sorry, I'm Stephanie, it's so nice to finally meet you. You are most certainly not a little girl and I'm so sorry I pictured you that way. I won't anymore." Her grin returns. While she was talking, I closely examined her brown hair that sparks red and gold when the sun hits it. Pale, maybe silver or the lightest blue eyes twinkle with an inner light. There's the smallest hint of a tattoo around her ankle I spotted as she stepped from the car. She seems kinda perfect, if I hadn't already looked into her, I'd be suspicious. I think this is a genuinely nice person, being nice. Wow, that triggered a reel of my mom smiling, helping me, helping others, being the nice person she was, it's been a couple weeks since I had a flash like this.

"Are you okay?"

I snap back to the present and steady myself as I answer, "Yeah, of course. It's nice to meet you. I didn't picture you, I'm sorry, but I will now." Shit, that sounded like something a serial killer would say, hmmm, that checks out. I want to face-palm so hard right now; I plaster on a smile and hope she didn't notice.

"Randy!" She calls into the open house as she lets herself inside, I follow her lead.

Uncle Randy comes around the corner and takes everything left in her arms. His eyes light up and a smile cracks his face right before he kisses her.

"Hi," his voice is deep gravel, ugh! I don't want to know anything about their private life. He notices me and almost looks guilty, which is weird, but also kinda sweet. He's worried I'll get jealous like a spoiled child. To be fair, this is new territory for us but I'm completely confident that I have his fatherly love, for life. I want him to fall in love and be happy, and if she's awesome and I get along with her, even better. But I know he loves me unconditionally and that's never going to change.

"Violet, hi sweetie. I still can't get used to how grown up you look with your haircut. Just put those in the kitchen." I followed him and we both set down our stack of plastic. He looks towards the doorway and there's no sign of Stephanie. He examines me and I grin at him. He grins back.

"Well?"

"We only exchanged one sentence; how can I have an opinion already?" I retort.

"Come on, I know you better than that, give it up."

"Fine. I like her, and you're being weird, stop it. Do you need my help?"

"Nah, go chat with Stephanie, I'll get the food ready."

"Okay, hurry up I'm not the best at conversing."

"Yes ma'am. Turning on the turbo as we speak." I roll my eyes at him. For someone who's never had a kid, he's got the dad sense of humor down. When I enter the living room it's empty. I continue on to the Florida Room. She's sitting on the corner of the couch and reading a book. Not wanting to interrupt, I backtrack.

Before I take two steps she asks, "Where 'ya going? Have a seat." She closes her book; a leather bookmark protrudes from the pages.

"I didn't want to interrupt."

"I'm always reading, if you don't interrupt, I won't stop. Never worry about interrupting me, okay?"

"Okay. So, Uncle Randy says you're new to the area, how do you like it so far?" I ask.

"I work so much I haven't been able to see anything yet. Randy took me to the springs and the beach, but we haven't gone paddle boarding or hiking. Is that really what you wanted to ask me?" She smiles with a mischievous grin that looks like someone who knows everything.

"I was curious about that, but no, I wanted to ask why you moved here." I lay it on the line and figured I'll learn a lot from her next words. Her face crinkles into a frustrated sort of scowl.

"That's a tough one. I'm going to give you the quick and clean version, but you're welcome to ask more questions and I'll answer anything you ask. Randy knows everything, and you're free to ask him if you're more comfortable. I won't treat you like a child, and I won't lie to you, fair?"

"Great, yeah."

"I moved here because my parents aren't too far away. I left my old life because I had a problem at work. I found out some co-workers were breaking the law. I was threatened and harassed not to turn them in, and I did."

"Thanks for telling me the truth. I appreciate your honesty, and your pledge to treat me like an adult," I smile without showing any teeth.

She smiles back, understanding how important it was to tell me the truth. She is smart, Uncle Randy said it, but he brags about how smart I am, so I can't trust his scale. I like her a little more and I trust her a teeny tiny bit. Not many people make it into my circle of trust, like four. Or five? Doctor Stephanie will probably make six.

"Tell me something about you. How're you doing living on your own?"

"I'm good. I rescued a cat from the alley, and he keeps me company. I like my job, they're nice and pay well. The customers usually tip well too, and I make enough to support myself. I've made a few friends. I'm pretty happy with everything," I say as Jackson and Austin flicker through my head.

"What time does the game start?" She asks looking at her watch, it must be a doctor thing; I've noticed they all wear watch-es.

"It starts at four, but the pregame show should be on now. I'll put it on." I found the channel and try to think of something to say. She's chewing on her lip. I wonder if she's nervous talking to me. I suppose that would make sense. I am Uncle Randy's daughter for all intents and purposes as he says. It must be so hard to date when you're old.

"When does school start for you? Randy says you're going to Henry Plant in town, I've heard it's a good school. Do you know what you want to study?" she asks.

"Yeah. I graduated high school with the credits for an AA degree, so I'm starting on a BA with a major in Computer Science and a minor in Programming. School starts in a couple weeks, it seems like the summer has flown by, with everything." I feel a sharp pang in my heart as memories of my parent's flash through my head, and it takes my breath away. I feel my eyes burn with tears. Damn, I've been so good at keeping my emotions in check. I know Uncle Randy will say they have to come out one way or another. I thought I had them focused on another way, a physical release of epic proportions when I slice into an asshole who deserves it. I force a smile and hope she doesn't notice.

She swallows hard I can tell she noticed. She's probably trying to think of something considerate to say. Ugh! I hate pity, please don't say anything filled with pity, Stephanie.

"I'm almost set up for lunch, what do you ladies want to drink?"

Uncle Randy to the rescue, a genuine smile graces my face. Stephanie and I both ask for iced tea at the same time, only my request is for sweet tea like a true southerner. We laugh at ourselves and Uncle Randy smiles and winks at Stephanie. I think he's happy we have something in common.

"I've never had iced tea until I moved here. Being from Seattle, I've always been more of a coffee drinker. Especially during medical school and my residency, since the hours you have to put in are brutal. Some days, the only thing holding me up was coffee. But I'm really liking the tea. It's so refreshing in the heat. I don't care for that sweet stuff though. It's just too sweet for me."

"You might need to have southern blood to drink sweet tea. I like coffee sometimes, if it's cold out, or I want one of those super sugary mocha, frappe, things. It's like dessert instead of coffee."

"Yeah, you can thank Seattle for those expensive, thousand calorie coffees. Do you guys serve fancy coffee at your restaurant?"

"No! Thank God, we just serve sodas and there's a bar. Sangria is popular. We also have margarita night, it's sort of a Mexican place with a twist of American. Maybe it's Texmex, I'm not really sure what constitutes that combo."

Chuckling at my description, she asks, "Do you plan to keep working once school starts?"

"That's the plan, but if it's too hard I may adjust my hours. They're pretty flexible and I did tell them I was starting school soon when they hired me."

"Okay ladies, everything's ready!" Randy yells from the kitchen. We make our way to the dinette table where we usually eat breakfast and lunch.

After the game is over and we have everything cleaned up, I'm ready to go. I had a really nice time getting to know Stephanie. I like her and I can tell Uncle Randy is smitten. He tried to keep the PDA to a minimum, but I caught them kissing twice. It was cute that they couldn't keep away from each other. Maybe she's the one for him. I say my goodbyes to her, and she hesitates before giving me a one-armed hug. I'm not a hugger, but if I like you, I'll put up with it. I still like her even though she hugged me. Uncle Randy walks me outside.

"All right, let me have it."

"Wow, I'm barely out the door dude," I smirk at him enjoying his discomfort as he waits for me to answer.

"Come on, just tell me. I can't take the suspense."

"I would think you would have more patience than this, Doctor Nercy. Okay, okay, I've tortured you enough. I really like her. She's very nice, smart, funny, and even though she likes the Seahawks of all things, I think I can get along with her. There, are you happy?" I can't keep in my laughter.

"Seriously, Uncle Randy, she's great. I appreciate how she treated me like an adult, and she didn't hesitate to tell me the truth about why she moved here." His eyes widened with surprise at my admission.

"I'm glad. Drive safe, and please text me when you get home. We need to make this a regular thing, I miss you."

"I miss you too. Why don't we alternate weekly meals between here and in town? We can try some of the restaurants and maybe some of the entertainment. I promise I'll text when I get home."

"That's a great plan, I'm in. Can Stephanie come if she's free?"

"Of course. I told you I liked her. Also, I think I'd rather you tell her about my history. I've been having a few flashes of my parents today and I think it'll be hard for me, okay?"

"Should I be worried?"

"No. It's nothing like that. I think it's just that she reminds me a little of mom and it triggered some memories. Nothing debilitating or anything to worry about. Promise."

"Okay." He encloses me in a tight hug. "I love you, don't forget even though you're all grown up, I'll always be here for you. If you need to talk or anything else, call me or just come over, okay?" "Yes. I know. I love you too, you're my favorite uncle." It's our usual joke.

"I'm your only uncle," he chuckles and releases me. We smile and I wave before I head home, after a small detour.

CHAPTER THIRTEEN

The lights glow softly from the first floor even though the sun hasn't really gone down yet. It's that perfect time of twilight where the sun is low enough not to blind you anymore, and everything has muted colors as the world waits for night to drift in like a dark fog. I imagine the occupant of this historic mansion is worshiping at an alter to Satan himself, probably with candles flickering and a bloody sacrifice twitching and wishing for death. This particular target is the evilest of the monsters who tormented me as a child. He didn't hold his current highly respected position back then, but he was a trusted member of the community. He was a mentor to many, and a confidant to the vulnerable. I didn't know he was dangerous until the Beast brought him home. I actually thought he was there to save me. In my childhood mind I imagined that my biological mother actually loved me and somehow, she had told him to rescue me from the hell the Beast kept me living in. I remember he sat at our dinner table and shared our meal while he spoke kindly to my mother and the Beast. He looked at me strangely and I thought it was a secret signal that he would help me escape and take me someplace safe. I couldn't have been more than eight years old.

I used to attend the academy he oversaw when I was allowed to go to school. I trusted him. It made it so easy for him to do what he did, and it might be the thing that finally broke me. I might have never sliced the Beast open and reveled in his blood, if it weren't for this particularly evil monster. It's why I think he's the worst of them all, and it's why I need to make him pay, and soon. As I drive away, my mind fills with the details of how I want to torture him. I need something truly mind bending and painfully slow, to make him suffer just half of what he did to me. I have some ideas and my lips curl into a wicked grin as the blood flows in my imagination.

By the time I pull up to my warehouse, I've got the outline of a plan formed and I'm excited to get to work on all the details. I need to start with his daily schedule and find his vulnerable times of day and locations. I need a secluded place to get him into a transport vehicle. I'm strong but he's a big guy, and he won't be easy to move. Maybe I can convince him to get into a vehicle somehow before I knock him out or tie him up. I need supplies. I need to test the room where I want to keep him for soundproofing and escape proofing. Yeah, this may take a few weeks, and I'm probably going to have to deal with the auction winner first which is fine, since he deserves my attention too.

After I fed Sawyer, I get to work on my plans for the evil one and the auction winner. The Bait and Slice Inn is going to be filled to capacity soon. I spent the next three hours poking at the keys on my laptop. Once I have all of my plans laid out, encrypted, and in code, I work out with my music on full blast. Sawyer doesn't even react to my playlist anymore. He perches nearby and watches while feigning disinterest. I push myself hard beating the hell out of the bags and sweating gallons. It helps me release the stress of remembering the events I've survived. I spend at least a half hour bouncing around the warehouse honing my parkour skills. I have to say I'm getting pretty good. I'm able to scale up to the second floor with ease and I can jump really far now. I'm working towards being able to navigate the rafters and beams along the warehouse ceiling. I need to do some practice in the wild, on some real buildings. I should have time for that on Tuesday, my next day off.

Once I cool down from my workout, I take a quick shower and microwave a bowl of leftover spaghetti. I round out my meal with some salad and stream the news and weather while I eat. I change to a cooking channel when the news becomes too depressing one minute later. Much better. Sawyer is curled on my foot waiting for me to drop something. My phone chimes with a text message. I finish chewing before I look at the screen.

Cousin Austin- Hi Violet, it's Austin. Are you busy?

Me- Not particularly, what's up?

Cousin Austin- I was wondering do you have any time off this week?

Me- I'm off Tuesday, why?

Cousin Austin- Jackson and I were talking, and we wondered if you would hang out with us, like we talked about?

Me- What do you have in mind?

Cousin Austin- We thought you could choose this time, and we'll pick next time. What do you think?

Me- Hmmm...

Cousin Austin- You can text me later, no rush.

Me- Would you guys want to work out with me?

Cousin Austin- At your place?

Me- No. In town.

Cousin Austin- Sure! Just tell us when and where. We should be finished at work early Tuesday, so any time after 2.

Me- Ok I'll send you a location and time when I get it set up.

Cousin Austin- Cool. Jackson will be thrilled-he hates to work-out.

Me- You have a mean streak. Me too.

Cousin Austin- I knew it. Catch ya later

*Me- *thumbs up emoji**

I grin at the phone. I'm going to take them to town for parkour practice, this should be fun. I wonder if either of them knows any moves.

"What do you think Sawyer? Do they know anything about parkour, or will they kill themselves trying?"

Mooowow.

"You're probably right. Men can't seem to avoid trying to show off, but even if they know some moves it'll probably turn into a competition and be very entertaining. I'm looking forward to it. Having some friends might be just what I need to keep me from going full dark. Unless I'm already there. Come on cutie, let's clean up and head to bed. I have the early shift tomorrow and I don't know how much sleep I'll get with the memories I visited today." He follows me into the kitchen, and I let him have a couple bites of a meatball and a small cube of cheese.

He purrs when he eats if it's something he really likes. It's hilarious and he makes me think of a lion, but his tiny little body is too adorable to be that fierce. I told him all about meeting Stephanie and how I kind of like her. He doesn't weigh in. Every night I place him in his bed on my bed. Sometimes he lies down there until I fall asleep, other times he doesn't even pretend, and he just hops right out and curls up on me. He doesn't care if I put him back ten times, he does what he wants. He's so freaking cute I can't get mad.

I know it's my fault he keeps doing it because I give in. I find myself locked in the torture dungeon from my childhood and I'm chained to a bed. A huge man dressed in black with a hood covering his head so I can't see his face, arranges instruments of torture on a small table. I plead with him not to hurt me, and he chuckles an evil laugh as he chooses a shiny, metallic, implement and steps towards me. I'm crying and begging him not to hurt me, but he keeps approaching. He leans over me; his size alone is imposing and when you combine it with the weapon in his hand, I'm terrified. When his other hand reaches for me, I spot a large gold ring on his finger, with a red stone sparkling in the dim light, I scream. I jolt upright, awake and shaking in my bed. Sawyer quickly curls in my lap and rubs his face against me. I lift him to my chest and hold him close while I catch my breath.

I chant my safety mantra, "I'm free, I'm safe, they can't hurt me anymore. I'm strong, I'm a warrior, I'm a badass, they can't hurt me anymore." Once I've repeated it five or six times, my breathing has returned to normal.

The tears have dried at the corners of my eyes. Sawyer watches me and relaxes when I do. Uncle Randy helped me come up with my safety mantra. I thought he was crazy when he first mentioned it, but it really helps soothe and calm me after a traumatic dream or flashback. It changes over time, but the message remains the same. He might be a genius. I'll have to tell him about my dream. He always knows when I've been having bad dreams, but I won't tell him why. I can't ever let my revenge taint his life in any way. I settle back down and try to sleep. After I drink some water, I use my other tools and imagine my happy place until I fall back asleep. It always works like a charm. Another gift from my ersatz parent. He got me to admit that I have an ideal place I would visit in my imagination any time I was trapped in an uncomfortable, abusive, or traumatic situation. Once he knew that, he got me to expand it and add to the structures so I had safe rooms with locks I control, and I can go there and be completely relaxed and safe.

At first, I struggled with flashbacks of why I started imagining it in the first place, but he helped me see that my mind set it up as a safe escape and I can still use it. Once we reinforced all the walls and doors and put in locks, it was easy to be safe there. He doesn't know about my weapons room or my torture room, but he doesn't need to know. They work for me when I need a little revenge. Nowadays I prefer the real thing, but it still works in a pinch.

I wake up refreshed, well rested, ready to face my early shift. After I make sure Sawyer is good for the day, I head to the Cantina hoping this day goes by smooth and quick. Right when I arrive at work my phone rings. I'm a few minutes early so I answer, only for Harmony.

"Hey girl! How're you?"

"I'm good. I just got to work so I can't chat long. I've got about ten minutes until my shift."

"Okay, I'll get right to the point. I found my perfect *666 rule* guy, and I'm getting married!"

"Oh my God! Congratulations! I'm so happy for you and Mike. Do you have a date picked out?"

"Yeah, next year, summerish. I hope you know you're my Maid of Honor, okay?"

"Of course. But you know I'm clueless about all that bachelorette stuff, I'm going to need guidance. Lots of guidance."

"No worries, babe. I got you. I'll plan everything and you can just execute my plans, 'kay?"

"That'll work. I'm so excited for you guys, you're the best couple. What's the 666 rule?"

"You know, over six feet, over six inches, over six figures. Well, he'll earn over six figures once we graduate."

"Oh damn, how're you gonna be like grown up and shit? You're ridiculous! Holy crap, are you gonna have kids?"

"Geez, Vi, way to make it serious! I mean, probably, yeah, some day. Definitely not any time soon. I want to work on my career for a few years before we do that. Umm...I need to tell you something. Promise you won't freak out, okay?"

"What the fuck, Harm? Why would you say that?"

"I'm sorry sweetie, it's about Max."

"What about him?"

"He got into a fist fight with his asshole father and took off to Europe. He says he's going to travel around for a while and if he decides to go to school, he'll come back. Mike tried talking him into staying with us and not ditching out on school, but he says he can't be on the same continent as his dickhead father. I'm sorry, Vi."

"Shit. Why are you sorry? He's always had major issues with his father, he's an abusive prick. I'm actually kind of proud of him for fighting back. Do you think he's going to be okay?"

"Mike spoke to him, not me, but he says he seemed good and positive. Looking forward to a different future than he had planned. He says he's okay about you, he understands. He said he'll always love you, but he knows why you guys couldn't stay together and he misses you, but he knows it's for the best. He said he'll be at the wedding no matter what. Are you all, right?"

"I'm okay. You know, I think our love was more like best friends or siblings and when we tried to make it something it wasn't, it just didn't work, it sounds like he gets that. Maybe we can be friends again someday. I miss him too. But my feelings aren't romantic if that makes sense. I just don't think we were meant to be more than friends. We liked each other so much as friends we kind of gave in to the pressure to date and be more. But it just wasn't gonna happen. If you speak to him, please tell him I'm happy for him and I hope we can be friends someday. If he ever needs me, I'll be there."

"I get what you're saying, and I think you're right. With your past and his, you guys didn't know what you had or what you were meant to be. I'm glad you figured it out before you made any major, life changing choices. It could've ended up being really bad, I think you guys will be friends in the future, you're too great at being close to each other. Besides, you're an awesome friend and if he doesn't remember that he's a dumbass."

"He's not a dumbass. I think we'll figure out how to be friends again. I'm sorry Harm, but I've gotta get inside, my shift is about to start. Thanks for calling. Please give Mike a big congratulations hug for me. We'll talk soon. Yeah?"

"You got it babe. Love you!"

"Love you too!" I enter the building and stow my things. While I wipe down the tables and refill the condiments... and I think about Max. I hope he's really doing okay, better than okay. He's a good guy and I know he's going to find the right girl, and she better be amazing because he's the best. I can't believe he hit his dad. That must've been some fight. His dad is such a piece of shit. Rich beyond rich, but abusive, racist, condescending, just vile to everyone, but most of his anger has always been focused on Max. He wanted Max to be someone else.

Max's personality is gentle, funny, and kind. His father always called him a *'faggot, sissy, nerd, with no future.'* My blood boils just thinking about that asshole. I hope Max knocked his ass out. I smile as I imagine him with a broken jaw that had to be wired shut, finally keeping him from spouting his repulsive hatred.

"What're you so happy about?" Danielle asks as she passes me with a tray of freshly refilled saltshakers.

"Got some good news on my way to work about some friends. What's new with you?"

"Girl don't even get me started. My youngest's baby daddy hasn't paid child support in two months and I think I have to take him to court. He has three warrants, so if I file, they're gunna arrest him and then I definitely won't be getting any support. What is wrong with men? I swear they can be so stupid sometimes..."

My shift flies by as I nod and respond with the appropriate outrage to Danielle's stories, for the entire eight hours. When the clock strikes four joy fills my veins and bursts out of my mouth in a cheer. How lame am I?

When I arrive at home to check in with Sawyer, I call Uncle Randy and update him on my dream and how I coped with it. He feels good, like he's taking care of me and I'm happy to connect with him. I assure him how much I like Stephanie, and he shares that she likes me too. I get a little tingle in my chest. If she marries Uncle Randy at some point, she could be Aunt Stephanie, and maybe an adoptive parent just like him. I stop my thoughts from going there. Just because the happiest time of my life was when I had my mom and dad, it doesn't mean things will ever be that good again. I need to remember, when people love me, they either die or end up being wolves in sheep's clothing. I can't fall for that again, I'm too old to be so naïve.

When I hang up, I text Austin and tell him when and where he and Jackson can meet me tomorrow. Then I leave for the store with some very specific purchases in mind. I need some supplies for the Bait and Slice Inn, this Friday is going to be a blast.

CHAPTER FOURTEEN

When I pulled up next to the truck with Jackson and Austin sitting inside, they both watch me climb off my beautiful bike and remove my helmet. There's a group of young guys playing shirts and skins on the basketball court and some goth looking kids hanging out underneath the pavilion smoking something. Some of the basketball players whistle at me. I ignore them, and the kids dressed in all black and spikes, with rings in their ears, noses, and lips don't notice me in their anarchistic aloofness. I smile brightly at Jackson who's closest to me in the driver's seat of the fairly newish looking white truck.

His mouth snaps closed. "Hey. Violet. I, I didn't know you ride a motorcycle. That's um, a nice bike."

"Thanks, it was my dad's. You guys ready to get started?"

"Uh, yeah. Come on Austin."

Both guys climbed out of the truck. They're dressed in sweats and tank tops. I'm in yoga pants, a sports bra, and a cut up t-shirt over it. Austin makes his way around the truck and greets me with a fist bump. I try not to be obvious as I check them out. They're toned and muscular but in a hardworking way, not a bodybuilder look at all. I feel something fluttering in my stomach as my eyes scan their defined bodies and tattoos. They're very attractive and I've tried so hard not to notice. I hope my face isn't betraying my inner thoughts. I realize I'm staring, and Austin is waiting for my attention to greet me, and I finally focus on his eyes as my cheeks heat.

"Hey. Cool bike. What're we doing? I don't see a gym or any equipment in this park, and you were a little vague."

"Sorry. I was kinda going for a surprise. We're going to practice parkour; do you have any experience with it?"

Jackson answers first, "Yeah, a little, we used to do it in his backyard when we were kids until he fell and broke his arm. After that we had to do it away from our houses." He points his thumb over his shoulder towards Austin.

"It was your fault I fell! You moved the branch right when I was jumping. I would've had it if you weren't being a dick."

"Yeah, okay, Spider-Man. You would've made that jump if not for me." Jackson shakes his head while Austin smirks behind him.

"Where're we doing this?" Austin asks, looking around.

"I thought we'd stretch out a little and then jog over a few blocks to warm up. There're a few empty buildings over there where people practice parkour and skateboarding, basically anything society frowns on. What do you think?"

"Lead the way," Jackson answers.

After we stretch and do a few pushups, sit-ups, and jumping jacks, we race to the empty buildings. We don't find anyone else practicing anything when we get to the first building. I speed up and leap onto a wall and then scale over to an out-cropping with some metal attached to it. Then using my arms and my momentum, I swing upwards to a balcony. When I stop there, I turn to see what the guys are doing. Jackson follows right behind me and lands next to me smiling. Austin swings down from above us and lands on my other side a moment later. Color me impressed.

"I thought you said you haven't done parkour since you were kids?"

"I didn't say that. Did you say that, Austin?"

"Nope, I didn't say that, and I didn't hear you say it either." They both offer me smug smiles and it makes me laugh.

"Oh boy, I'm going to have to watch out for you guys, aren't I? You two are trouble, I can see it clearly now. Okay, let's try this again. How much parkour experience do you both have? And how recent is it?"

"Jackson, did that sound like two questions to you? Isn't that against the rules?"

"Why yes, Austin, it was two questions and definitely against the rules." Again, they both look at me, this time with wide grins on their faces. They look like Cheshire cats from Alice in Wonderland. Oh man, this isn't fair, the two of them ganging up on me with their smartass remarks. I bet they've been doing this their whole lives, especially since they grew up together like brothers. I think over my options, and I make a quick decision.

"New rules! If you catch me in less than a minute you can ask three questions, if I can avoid you for more than a minute, I get three for each of you!" With that, I bolt and leap from the balcony onto the next one and then using a drainpipe, I scale up to a third-floor window. Stepping carefully along the narrow sill, I climb across the next window to a fire-escape. Then I swing out and fling myself upwards and to the side, climb to the next level, and then I hop through an open window and stop counting in my head. Sixty seconds have passed, and I'm alone. Not for long, just a moment later both guys step through the same window.

"That wasn't fair, you changed the rules and took off before we could agree or disagree. Once we got our heads out of our asses, we were right behind you, but nobody set a timer."

"I counted in my head. If you're willing to trust me, I was here for eighteen seconds before you guys arrived. So, I should get three questions for each of you." I look between them my eyes wide, brows raised, a pleading grin of innocence on my lips.

"Aww, man. She has those puppy-dog eyes that I can't say no to, and that's going to be a problem. What d'you think Jackson?"

"Fine. We'll give you this round. I can't fight that look either. It's the same one your little sister uses on me, Auz. Ask away, Violet." He looks a little defeated when he turns towards me, but I know he's just being dramatic.

"Answer the questions I already asked about parkour."

Austin clears his throat, "Yeah, we practice pretty regularly. We like to be ready for anything, and it helps us get out of a bad situation quickly when our opponent doesn't know we can scale walls and jump around like monkeys. We've been doing it since we were kids and we're pretty good at it. Our height helps our reach, but it also hinders us sometimes being this size. We can't be as fast as you or flip around with as much acrobatic grace as you, but we do pretty well. Any more questions?"

I look them each in the eye, assessing them and their honesty. I look at their size and I can see what he means by their reach and they're likely much stronger than me. Even though they have more weight to lift, their strength probably balances it out nicely. A question comes to mind, and I look at Jackson while I ask it assuming he'll answer since they seem to enjoy alternating who speaks. I suspect it's another leftover childhood habit.

"Do you get into bad situations that you need to escape quickly very often?" He glances at Austin, and they exchange some type of silent communication before he responds.

"We have some hobbies that can be a little bit dangerous sometimes," he smiles at me like he gave me a complete and sensible answer.

Trying not to show my frustration, I spout, "Round two!" While I take off running. I bound up onto the landing of the stairwell and bounce off the wall reaching the threshold of the next floor. I ran through a doorway and into a large room. The windows are missing so I grasp the opening and step onto the sill. I'm on the fifth-floor fire escape in no time and I continue to count in my head until I step over the barrier surrounding the roof. Standing before me are two men who look like they've been here for twenty minutes, not the more likely twenty seconds.

"Shit! How did you guys do that? It wasn't even sixty seconds yet."

"Yeah, we use our long legs to climb fast. It's our turn for questions," Austin states.

"Why do you use parkour?" Jackson questions.

"I'm still learning, I haven't really used it yet."

"How long have you been, learning?" Austin takes a turn.

"A year or less. I started fooling around with it at first but over the last few weeks I've stepped up my training," I automatically look to Jackson for the next question.

"In what activity do you partake that makes you want to learn and use parkour?" Shoot, Jackson finally phrased his question in a way I can't squirm past.

"I have some hobbies in which I would benefit from being able to escape quickly if the situation warranted it. I'm working on a special project right now that is particularly wrought with possibilities for situations that may require the use of parkour. Plus, it's fun and I want to be in the best shape possible," I try to give them my puppy-dog smile. They exchange another look filled with some type of communication only they can understand.

"I think you may have some interesting secrets, Miss Violet. But I suppose we have time to figure it out. One-two-three-go!" He takes off and dives over the edge of the roof. Jackson runs off in another direction. I stand stunned for a moment too long. Then I follow the direction Jackson went; I'm rewarded wit. an open door to a stairwell. I make my way down the stairs as fast as I can go, barely touching any steps. I leap and slide my way down again and again.

Before I reach the bottom floor, I veer down a hallway and run towards the far end of the building. When I find an open door and an open window, I jump through it and using some type of plumbing or electrical pipe fastened to the exterior of the building, I swing down and land on the ground. I rush to the area I think the guys will be waiting. Then I slow and stroll up behind them. Before they have a chance to notice me, I'm there. I reach out and point my finger into Jackson's back like it's a weapon.

"Freeze. Put your hands up," I can't keep from cracking up and I drop my 'weapon' and bend over laughing like a loon. I don't think I actually scared either guy, but they were surprised I came from behind them. Even though I'm pretty sure they knew I was there long before I touched him, they don't bust me for being the last to arrive. I think they're honestly trying to build a friendship with me. Maybe they realize the disparity between us when it's two against one.

I venture a question to see if they'll answer or call me out, "Do you both always carry a concealed firearm?"

That look flashes between them again before Austin answers, "We're both licensed to carry and conceal. When you gave us the meetup address, we decided to bring our firearms. Does it bother you?"

Even though it seems they're letting me ask the questions I decide not to call them out either. I figure if they're letting me get away with it, I can reciprocate. I notice some odd warmth in my chest and sort of a twinge between my thighs. It's not a feeling I'm familiar with and I freeze for a moment.

"Are you all, right?" Jackson asks concern lowering his brows. I can feel my face flush with embarrassment, and I shake myself a bit to dispel the color in my cheeks.

"Oh. Yeah. I'm fine, sorry. No, it doesn't bother me, I don't mind at all. I have experience with firearms, knives, and swords from my martial arts and weapons self-defense training. I've been learning that stuff since I was thirteen." I give him an innocent grin and hope he doesn't ask why.

We decided to get a smoothie before going home and walk to a place down the block from where we parked. After we're seated the guys start teasing each other and we spend the next forty-five minutes laughing and sharing more about ourselves. Before I know it, I've told them I have no siblings, and I ask about theirs. Jackson has an older half-brother who's married and lives in Tallahassee. He's not blood related to Austin at all. Austin has two younger sisters, and one older. Two are still in school and the older one is away. He doesn't elaborate and they both get quiet after mentioning her. I take the hint they don't want to talk about her, and I redirect our conversation. Since it's getting late, I need to get home. I have things to do, and Sawyer needs to eat. The guys are agreeable, and we say our goodbyes at our vehicles.

"I'm glad we did this, it was fun," I say.

"It was fun. It was also nice getting to know you better, you're funnier than you let on at first glance," Austin compliments.

"You're pretty funny yourself." I smiled at him, feeling that awkward heat in my chest and along my neck.

"What about me?" Jackson asks.

"You're funny, looking," Austin teases him. Jackson punches his arm, and Austin grabs the injured part of his biceps.

"Dickhead."

I chuckle at them, "You're both funny, dickheads. Don't worry, it's totally a tie. No need to battle it out." They both look at me with mock shock, then smile.

I climb onto my bike and before I pull on my helmet I say, "Text me when you decide what we're doing next. I'll see you guys. Thanks again for working out with me. I had fun. I'd love to do this again, and I need more work on my parkour skills. Bye guys, drive safe." With that, I pull on my helmet, rev my engine as my bike comes to life, and wave before I take off. They wave as I pass them and then open their truck. I turn a corner and lose sight of them. The smile doesn't leave my face the entire drive home.

Lost in thought, I don't remember the entire drive home and I'm at my warehouse before I know it. I park my bike in the vehicle bay and stow my stuff. Sawyer greets me from his post on the stairs where he was lying completely relaxed and not waiting for me at all. He follows me to the kitchen after I step over him. I open a can of food for him, and he meows loudly urging me to move faster. Once his dish is in front of him, he dives on it, growl-purring in his usual way.

I smile at him. "You're the cutest, little guy. I'm going to do some work in the Bait and Slice Inn. You're welcome to join me when you finish." I grab a bottle of water and my toolbox on the way to the construction zone.

Once I'm inside I start a playlist on my phone and survey my supplies. I'm installing extra soundproofing in this room on the walls and ceiling. I get busy nailing up the waffled material and quickly get into a rhythm making fast work of the job. I seal all of the joints that don't line up perfectly for extra sound dampening. Starting on the ceiling was definitely the way to go, it's the hardest part. By comparison the walls are easy and I'm finishing in just a few hours. I notice the time when my stomach growls, as I hit the last nail on the head. It's later than I thought but I'm really happy with the end result.

I want to test how well it works, so I turn up the volume on my phone as loud as it goes. I close the door and stand right outside. I can't hear anything, and I smile satisfied with a job well done. I need to call Colby at some point and have him listen over the phone while I bang around in there to be sure it's completely secure. Exhausted, I collect my phone and tools before heading back upstairs for a shower. Sawyer follows me and waits for a bite while I eat.

Once I'm showered, I join a sleeping Sawyer in my bed. For once he's actually curled up in his own little bed, I hope he stays put. When I plug in my phone on my nightstand the text chime sounds.

RobNdaHood: How did the installation go?

Me: Good, we'll test it tomorrow, I'm going to sleep.

RobNdaHood: Cool. I got Nemo all set up for Friday. He says all he needs is a sink and an outlet. I also got Dozer to be the chauffeur. Everything is ready on my end. Let me know if you need anything else. Sweet dreams!

*Me: Sounds perfect-thanks RobN *heart emoji**

*RobNdaHood: *spider emoji**

When I set my phone back on the table my eyes fall closed.

Chapter Fifteen

By Thursday night I've driven past the *root of all evil mansion* several times. I hate thinking about him, imagining him just living in his evil lair, pretending to be a normal, law-abiding citizen. I refuse to say his name and I try not to even think about it. Maybe I need to do what J.K. Rowling did in Harry Potter and just call him *He-Who-Must-Not-Be-Named.* Oh, I've got it, I'll call him *Voldemort.* It's actually quite fitting. He's vile and evil as evil can be. He pretends to be a leader but uses his absolute power to corrupt. Was it Lord Actor who said that? No, it was *Acton!* Why do I remember such weird little bits of information? Can you get A.D.D. as an adult? I know I was tested for everything as a kid during my hospital stay, and you'd think if I had it, they would've found it. I'll have to ask Uncle Randy.

I've also hacked everything I can get my virtual hands on that belongs to Voldemort or his local organization. I'm monitoring his every move and I've actually been surprised by his efforts to avoid detection. He definitely hired someone, bribed them, or black-mailed them to set up all of his electronics. Between me and Colby he couldn't avoid our hacking prowess, but it wasn't as simple as I thought it would be. My modified *Comet* program is hard at work documenting every click of a key, and I've got some cameras set up to watch his comings and goings. I even managed to attach a GPS locator to his car so I can follow his every movement in the real world too. My plan is coming together and I'm excited to move forward. But before I can do anything with him, I have to get through this weekend with my auction winner.

I have everything set up and I'm as ready as I can be for tomorrow. Colby's got everything on track to broadcast as I get the tattoo. I'm excited to have another scumbag predator in my clutches. I wish I had a ghoulish laugh to enjoy the moment.

Me: Hey, I'm all set. I think I'm going to bed, after a shower. Thanks for all your work, I couldn't have done this without you. Are you nervous?

RobNdaHood: Nah, why would I be nervous? My best friend is just going to be alone with a predator while I watch on camera and can't help.

Me: Dude! Don't do that, you know you wouldn't be any help even if you were here. JK-seriously, you'll be tons of help monitoring everything, filming, broadcasting, and keeping a look out. I couldn't do this without you! I love you dude. I wouldn't trust anyone else. Good night.

RobNdaHood: You too! Sleep well, this is not a drill.

As soon as I put my phone in my pocket it chimes again, "Ugh! Come on Colby, I'm tired. Oh. Hey look at that, Sawyer, it's Jackson."

Jackson: Hey how are you?

Me: Good. You?

Jackson: I'm good too. Work's been super busy, I'm looking forward to the weekend. Do you have plans tomorrow?

Me: Yeah.

Jackson: How about Saturday?

Me: I have work in the morning, but my afternoon is free. What's up?

Jackson: We came up with an activity we think you'll like, but it's a surprise. Are you game?

Me: Sure.

Jackson: Cool. One of us will send you the address. See you then.

Me: Cool.

This should be interesting... I'm curious to see what they think I'll find fun. I smile all the way to the shower, and I may try to indulge in a little self-care with them on my mind. I'm not really ready to think about that, I've never felt attraction before. I have so many confused feelings about them and my own body, I don't know how to process it. I'm definitely feeling an attraction to both of them, which is weird by itself. Then add in my past, Max, my lack of experience, and my too many traumatic experiences, and I get overwhelmed and just feel stabby. I may need to bite the bullet and talk to Uncle Randy about them.

With Sawyer curled in his bed again I close my eyes and imagine how the conversation will go. I'll be embarrassed, but very blunt. He'll be embarrassed but very professional with his psychiatrist voice. I can't help teasing him when he gets all serious in his doctor mode. Plus, our goofy banter helps me talk about uncomfortable topics. I don't know what he'll think of me having an attraction to two men at once. Who does that?

He'll be understanding and non-judgmental because he's the best doctor ever and he loves me. I can't imagine what kind of advice he'll give me. With Max, he just offered a lot of support and pledged to be available if I needed him for anything as our relationship developed. I told him when Max and I decided to date and when we kissed and thought about more. I told him how sweet and patient Max was about my history. That's the thing, Max knew my history and was there for me through my treatment.

He never pressured me about anything, and he was a wonderful friend. I wish we didn't confuse our friendship with a romantic relationship, but he was exactly the person I needed then.

I miss my parents so much. Lying in bed at night is when all of my thoughts swirl in my head and good memories get plowed over by the bad ones. These kinds of thoughts are exactly what leads to nightmares for me. I could've talked to my mom and dad about them. I chuckled out loud a little, thinking about them grilling Jackson and Austin. I'm not sure who would've been harder on them. My mom was a serious badass, but my dad would blow up the world for me. I remember when he met Max for the first time, and we were only friends. With the good memories filling my thoughts I drift into a dream.

I know it's a dream, but I'm not sure how I know. I'm excited because I'm meeting my parents. We're supposed to meet at the cabin we rented in California one time. It's this beautiful log house nestled in the giant redwoods at the base of the Sierra-Nevada Mountains. We're the only ones around for miles and the snow is deep and sparkling in the sunlight. Our voices echo through the woods as we swish our skis through the packed powder. I never tried cross-country skiing before. It's so much fun. We're laughing and enjoying our time together, but I know we only have a short time to spend with each other.

They're only allowed to be here for one day and I want to make every moment count. I tell them about Max and me breaking off our relationship. I tell them about moving into my own place and changing schools. They're okay with those choices and encourage me to work out a friendship with Max. I decide to tell them about Grandmother Joyce and her freak out over their will. They promise it'll all workout, and I have no reason not to believe them.

Then I decided to tell them about Jackson and Austin. At first, they look a little confused, but mom eventually understands and explains it to dad.

"Sweetie, they're good guys. What you're talking about is called a polyamorous relationship. There's nothing wrong with it, if all the parties know about each other and agree, it's fine. Besides, they might be your soul mates, and you can't overlook that because it's a little different. True love is to be treasured when you are lucky enough to find it. Talk to them. I think you'll find they feel the same about you more than you think. Follow your heart and don't be afraid to go to Randy about anything. He loves you so much. You're really his daughter as much as ours." They hug me and my heart sings with joy in my chest. I've missed their hugs so much.

We hear a noise, branches breaking, and we look towards the sound. A black bear comes running out of the woods and right at us. I want to panic and flee but we just stand there and watch as it runs right by us. It occurs to me that bears shouldn't be out yet, it's not spring. It should be curled up hibernating in a den somewhere.

Dad leans close to my ear and whispers, "Look how brave you are Violet. You're stronger than anyone I've ever known. You have enough fight to be victorious, and enough love to be happy. Don't ever give up on either one, keep fighting. Fight for yourself, fight for joy, fight for love, and fight for those who can't fight for themselves."

We turn when there's another crack of wood. In the distance we see smoke and the popping and sizzling of a large blaze reaches us in a gust of wind. The fire grows with the influx of oxygen, and I feel the heat on my face. I turned back to my parents, and they're gone. I'm alone. I didn't get to say goodbye. I want to cry and plead for them to come back at least long enough for a hug. But I know they can't, they're dead, and heaven doesn't expel the good ones. I find myself right in front of the cabin, no skis on my feet. I'm wrapped in a blanket, and I can hear Sawyer crying from inside.

"Sawyer! I'm coming! Mommy will save you!" I dash up the steps and use the blanket to grasp the hot doorknob. I throw it open, and the flames are so hot on my neck and face. I put my hands up to protect my face and force my way into the flames, determined to rescue my furry boy. My eyes pop open and I struggle with my blanket I'm in my room, in my bed, with Sawyer clutched against my neck and face.

I hold him close, "Oh thank goodness! I thought I lost you, baby boy! Mommy will always run into the burning building to save you, but please try not to be in any, okay?"

He looks at me like I'm crazy for disturbing him. It's as if he's feeling sad I'm a total nutcase and he hopes I get help, but he's going back to sleep because I'm not his problem. He's so adorable I can't be annoyed with his cute little face. Screw it. I let him stay on my neck and snuggle back into my covers. I fall back asleep remembering everything my parents said, feeling happy they came to see me. I'm pretty sure I spent the rest of the night with a grin on my face.

After my early shift is over, I head straight home excited for the events planned for the night ahead. After a shower, I dress in my purple bikini and wig. I pull a cute, opaque, cover-up over it. I have a mask to wear while the high bidder is here, it's like a masquerade mask, but it's longer. It covers from just above my lips to my hair line at the top of my forehead. I almost went with a purple one, but I fell in love with the black sparkling one with fluffy feathers along the edge and rhinestone outlines. It makes me look like a little girl trying to look older, like I'm dressing up in my mother's clothes.

I locked Sawyer in my bedroom so there's no way for him to accidentally be involved. I make my way down the stairs without my shoes, so I don't break my neck. They match the mask, black with sparkles. In the *Bait and Slice Inn*, everything is hidden that needs to be and everything that should be visible is, including some obvious camera equipment. Hidden cameras are everywhere. I even have a panic button wired to the alarm system so I can call the cops as a last resort. I feel ready, so I check in with my partner.

Me: Hey, you ready?

RobNdaHood: all set. How are you?

Me: I'm great, ready to do this! When will they be here?

RobNdaHood: Dozer checked in after he picked up Nemo and the high bidder. The ETA is 10 minutes. I'm following all feeds, I'll broadcast the tattoo video as soon as it's done. Be safe!

Me: you know it!

Feeling like I'm abuzz with energy. I tap my foot as I wait for them to arrive. I mentally go over the location of every hidden blade, camera, and emergency implement. I have the door open so I can hear any noises outside. The soundproofing works both ways and when you're in the *Bait and Slice Inn,* you can't hear anything outside these walls. My phone is in my pocket, I'll have to take off the cover-up most likely, but I'll keep it close.

"Look lively, they're pulling up now," A disembodied voice I know very well announces from a visible camera in the corner.

I show him a thumbs up and reply, "Here we go!"

I make my way to the side door that faces the alley. Before Dozer can knock, I open it and observe a blacked-out limo, it's sleek and classy, not flashy. Dozer is a huge guy. Colby warned me he was big, but damn, he's probably taller than Mike and has a hundred pounds on him. He's got ear piercings and neck tattoos that I assume flow beneath his sleeves and come to a stop at his fingertips. His bald head is smooth and buffed to a dull shine. He kinda reminds me of a cross between The Rock and Vin Diesel.

"I'm Dozer. Who do you want first?" A man of few words, I like it.

"Bring Nemo first, please. I'll show you the way." He nods and goes to the far passenger side. He guides a tall, but shorter than him, lanky guy towards me. Nemo has gages in his earlobes and fewer visible tattoos than one would expect. Although he's also wearing long sleeves so maybe I just can't see them. How are they both wearing long sleeves? I can barely wear them in winter, it's freaking Florida!

He follows me silently and Nemo doesn't speak either. I wonder if Dozer threatened him or if Colby gave him specific instructions. I'm ready to bust with excitement and I can't keep from talking.

"Hey, Nemo. You can call me Violent. Stay still, keep your mask on please, and I'll be right back, okay?"

"Yes, ma'am." I smile at Dozer thinking if only Nemo could see who he's calling ma'am. We do the same to get the high bidder into the room. We seat him in a chair that has restraints, but you can't tell unless they're in use. Dozer nods at me. He's been instructed to wait outside for Nemo and return him to where he collected him. He won't be transporting the high bidder again. I nod back and he leaves the room, I lock it behind him. I survey the masked men and wink at the camera in the corner.

"Hello, I'm Violent or *V.* I'm going to allow you to remove your blindfolds in just a moment. First, some instructions. You're being recorded, both video and audio recordings are being made. You will sign the release forms I have ready for you, or you'll be asked to leave. You'll remain seated and you will not touch me. Nemo, obviously you'll need to touch me, only for the tattoo. Any questions?"

They both say no. I look closely at the bidder and see he is probably in his mid to late fifties. His hair is dark, almost black, with some silver streaks mostly around his temples. He's dressed in a fancy suit and wearing only one piece of jewelry, a simple gold wedding band. I feel sorry for whatever woman married this creep. Hopefully she'll be happy when he doesn't return home.

"Okay, go ahead and remove your blindfolds. Please immediately sign the release in front of both of you," They do as I ask. Nemo grins at me once he's finished. The bidder looks up and a grin, the likes of Batman's Joker, crawls across his face as he eyes me.

"I have an agreement for you to sign," I hand him the next forms. He quickly glances at the forms; I assume to confirm it's what we emailed for him to review. He signs without question. I stare at my phone, when the time changes to the top of the hour, a notification of a bank deposit flashes on my screen. The balance of the auction amount has been delivered and we can proceed. I replace my phone into my pocket and slide all of the signed documents through a slot I can open, or seal closed. It just goes into the next room, but they don't need to know that.

"Hello, Mr. *Daytripper7*. What would you like me to call you?"

"You may call me, Trip. I think I'll call you V. As in V-card, all right?"

I desperately want to roll my eyes. He has that same slimy thing about him as the Beast's friends always had and it makes my skin crawl and my stomach twists and churns a bit. I look at his face now that he's looking into my eyes. He has bruises around his eye and cheekbone on the left side of his face. His lower lip is split but healing, and I suppose his bruises are healing too. They're more blue-green than black and purple. He has eyes that shine with a beautiful color even though they measure me with cruelty. They light up when his gaze drifts down my body to my bare legs. I try to keep from vomiting in his lap. I focus my attention on Nemo. Dozer searched Nemo's bag before bringing him here, I have no concerns the artist has anything he shouldn't have in it.

Pointing Nemo to the work area I say, "There're some outlets above the counter and the sink's in the corner. Why don't you start getting ready while Trip tells me about his choices." My gaze trails from Nemo, the tattoo artist, to Trip, the highest bidder.

I look at him intently, "Please tell us where the tattoo is going and what design you've decided on. Remember all the rules you agreed to, and remain in your seat, please."

He clears his throat and fights off his sickening grin before he begins, "I've thought about this for a very long time. Of course you're just the final piece. I've wanted to leave my mark on virgin flesh since I was a horny teenager. But marks heal no matter how hard you try to make them permanent. I've tried everything, even burning a mark into pristine flesh. The problem with burns is that you can't completely control how they heal, and they're never left with crisp edges, the way I really want them to be. A tattoo is perfect. It'll be exactly what I want in the exact way I want it, forever. My next decision was the location, of course I thought about every inch of your flesh. You realize in this moment, I own you, don't you?"

I smile at him, imagining how I'm going to own him later. How I'm going to carve exactly what I want into his flesh, exactly how I want it. I tilt my head and flutter my eyes as if I'm enjoying his claims, he smiles salaciously in return.

"Of course, Trip. Please, go on."

"I thought about putting my mark on your firm little tits, then your ass, and I would love nothing more than to stake my claim right on the lips of your sweet, little pussy. But I agreed to your rules. I understand I can only choose an area below your neck, and not beneath your bathing suit. That seems like a restriction of the very best parts, at first. Then you think about the pain level of certain spots. I understand bony areas can be some of the most painful. Plus, visibility of areas like your shoulder blade, collar bone, or ribs could be much higher than your foot or ankle if you don't wear sandals very much. Since your feet aren't showing any sandal tan lines, I'm guessing you don't. The most painful place I could find is the armpit. It has lots of nerves and sensitive lymph nodes just below the delicate skin, bringing it to a ten out of ten on the pain scale. Since I'm limited in my choices for now, I want to see if I can make you cry. If I can make you scream. Will you cry for me V?"

Nemo gasps and his mouth falls open with concern. He looks at me with pity on his face but says nothing. I appreciate his professionalism in these bizarrely unprofessional circumstances. He may earn an extra-large tip. My jaw is clenched so tight I'm surprised my teeth aren't crumbling in my mouth. He's exactly like the monsters the Beast used to bring to abuse me. I can feel the flood of adrenaline filling my veins, I'm trembling with anticipation to slice him open with my favorite blade.

Doing my best to keep my voice steady, I answer, "I suppose you'll just have to wait and see, Trip. Please tell us about the design." I can no longer force myself to smile. I concentrate on not frowning or even worse, grimacing. His type always wants you to suffer mentally as much as physically, if not more.

"I debated the design most of all. I thought about putting my face on your skin, my initials, anything that would mark you as mine. I want everyone to know it was me who took your virginity, but then I realized that may not be the best plan. Since our agreement has a nondisclosure section, I thought it would be best not to have my identifying information permanently on your skin. But you'll know exactly who took your virginity, you'll see my mark and know it was me, forever. That's good enough for me. Here's the design. It's exactly the measurements allowed in our agreement." He reaches into his pocket and pulls out a folded piece of paper. He places it on the table in front of him. He wants me to step close and take it.

When I reach for it, he inhales loudly and groans softly under his breath. I don't want to know what he smells or how it affects him. He doesn't disguise adjusting his crotch, and I feel disgusted. I take a few deep breaths and focus my thoughts back to his demise and I calm instantly. I unfold the paper slowly reminding myself not to react to the image. No matter what it is, it doesn't matter, it'll be covered over as soon as it heals.

Despite my best effort, the design is soul crushing, and I begin to tremble, the paper vibrates in my hands. He smiles with satisfaction, and I want to thrust my blade into his eye. I place the paper in front of Nemo, who chokes and clears his throat a few times.

"Violent? Are you sure about this?" He asks, pleading for a sensible reply from me. I can't give him one, we have an agreement and I'm going to be paid so much more than this monster's money... I'll be paid in blood. His dying breath will rush past me, his dying screams will be my reward.

"I'm sure. Let's get to it, right now," I say with force. Even though I'm young and female, my voice in this moment is the growl of a demon who fears nothing. Trip jolts in his seat and I smile a genuine grin. Nemo doesn't question me further. He gets to work making the stencil and preparing the ink. I sit still and silent, I don't invite conversation and both men remain quiet.

It's going to be a painful procedure to get this tattoo. He made sure to use up the entire space allowed. It'll be a solid two by three inches, mostly black with red filling in the rest. It's going to be painful to cover it later and he knows that. He wants me to suffer as much as possible, just like all of the Beast's friends. They wanted me to suffer not just the physical pain, but the humiliation and mental pain, they taunted me and laughed at me while they made me scream. They tried not to physically scar me on the outside, at least anyplace you could see if I was wearing a swimsuit. Although I do have a few scars on the backs of my thighs and my back, you'd never guess they were from anything other than a childhood accident. The Beast got so pissed off when they left permanent marks, I think he killed a guy once. I'm not sure because he knocked me out during the fight, but I never saw Kevin again. I wasn't sad about that at all.

Once Nemo is finished, he asks, "Are you ready?"

"Yeah."

"I know I'm not allowed to touch you and I won't, but I want to be next to you while it's done. I need to see it come to life on your skin," the monstrous high bidder says.

"That's fine. You can approach on the opposite side from Nemo once he begins. Your hands will remain on the armrests of your chair. Got it?"

"Sure thing, my little V."

After I removed my cover up, I turn away from him to situate myself on the tattoo chair. I can't keep from rolling my eyes. Once I'm settled, I repeat my safety mantra in my head a couple times while I take some deep breaths. Feeling much more relaxed, I nod at Nemo, and he nods back. I made a show of beginning the video feed so they both know they're now live streaming on *ITZYuu*. I wonder how many sick fucks Colby will catch this round.

"Okay Violent, I'm going to clean the area first so it's sterile. I'm sorry it's cold, just hold your arm up and make yourself comfortable." He adjusts my arm so it's flat where he needs to work and I'm in a position that I can easily keep without fatigue. He begins cleaning my skin and I can't help making a noise, he wasn't kidding it's cold.

"You doing, okay?"

"Yep. Just cold."

"I know, I'm sorry. Next, I'm going to put the stencil on your skin. It will just take a minute... hold still."

"No problem." It tickles a little while he's tracing the design onto my armpit, probably another level of torture planned by this asshole. I'm able to fight laughing or moving.

"I'm going to start by outlining the design. I'll begin by doing all of the black outlines first. Then I'll fill in the black. We'll take a break while I load the red. After the break, I'll outline the red before I fill it in. I don't expect it to take longer than an hour and a half. If you need any extra breaks or water or anything at all, just let me know, alright?"

"I will, thank you." I try to tell him with my eyes to make it as quick as he can. I just want to get it over with.

"Do you want to see the stencil? Make sure it looks right?" he asks me, but the monstrous Trip butts in with his own thoughts.

"Don't ask her that! Ask me. I'm the one it belongs to; it's going on skin I own. I'm the one who decides." Nemo freezes and looks to me for guidance. I give him a subtle nod and he looks to Trip.

"I'm sorry. This is a new situation for me. I'm only used to checking with the person I'm tattooing. Mr. umm, Trip, does it look right?" He steps up close to me and inspects my armpit. He's way too close to my face, and I try looking down to avoid his eyes.

My glance catches on the tent in his trousers, and I instantly feel sick. What the fuck is wrong with him? He's just vile, disgusting, and I want to slice it off and watch him bleed.

"Are you all right Violent?" Nemo asks me.

"Fine," I grit out between clenched teeth.

"It looks perfect. You may proceed," Trip tells Nemo in a condescending tone.

"I'm going to start the machine. Sorry, but it's a little loud." He turns it on, and it sounds like a pump for a small pool. It has that motorized vibration to it which echoes off the ceiling a little bit despite the soundproofing. I repeat my mantra again and take a few deep breaths.

"I'm going to begin." I breathe slowly and try my best to stay still. The high bidder slides his chair next to me opposite Nemo. I still avoid his eyes and watch Nemo's face while he works. The pain is intense, but I've suffered worse and under much worse conditions. This is a situation I control. Colby is watching very closely. If I need help, he'll have Dozer in here in a flash. He's also prepared to send the cops if required. That's the last thing I want, so I project a calm facade. I don't let the pain show on my face nor do I wiggle or make a sound.

Nemo looks at my eyes and says, "You're doing great. I've got the black outline done. It's going fast since you're being so still. Do you need anything?"

"Nope."

"You're doing very well. Please tell me, how does it feel?" I don't want to talk. I'm keeping it together by visiting my happy place and reciting my mantra. Interruptions break through my walls and make the pain burst through. I suspect this asshole knows that and he's doing it for that reason. He wants me to suffer, to cry.

"Great," I grit out. Refusing to engage any further. He tenses and I hope I'm annoying him. I hope my lack of tears pisses him off. I want to deny him the climax he seeks.

"Come on V, tell me. Does it hurt? Is it the most painful thing you've ever felt? Are you holding in screams?" The highest bidder asks.

"No." I refuse to give him what he wants. I'm not going to play his games. I can do this without tears and without screaming. It does hurt like a bitch, but I've felt worse. Much worse. I won't let the pain I agreed to, take me down. I've had so much pain against my will, and I'll never allow myself to be in a position where someone else can inflict pain on me again.

"You're doing great. I'm almost halfway finished with the black."

I'm not sure if it's helpful to know how far along we are or not. On the one hand it's good to know he's making progress, but on the other it's like a punch in the gut knowing how much longer it's going to take. I think he's pressing very lightly and not filling it in as much as he would if I wanted this tattoo. I appreciate his help. I wonder what Colby told him about me and this weird situation. I know he's getting a nice chunk of change. Probably way more than his usual fee.

Colby told me he's a great guy with a shady past. He has a kid that he's trying to provide for as part of his reformation. I find that admirable and I appreciate his willingness to push legality a bit to help me out and take care of his child. Most people deserve a second chance when they screw up. He seems very professional, so I know he takes his work seriously. Anyone who properly cares for their kid is aces in my book. Coming from my bio-mother and invisible bio-father and all I've been through, to being loved by mom and dad and Uncle Randy, I think I'm in a good spot to know when someone is or isn't a good parent.

"You're doing so great. I'm finished with the black. You're going to have a break while I set up the red. Do you need some water? Bathroom? Anything at all?"

"Nope. All good." When he wipes off the blood and moves to the sink, I stretch my arm out above me and move a little, so I'm not stuck in the exact same position. When I reach my arm out in front of me, I flinch from the pain under my arm. While he was working on it there was a constant sharp pain. Now the whole area burns and radiates along my inflamed nerves like a hot poker. Wow, I had no idea tattoos hurt this much. I have a whole new appreciation for people who have large designs across their skin.

I glance towards Trip to check what he's doing. He's watching me closely. His smirk tells me he noticed my pain and is reveling in it. Now I'm frustrated that I forgot to keep my emotions in check for a moment. I watch Nemo for a minute while he messes with his machine. I shake out my hand trying to get the nerve pain to stop traveling up my entire arm. I see now why the bastard chose my right armpit, so it'll hurt every time I use my right hand. Since I'm right-handed that's all the time. It didn't occur to me to not reveal my dominant hand. I wish I had thought of that. I hope this doesn't mess up my knife or fighting skills. No matter what it's going to hurt like a bitch when I slice him open, but I'm willing to suffer through it. Smiling, I have to hold in a chuckle. I hope my mirth bothers him.

"Okay, are you ready to get back to it?" Nemo asks.

"Yeah."

"Can you move just a little more to the right. Perfect. Here we go..." The first touch of the needle brings back all of the throbbing pain traveling up and down my nerves. It feels like when the dentist digs in with that sharp thing right on a nerve where you have a cavity. I can't keep from flinching again, which makes me mad. My eyes water from the pain and a tear escapes beneath my mask then rolls down my cheek. I'm not crying, it's just such a sharp pain my eyes are instantly filled with liquid.

"That's my girl. I knew you would cry for me and it's worth every penny." I fight not to respond to him. I want to set him straight. I have the strongest urge to scream at him while I throat-punch him over and over. If I react it'll just give him more of what he wants. I use my left hand to wipe my eyes through the holes in my mask. Nemo hands me a tissue and I'm able to dab my eyes dry with a sniffle. The monster next to me groans in the most lewd and disgusting way. My skin crawls and I involuntarily shiver. Nemo just keeps working without comment. I think he's caught on that this dickhead is enjoying every minute of me suffering.

"You're doing great. I'm almost done with the outline."

I refocus and repeat my mantra silently a few times while I ignore the asshole next to me. I regain my control over the pain and feel myself enter the zone. I close my eyes and picture my safe place. It fills in fast with bright colors and warm sunlight. Sawyer joins me and curls in my lap purring. It blends in with the hum of the tattoo gun and becomes one with the rhythm of the machine.

When he stops, Nemo breaks in, "Okay. We're finished. Here's the mirror so you can see it." His gaze shifts down, and I swear he's ashamed. I take the mirror and he helps me hold it so I can see his work.

Yep, there it is, the black and red symbol of hate with the black words on a red background. This man needs to die, so fucking hard. I cull my anger and force what must look like a pained grin.

"Thanks Nemo. You did a great job."

"Let me flush this and then I'll wrap it and go over the instructions." Nemo steps to the sink.

"Are you satisfied, Trip?" I ask for the benefit of the live audience.

He looks into my eyes through my fancy mask and straight into my dark soul. He has satisfaction glowing in his unfairly beautiful eyes and smiling across his face. He stares at me far too long, but I won't glance away. I refuse to give in first. He licks his lips and tilts his head. He seems to be considering something carefully and I don't like it.

"Oh yes, my dear V. I'm quite satisfied. I wonder, will you share the design with your audience or keep it between us?"

"I think it should be our secret for now." I touched my shoulder to relay the signal Colby and I arranged to cut the live feed. Trip doesn't know he's no longer being broadcast. Colby put one of those blurry squares over Nemo and his tattoos so nobody will be able to identify him. He also dubs over any audio with his name being said. I tried not to say it once we were broadcasting but just in case I slipped or the high bidder said it, we wanted to keep Nemo anonymous and safe.

I smile invitingly at Trip and say, "I'm going to have Nemo head out. You can stay for a while, if you like."

"That's intriguing. I think I'd like that."

"Good. Nemo, quickly explain the instructions for me and wrap it. I'm going to call your ride to collect you."

I texted Dozer to give us ten minutes. Nemo works quickly and efficiently, and we're finished when Dozer taps on the door. Both men are seated and wearing their masks. Nemo clutches his case of tricks. His bank account is ten-thousand bucks richer thanks to Trip's deposit in my and Colby's business account. I think he'll be pleasantly surprised. We agreed on seven.

"Okay gentlemen, please keep your masks in place, and remain seated until you're told otherwise. Nemo, thanks and don't jump, your driver is going to guide you out to your ride." Dozer nods at me. He carefully guides Nemo from the room, and I lock it behind them. I checked my phone and Colby sends me a message that they're clear from the building and all the cameras are working.

"Trip, please stay seated and keep your mask on for just a few more minutes. I'm going to fix us some drinks. Do you have any preference? I have scotch, vodka, and tequila."

"Scotch. Neat, please."

"Coming right up." I take two glasses from the cabinet then I pour some scotch in each glass. I replace the scotch on the shelf and close the cabinet. I mix his cup with my finger. There's the smallest difference between the patterns on the cups so I can easily identify which is which. His glass has some Ketamine in it. Not enough to knock him out for a long time. Just enough to make him extremely agreeable and not very steady. Just enough for me to overpower him if I need to.

When I approach him, I say, "You can take off your mask. I'd love to chat a little. Tell me something about yourself that I wouldn't guess." I hand him his glass and take a sip of my own, he follows suit.

"You're much more talkative now. Why?"

"We're alone, I didn't want to say much while we weren't."

"I see. I have a worthless son, close to your age." I must look confused. "You said to tell you something you wouldn't guess. Does it bother you that I'm old enough to be your father?" My stomach wants to revolt at the thought, but I wrestle it into submission.

Answering with a sweet grin, I tell him, "Not at all. I never knew my father." He swallows another mouthful.

"Tell me something about you. Was your skin the only thing virginal about you?"

"No," I answer not exactly lying. He asked me to tell him something about myself and I said *no*. I didn't answer his second question because it doesn't deserve one. I continue to smile and sip from my glass. He gulps the last of the liquid in his cup and I just keep on smiling. He's smiling back at me, oblivious to my intentions. I decided to ask a few more questions, since it won't hurt to know more incriminating information.

"Have you done anything like this before? Met someone from *ITZYuu* in person?"

He smiles, looking me up and down, and I shiver with disgust. I hate that I can't control that reaction. His smile grows. He must confuse my shiver for arousal. Ick, bile tries to fill my mouth and I force it back down my throat.

"I've been around. You may be the youngest person I've met from that site though. I have to say, you're not what I expected. You're very mature and business like for someone your age. I know you have to be at least eighteen to be on the site, so how old are you?"

"Would it bother you if I wasn't eighteen yet?"

His lips stretch into a bigger grin, "Not in the least. How did you manage that? I've been told you can't get past their screening process."

"Is that really what you want to discuss?" I run my finger along the rim of my glass and peer at him with my most innocent expression. His eyes light up.

"What did you have in mind when you invited me to stay behind?" His teeth appear in a wolfish smile.

"Why don't you remove your jacket and get comfortable?" I watch him closely for signs the Ketamine is taking effect. He struggles to stand and remove his jacket. Once he's out of his jacket he falls without any grace, back into the chair.

Patting his thigh, he suggests, "Why don't you come sit over here with me?" His words are thick or maybe it's his tongue. A good sign. I approached him still smiling.

"How would you like it if I remove my mask?" I ask.

"That would be purrrfect," he slurs.

I lift it over my head and shake out my fake hair. I step closer to him, and he leans towards me in anticipation. Using my left hand, I trace the collar area of my top in what I hope is a sexy move. He licks his lips and follows my fingers with his glassy eyes.

"I have a fantastic idea. Would you like to have my virgin mouth on you?"

Nodding fiercely, he mumbles words I can't decipher, but his excitement is easy to see. I place my finger on my lips to shush him. His nods are exaggerated as he silently agrees. I step in front of him and then lean down putting my face close to his but not touching him at all.

"Stay still Trip, I'm going to restrain your arms for this part. I don't want you to be able to move or touch me with your hands. Okay?"

"Y-yes." He answers then snaps his lips shut, in what I believe is a move to show his obedience. I place a hand on his right forearm. He's not the only one who notices which hand is dominant. I quickly strap down his arm with the mechanism housed in the arm of my special chair. He tests it immediately and looks back at me, startled when he can't get free. I strap down his left arm before he can try to escape.

"Hey. I c-can't get my arm out."

"I know. Do you remember me saying that I wanted to restrain you for this part?"

"Oh. Yeah, I remember."

"Good job. I'm going to put on my special outfit I picked out just for you, okay?"

"Yes! I can't w-wait."

I step behind his seat and collect my clothes. I pull on a long sleeve black t-shirt and leggings. Socks and shoes cover my feet for safety. Then I put on a butcher's apron. I put some of my blades in my apron pockets and picked up my favorite. It's the one exception to using items of sentimental value for hunting. A Bowie knife my dad gave me when we were camping. He said it belonged to his grandfather and he wanted me to have it so it would stay in the family. It touched my heart that he thought of me as his family. Every time he or mom did something to demonstrate the love they had for me; I would wait for something awful to happen. It took a lot of time and work with Uncle Randy for me to believe how much they truly loved me and that I was without a doubt their daughter. Dad called it his *David Bowie Knife.* His dad jokes were always the best, and this blade will be forever, *David Bowie* to me.

When I get close to my prey, he's slumped in the chair. His head is flopped on his shoulder and his legs are awkwardly splayed in front of him. A small dibble of drool hangs from his bottom lip. I take the opportunity to check the pockets of his jacket. His wallet is in the upper pocket along with a strip of condoms. In his lower right pocket, I found a prescription bottle without a label and three pills contained inside. I set the bottle and condoms on the counter.

I set down *David Bowie* and look through his wallet. He has two thousand dollars in hundreds, a Florida driver's license, and a black American Express Card. I looked over his ID and see that his name is Maximilian Alistair Hale III. The air rushes from my lungs as if I've been kicked in the gut. The ID blurs in my hand for a moment as darkness tries to close in on me. I take a deep breath and look at Trip. I examine him closely. His face is relaxed while he's not quite conscious. His lips are the same. His hair color, where it hasn't turned to silver, is the same. I think about his beautiful eyes, the only attractive thing about this monstrous asshole; they're the same. I'm looking at the father of my ex-boyfriend and hopefully not ex-friend, Maximilian Alistair Hale, the fourth. Max. Now that I look at him, I see the resemblance, but where Max is gorgeous, this man reeks of evil. His bruised face is the final clue, Max got into a fist fight with his father before he took off for Europe.

Me: Holy fuck dude!! This evil asshole is Max's dad!

RobNdaHood: WTF!?! No!!!!!

Me: I swear

I texted a pic of his ID to Colby.

RobNdaHood: Holy fuck dude!!

Me: I said that already. Do you think Max'll care if I dispatch this asshole?

RobNdaHood: He hates his dad. He'll probably throw you a party.

Me: Any problems with the plan because of this complication?

RobNdaHood: No. We followed the plan, nobody but us knows he's here. Dozer doesn't know who he is and wouldn't care. We're good to go if you're okay with it.

Me: I'm good. I just want to make sure it won't hurt Max.

RobNdaHood: I don't see any reason it would.

Me: OK I'm getting started.

I'm not even worried about our conversation being on text, we have some CIA level encryption on all of our communications. I'm kinda excited that this slug is Max's father. I've hated that guy for a long time, since he's only been neglectful or hateful towards Max, and nothing else. It's going to be fun to tell him I'm ending his life for all of his victims and most of all his son, his most tortured victim.

I carefully strap Trip's legs to the chair after I remove his shoes. I slice away his shirt from his torso. Gross, his skin is saggy and wrinkly with gray hair on his chest. It's weird because he does have some defined muscles below his loose skin. He appears to be tattoo free.

I drag the tip of my blade down his forearm letting it scratch into the top few layers of his skin. Blood oozes up slowly from the cut, but he doesn't stir. I trace his collar bone next leaving a trail of drips and drops of blood. He flinches a little and his eyes flutter but don't open. I continue my path up his neck and onto his cheek. I press a little harder and make a slice just above the bone below his eye. Blood flows a little faster from this cut. His eyes flutter again and open wide in surprise.

"Whad-der you doing?" he grumbles out in a gruff slur.

"I'm showing you what I like to do with men like you. But you're sleeping through it when you should really be paying attention. How do you like my favorite? His name's *David Bowie,* isn't that a hoot?" I show him my blood-stained blade in front of his eye, much too close. He definitely doesn't like seeing it at this angle. He struggles wildly in the chair trying to break his legs and arms free from their prisons. He presses his body upwards and moves his face away from *David Bowie.*

He continues to struggle while I just stand above him and watch calmly. My anger and outrage are nowhere to be found. I feel an elated flutter in my chest and a bright smile won't leave my lips. There's nothing else, no other activity that brings me this level of peace, since I lost mom and dad. Slicing into the flesh of evil monsters is my greatest joy. I don't think Trip feels the same. He growls loudly as he begins to understand there's no escape. My face aches from smiling so hard and I revel in the pain. He stops moving suddenly and looks me over. I can tell he's calculating his odds of getting *David Bowie* away from me and escaping. He's trying to figure out a way to get the upper hand. He examines the restraints and not finding a weak link, he looks at me again. He must think the key to being released lies with me. It does, but I won't be releasing him until after his last breath has left his tainted body.

"You're very pretty. I couldn't tell how beautiful you were when you were wearing that mask, but now I can see you're a stunning young woman. I would be so proud to have you on my arm. I'm incredibly wealthy, did you know that?"

Humoring him. I answer playing shy and innocent. "I didn't think you were poor, considering how much you bid on the tattoo. It's going to pay for more than a year of college, including all of my expenses."

"I'm happy to help, especially a young lady working towards a noble goal like a college degree. Too many people these days think they can just get any old degree and be successful. What are you studying?"

"Computer Science. I like programming and technology."

"That's an excellent choice. Plenty of good jobs in that field."

His eyes shift around checking out the room and me while he pretends to give a crap about my major. The blood is drying on his face, and I feel like he needs a freshly decorated eyebrow. Anything close to the scalp bleeds a lot, which makes me anticipate my next cut like I'm waiting for my name to be called by the barista at the coffee hut. I want that sweet fix.

He trembles when I shift towards him. He pulls against his restraints again and grimaces. I reach out with *David Bowie* and press his sharp tip to Trip's left eyebrow. I don't press hard enough to break his skin. He shivers and the tip of my blade enters the skin just below the arch of his thick silver highlighted brow. He jerks his head back from my knife and it leaves his skin dripping blood down to his eyelid. I tilt my head and follow the flow with my eyes.

"What the fuck? Why are you doing this?" he shouts at me, less in control of his fear.

"I'm doing what I enjoy doing with men like you."

"What the fuck does that mean, men like me?" I'm thrilled he's asking the right questions, because I want to tell him. I want to watch as it dawns on him there's no way out. I want to watch him discover his life is in my hands and I have no intention of letting him continue breathing.

"It means I'm the deliverer of justice. I'm the reckoning for evil monsters who like to harm those who are vulnerable because they're too young or too weak to fight back. You've been judged by me and found guilty of the worst kinds of treachery. I'm going to dispense your punishment."

"You can't do that! You've no right! I haven't done anything to you!"

"Oh, no? What were you trying to do with this?" I raise my arm so he can see my fresh tattoo. "Was this supposed to make me happy? Am I supposed to feel good about what's been perma-nently inked into my skin? I believe you said you wanted me to scream and cry. That you wanted me to feel pain every time I look at this mark. It's a sick and twisted thing to mark me with don't you think?"

"It's no big deal. I let you get it in a place not many people will see."

"Only because your Google search told you it's one of the most painful places to get a tattoo!" I laugh an incredulous sound. His excuses are ridiculous.

"So, what, you're going to give me a few scars as payback?"

"No! I won't leave any scars at all."

"I think what you did to my face is going to leave a scar. It feels like you made a deep cut on my cheek and my eyebrow. How can you know if it'll leave a scar?"

I lean in close to his face and say, "Scars don't form if you're dead."

"Bullshit! You're trying to scare me! I'm not falling for it, there's no way a little girl like you has the balls to kill a man like me."

"There's where your wrong Dumb-daddy Trip. I've got everything I need to kill you. *David Bowie* here loves to cut through beastly monsters who have nothing but evil in their veins."

"Hasn't anyone taught you not to lie? You're not going to kill me, but I promise when I get out of here, I'll make you wish you were dead! Come a little closer bitch!"

He tries to grab a handful of my hair, my fake hair, and my wig falls off in his hand. He flinches and drops it like it's a rat and I can't help it, I burst into hysterical laughter while gasping for breath.

"Holy fuck! What the fuck is wrong with you? Are you fucking crazy?"

Without hesitation I answer, "Yeah, I am, Daddy Trip. I'm looney toons, bat crap crazy, out of my fucking mind, bonkers. And I promise... I am going to kill you. Then I'm never going to think of you again."

"Fuck you! You're going to think of me every time you see my mark under your arm. I chose mostly black to make it virtually impossible to cover. In case you didn't like my Iron Cross and

Swastika or my sentiment, you won't be able to cover it! It'll show through anything else you put there!! I'm going to own your skin and your fucking soul forever you little cunt! If you know what's good for you, you'd let me go right fucking now!"

"Tsk, tsk, tsk, Daddy Trip. Didn't anyone ever teach you how to catch more flies with honey?" I ask in my sweetest tone.

"Fuck you! You catch more flies with shit! I don't play games. I do what I want." Aiming carefully to avoid any major arteries, I arc my favorite blade through the air and skewer his thigh.

"Ahhh! Fuck! You fucking bitch! What the fuck!?! You're so fucking dead..." I tune him out, take my blade, and move to the counter where I lean, waiting for him to finish screaming at me. He's yelling so loud that spit flies out of his mouth, and I'm glad I got out of the splash zone.

When he runs out of steam I ask, "Do you have anything else you want to say, or are you ready to listen?"

He lifts his head, his eyes are watery, and red. Blood has leaked from his brow down his eyelid and around his eye to drip onto his cheek like he's crying tears of blood. It sets off a rush of happy endorphins through my system, and I feel so strong and satisfied in that moment.

"I guess that means you're ready to listen. I know you're Max the third." His eyes widen in surprise and the blood looks more interesting as the pattern in his wrinkles is revealed.

"I also know Max the fourth is your son. I know most of the terrible things you've done to him. Did you need to come here and hurt me because you can't hurt him anymore? Huh? Is it because he fought back that you needed to hurt someone weaker than you?"

"I'm not talking to you anymore. Do whatever you think you're going to do so we can get this over with. You'll never get away with this. I'm a wealthy man. I'm a member of the community, and everyone knows me."

"That may be true. But nobody knows you're here. This is your dirty little secret. You didn't tell anyone, did you?" I see regret cross his face. Dozer had them turn off their phones. Nobody can track him here or anywhere along the way.

"I'm guessing you just remembered that you were required to turn off your phone. I bet you're trying to figure out how to get it out of your pocket right about now. You're thinking about turning it on and calling for help. Who can you call? The police? Some lackey? What will you tell them? The truth? That you paid a ton of money to tattoo a mark onto the virgin skin of a minor?" His eyes jolted to mine once again surprised. This is fun.

"Will you tell the cops you wanted to hurt me as much as possible? Do you think they'll believe you? A full-grown man against a young girl? Will you tell them why I'm dressed this way?"

"All right!! Stop! No! Okay? No, I can't call the police." His head flops forward, he's breathing hard, his shoulders are rising and falling. Good to know, he must have a lackey he could call, so someone in his circle knows what he is and what he does. But they don't know he's here because he didn't need a ride or any help dealing with a girl from the internet. Just goes to show you, never trust anyone online!

"Do you have any questions?"

"I can double your money right now. I can transfer as much as you want, please. What do you need? I can pay for your entire college education, buy you a car, a house. Anything you want. What'll it take for you to let me go?"

"Not gonna happen. I'm done talking to you now. Time to finish up."

"No! Wait! Please! Listen... I'm *very* wealthy. I can give you a million dollars!" I shake my head as I approach, and he keeps yelling higher numbers at me. If he wasn't Max's dad, I'd let him give me as much as I could get. But he's trying to bribe me with Max's money, and I won't take a penny.

The closer I get, the higher pitched his voice climbs. Holding *David Bowie* with his blade up I thrust it into Trip's armpit. What can I say, payback's a bitch. I know he's feeling an excruciating sharp pain burning down his nerve pathways all the way to his fingers. He's squealing now. It's a horrible high-pitched sound like a pig when you chase it. They're such dramatic animals, if they get scared, they'll run away squealing the whole time. If you catch them, it shifts into a higher gear, and they wiggle their bodies trying desperately to get away. As a last resort they'll try to bite you with their fairly blunt teeth. They may or may not puncture your skin, but they'll pinch you with their flat teeth hard enough to draw blood. Trip is thrashing and squealing like a caught pig. I keep a close eye on him, so I don't get near enough for him to bite.

"Pllleeeeeasse...pllleeeeaaassse...I'm begging you..."

I stick him in his hand; a fast in and out hole about two inches long. Before he knows what's happening, I puncture his other hand. He yanks his hands against the metal cuffs holding them and desperately tries to work one hand free without success. Next, I thrust the blade into his other thigh and leave it there while I grasp the handle.

"You know, Trip, there is something you can do to make the pain stop."

"A-anything. Please, I'll do anything. Just...please...stop," his plea does nothing to my black heart. But I removed *David Bowie* from his leg.

"Answer my questions and remember... I know a lot about you. I may even know the answer to the question I ask, so don't lie to me."

"Anything. Please," he pants. He's a disheveled, sweaty, and bloody mess. A far cry from the well-groomed slick asshole who arrived just a few hours ago. I wonder how many times he scared Max this much. How many others has he tortured to screams and tears?

"Have you ever physically abused your son?" He flinched, and swallows hard.

He tries to focus on me through the drips of blood and sweat, "I... have." He immediately looks down. It almost seems like shame keeping him from meeting my eyes, but I know it's only fear.

"When? How old was he? How often? How did you hurt him?"

"Please. I'm begging you, please don't make me, please. I can't." His head shakes hard from side to side, I give him a fierce look and I feel like I'm trying to enforce the rules for a toddler.

"I don't remember when the first time was, but I b-broke his arm when he was... t-two. He had a cast for his third birthday. I dislocated his elbow maybe a year later. I broke his collarbone, two or three fingers, and some ribs." He glances at me quickly before he continues.

"I think those are the major injuries. But he had bruises most of the time. Listen, you have to understand, he would defy me and push me on purpose. He poked and poked until I snapped. It wasn't just my fault you know. He was always arguing or rebelling and he's so stubborn. He needed discipline. But I was relieved when he took off and I cut him off for hitting me."

"Who else?"

"Who else what?"

"Who else have you hurt? I want them all."

"No. I'm done."

My hand shoots out without my direction and lobs his ear off. It falls to his shoulder and sticks for a few seconds. Then it tumbles down his chest, end over end, and lands with a soft splat on his forearm. He instantly jerks his arm like a cockroach just fell on him and sends it a few feet away where it lands quietly. His face goes gray, and his eyes look vacant.

I slowly bring my favorite blade in front of his face and bring it to his other ear, before I request an answer, "Look Trip, I want an answer. Are you going to answer me? Or do you prefer matching ears?"

Resigned he says, "Okay, I hurt my wife. I hurt four of our housekeepers. A babysitter, nanny, and girls a friend would setup for me."

"Good job. Just a few more questions. You're almost done. Which of these women that you hurt, have you sexually assaulted?"

Looking down refusing to look my way, in a very quiet voice I can barely hear, he answers reluctantly, "All of them." I take a moment to breathe deeply and repeat my mantra. I bite my lip hard and try to regroup to ask my last questions.

"I have just a couple more things I want know. I'm going to ask, you're going to answer, and then we'll be finished. Who sets up girls for you?"

"He's going to kill me."

"No, he's not. I promise you, on my life, he won't kill you. Now, answer my questions, or we can play with *David Bowie* a little more."

"He goes by a street name. I know him as *The Cuban*. His first name is Marc. His last name is something Spanish like Gomez or Torres, maybe Perez. I'm not sure, but he's from Oakdale."

"Okay. Good job. What's the age range of these girls?"

"I don't know because they lie, but some say they're as young as fifteen. I don't think that's true...but I don't know." His voice is scratchy from screaming. He looks exhausted and defeated. But I keep a sharp eye on him for anything he might try.

"What about the nanny or the babysitter? How old were any of those girls?"

"The babysitter was the youngest, I know for a fact she's fourteen, but I only touched her a little. She wanted it. She came on to me and then begged me to fuck her. I didn't." His energy is renewed with his excuses, and I remember how the Beast and his friends would humiliate me by saying I wanted what they were doing. They would force me to climax and then say how much I liked it and how I wanted them. Voldemort was the worst about that. He always said I was evil because I wanted what he was doing. He said he was going to beat the devil out of me, and I believe he tried his best, and most of my scars are from his punishments.

Something snaps inside my head at that memory, and I slice *David Bowie* across Trip's throat. He makes a gurgling protest as the final pints of his life's blood crashes down his chest just like a wave rolls its way down the shore. Blood splatters as it hits the chair and the floor then pools beneath his seat. It spreads to my shoes before I can get out of the way. The trail of blood flows like a stream before it gathers in a puddle in the center of the room.

I carefully make my way to the sink and place *David Bowie* into the basin. I run the water over the blade and wash my hands, arms, and face with soap. I wipe off my apron and make sure there's no obvious blood on me. I pour alcohol over *David Bowie* and then looking in the mirror, I use his sharp tip to carefully carve the swastika from the center of the iron cross under my arm. I don't dig very deep, just enough to take off the top few layers of skin and red ink. I douse it with alcohol and bite my lip to hold in a scream. My eyes water, but my armpit is numb from the sting. I drop my blade back into the sink and put some paper towels under my arm and hold it down. After a moment I wash my hands again.

Once my hands are dry, my cellphone chimes.

RobNdaHood: Are you alright?

Me: Fine. Please call them.

RobNdaHood: Done.

Me: Thanks, I'll call you after my shower

RobNdaHood: cool

I stay until the cleanup crew is finished with everything. Dozer is on the crew, I'm not surprised. He suggested I get a drain installed in the floor for easier cleanup. It's something to think about, watching them mop it up for an hour was quite an incentive. Once they're gone, I finally go upstairs for a shower.

Chapter Sixteen

Sawyer is curled on my lap, watching me carefully. I'm keyed up and tired at the same time. Normally I would go work off my anxiety in the gym, but I just feel like snuggling Sawyer tucked under the covers right now. I hit Colby's number, and he answers before the first ring finishes.

"Hey. How're you feeling?"

"I'm okay. Just had some unpleasant memories pop up and it made me a little anxious, but nothing too bad. How's the footage from tonight?"

"It's perfect. The tattoo video is viral on *ITZYuu*, everyone wants to tattoo you and they're offering huge amounts of cash. Some other girls are auctioning off space on their bodies now."

"Can you track their bidders?"

"Yeah, they're all originally from your auction. Well, except for the ones overseas, there's a ton of new ones. Chinese men really like this idea and they're going crazy bidding on the other tattoo auctions. There's also a few from some middle eastern countries that are wound up and bidding non-stop. I'm tracking as many as I can, I'll send them to the authorities, but I doubt anything will come of it. Nobody gives a shit about trafficking victims."

"That's for sure. But we're going to change that. If we can steal their money and put them in jail or 6 ft. *lower,* I think some may decide it's too risky to continue. The problem is there's always more. New pedophiles, monsters, and more victims. I'm ready to spend the rest of my life taking them down."

"Me too. I'm with you all the way," Colby replied.

"Dozer was a good find. He's professional and quiet."

"Yeah, he's got some serious connections, and he does a good job. He has an excellent reputation and is all in on removing bad guys any way necessary. He was happy with his tips tonight. He said we can call him anytime."

"Great. How's Nemo? He definitely struggled with the subject matter of the tattoo."

"He's okay. I think he suspected Trip wasn't making it home. He alluded to it with something along the lines of *good riddance.* He said you can come by whenever you want to have him cover it."

"I will, as soon as it's healed."

"Do you need anything? You know I'll come there if you need me."

"I know. But you don't need to do that. I'm all right. I'm going to work out if I can't sleep. I have work tomorrow which keeps my mind busy. I'll be fine. We need to work on *Operation Voldemort.*"

"Your cameras and tracker are sending in lots of data. I've got *Modified Comet* tracking his virtual moves. We just need to work out logistics, especially since you're saying he's going to be an extended stay guest at *BASI.*"

"Still not sure I like that acronym. Bait and Slice Inn is poetic. BASI isn't."

"How 'bout BSI, like FBI?"

"Maybe... I'll think about it."

"I know! What about *BASIL?* Bait and Slice Inn Location?"

"That's better. I'll let you know when I decide. Thanks for everything. I'll talk to you tomorrow, RobN."

"You got it, Batman, night."

"Goodnight."

He's the best. Colby has been such a good friend. I know he would come here if I asked, but it's so difficult for him. I'd never ask. Having him on the other end of the phone, web, or the lens is huge. A friend I can trust completely is worth more than anything to me.

That thought leads me to my new friends. I've been avoiding examining my strange feelings when I was last with them. It was so strange to have those electric sparks traveling my nerves, with tingles in my chest, and lady bits. I never feel any excitement in my sex organs. No one has ever made me feel anything at all there since I was abused. The shame and humiliation involved with the things I felt back then, have left me numb in my groin area. Max never aroused me. It never felt right.

But Jackson and Austin had my panties ready to burst into flames without even touching me or saying a word about anything sexual. My cotton briefs were soaked in the crotch when I got home. Thinking of them now has me heating up and quivering. My arousal is hot and pulsating right on my clit, and I'm amazed it's possible. I've never masturbated. Never had a reason to because I've never gotten excited in a sexual way. I lie awake, for I don't even know how long, contemplating if I'd even be capable of getting myself off.

Uncle Randy is going to be thrilled when I tell him I want to talk about sex. I hope I don't give him a heart attack. Hopefully I'll have a chance to call him before I see the guys tomorrow.

Thankfully, I was able to sleep like a rock once I nodded off. Work was quick. It was really busy because Danielle was off and the girl they hired to fill in, called off sick. Jackson sent me the address of where to meet them with specific instructions to dress in comfortable, casual, long pants, long sleeves, and closed toe shoes. I ignored the urge to Google the address and spoil the surprise.

It's a thirty-five-minute drive from my place so I shower and get dressed before I call Uncle Randy. I figure if my call runs long with him, I can take my SUV and finish from the car. I prefer the bike usually, but I need to have this talk before I see them again.

"Hey, how's your week been?" He greets.

"Good. I have something I want to talk to you about and it might be a weird conversation. Do you have time now?"

Knowing me and my voice, he can probably tell I really need to talk now. He clears his throat and after a moment of silence I can hear a little shuffling and a door close.

"Yeah. Stephanie's here but I'm closed in my room. What's up?"

"Have you told her about my history yet?"

"Yes. It seemed like you really wanted me to do it. Is there a problem?"

"No, no problem with that. I did want you to tell her. What I need to talk about has to do with the opposite sex."

"Okaaay."

"I met this guy while I was at work. He's nice and asked me out. I said no. He brought his cousin in, and they're both nice, funny, good-looking guys. I told them I'm only interested in friendship. They both agreed to be friends with me. We've hung out a few times and we're going out in a little while again."

"I'm sorry, we who? The guy or his cousin?"

"Both of them. The thing is...wow, this is harder than I thought. Okay. The thing is, I'm having some weird feelings for both of them. Like weird sex type feelings. I really like them both and I'm attracted to them both. What should I do?"

"Do they know you like them?"

"No. I was very adamant that I would only be friends with them."

"What about Max? Do you still have feelings for him?"

I quickly explain the status of my relationship with Max and his current whereabouts. Uncle Randy doesn't really say much beyond, uh huh. What the hell?

"Did you and Max ever have any sexual interaction?"

"No. We kissed, a lot. He wanted more but he was willing to go at my pace, which was zero. I was never attracted to him that way. When I look back, yes, I love him, but as a friend or like a brother. It's the same way I feel about Harmony."

"Okay. Let me make sure I understand. You're attracted to two men, feeling arousal, and you're confused by those feelings, correct?"

"No. Yes. I mean, I'm confused because there's two of them and that's not normal to have feelings for two people. But I'm also worried about sexual feelings because I've never had any before. What if I kiss one of them or they try to touch me, and I completely freak out? I'll scare them away. What if I end up back in the mental hospital? What if I have a total breakdown? What if I can't enjoy sex?"

"Whoa. Calm down. We've talked about this before. Remember, you're in charge of what happens with who and when. You set the pace. If it's the right person, or persons, they'll let you direct what happens. You don't know what you're going to like or not until you try. All things considered, you're a virgin. Completely new to caring and loving sexual interactions. First of all, cut yourself some slack. You have no experience and that's okay. You'll need to talk to them about your past, only to the degree you're comfortable with, before anything happens. They need to be aware that you need extra care, patience, and guidance. If they're not okay with that, then they're not the right partners. As far as there being two of them, it's not weird. It happens all the time and if they feel the same, there's no reason not to try it. The more people in the relationship, the more communication will need to take place. Misunderstandings occur in every relationship; the more humans involved the more misunderstandings can be an issue. My advice is to relax. See if they give you any signs they're attracted to you, then talk about it."

"Would you want a woman with a past like mine?"

"Violet, if I cared for a woman with a past like yours, it wouldn't keep me from her. I would want to do what I could to make her comfortable. Your past doesn't define you. You're an amazing person and nothing that happened to you changes that. It would make perfect sense for lots of guys to be attracted to you."

"Are you going to tell Stephanie about this?"

"Do you want me to?"

"Honestly, I may want her advice in the future. You're the best, but you're not a woman. Sometimes I might need some advice from a female and she's one I trust."

"I'm glad. I'll tell her so she's ready if you want to talk to her. I'll never tell her anything without your permission. I know I'm more your parent than your therapist now, but I'll always keep our conversations between us. Do you have any other questions?"

"I don't think so. I guess I'll see how it goes."

"As your parent, I feel I have to say, make sure you use a condom."

"Oh my God! I know. I don't need *the* talk."

"You'll understand if you ever become a parent. I wouldn't be able to relax if I didn't say it," he chuckles.

"All right. Thanks Papa Randy. I love you and I promise to be safe."

"Thank you, that's all I ask. I love you too. Have fun and call me tomorrow."

"Okay. Bye"

"Bye."

Feeling as well as possible considering my nerves, I decided to take my bike. It'll help me relax before I meet them. After I feed Sawyer for the night and say goodbye, I head off to meet the guys. I travel at or below the speed limit and take the time to enjoy the ride. The air is warm, the sky is blue, the trees sway in a pleasant breeze. By all accounts a beautiful day. When I pull into the parking lot, I don't see the truck they were in for our parkour outing.

I'm surprised to see *Mystic Range* on the sign above the door. Instantly a knot forms in my stomach. Shit, what if they require ID for me to use the range? I wasn't planning on being outed to the guys before I have a chance to tell them my story. I gulp my fear and decide to face whatever comes my way. I wish they told me this was the plan for more than just my age, I would've brought my gear. They rent it here so it's not a big deal, it's just always preferable to have your own eyes and ears at a minimum. When I'm about to text Jackson to see where they are, I hear someone call my name.

"Hey Violet! We're over here."

Austin is at the end of the parking lot under a big oak tree. He looks handsome in a pale blue hoodie and blue jeans. I walk towards him and spot Jackson's back; he's getting something from a saddlebag on what looks like a Harley motorcycle. I smile. I guess they had the same idea as me. It's the perfect day for a ride. When I get close, Austin smiles at me. "Are you surprised?"

"Yeah. Totally surprised, I didn't check Google or anything." I want to kick myself for not checking now that I'm faced with a place that may have an issue with my age. I'm emancipated for legal things like court and school. I can even have my own bank accounts without a parent's signature, with just my court order, but I can't vote or buy cigarettes. I can own an inherited firearm, but I can't purchase one. If they wanted to be assholes, they could really harass me at a gun range.

"Is it okay if I give you a hug?" Austin asks with some puppy dog eyes. He acted all offended when I tried that.

I can't contain my smile, "Yeah. It's fine." He leans in and gives me a one-armed friendly hug, which I return with two arms. It sends sparks right to my panties and my face heats up. I turn my face away so he can't see my blush. I'm aware of a twinge in my healing armpit.

"Which bike is yours?" I ask while I look at the bikes on either side of Jackson.

"The black one with the design on the tank," he points it out.

"It's nice. Hi Jackson," I call to him. He turns and looks at me over his shoulder, his face lights up with a friendly smile. His hands are full of small cases and bags with handles.

"Hi Violet. Glad you made it. Both of you come help me!" We both hurry over and grab things from him. Once his hands are free, he hugs me, without asking permission. I don't mind, I look up at him and give him a smile of approval.

"Anything else?" I ask him, looking at his saddlebags.

"Nope, I've got the rest." He hefts a heavy bag from the far side of his bike and rests it on his seat while he closes his saddlebags. I follow them through the door, and we set everything on the counter to be inspected. They each display their carry and conceal permits and their firearms from their holsters. Some ranges want to check everything. Others only allow firearms in bags until you're on a lane in the enclosed range. A short muscular guy, with a bald head, finishes with a middle-aged couple and looks at Jackson.

His face breaks into a friendly smile, "Hey Jackson, how's it going?"

"Hey Mitch, great. How's the baby?"

"She's amazing, but my poor wife is exhausted. I have some photos on my phone..." he pulls his phone out of his pocket and swipes at the screen. "Here she is, she's already growing so fast. She's three months on Monday."

"Wow! She's adorable and she's changed so much. I'm really happy for you, man. Here Auz," Jackson hands the phone to Austin and I peer over his arm to see the bald baby with a big toothless smile. Austin leans the phone so I can see better.

"Awww, she's so cute. She looks really happy," I smile at Mitch.

"She's a doll. I'm Mitch, and you are..."

Jackson jumps in, "Sorry, this is Violet. She's a friend of ours, it's her first time here. She's going to use our gear."

Mitch looks me over. "Welcome, Violet, it's nice to meet you."

"You too," I chew my lip. My nerves are swirling in my stomach waiting for him to ask a dreaded question.

"Have you ever been to a range before?"

"Yeah. My parents used to take me when I was a kid. I've practiced with a few different firearms. A Glock 9mm, a Sig 380, and a .22 rifle."

"Great. Do you have eyes and ears?"

Austin speaks up this time, "We brought some for her. That's an adorable kid dude." He hands Mitch his phone.

"I'll need you to read over the rules since you haven't been here before." Mitch hands me a laminated page with the rules from a stack of them on the counter.

I carefully read through them, and I chuckle when I see rule 13. *When on the range I may not shoot unicorns, but I may shoot badgers because they're assholes.* When I finished, I hand it back to Mitch with a grin.

He looks me in the eye and says, "You passed our rule thirteen test. It's how we know if people are actually reading the rules. Just one more thing, tell me the three fundamentals of firearm safety."

My eyes widen and the knot in my stomach tightens a little, but then I remember my parents teaching me exactly that. It was in the car before we got to the range the very first time. We were going over the basics and my mom explained the fundamentals.

"Never keep a firearm loaded when it's not in use. Never point a firearm at something unless you want to destroy it. Never put your finger on the trigger unless your firearm is pointed down range and it's safe to fire?" I finish with a questioning tone hoping I got it right. Mitch smiles broadly and my stomach relaxes a little.

"Good job! Okay you guys are all set. Violet, I'm sure they'll show you what to do, but we have an entry where you put on your eyes and ears before you enter the range. You guys have lanes twelve, thirteen, and fourteen at the end. Let Ashley know if you need anything on the range."

Looking at the wall behind Mitch, I spot a target with an angry cartoon badger on it, next to the zombie targets. That's pretty funny. There's also a bumper sticker above them that says: *I never shoot unicorns!*

I like this place. The owners must be cool. I follow Austin into the entry area, we place our bags on the large counter for that purpose. There are tape dispensers and staple guns lined up. There are also pads with score cards and those little golf pencils in a cup. Jackson comes in behind me and sets his heavy bag next to ours. He removes ear protection from one of the bags I carried and places a set of headphone style ear protection gently on my head. He's careful not to pull my hair. I move my hair out of his way and together we get my ears covered. The world goes quiet. I can still hear the banging sound of rounds being fired but it sounds far away now. Next, he hands me some protective glasses. They're tinted to help with glare.

They each put their own eyes and ears in place and using hand gestures ask me to follow them through the next door. When the inner door opens directly into the range, the shooting sounds become louder but remain muffled. There's a strong odor of gun powder in the air. It's an acrid and slightly burnt smell. We make our way down the row of lanes to the end. They each set bags on the various counter height tables made for that purpose. They place only firearms on the counter for each lane.

All the firearms aim down range. The range master, a red-haired masked woman, apparently named Ashley, waves at us and gives us a thumbs up from an elevated area in the middle of the lanes. I waved back, and the guy's nod at her.

"I'll set up your target. Do you want to try my nine?" Austin shouts at me. I nod.

He presses a button, and the target bracket glides to us on its rail. He attaches a piece of cardboard from the bin behind us then staples a target onto the supportive cardboard. He presses the button to return the target to the far side of the lane. You can go as far as twenty-five feet on this side of the range. He lets it go ten feet. I stared at him waiting for him to move it further. He doesn't.

"Can I please have it further out?" I shouted.

His brows raise. "Are you sure?" he shouts back.

I nod. He presses the button and moves it two more feet. I rolled my eyes and gesture for him to move it further. He watches me until I say to stop around eighteen feet. It's been a while and I've never fired their firearms before, so I decide that's a good start. He shakes his head like I'm ridiculous. I ignored him and stepped up to the bay. The sides are enclosed with bulletproof glass. Thank goodness, because the older man a few lanes down is trying to fix a misfire and has his .45 pointed this way. The range master is already running towards him. I can't hear what she's saying, but her arms wave in the air while she yells at him. He hangs his head and appears chagrined.

I look over the target, then the firearm. I check that the safety is engaged. I lift the firearm keeping the barrel pointed downrange. I checked the clip and confirm its full and loaded properly. I check the sight and line up the target to take a shot. I settle my grip so I'm holding it correctly. I take an extra breath to get past the temporary pain in my armpit from the movement. When I feel I have it properly sighted, I take a breath, place my finger on the trigger, and then I gently squeeze. I hit the top right edge of the center of the bullseye. I adjust my sight and squeeze again. This time I hit just below and left of the center. I adjust, splitting the difference and squeeze once more.

I hit dead center and smile. I'm happy to see my absence from the range hasn't completely destroyed my aim. I empty the clip, remove my finger, re-engage the safety and gently set the firearm down. I'm pleased with my grouping so far. I'm about to reload the clip when I hear a voice on my right.

Jackson yells, "Nice work! Do you need any help reloading?" I shake my head in response. He nods.

"Okay! I'm going to shoot next to you! Wave at me if you need any help with anything!" He gestures with his hands to accentuate everything he says. I nod in agreement.

He moves to his lane and gets himself set up. Austin is past him and he sends his target down the lane. Before I'm done reloading Austin begins firing. Jackson sends his target down the lane and then he begins firing a moment later. When I'm finished, I move my target to about twenty-two feet. I go through all of my preparation and begin firing. My armpit is barely a discomfort now.

We spent the next half hour repeating our actions. Austin taps my shoulder while I'm reloading, and I look at him with my brows raised in question.

"Do you want to try my .357 next?"

I nod, "That sounds fun!"

He swaps my gun and trades my ammo supply. I installed my fifth new target and line up the sights again, going through my same routine. Austin stays and watches me shoot. Probably in case I need any help. Whenever either of them is close to me, my heart starts beating faster and my skin heats. Thankfully the brightest lights are aimed downrange.

When I'm done, he shouts, "You're a great shot! Want to have a competition?"

"Yeah!" I nod smiling like a loon.

Jackson comes over and asks, "What's up, everything okay?"

"We're having a competition! Want to join?"

"Okay! What's the prize?" I look at Austin; we hadn't gotten that far. He scrunches his brow in thought and then I swear it's like a lightbulb goes off above his head.

"Loser buys dinner! Okay?"

I nod then ask, "How are we scoring it?"

Jackson yells, "Nobody has fired the .32, let's each take three shots with it and lowest score buys dinner!"

"I'm in!" I shout at them.

"Me too!" Yells Austin.

I step back and Jackson sets up the first round. He takes his three shots and sets up a fresh target. Austin gestures for me to go next, I shake my head and gesture for him to go. We both end up laughing and he takes his turn. He sets everything up for my turn and I hit the bullseye with each round. I empty the final round of the ten-round clip onto the countertop. Then I press the button and my target flies at me like a ghost in a haunted attic. I take it down and dispose of the holey cardboard. We decide to exit the range before we determine the winners and losers. After we load everything up, collect our brass, and deposit it in the appropriate bin, we exit the range area and wave goodbye to Ashley who waves back.

We set our bags on the clean-up counter while we scrub our hands with soap and water. Then we use the provided wipes for our faces and clothing. Just a quick once over can get rid of any lead debris stuck there. They'll need to clean all of the weapons we fired tonight or tomorrow. Improperly cleaned or maintained firearms can be unsafe. I hear my dad's voice in my head.

Once we're outside in the fresh air I feel a huge relief. The darkness on the lanes was oppressive and I didn't even realize it until now. They aim all the light down range and where you reload your firearms. The rest of the range is dimly lit. Not to mention the sensory deprivation of the safety gear.

We make our way to their bikes and put all of the gear away in their saddlebags. Once everything is stowed, we just stand there looking at each other. They each have a little smirky smile on their faces while I examine them suspiciously. My insides are swirling, and my face grows hot.

"Okay, let's hold them up together and see who did the best!" Jackson shouts.

"Stop shouting, dude," Austin admonishes.

"Oh, sorry," Jackson says barely above a whisper. Austin rolls his eyes, and I giggle.

"Okay, yeah, let's do it," I agree with enthusiasm.

We all hold our targets next to each other. Jackson obviously scored the highest. For mine and Austin's we have to calculate and add our scores. I beat him by one point. It was so close I felt bad accepting the win.

"Come on Violet, let me lose with dignity. You're a great shot. I'm not at all embarrassed that I lost to you. Seriously, be happy, you didn't lose!" I can't help grinning at his logic. He's so cute when he's trying to argue with me out of kindness, it's sweet.

"Man! Not fair, you ruined all the fun in ragging on you for being a loser. What's the plan? Where are you buying us dinner?" Jackson questions.

"Um hmm... do you like barbecue, Violet?"

"Yeah, I love it. I'm a carnivore."

"Great. What d'you think about going to my house for a barbecue? I just got some steaks; I can throw those on the grill, and I've got vegetables and some pie for dessert. How does that sound?"

Jackson answers first, "Sounds good to me, you're the grill master."

"Well, how can I possibly turn down a chance for steaks cooked by the master?" I question.

"*Grill* master, and you can't turn it down. You'd regret it forever."

"We wouldn't want that. Where's home?"

They tell me directions just in case and Austin texts me his address, we ride there together, the three of us enjoying a leisurely ride on a beautiful day.

Chapter Seventeen

We pull up to an unassuming ranch style home with a circular drive. He opens the garage and pulls inside. Jackson follows and parks next to him then gestures for me to pull inside as well. We enter the house through the garage into a laundry room, and they leave their helmets on a shelf next to a few others. I left mine with my bike. We make our way into a kitchen and family room combination. Austin points at some barstools in front of the island.

"Make yourself comfortable, I'm gonna go light the grill. Jackson, get her a drink."

"Already on it," Jackson says from inside the fridge. I check out the house. It's painted with neutral grays and has wood plank ceramic tile as far as I can see. It's not overtly masculine, or the way I would imagine a bachelor pad, but there's nothing feminine about it. There's a nature painting hung above the leather sofa. A massive flat screen takes up most of the wall opposite the seating area. I guess that's a guy thing since my TV is human sized.

Jackson asks, "Do you want soda, milk, orange juice, or beer?"

"What kind of soda?"

"Coke or something purple."

"I'll try the something purple," I answer with a goofy giggle, it makes me roll my eyes at myself.

He hands me a can that turns out to be flavored seltzer, it's not overly sweet and hits the spot. He opens a beer for himself. Austin returns and begins chopping vegetables and he marinates the steaks. We chatted about the ride and the range. I feel relaxed with them, like we've known each other for a long time. My nerves are calm, and I decide I need to tell them some more about myself. Things I've been keeping quiet. I initiate our favorite game, with the first of three questions.

"Austin, you haven't said much about your sister who's away, where is she?" His eyes snap to mine and then he looks at Jackson who nods. I watch the two of them carefully watching their expressions.

Austin looks down then takes a deep breath, "Megan is my older sister. The other two, Kristin and Tori, are younger and live at home with my parents, they're fourteen and fifteen. Megan and I have a different father than our younger sisters, and he passed away when we were young. My dad was Jackson's mom's brother. My mom remarried and had my little sisters. Their dad, Miguel, raised us. He's a really good guy and never treated us like we weren't his. He was also like a dad to Jackson while we were growing up. We both call him dad. He was dad to our friend, Pierson too. He grew up with us. The three of us were like brothers. When Megan was sixteen, she was assaulted, and she had some mental health issues after that. She tried to kill herself, that's why she's in a facility now. She's been there two years. We had no idea what happened to her until after she started getting help."

"I'm so sorry. You know you don't have to answer every question, right? You can pass."

"I know. I wanted to answer. It weighs on us every day. Jackson was practically living with us when it happened. We feel so guilty that we didn't know what happened to her, and that we didn't protect her or help her after. She changed and got distant, but we thought it was girl stuff, you know, like hormones or whatever. When she screamed at us to leave her alone, after like twenty times, we did. We can't forgive ourselves for it."

"You know none of it is your fault, right? Even the fact that you didn't do anything when she was having issues after the fact."

Jackson speaks up, "We know. It just doesn't make us feel any better. I found her when she was unconscious. She swallowed a bunch of pills... we did CPR until the rescue got there."

"You saved her. All you can do is be supportive. It sucks, but it's what she needs... your love and understanding."

"Yeah, that, and we want to kill the motherfucker who hurt her," Austin adds. Jackson nods his agreement.

"Do you know who it is? Was he caught?"

"She accused him, and nobody did a damn thing because he's got power behind him," Jackson growls.

"We know exactly who he is and where he is, but he's untouchable," Austin continues.

Jackson changes the subject, "Your turn. I've noticed you talk about your parents in the past tense. Are they not around anymore?"

"Okay. Right to it, huh? They died a couple months ago, car accident. My uncle is all I have now. He's great. We've been close since I was a kid, but I really miss my mom and dad." I end with a forced smile trying not to be sad and bring the mood back down.

"Shit Violet, that sucks I'm sorry. We can stop with the questions."

"No. I'm good. It sucks but nothing's going to change it. I want to continue."

"All right but please speak up if you don't want to answer something. I'm really sorry for your loss," Jackson says, and places a comforting hand on my arm.

I offer him a genuine smile, "Thanks. I'm good I promise."

Austin examines my face, "I'm sorry too."

"Thanks. New question. Jackson, you said you grew up practically living with Austin. What's the story with your parents?"

"They suck. My mom's an addict and she'll get sober for a while then she goes back to drugs after she starts drinking again. My dad's never been around much. He used to try when I was little, but my mom made it so difficult he eventually gave up. My uncle, Austin's dad, had substance issues too. He overdosed while he was partying with my mom. Our grandparents were alcoholics, and they died pretty young from cancer. That whole side of our family is messed up. I talk to my dad, but he lives in Texas, and I never see him. He has a kid from before my mom, my half-brother, but he's not around either. My dad's married but he never had any more kids. His wife has two, but I've never even met them. Austin's parents took care of me most of the time. I call them mom and dad. I call my biological mother Lois."

"Geez, we're both from fucked up parents." Both guys look at me confused, so I elaborate, "My mom and dad were my adoptive parents. My birth mother is not a good person, and she gave me up when she didn't want me anymore. I never knew who my father was." I look between them and decide I'm going to get this over with.

Austin, speaks first, "I have a feeling you've got a story to tell. Let's get this cooked and we can continue while we eat, okay?"

Relieved, I agree. We help him prepare everything while he uses his master skills on the grill to cook our steaks perfectly. Once we're seated at his dining table with our plates full, they get quiet, and I take it as my cue.

"Austin, you weren't kidding, this is great. You're definitely the grill master. Thank you so much for cooking dinner."

"It's my pleasure. I love cooking, but grilling is my favorite. Do you cook?"

"Not really. I'm learning, but so far, I can heat up soup, cook jarred spaghetti, and build a sandwich. I just moved into my place after my parents passed away. My mom and dad were both pretty good cooks, and I thought I had plenty of time to learn from them," I shrug.

Jackson speaks up, "I'm sure you'll learn fast. I'm not much of a cook, but I can make enough to keep myself alive. The rest of the time I eat here or at mom and dads. Does your uncle live close?"

"Yeah. He's not very far. He works at Mystic Cross Medical, he's a psychiatrist."

"That's interesting. Does that make it easier or more difficult to talk to him?" he asks.

"Actually, I'm pretty comfortable talking to him. Are you guys ready for my long story?"

Austin answers me, "Yes. But if you're going to be talking, take a few more bites before it gets cold."

Jackson smacks his arm, "Dude! What are you, her mother? She can feed herself."

"I know. I just want to make sure she gets enough to eat. Sorry Violet. I didn't mean to imply you're not capable."

I chuckle at them, they are like brothers, teasing each other constantly. I wish I had a sibling.

"I'm good. Don't worry, no offense taken. Look, I'm eating," I shove a huge bite of rib eye into my mouth. It's so delicious. They both smile at me and then Austin gives Jackson an, I told you so, look. I might be starting to understand their nonverbal communications. A warm feeling unfurls in my chest, and I feel a burst of happiness blooming there. It makes the corners of my mouth curl up despite the fact I'm chewing like a camel.

Once I swallow, I begin, "I lived with my mother until I was twelve. I had a stepfather, Jerry, since I was younger. I don't exactly know for how long. In my memories he was always around.

When I was little, he was nice and father-like. Later, after I was in school, he started abusing me. Eventually, he took over everything and he wouldn't let me attend school anymore. Looking back, I wonder if a teacher saw signs of abuse and he got nervous about getting caught. I told my mother what he was doing, and I begged her to make him stop or take me away. She didn't believe me. She wasn't physically abusive herself, but she was mentally and emotionally abusive. Plus, she let him hurt me." Both guys have stopped eating and they're watching me intently.

"I was allowed to walk to the library for one hour a week. I learned how to use a computer there and I learned everything I could on the internet. I also checked out as many books as I could carry. They let me take up to thirty at a time. I read them all and got thirty more the next week. I taught myself all types of things, from math to spelling, science to grammar. I couldn't get enough. The books were my only connection to the outside world."

Some of my story makes them gasp and some makes them scowl. I need to say it all and find out if they still want to be my friends once they know some of my dark secrets, at least the ones from my past.

"When I got a little older, the Beast, that's what I called my stepfather, started bringing his friends around and he let them hurt me too. I began exercising and trying to build enough muscle to fight back. The Beast didn't like that, and he started limiting my food. If he saw me exercising, I was punished worse, so I quit. I'd do anything to continue my trips to the library, and he used that to control me."

I can tell they want to say something. Jackson's hands are fisted so tightly his fingers are white. Austin's face looks red, and he seems a little nauseous. They hold fast and don't say anything, they let me continue.

"When I was twelve, he accidentally left me alone and free in the I found a knife and hid it in my room. I figured if he came to take me to the dungeon in the middle of the night, I could protect myself and fight him off."

"Holy shit," Austin blurts.

"Be quiet, let her finish," Jackson admonishes. Austin looks ready to cry, and his eyes are glassy and watery. Jackson nods to me to continue.

"A few days later, mother left early in the morning to go out for the day. I was asleep in my bed when the Beast came to get me. He only came to get me for one reason, to take me to his dungeon. He always called it the playroom, but it was a dungeon. I didn't hesitate. I stabbed him. He was shocked and fell back, then he tried to get away from me. I was like a wild thing. I pounced onto his back before he could get up and run away. I stabbed him until he stopped yelling and moving. I'm not sure how long I stayed there, curled up in his blood. But I woke up to my mother screaming and calling me names. She called nine-one-one. She was mad at me for freeing us from the Beast. I couldn't understand that. The police sent me to the hospital and when they figured out, I wasn't bleeding and I was the one who killed him, they arrested me. My mother immediately disowned me and gave me up. She even became a witness against me. Since I was a child, they admitted me into the psych ward while they decided what to do with me. Uncle Randy was my doctor. He's friends with my attorney, and he introduced us. Krewe took my case and he's been my attorney and friend ever since."

"Holy fuck! I'm so sorry. I don't even know what to say," Jackson blurts. Austin gives him a look and then he admonishes Jackson for his outburst.

I continue, "My first hearing was horrific. When the judge came into the room, I recognized him as one of the men who had hurt me. I became ill and was rushed back to the hospital. He ended up going to jail and the new judge dismissed the charges against me and allowed me to be emancipated. She was nice and saw that what I did was self- defense. I remained in the hospital for a while.

Once they were ready to release me into foster care, Uncle Randy introduced me to his best friends. They had been trying to have a child for a long time. When they heard about me, they wanted to meet me. They became my foster parents and then they adopted me." I search their faces, hoping I won't see pity. It will break my heart if they reject me now. But I sit up straight and steel my jaw, ready for their reactions, well, trying to appear ready anyway.

Austin speaks first, he swipes his arm across his eyes and says, "Damn. That's so fucked up. I'm so sorry your parents are gone. I can't imagine going through everything you've been through and still being so strong. You're amazing. Can I have a hug?"

He jumps from his seat and pulls me up and into his arms. Tears fill my eyes against my will. I feel him shudder and I assume his tears are falling freely. We hold onto each other so tight, and I've never felt safer. The feelings inside me explode and spark all over the place. I feel hot and cold. Happy and sad. Crazy and sane. Most of all I feel a bond connecting me and Austin. It's instantaneous and as sturdy as a bridge made of diamonds. I feel another set of arms pulling me into another hard, warm body. Jackson holds me close and somehow Austin is still holding me.

The bridge made from the hardest substance on Earth expands and joins me with Jackson as well. The three of us hold each other with me in the middle, it feels so right. It feels like this is where I belong. Austin kisses my temple and he's mumbling something reassuring. Jackson kisses my head and rubs my arm, comforting me to my soul. I feel the darkness there accept a shard of light brighter than the sun. It heats me and excites me. I want to kiss them. I've never felt like this before. I'm not sure how, but we all end up cuddled in Austin's bed.

Jackson is propped on the pillows with my head on his stomach. His fingers are twisted in my hair as he twirls it round and round. Austin's head is on my belly with my hand moving between his neck and his shoulder. His hand is curled on the back of my biceps. We've all been lost in our own thoughts, while sharing soft touches.

"I have some questions. Do you feel like answering them?" Austin asks me.

"Sure. Shoot."

"If I ask something you don't want to answer, please tell me. I want to know everything about you, but I don't want to trigger any flashbacks or anything."

"I'm pretty good at talking about everything. I've been in therapy for a long time, and I've worked through all of my trauma upside down and sideways. I promise to tell you if I don't want to answer something, but I doubt that'll happen. You may have noticed I'm a little blunt. I don't shy away from tough topics."

"I've noticed," he says with a chuckle. "You said there was more guys than your stepfather who hurt you, did any of them go to jail?"

"No. The case was bungled by the cops. Being a little cynical now, I think it was on purpose. They found video tapes that put the judge in jail. I think they accidentally lost some of the evidence that showed the men involved. But some of them eventually ended up in jail. Some are dead." I can't keep the grin from my face as I recall slicing some of them.

"Do you ever think about doing something to them yourself?" Jackson asks.

"Sure. Who wouldn't? I mean, that would be perfect justice, right? If I could torture them to the same degree, the way they tortured me, you know, sentence them to the fate they actually deserve it would be like self-made karma and very satisfying." "If you could actually get a hold of them, literally have the opportunity to kill them, would you, do it?" Austin asks.

"In a heartbeat. I learned a lot of self-defenses from my parents. I've studied MMA style fighting, knife throwing, sword fighting, target shooting, and parkour. I'm especially partial to using knives."

"Geez. You're a dangerous woman," Austin says as he raises himself off of my belly. He props himself up on his elbow and is now leaning over me and very close to my face. His bottom lip is pulled between his teeth as his eyes shift between mine. I want him to kiss me.

The thought makes me lick my lips and his eyes follow my tongue, then he swallows hard.

"When we met, you told me you didn't want to go out with me because you just broke up with someone. Will you tell us about that?"

Jackson asks. When he speaks his stomach moves, and it makes me giggle. Austin smiles at me.

"Okay. When I was in the psych ward I made a few friends. My roommate Harmony is still one of my closest friends. A guy named Colby who's into computers and nerdy stuff I like, we're still very close too. Harmony is actually marrying another friend from there; his name is Mike. Max was new shortly after I arrived. He was Colby's roommate. We all used to hang out inside. Once I was adopted, I went to a private school and Max showed up there eventually. Turns out it was his school. Our friendship continued and eventually we started calling each other boyfriend and girlfriend, since everyone pressured us into it. After a while we started kissing, but it just didn't feel right. He was more like my best friend. We love each other, but it's more like sibling love than anything romantic. I finally realized it wasn't what I wanted and broke up with him. He's in Europe now, according to Harmony. I figured out recently that my feelings for him were not romantic at all. Because of my past, we went glacier slow, and never did anything more than kiss. He said he was fine with waiting until I was ready, but I just didn't ever feel that way about him."

Austin looks thoughtful and asks, "Have you ever done anything sexual, with a guy, voluntarily?"

I look away from him and chew on my lip before I answer, "No. Uncle Randy says my past doesn't change the fact that I'm technically a virgin. I don't know the first thing about romantic love or sex. Ugh! It's so embarrassing." I cover my eyes with my hands, mortified that I just told them about my lack of knowledge in the sex department. I feel them shift around and beneath me. One of them, I think it's Jackson, lifts me into a sitting position and then peels my hands away from my face. Jackson continues to hold my hand, and Austin takes my other hand. I keep my eyes scrunched closed tight.

"Violet?" Jackson probes gently. I peek at him by opening one eye. He smiles softly. I slowly open the other eye. They're both smiling at me. They're not running away, that's got to be a good sign.

"Yeah?"

"It's okay. It doesn't change who you are, and we really like you... exactly this way," Jackson states.

"A lot," Austin adds. I look between them, they're so sincere it makes my heart flutter wildly.

"I like both of you." There. I said it. They both smile, so I smile. Now we're sitting here smiling like idiots.

"Not to sound stupid, but because of everything you've told us, I want to be perfectly clear," Jackson declares.

I hold my breath and nod. My mind races with terrible thoughts. Are they sending me away? Do they want me to choose between them? Are they going to refuse to touch me? I want to run away screaming.

"When you say you like us both, what does that mean?" I gulp hard and tell him the truth, "It means I have romantic feelings for both of you. I can't... I won't choose just one. If you don't want anything romantic to do with me, that's okay. I'll absolutely respect your decision. But if that's the case, I hope..." He leans in and kisses me. A soft and slow kiss right on my lips. He takes my hand into his, and it makes a warm vibration zing up my arm and straight into my sex. Feeling his lips on mine is similar to the time I rode a rollercoaster.

My stomach feels like I'm heading downhill at the fastest speed, it's that thrill of excitement that is unmatched, and makes you want more. It leaves me breathless. My eyes open and look deep into his, "What was I saying?"

Austin places his fingers on my cheek, he turns my face towards him and says, "You were saying you like us both and we're agreeing with you."

He rubs his thumb across my bottom lip then looks into my eyes. Just like in a movie he bends towards me, and we fall into a kiss. My eyes close and his fingers move into my hair. His tongue presses against my mouth and I open for him. Jackson's hand squeezes mine. I can feel my panties growing damp. When our kiss ends, I feel a bit foggy and a lot elated. I've never felt anything so exciting in my life, I want him to keep touching me, kissing me. I want them both rubbing against my skin. I feel a need deep inside that's taking over all of my nerves.

"Did we make our feelings clear?" Jackson asks. A wide grin stretches my face as I nod. Both of them smile in return.

"We want to know everything about you. We want to go as slow as you need. We want to teach you how... to use your words, romantic sex can be good. You aren't your past. We care about you, and we want to keep you safe. That means guarding your emotional and mental health. You're in charge of what happens, and we'll ask before we try anything new. If you get scared or you don't want to do anything, just tell us, alright?" Austin asks.

"Yeah, okay. Will you please kiss me some more?" They both laugh out loud and my face hurts with the force of my grin. When his laughter dies off, Jackson pulls me onto his lap. I end up straddling him with my knees bent near his hips. He wraps his arms around me, then he pulls me close, so I'm pressed against him. His lips meet mine in a warm connection. I push my tongue into his lips seeking entrance. He obliges and our tongues dance in each other's mouths. My hands squeeze his shoulders as I try to pull him closer. I need something I can't articulate. I have a burning desire in my chest, and I want his tongue to lick it.

I wiggle in his lap trying desperately to connect with his entire body. My damp panties become soaked almost instantly. I start to worry he'll feel it and be grossed out by me.

"What's wrong baby?" Austin whispers into my ear. His hands wrap around my hips from behind me.

I release Jackson's mouth and try to answer Austin, "I don't know, I need...I...I need something. I..."

"Can I feel you? Can I touch you with my hand? I want to feel if you're wet for us." Austin asks. That sounds good. I need someone to touch me.

I try to smile with confidence, "Yes. Please touch me," I nod. "Is it normal to be wet?" I feel stupid asking, but I've never read or researched anything about sex because of my past I never wanted to think about it. It seems like a really dumb move now. Harmony tried to tell me things so many times and I shut her down, what a boneheaded move.

"The wetter the better," Jackson responds. Austin unbuckles my jeans and moves them so he can get his hand into my panties. His fingers travel down until he touches something that jolts me up off Jackson for a second. It feels amazing having him touch me. His finger slides lower and then it moves in circles. It feels so incredible. I think I'm making some kind of sounds, like tiny moaning panting noises. I'm also grinding against his hand.

"Babe, can I touch your breasts? I want to feel you." Jackson questions. I nod my response. I couldn't speak a coherent word right now if my life depended on it. He gently rubs his hands over my chest, and he's watching my face carefully every time my eyes open. His intense scrutiny adds to my excitement. Knowing I'm the sole focus of these two gorgeous men is making me hotter. His hands gently squeeze and pinch at my nipples. They're hard and pointed, and it seems very interesting to him. He pushes one hand under my shirt and his fingers against my skin send shocks of sensation zipping to where Austin's fingers are making me crazy. Every touch is building up to an explosion. My moans are loud, and I can't control them. I give up trying and just enjoy the ecstasy these men are giving me.

Their fingers are magical and it's like they know exactly the right place and way to touch me to bring the most pleasure. The pure bliss builds and reaches a climax that has me screaming. A flood of thrilling sensations burst from my loins, and I orgasm in a rush of fluid and energy. A colorful blur of lights and feelings takes me over and I leave my body in a flight of pure enjoyment like I've never felt before. When I come back to my senses, my body continues to shudder and warm tingles travel my skin in the most pleasant way. Both of them are staring at me in awe while they hold me close. I'm not sure if I should be embarrassed or happy. The joy I feel is the dominant emotion, so I go with it.

"Wow. That was...just wow."

"You're the most beautiful woman I've ever seen. You have no idea how amazing you are..." Jackson whispers, his eyes are glued to mine.

Austin speaks softly into my ear, as he leans back a little, "Violet, that was incredible! You're so stunning when you come. It makes me want to spend every minute making you come." He puts his finger into his mouth and sucks on it. "Mmmm, you taste amazing too. Next time I want to lick you until you come on my tongue." I feel my cheeks blush and I look down.

No one has ever put their tongue on me before. The thought of it makes me feel warm, excited, and embarrassed.

"Hey, don't be shy. We want to make you feel good, not self-conscious. Don't feel ashamed of your body or your feelings. We care about you, and we want you to feel good, okay?" Jackson tilts my chin so I'm looking at him. I can see the sincerity in his eyes, and it eases my awkwardness.

"Okay. I just feel kind of dumb for not knowing what I'm doing or what I'm feeling. I wish I had let my friend, Harmony, tell me about sex stuff. Are you sure I'm not a disappointment, since I'm so clueless?" Austin huffs behind me and pulls me next to him, so I can see both of their faces.

"You're not dumb. You have a history that's tragic, but it's not your fault. We understand and we want to help you learn and enjoy being with us. We don't care how long it takes or what we need to do to make you feel good and comfortable with your body. We care about you; we want to be with you. Do you understand?"

"I understand. I mean, I understand what you're saying. I'm not sure I understand why you want to be with someone like me," I shrug.

Jackson speaks next. "Violet, you're smart, funny, hard-working, and beautiful, who wouldn't want to be with you? You've no idea how long we've wanted to find someone like you. I mean, you're a dream come true for us. Since we were kids, we've had this image of the perfect woman in our heads. We always wanted to find her and share her. We know that's not the average idea, but it's how we always pictured our ultimate future. You check every box. You're her, and you like us both, which is amazing. Especially since Austin's a jackass."

We both laugh while Austin punches Jackson in the arm, "Dickhead! We're having a nice conversation, and you have to be a dick." Austin shakes his head and tries not to laugh. I laugh harder, but Jackson grasps his arm in pain. This gets Austin laughing. They're so funny. I really do like them so much. Jackson starts tickling me and he reaches under my arms to tickle there.

"Ow!" He jerks his hand back.

"What's wrong? Did I hurt you?"

"No. It's just, I have an injury." Austin takes my hand and lifts my arm. He investigates my armpit, trying to move my sleeve but it's too long to move out of the way.

He grasps the hem of my shirt but stops to ask, "Is it okay if I look under your shirt at your injury?"

"I...uh...oh-okay. Just...I think I should explain."

"Explain what?"

"Well, um, you both like me, right?"

They both nod and say, "Yes."

"Would you say you want to have a relationship with me?"

Jackson speaks first, "Definitely. We want you to be ours, just ours. A committed, exclusive relationship. Is that all right?"

My face breaks into a huge smile, "I never would've thought I would want a relationship with anyone, and I certainly never considered two someone's. But, yes, I want to be with you both very much. A committed exclusive relationship with both of you sounds wonderful."

They both smile and Austin kisses me. Then Jackson kisses me. Austin asks, "Does this mean you're our girlfriend?"

"Is that what you want?"

"More than anything," Jackson states.

"Absolutely," Austin answers.

"Then yes. I'm your girlfriend and you're my boyfriends, right?"

"Yes," they both say, then Austin continues. "So can I look at your injury?"

"You can but let me explain first. It's a tattoo."

"Under your arm? Why would you get one there? That's such a painful spot. Didn't it hurt while you were shooting?" Jackson questions.

"Yeah, it hurt a little. I didn't choose the location."

"What does that mean?"

"Well. I...oh. I guess we need to talk about some things."

"That sounds ominous. Are you all, right? Do we need to kill someone?"

"Definitely not. It's all taken care of."

"I'm so confused," Austin interjects.

"Sorry. Let me try to explain. Were you guys serious about wanting to kill Megan's attacker?"

They look at each other and Jackson answers, "One hundred percent. We plan to kill him at some point, we just haven't figured out how to get close enough yet. He deserves to be tortured and killed for what he's done to Megan, but we don't think she's the only one."

"In my experience, if they're molesters they're that way all the time and would take advantage of any situation to molest a vulnerable victim."

"That's what we've discovered too," Austin adds.

Chapter Eighteen

"**I**'m thirsty, do you think we could get something to drink? Plus, we need to sit so I can see both of you at the same time. I feel like I'm in the middle of a tennis match." They both chuckle.

"Yeah, come on, we'll sit at the table and talk. Do you want a snack?" Austin asks.

"Sure." We sit at the table, each of us with a drink and a tray of vegetables and cheese in the center. I can see them both now and I can't believe they're my boyfriends. I won the lottery.

"Can I look at your injury before you start?"

"Okay. I probably need to put something on it, I'm supposed to every few hours."

"I think I have some tattoo balm in the bathroom cabinet, will you grab it, Jackson?"

He nods and leaves the table. Austin turns his chair towards mine and helps me get my shirt over my head without hurting my armpit. He sucks in between his teeth when he sees it. I haven't looked at it since before we went shooting.

"I'm so sorry I touched it. How bad does it hurt?"

"If nobody touches it, not too bad. But shooting was a little painful. How red is it?"

"It's not really red, it doesn't look infected or anything. Just kind of raw. Why's there a hole in the middle of the cross?"

"I kind of cut that part out."

"Holy fuck! Why?"

"Here's the stuff from his cabinet. Damn, that looks painful. What happened in the middle?" Jackson asks.

"You wanna put it on for me? Or can I, do it?"

"Whatever you want, but I can see it better than you."

"True. Okay, you can do it."

Austin carefully applies some of the cream, "How's that?"

"Thanks. It's good."

"All right, spill it beautiful," Jackson demands.

"Okay. Have you heard of the website ITZYuu?"

"Yeah. It's the one where people pay to get people to show them their feet or the rest of their bodies, right?" Austin questions.

"Uh huh. I thought it might be a good place to catch molesters. I figured if I posed as a younger girl, willing to show my feet, I could catch people who wanted to molest me. So, me and my friend Colby set up a page we charge for, and we started collecting information on all the donors. Colby's a computer genius and I'm not too shabby. Then I had this idea to auction off my first tattoo."

"What information do you collect?"

"I developed this program that acts like a virus and once it gets into their system it collects all of their activities and their banking info. We can then send their predator behavior to the authorities, and we can steal their money and donate it to charities that help victims of assault." I hold my breath while I wait for their reactions. This could make or break our brand-new relationship and I'm terrified of losing them which freaks me out. As usual they look at each other and communicate in their silent way. They both look at me and I freeze.

"Explain how you auction a tattoo," Jackson prods. He reveals nothing about how he feels regarding my explanation so far.

I nervously swallow and continue, "I offered to let the highest bidder choose where they could put a tattoo on my body-"

"What the fuck?" Austin spits.

"No! They had rules. They couldn't put it anywhere a swimsuit would cover or above my collar bones and it was limited to no bigger than two by three inches. They had to sign a contract and they weren't allowed to touch me."

"How much was the highest bid?"

I'm embarrassed to admit, "Eighty-seven-thousand dollars."

"Mother fucker! That's insane! I mean, you're gorgeous, but what kind of sick fuck wants to tattoo a girl?" Jackson blurts.

Austin whistles and adds, "That's a lot of money. What're you going to do with it?"

"It's already been donated; I mean after I paid the help."

"We can get back to that. Tell us why you cut out the middle," Austin pushes.

"Well, the highest bidder wanted to hurt me. I guess his kink was pain. He chose the location and made it solid dark colors to inflict as much pain as possible, even if I want to cover it, he'll still be responsible for the pain. He also seemed pretty excited about putting a mark on me. But he also wanted to cause emotional pain. The middle of the cross was a swastika."

"Son of a bitch! Where's this asshole now?" Austin growls. Jackson looks just as ready to rip his head off. Oh boy, I don't know how much to admit. What if I tell the truth and they hate me? What if they turn me in? I couldn't bear either one, but most of all I don't want to lose them. I won't lie to them if they ask; I'll tell the truth.

"He's gone. I'm fine, and I'm going to cover it as soon as it's healed. I thought I could make it until then with the hate symbol on there, but it bothered me too much, so I cut it off. I was careful not to cut too deep and I sterilized the blade."

"Okay. So, you catch molesters online. Does that help you, mentally, because of your past?" Jackson queries.

"Yeah. Colby is really the one who does the stealing from them, he modified my program and he's been very successful getting ahold of the bad guy's money and donating it to worthy charities. I do the luring when needed."

"Do you want to catch the molesters and send them to jail?"

"It would be great if they went to jail."

"You didn't really answer his question," Austin helpfully points out.

"Yes, I want to catch them. Better?" I smirk at Austin.

Jackson realizes I'm still avoiding half of his question. He inspects my face and then my fisted hands. Looking into my eyes he asks again, "Do you want them to go to jail?"

"In an ideal world they would go to jail forever. But that doesn't happen and even if they go to jail, they get back out. Child molesters and rapists don't change, and if they're released, they offend again. I prefer a more permanent solution."

"I feel like we're dancing around the full story. I'm just going to ask what I want to know. I hope you'll trust us with an honest answer. Have you had someone kill a molester?"

"No. But you know I killed one, my stepfather. He's not the only one. Do you hate me now?" I can't look at them, if they're disgusted with me, I don't want to see it on their faces.

"What? No. Of course not. Do you want to tell us what happened?"

"I'm afraid you're going to think I'm crazy and that you're going to dump me." I brave a look between them, and their faces are soft, caring, definitely not disgusted. I relax a bit, the breath I was holding rushes out and I feel better.

"Not going to happen. We told you we want to kill the bastard who hurt Megan. We weren't kidding, we seriously plan to kill the asshole," Jackson states. I inspected his face. Then Austin's, they're completely serious, no smiles no hint of humor.

"Okay. After my parents passed away, I decided I needed to get rid of the monsters who hurt me. Colby and I tracked down the worst ones and found that two of them weren't in jail but still hurting girls. I hunted them down and I... kinda... unalived them." I shrug.

"You're amazing. So brave, so strong. I think I like you even more now if that's possible," Austin tells me.

"I agree. I mean, you saw a problem and you took care of it. That's so hot," Jackson adds placing his hand on my thigh and squeezing.

"There's more," I offer.

"Hold on, before you tell us, I really want to know the details. If you're comfortable telling us," Austin requests.

Checking the time, I can't believe how late it is. Sawyer's probably very unhappy with me. I've been gone for hours and it's past his dinner time. Not that he doesn't have food available, he won't starve, but without his can at dinner he convinces himself he may. I wonder if they'd be willing to go with me.

"It's much later than I thought I'd be out, I need to get home to Sawyer before he starts plotting my murder," I smile at the joke. Their faces fall.

"Do you really have to go?" Jackson asks with his own puppy dog eyes.

"Would you want to go with me?"

Austin looks at Jackson and they both nod and look back at me, "Yeah, we'll go with you. Are you sure?"

"I'm sure. I live about a block and a half from the restaurant. It's got a garage so just pull in with me. Do you want to bring a change of clothes?" I aim my question at Austin since we're at his house.

"Yeah, give me a minute. You wanna borrow something, bro?"

"I guess, some sweats and a t-shirt, thanks man." Jackson and I clean up the snacks, rinse our cups, and put them in the dishwasher. By the time we're finished Austin's back with a small bag.

We quietly make our way into the garage, and we head out on our bikes. I wonder if Austin's neighbors hate him. Three bikes starting this late would be really annoying. At least it's the weekend. My bike isn't as loud as theirs, and Harley's are just inherently noisy. My beauty isn't quiet, but she purrs at a much lower decibel. We have a pleasant ride home. I'm glad I keep a jacket in the compartment under my seat or I'd be too cold. The small leather jacket helps a lot.

When we pull into my warehouse the roar of motorcycles echoes off the metal walls and roof of the uninsulated garage and it rattles my home. Poor Sawyer, I hope it doesn't scare him. Though he's used to fairly loud noises from me between my bike and music. When I'm out I leave him closed in the apartment for safety.

The guys are quiet and looking around at everything. They inspect my workout equipment as we make our way to the stairs. I'm glad I told Uncle Randy about them since he can see my apartment entrance on the security camera. I hope he's not looking though, we kind of agreed it would only be for emergencies.

"I'm not sure how Sawyer will react to you guys. He's not used to having strangers in his home. It's just been me and him since I found him, and he's only met my uncle once."

"Okay, be on the lookout out for an attack feline, got it," Austin quips.

"I'm not worried, animals love me. He's still a kitten, isn't he?" Jackson asks.

"He's like a teenager now, not quite full grown, but he thinks he's in charge. Once I feed him, he should be fine. I just don't know if he's going to be mad since I'm late with his dinner, and I'm bringing strangers home."

I get the door open, and they follow me inside. I hit the light switch near the door, and he comes running from the bedroom meowing loudly. He freezes when he notices the guys. I put my hand up to signal them to wait. I go into the kitchen area alone and open his food and put it down for him. He dives on it like he's been starved for days and growls while he eats like usual.

When I get back to the living room area, I find the guys still standing just inside the door.

"Come in, oh, yeah, I forgot I don't have furniture out here. Sorry about that. When I moved in, I definitely didn't have any plans for guests. We can go in my room and sit on the bed, or I can round up a few chairs for out here."

"Show us your room and we'll figure it out," Jackson offers. I decide to take a quick shower, the lead dust from the range is gross. They each take a turn after me. While I'm alone with Austin, he corners me and kisses me, constantly checking that I'm okay. When he's in the shower, Jackson kisses me and holds me close on my bed. He doesn't try to touch me; he just keeps kissing me. It's sweet and I'm surprised because Jackson is usually more forceful. I like it and I'm happily snuggled with him, when Austin comes back with damp hair.

Austin climbs in and spoons me from behind. I feel safe and content. Sawyer enters the room silently and perches on the back of the chair. He watches us with his tail twitching. Jackson is watching him back.

"Com'ere Sawyer, pspspsp," I call. He ventures onto the foot of the bed and sniffs my foot. He looks at Jackson, then Austin, sizing them up I suppose. He smells Austin and then hops onto his hip. He flops down on him and starts purring. Austin pets him and their bond is forged.

"Sawyer, dude, I'm deeply offended that you chose Austin over me. What's up with that?" Jackson reaches out his fingers so Sawyer can sniff him. Then he attempts to scratch his cheek. Sawyer lets him for a moment then turns his head out of reach.

Austin laughs and smirks in triumph. Jackson gives up and places his hand on my waist.

"Do you want to talk more or go to sleep?" Austin asks.

"I won't be able to fall asleep yet. Having you guys here is way too exciting and I'm not sure how to relax," I answer completely honest.

"We can help you relax, but if you want to talk, we want to listen. I really want to hear about how you unalived a guy," Jackson says.

"It wasn't just one guy."

"How many have there been? I mean if you want to tell us, don't feel pressured," he adds.

"Not including my stepfather, three. I hunted down two of the assholes who abused me as a kid. They were together when I took them out. The third was the highest bidder."

"Do you plan to hunt down any more abusers?"

"Yeah. I've been working on the worst one since my childhood. He's a difficult target because of his standing in the community. I call him Voldemort."

"From Harry Potter?"

"Yeah. I refuse to say his name. It seemed fitting, the evilest being ever, it's just like him. J.K. Rowling knows how to name a bad guy," I watch them carefully. I'm still afraid they'll be disgusted by me and dump me.

"You're not tiny, but you're not a huge girl either. What are you, like five foot seven? How did you handle two men?" Austin questions.

"I'm five foot seven and a half. I snuck up behind one while the other was out of the room, and I stabbed him before he had a chance to fight me. The other one came at me with a bat, but I outsmarted him and stabbed him before he could hurt me back. Then I burned the house down."

"Holy hell, that's sexy as fuck. You're a total badass. How did you take care of the third one?" Jackson asks.

"He was the highest bidder. Colby and I hired a tattoo artist and a driver. The driver is a highly recommended jack of all trades in the crime world. He's well known for keeping his mouth shut and doing whatever job is needed for the right price. The driver blindfolded the highest bidder and the artist and brought them here."

"Whoa! Here?" Austin sits up with his surprise.

"Yeah. I have some storage rooms that I made into what I needed. I use one as a studio for my videos online. The other room is extra sound proofed and set up for a tattoo artist to work and a killer to kill."

"How did you dispose of the...evidence?" Jackson wants to know. They seem like they're taking notes on how to do it, they must be serious about taking out the guy who hurt Megan. I'd be happy to help them.

"Colby hired a cleanup crew. The driver was a member of that group, so I felt good about them. He didn't say much, but he was thorough and did everything I asked without question. He was also willing to rescue me if I needed help. Do you want to see my rooms?"

"Yeah!" Austin exclaims and hops out of bed. I guess he's excited. I climb out after him and Jackson joins us. Sawyer just rolls over on the bed giving us his back.

We make our way back through the apartment and down the stairs. This time I turn on the workout lights. The guys look over my stuff and Jackson punches my heavy bag. They followed me into the hall where the storage rooms are located. First, I show them my little girl's room with all my fluffy pink accessories.

"Damn, this is definitely little kid central. What a bunch of sick fucks to bid on tattooing the child from this room. You said there were hundreds of bids, right?"

"Yep. Colby is tracking them, turning them in and stealing their money where he can. Some were out of the country so there's not much we can do about them. But he can still steal from them, so hopefully it hurts enough that they won't go back to ITZYuu."

I lead them into my BASIL. I decided it makes the most sense to call it that. I explain it to them, and they like it. They carefully look over the tattoo chair, then they open cabinets and check out my supplies. I have some of my knives in this room, so they scrutinize them too. Jackson spies my hidden firearms and I'm impressed.

"What's your plan for Voldemort? Are you going to bring him here?" Austin asks.

"That's my plan. I'll need to make some modifications to the space and remove the firearms. The driver suggested I install a drain. I've been working on a plan that'll allow me to get him here somehow without me needing to lift his unconscious body. As you pointed out, I'm not that big. He's not small, but even a small man would be really difficult to move alone."

Jackson stops checking over the room and walks to me. He looks me in the eye and folds his arms.

"What if we helped you?"

"That's really sweet, but I don't want to involve you guys in my vigilante revenge. I've been locked up before and I've got all the history of a crazy person. Chances are I could plead insanity if I got caught. But you guys would get a prison sentence, or worse. I can't ask you to do that."

"What if we help you before the fact, help you get everything ready and set you up for success? But you could do the actual, unaliving?"

I look between them; they're both standing before me, arms crossed, and very serious. They're waiting for an answer and I'm not sure what answer to give. I need some help. I don't want to risk them, but if they're going to kill a guy anyway, maybe I can't stop them. Or maybe we could work out a deal... they help me with things that don't involve killing anyone and I kill their guy for them.

"I have a thought. You guys are determined to take out Megan's attacker. I'm an expert at doing that, plus I have the background to plead insanity if it came to that. What if you guys help me and I help you, but we keep you away from any actual, un-aliving so you won't end up in prison if something goes wrong?"

I can tell they want to shoot down my idea flat out, so I blurt, "Please think about it. Let's work on our plan and we'll decide that later, okay?"

They look at each other and nod in their usual way. "Yeah, we'll think about it. We'll help you, and see where we end up," Jackson agrees. They walk to the center of the room and then to the outside wall. They put their backs against the wall and begin talking about drain installations. Before we head back to my apartment, they've figured out exactly how they're going to install a bathroom and a drain in my BASIL.

I'll even be able to get a permit for the improvements. I could apply for a loan if I needed to with legal permits and plans. I haven't told them about the money I have or the inheritance my grandmother is trying to take from me. I decided I may as well fill them in, they already know my worst secrets and they seem even closer than before.

After we each choose something to drink, we go back to my room. We make ourselves comfortable on my bed again, and Sawyer decides to lie on Jackson this time. Jackson grins with satisfaction now that Sawyer has accepted him. It's adorable. We talk into the night, and I tell them about my family, my money, and anything else they want to know. They fill me in too and we expand our connection on a whole new level, and I love it.

We hit one snag and I'm not quite sure how we're going to handle it. When I finally admit I'm not eighteen yet, they freak out a little. But when they discover my birthday is just weeks away, they relax. They don't run away and that's good enough for me. It was my final hurdle, the last secret that filled me with fear of losing them. I think we're going to be all right. Happy and content in each other's arms we fall asleep at some point, and I sleep soundly, not a single nightmare.

CHAPTER NINETEEN

My neck is hot, and I'm used to Sawyer trying to strangle me, so I don't move. Slowly, I realize something is poking me in the ass and my arms are wrapped around someone, not Sawyer. I pop one eye open and see an ear and some messy curls. Memories of everything we talked about and all the kisses and touching flood me and I smile. I've never slept in a bed with anyone before. I've had a few different people lying in my bed while they slept, but I never did. When a grown man hurts you then falls asleep on you, how can you possibly relax enough to sleep? But I didn't have any trouble at all with these two.

I'm not sure whose hands are where. My front is pressed to Austin's and my back is pressed against Jackson's front. I'm the center of a cousin sandwich and it feels like home.

I wriggle a little and a gruff voice in my ear tells me, "Don't do that. I'm trying very hard to think about baseball and old ladies."

"I don't know what that means."

"Guys get hard in the morning, maybe you've heard of morning wood? If you touch it, you're going to make it very difficult for it to go away. He's trying not to do something he shouldn't," Austin explains.

"Really? Do you have it too?"

"Mines gone down. I thought about golf. It's so boring it helps me."

"Can I see it?" I asked Jackson.

"Are you trying to kill me?"

"What? Why can't I see it?" Austin bursts into laughter I don't understand.

"Aaaaahhh! Babe, you're truly killing me." He flops onto his back and covers his crotch with a pillow. Austin hugs me close while his laughter fades.

"It's not that he doesn't want to show you. We just agreed that we don't want to go any further until you're eighteen. It might sound dumb to you, but it seems like the right thing to do for us. Understand?"

"I understand. But can I make a counteroffer?"

He shines a brilliant grin my way, "You can do anything. What's your offer?"

"What if we wait until I'm eighteen for intercourse? But we can do other stuff until then? I'm emancipated. I could get married if I wanted. I think it's okay if I consent to some stuff, but if you guys want to wait to go all the way." I place myself so they can't do their silent communication about this. I want his answer not a consensus between the two of them. He tries to see Jackson and gives up.

"Are you sure that's what you want? It might be very difficult to keep from taking things over the line if we're in bed naked and doing other stuff."

"Dude! You're literally killing me!" Jackson groans from my other side.

"Sorry, man. I just want to be clear about what she wants."

"Fuck it!" Jackson growls and leaves the room. I catch the briefest glimpse of his tented sweatpants, and I bite my lip at the thought of him.

"You're going to make this as difficult as possible, aren't you?"

"What? No! Sorry. I just really want to touch you both. I don't know if I can wait without being able to do some things. I want to see you and touch you. I feel so clueless because of my history, and I hate it."

"I understand, because I do have a clue. I know that it's going to be very difficult to do some things without doing everything. You've been driving us crazy since we met you. The first time I saw you, in the market, I thought you were the most beautiful woman I've ever seen. When Jackson brought me to your restaurant and I got to talk to you, I found you even more attractive. I'm so excited to be dating you, and I want to hold you all the time and make you come non-stop. But I think it's good for us to wait. With your past, your age, and our long-term goals, I think it'll help us build a strong foundation for a great relationship. It's definitely not that we don't want to do everything with you, because we do. More than anything," Austin kisses the tip of my nose, and I blush.

"I understand. What long-term goals?"

"We really mean everything we said. You're our dream come true; we want to be with you for as long as you'll have us. We don't want to rush anything and risk messing it up. We especially want to spend quality time with you, get to know you better and for you to know everything about us. We want to meet your uncle, and we want you to meet our parents."

"I like everything you're saying, and I agree with all of it. However, I want to go on the record with my feelings about sex. I don't care if it's now or a few weeks from now, when I'm eighteen. When I'm ready, I'm going to want to take that step, and I hope you guys will be okay with that."

Jackson returns, tentless. He and Austin share a look, and I can't decipher it. But they both smile, and it makes my chest fill with sparking butterflies, and I don't care.

"I'm good now. We're okay to decide when the time comes. For now, let's get some breakfast," Jackson inserts like he's been here all along.

"Okay, give me two minutes I'll be right out," I announce as I rush from my room. I brush my teeth, my hair, and use the facilities as quickly as possible. When I exit the bathroom, I hear them in the kitchen. The sound of dishes and pots or pans moving around reaches me and when I enter, they're facing the stove. I enjoy the view; their strong backs and tight asses are incredibly attractive. Sigh.

"Did you find something to cook?"

"Jackson found eggs and bacon, I found bread. Is it okay if we cook?"

"Yeah of course, any time. I'm still figuring out how to make most things, but scrambled eggs I've got down. Do you need any help?"

"Nah, we've got it. What do you want to do today?" Jackson asks.

"I've got to call in sick, then I'm all yours. We could probably go visit my uncle if you want. We could practice more parkour and workout or go for a ride. I haven't been to the beach in forever. Let's think about it while we have breakfast."

Javier is cool with me not coming in to work today. I've never called in before and I'm always the first one to fill in for everyone else. I'm starting school tomorrow and he was understanding that I needed today. He's a pretty good boss all things considered.

By the time we finish eating we've planned our day. They're both excited to workout in my gym. Then we're going to part ways to get cleaned up. They're going to pick me up for lunch and then we're going to meet Austin's parents who are basically Jackson's parents as well. I'm a little nervous about that last part,

I'm not much for social interaction with strangers. I've never met my boyfriend's parents before and I'm a little worried they'll think I'm weird or not good enough for them.

"I'm so full! I love this place I can't believe I've never been here before."

"Yeah, it's hard to beat a Publix sub, but they do a good job. I think it's the rolls, they make them from scratch every day. The bad part is when they're out, that's it, and they close for the day."

"I never would've thought to look for a sub place in a warehouse complex."

"We're here all the time, our shop is around the corner and the materials supplier we use most often is right there," Austin points to a warehouse across the courtyard.

"They don't advertise, they mostly serve the offices and warehouses right here. We smelled the bread baking one morning and followed the amazing scent until we found their shop. They say never trust a skinny chef, but I don't know if I would name my sub shop, *Two Fat Guys,*" Jackson speculates.

My nerves are vibrating beneath my skin, and I try to distract myself. I wish I had my toothbrush; I didn't think about kissing or meeting parents when I ordered onions on my sandwich. Worrying about onion breath isn't helping my nerves, so I try a physical distraction and reach out to take each of their hands in mine. Touching them soothes me and Austin raises our joined hands to kiss the back of mine, his kiss sends a pleasant sensation to my chest and a warm feeling climbs my neck and settles on my cheeks. When I glance at Jackson, he's smiling at me and kisses my hot cheek.

A short while later we pull up to a modest modern style home, with neatly trimmed landscaping. I feel instantly enamored with the neighborhood, and there are kids playing ball in the street at end of the cul-de-sac. Large oak trees hang over the road and the Spanish Moss hanging from them lends a homey feel to the welcoming community. I just hope I feel this good once I meet the occupants of this attractive residence.

Jackson drove us in his truck, Austin opens my door before I have a chance to even fumble with the handle. He offers me his hand and some confidence.

"They're going to love you, don't worry. My sisters can be moody, so don't be offended if they don't say much. My mom is a hugger, but she doesn't ask, she just swoops in, so I apologize in advance," he warns.

Jackson tacks on, "Mom is a sweetheart, she's going to think you're too thin and she'll keep trying to feed you, but it's okay to say no. Dad's a little reserved, but he's a great guy and once you get to know him. You'll see how warm hearted he and the girls are, well... Austin said it. They're moody as hell and they can be sweet or monsters. There's no in between. I would say it's because they're teens, but they've always been hot and cold."

Austin throws open the door and yells "We're here!"

Two girls with dark hair and eyes approach us and their eyes are locked on me. They look similar to each other, but not a lot like Austin. His hair is lighter, and he has more hazel green eyes. They're both pretty with glossy hair and smooth skin, one is smiling. I think she must be the older one.

"Hi, I'm Kristin, and this is Tori. It's nice to meet you." She points at her sister who nods but doesn't break a smile. I smile at them both and extend my hand to shake, Kristin takes it gracefully. Tori looks like I'm asking her to hold a toad, and she drops my hand as quickly as possible.

"Hi. I'm Violet." Before it can get anymore awkward, a tiny woman with golden waves and beautiful blue-green eyes steps from behind them and hugs me.

"Violet! I'm so happy you could come! It's wonderful to meet you. Are you hungry? Can I get you something to eat? A drink? Wow, you're even more beautiful than the boys said. Please come in and sit. What would you like?" She keeps her arm around my waist and directs me to a sofa. The house is just as warm and inviting inside, of course that may be because their mom exudes kindness and friendly hospitality.

"Miguel! Come meet Violet." Before I can say anything a tall, broad man, with dark hair and eyes matching his daughters appears before me. He reaches out to shake my hand and I'm thankful he's not a hugger. He gives a small grin and shakes my hand gently.

"Pleased to meet you, sir."

"Oh, there'll be none of that! I'm Angela, Angie to you or Mom. He's Miguel. You met the girls. Please sit. What can I get you?"

"It's so nice to meet all of you. I'm fine, Angie. We just had lunch. Thank you." I perch on the sofa and try not to look awkward. Austin and Jackson each hug Angie and lift her up in their arms, and Miguel shakes their hands with that man thing of patting their shoulders. The guys have huge smiles on their faces.

"Girls, have a seat and visit with your brother's friend." Kristin sits in a chair and Tori rolls her eyes and sits next to her on the floor. She puts ear buds on and ignores everyone.

"So, Violet, how did you meet my brother?" Kristin begins the inquisition.

"I met them at a market near my work, then Jackson came into the restaurant, and we started talking," I answer attempting to keep the nerves out of my voice.

"That's wonderful dear. Where do you work?"

"Mystic Cove Cantina, I've only worked there a couple months. I'm starting school tomorrow."

Austin cuts in before anyone can ask me another question, "Violet's studying computer science. She's got a knack for computer technology."

"That's so nice. Are you excited?" Angie asks.

"I guess so, I'm looking forward to finishing and being able to get a job in my field."

"Are you going to the community college?"

"No. Henry Plant University, also here local. I have an A.A. degree already so I'm working on my bachelor's now, I haven't decided yet if I'll pursue a master's degree."

"That's great. The boys tell me you have your own place in town. How do you like it?"

"It's nice, I like being so close to work and now school."

"Austin said you're close to your uncle, does he live nearby?" she continues.

"Yeah, he's over by the medical center. He's a doctor there."

"That's wonderful. It's nice to be close to family. Oh, I'm sorry."

"Mom! What did we say?" Austin scolds.

"I know. I'm so sorry for your loss. I'm terrible at saying the wrong thing. Please forgive me."

"Oh, it's fine. "Don't worry about it," I reply with lots of awkwardness hanging on tight to my movements.

Miguel speaks up, "The boys told us you ride a motorcycle. What is it?"

"It was my father's. It's an Indian Scout. We were hoping to restore an original vintage model someday."

"The boys helped me rebuild mine, it's a Harley," Miguel is a man of few words.

Angie is the talkative one, and she seems a little hyper. I wonder if she's nervous, had too much coffee, or is naturally this energetic and chatty. I spot her giving Tori a mom-look. She responds by huffing and rolling her eyes. Then she looks at me with resentment. Great, I'm so glad Angie's making her stay in the room to visit with me.

"It's nice to meet you, Violet. I'm glad my jackass brother was able to act normally enough to convince you to like him. Can I go now?" Tori directs the last part at her father.

"Victoria! Apologize to Violet and Austin this minute."

"Fine. Sorry. Can I go now?" Jackson whispers in my ear, "Just ignore her. She's been a little shit for a while now. She's fourteen."

"Just go!" Austin answers on behalf of his parents. Tori stomps out of the room and a door slams down the hall, and the pictures hanging there rattle.

"I'm so sorry for her attitude. She's at that age. Can I get you something to drink?"

I don't think she's going to stop asking until I agree, so I accept, "Sure, I'd love a glass of water. Thank you." She scurries off towards what I assume is the kitchen.

Kristin laughs, "Good call, she won't leave you alone if you don't give in and let her get you something. But fair warning, she's gunna harass you until you have a snack, or a four-course dinner."

"Thanks for the warning. I'll make a mental note to come here hungry in the future."

Miguel speaks up, "I like her, she's smart." He says it to Jackson but Austin nods too. They seem like a fun group; I like them too. When Angie returns with my water, she starts grilling the boys as she calls them, about work and what they've been eating. Kristin wanders off at some point and Miguel puts the game on without the sound. We all chat about random things; Angie tells everyone about the news in the neighborhood.

She seems to know everything about everyone. Whose house sold and for how much, who's getting a divorce, and who died. Austin seems to know some of the people she mentions while Jackson rubs my lower back and watches the silent game. Eventually the water kicks in and I excuse myself.

Austin shows me to the restroom after he points out his room. He and Jackson shared a room since he wasn't always here. It makes me wonder why they don't live together now. When I leave the bathroom Tori opens her door and almost bumps into me. She jumps surprised and quickly closes the door behind her.

"Sorry I didn't see you," I offer in peace.

"It's okay. How old are you anyway?"

Not wanting to answer, I decide to fib slightly, "Eighteen."

"How did you get your own place already?"

"Mostly a series of unfortunate events. My parents left me some money, it was enough to get a place, and my uncle was okay with it." I shrug.

"I like your hair. My parents won't let me color mine. The blue looks good."

"Thanks, it's fairly new."

"Cool."

She goes into the bathroom and closes the door. I guess I need to call that a win. She could've ignored me or cursed at me based on her behavior so far, I think that went well.

I'm dying to check out Austin and Jackson's old room, but I can't bring myself to snoop, so I just look at the family photos hanging in the hall. There's a timeline of the kids as they grew up. I don't see any pictures that could be Austin's father, but Miguel is with Austin in some from when he was very little. Jackson is there, as well as the boy I assume is their friend Pierson. There's a few of the three boys of various ages, and they're adorable. There's a Christmas photo of everyone that can't be older than this past Christmas or maybe the previous one.

Jackson finds me staring at Pierson in his military uniform. It says he's in the Navy. He's very handsome, dark hair and eyes with two dimples bracketing his barely there, smile. He was a cute child but scrawny now, and he's filled with some obvious muscles.

"That's our other brother, Pierson. He joined right after Megan tried to kill herself, I think he was struggling with it and needed some structure and goals. He used to work with Austin and me, but he seemed to get depressed when everything happened with Megan."

"I'm glad you and Austin had each other. This one's Megan, right?" I asked, pointing to a beautiful girl with auburn curls and bright blue eyes.

"Yeah, that was right before she began to change. She refused to have her picture taken, dyed her hair black, and got really quiet. I think she was using drugs, and they made her swing from silent to angry. It kills me seeing her like this and knowing how far she went down a dark path. It makes me want to hunt that bastard down right now."

"Preaching to the choir. I'm so sorry, I can't imagine watching such a dramatic change in someone you love and not being able to help them."

"Yeah, it sucks."

"Do your parents know that I'm dating both of you?"

"We told them, but I'm not sure they understand. Sorry if it's uncomfortable for you."

"No, I'm fine. I just didn't want to say the wrong thing. Since we're here, can I see your old room?"

"Okay, but you need to know Austin was in there still after I left, so, the posters are his." I can't help giggling at his warning.

"Did Pierson stay in there too?"

"No, he had his own room. It's Tori's now. The girls used to share when they were little. Most of the time if I was here Pierson would bunk with me and Austin. We had two sets of bunkbeds in here back then." He opens the door Austin pointed out earlier. There are two twin beds, one against each wall now. The pale gray walls are adorned with a few bikini clad girls, Post Malone, and Imagine Dragons. It's what I would imagine a teenage boy would have in his room. There are a few trophies on a shelf for various sports, and some models of muscle cars on another. The corner has a baseball bat and glove leaned there as if the owner will be right back to collect them.

"You're the sole visitor to these hallowed halls, because we've never brought a girl home before. It's probably why mom's acting like a psycho."

"As a certified psycho myself, I like her. She seems really nice, and she obviously loves you guys."

"She does. She's a wonderful mom. I just wish Tori wasn't giving her such a hard time. I think it's because she's the youngest. We all spoiled her when she was little and cute. She had adorable curls, and she was always a sassy little thing. Now it's annoying," he chuckles, and leads me back to the living room.

Angie convinces us to stay for dinner, there's no way to avoid her feeding you once you step through the door. I'll be better prepared next time. Even Tori can't escape the mandatory meal. But it's delicious and we laugh through it. Kristin and Tori engage Austin and Jackson in a sibling war of sorts attempting to tell their most embarrassing childhood stories. My favorite is when Austin was twelve. He started hoarding Victoria's Secret catalogs and Megan outed him at a Sunday dinner that included the family priest.

Everyone got really quiet after that story, so I made a move to get us out of there. Not that we weren't having fun, but I start school in the morning and the guys have work. We can't spend all night there, no matter what. We all get hugs good-bye, even Tori says a polite see-ya. I leave their family home with a warm feeling of family in my heart. It's pleasant.

The guys drove me home and we decided they need to head home since they have to get up early. I don't have work until Wednesday since I'm starting school. They both kissed me, hugged me, and kissed me some more. It's physically painful not to invite them inside to bed. Once we're able to disentangle ourselves from each other, they leave for home. I spent my evening working out and playing with Sawyer.

Jackson: Hey beautiful. I wanted to say goodnight and good luck tomorrow. Text me when you have a chance and let me know how it goes.

Me: I will. I miss you.

Jackson: I miss you too. It was so hard to leave.

Me: It was so hard not to try to convince you to join me inside.

Jackson: Would it be okay if we brought you dinner tomorrow?

Me: That sounds perfect. Sweet dreams.

Jackson: Good night beautiful.

When I set my phone on my nightstand it chimes again.

Cousin Austin: Hey babe! I miss you.
Me: I miss you too.
Cousin Austin: It was really difficult to leave you.
Me: I had a hard time letting you go.
Cousin Austin: Can we bring you dinner tomorrow?
I laugh, they're so funny. I wonder if they discussed it or if they're just hoping it's all right with the other one.
Me: Perfect! I can't wait!
Cousin Austin: I hope you have a great first day!
Me: Thanks. I hope you have a great day too.
Cousin Austin: Sweet dreams gorgeous.
Me: You too, goodnight.

I decide to change his name in my phone, he's no longer Jackson's cousin. He's, my boyfriend. I changed his name to AUZ and Jackson to JAX. That's better.

After I checked my school supplies for the tenth time, Sawyer and I curl up in my bed and I think about my amazing weekend. I fall asleep remembering the kisses and touches I experienced and how good they made me feel.

CHAPTER TWENTY

My alarm startles me awake from a dream of me between two hard, hot bodies. I'm sad to find out I'm alone in my bed. I'm slow to get dressed and groom myself. Sawyer has no such issue and has his leg in the air while he licks his nether region. No shame at all.

I force a granola bar into my mouth and hope it keeps until I get a chance to eat lunch. My schedule isn't too bad, I was able to get all of my first-choice classes. I have classes four days a week. Three on Monday and Wednesday and four on Tuesday and Thursday. It sounds like a lot, but one of them is a lab. My guidance counselor was worried I wouldn't be able to keep up when he saw my date of birth, but my transcripts finally shut him up.

I just hope I'm not bored; I know a lot about computers and programming. I can set up an entire network, wiring and all, then program it. One of my professors is supposed to be a genius and

I hope he is, maybe I'll learn something from him. Thankfully nobody is privy to my thoughts right now or they'd think I'm a snobby know it all. But I'm just realistic, my high school teachers learned more from me than the other way around.

My phone chimes and my face breaks into a huge smile when I see it's a group text. They must've talked after they texted me last night.

AUZ, JAX: Hey baby, we wanted to wish you a good day.
Me: Thanks! I'm leaving now. Can't wait to see you tonight.
AUZ, JAX: Are you okay with pizza?
*Me: Sounds yummy. See you! *smiley emoji**
*AUZ, JAX: *tongue and smiley emoji**

I arrive at school with a huge smile. I find my class easily; all of the computer classes are in the same building. I literally have two classrooms and a lab for all of my classes. I'll never get lost. I choose a seat against the wall near the middle of the stadium style risers. Every desk has multiple outlets and cords ready to go. I connect my laptop and I'm all set to begin.

There're two other girls in my first class. I'm surprised there aren't more girls getting into this field, it seems like we're long past the stigma of no girls allowed in the computer nerd world. Neither girl sits near me or each other. A very skinny guy with glasses sits next to me. He introduces himself as Anthony and shakes my hand.

Two guys who seem to be friends sit in front of me and they chat until the professor begins our class. He goes over the syllabus and explains our projects in detail. We have two, one is due at midterms and the other at the end of the course. We have two weeks to decide on our first project topic. I've already decided to work on cyber security for this one. The guys in front of me want to build video games.

Class ends early since it's the first day. My next class is in the same room, so I don't move. A couple guys also stay put. I focus on my notes for the project I've already started for the class that just ended. The next class is the first one I have with the supposed genius professor. While I'm not paying attention the class fills up and there're four girls besides me this time. Nobody greets me or introduces themselves, which is my preference. The guy next to me is a large man with dreadlocks down his back. He has a lot of earrings in both ears, he smiles at me, and I smile back.

Our professor makes his way in, and I inspect him carefully. He's tall, with dark hair and has an athletic build. He's nice looking and when he begins to speak, he has a hint of an English accent. He emails us our syllabus and his bio, which I've already read. Our entire term is going to be based on cracking his code, solving a riddle, and using the answers to build something we'll find out when we get there. I'm intrigued. I don't know if he's a genius yet, but I'm looking forward to finding out. Everyone is chattering, it sounds like a room of excited chipmunks.

He ends the class by putting our first link up on the screen. Some of the class gets to work immediately and the rest leave, happy to be let out early. I have a break for lunch now, and I decided to check out where the link goes. It leads to a website with a black screen, which only contains a name. No obvious links, no other pages, just a name, *Babbage.* I recognize the name as the *Father of the Computer, Charles Babbage.* When I click on the third *B* in his name, it opens a search box that wants eighteen characters.

I try a few different combinations of computer terms and history of the programmable computer. Looking around, I see the black background with the name on most of my remaining fellow student's screens. There's one guy, two rows down and three seats over who's on the same screen as me. He's furiously making notes on a yellow pad. This might take a bit of time; I pack up and go for lunch.

My tuition came with a meal plan, so no sense wasting it. Student Center, here I come. The food court style cafeteria has nine options, one vegan, two Asian, one Italian, a deli, two Mexican, Starbucks, one Greek, and a burger place, one could argue is

American. I choose Mexican, I haven't had it in a while, and I have a thing for tamales.

My plate has a huge pile of rice and refried beans, a small salad of lettuce and tomatoes with a glob of sour cream on top, a falling hill of chips, and two corn husk enclosed tamales. They also gave me a cup of spicy salsa and a bottle of water. I find an empty table in a mostly unoccupied corner. When I'm up to my wrists in Mexican deliciousness, I hear voices approaching from behind me.

"Do you mind if we sit here?" Two guys from my last class stare at me.

I swallow my mouthful and wipe my lips, hope I'm not sporting a sour cream mustache, and answer, "Go for it."

One sits a seat away from me and the other sits across from him. The one next to me takes a huge bite of his sandwich while the one across from him pours dressing on his enormous salad. I take another bite of my second tamale. Once I'm finished with it, I clean off my fingers and lift my phone from my pocket.

Me: Hi handsome boyfriends, I'm at lunch. Two classes and still alive, only one more to go. How's your day going?

AUZ: Hi gorgeous, we're busy, and it's hot!

JAX: Yeah, it's hot as fuck out here. Do you like your classes?

Me: So far, it's mostly syllabus introduction, a few interesting projects coming up.

AUZ: Have you made any friends yet?

Me: what are those?

JAX: lol We might be a little late tonight, we're behind, hit a fiber cable that wasn't marked.

Me: that sucks, did you knock out everyone's internet?

AUZ: Nah, it's a vacant building they're retrofitting for a new tenant, but it has to be fixed. We had to move everything and start on a different part of the job. We shouldn't be too late.

Me: Okay. Should I take care of dinner? I can order it and pick it up so it's there when you guys arrive.

AUZ: Okay, we'll get it tomorrow.

*Me: I like it, already planning to see me tomorrow *smirk emoji**

JAX: Plan on it every single day babe!

AUZ: What he said.

JAX: See you later beautiful!

AUZ: Ditto gorgeous!

Me: Later handsomes!

The roar of a huge room filled with animated college students rushes back to me when I stop focusing on my boyfriends. It's still amazing to me I have two hot-as-hell guys and they're all mine, exclusively mine. It seems like a dream, and I usually have nightmares.

"Wow, who makes you smile like that?" The guy across the table asks.

"What?"

"You have the biggest smile on your face, I was just wondering what a guy has to do to get a girl to smile like that."

"Oh. Boyfriends don't need to do much more than make plans to see us, and call us pretty," I quip, completely honest.

Next-to-me-guy, says to his friend, "Told you! We need to get some girlfriends."

"I know, but you need to tell the girls, they're not cooperating with our plans," across-the-table-guy answers. They're funny, a laugh escapes me, and they both look at me.

"You're in our class. I remember the blue hair. Hi, I'm Wyatt," across-the-table-guy introduces himself then his friend, "That's Aiden, we're computer science majors."

"Nice to meet you, I'm Violet. Also, a CS major. What did you think of Professor Kunal's assignment?"

Aiden speaks up, "I looked at it for a few minutes, googled it, and that's it. Did you figure out what we're supposed to do?"

"Am I really helping you if I give you the answers?"

"So, you know, and you just don't want to tell us? That's so cruel, we're stupid, please, have mercy on us!" Wyatt adds.

I like them. I decide to be benevolent, "How about a hint. Did you ever play AdVenture Capitalist?" They nod. "Do you remember what you did to advance the game? Try something similar." I see the lightbulbs appear above their heads when they grasp my meaning. It's an old point-and-click game. I figured they'd understand.

Wyatt smacks his forehead. "Duh! I guess Professor Kunal likes history. We'll need to keep that in mind. Thanks, Violet."

"Sure."

Aiden asks, "Did you just transfer here? I don't remember seeing you before."

Not wanting to answer a lot of questions, I make it easy and use his story, "Yep. Do you guys live on campus?"

"No, we just got into Beta Chi Theta, our house is on Greek row. What about you? Are you in a dorm?" Aiden asks.

"No. I have a place off campus, I'm a local."

"That's cool. I'm from Indiana and Wyatt's from Oklahoma. Do your parents live close-by?"

"No, just my uncle," I clear the lump from my throat.

Wyatt starts a new subject and I'm relieved, "What class do you have after lunch?"

"I'm back in the same room for Algorithm Abstraction and Designs, what about you?"

"I have Computer Programming Fundamentals 1," Wyatt answers.

"I'm with you next class," Aiden tells me, "I have CPF1, tomorrow."

"Me too, do you have the lab?" I asked him.

"Yeah, right after the class. It's right across the hall."

"Good. It makes it easy when the whole building is Computer Science. I only have two separate classrooms and the lab. What else do you have tomorrow?" I query.

"After the lab I have Intro to Design. What class do you have first tomorrow?" Aiden questions.

"Digital Logic One, after the lab I have Programming Language Concepts."

"Wyatt's in your P.L.C. class. Professor Prinz is cool. We had him last year for Intro to Programming."

Wyatt adds his opinion, "You're taking all the hardest classes. Do you have no social life or are you a glutton for punishment?"

"I have a job. I have a life, but no it's not very social. Boyfriend's not in school, working instead, that's pretty much all I have time for with my schedule." Wyatt squints his eyes at me as he inspects my face. He doesn't question me further and I'm thankful.

Aiden pipes up, "Well, Violet, we better get a move on, our class starts in ten minutes."

I collect my things and toss my trash. I wonder how this class will be, but if we get out early, I'm gone. I want to see my guys. I say goodbye to Wyatt and walk to class with Aiden.

"How long have you been together with your boyfriend?"

"Not very long, we were friends for a few months and sort of recently decided we want more."

"That's cool. I used to have a girlfriend all of freshman year, and halfway through sophomore year. Then over the holidays I found out she was cheating on me halfway through freshman year. I was the dumbass who was totally faithful."

"Loyalty doesn't make you a dumbass, it makes you worthy. You'll find the right person, who won't cheat."

"You don't even know me. How can you make that prediction?" he grills me.

"I'm a really good judge of character, you're a decent guy. The perfect girl is out there hoping to meet you soon."

"You're an interesting person. I hope your boyfriend knows how lucky he is."

"Definitely."

When Dr. Hindri dismisses class a half hour early, I'm so ready to get home. He seems pleasant and didn't assign any projects, yet. Aiden and I sat together, so he walked me out. We say goodbye near the parking lot, then he walks back to his frat house. I sit in my vehicle for a minute to text the guys.

Me: Hey, I'm heading home. I'm going to study until it's time to get the food. Let me know if you want anything besides pizza with mushrooms, green peppers, and pepperoni.

JAX: Will you get one with pepperoni and sausage? Austin wants to know. I don't care, I'll eat anything. See you soon, drive safely.

Me: Will do

Checking the time, I've got at least a couple hours, so I take a minor detour and pass slowly by Voldemort's Lair. Usually, I can't see any cars parked outside of the imposing structure. Today there are three large black cars parked at the front entrance. The place looks like an ancient haunted French chateau. It's gloomy with the many hulking oaks draped in Spanish Moss lining its driveway and sprinkled across the property. The many windows and doors are accented with shutters and decorative metal. The upper floors have small balconies and the landscaping surrounding the building is lush, green, and covered with bright colored flowers which do nothing to pierce the gloom. In a symmetrical design, the four walls between the large windows of the first floor have large trellis' lifting bougainvillea up to the railings of the verandas above.

If I didn't know the evil within, I would probably find it inspiring, but darkly beautiful. Since I'm far too aware of the sinister villain who resides here, the stench of sulfur hangs in the air and the heat from the flames of hell radiate out until they heat my face in the most unpleasant way. The darkness is palpable, and it makes my skin crawl.

I've had enough and I turn towards home, ready to study my trail cam clips, and see if I can track down who owns those cars, and if they're someone to be feared or ignored. I depress the dial button on my steering wheel.

"Call, RobN," I say when prompted. The phone rings once before Colby answers.

"Hey! How was your first day of school?"

"It was good. I like my teachers so far. I've got a few projects to work on, and I even spoke to some people."

"Wow, that's a good day."

"Have you been watching Voldemort today? I passed his lair on my way home. There were some suspicious cars parked out front, I'd like to know who they belong to and what's the connection?"

"Easy-Peasy. Anything else?" he asks.

"Nope. How's it going with you? Is everything still all right?"

"Yeah, right as rain. I'm doing well on my current meds. Virtual psychiatric visits are so much better than in-person ones. I'm doing okay, I promise, Vi. You know I'd tell you if I wasn't."

"I know, I just wanted to check in. I was wondering, if you're feeling up to an outing?"

"What type of outing?"

"There's someone I want you to meet, well, someone's. What do you think? We can meet anywhere you're comfortable. If you want to go to Bugsy's BBQ again, that's fine."

"When are you planning this meetup?"

"This weekend? Your call."

"Are these someone's that have a significance in your world?"

"Yeah. They're my boyfriends."

"Is this a pronoun thing? Or is there more than one?"

"Jackson and Austin. They're cousins, and this past weekend we decided to try dating. I met them a couple of months ago when I first moved here. We've been hanging out, and lately I've been having some feelings. We talked it out and they like me too, so we're dating now. Does that freak you out?"

"That you're dating someone I don't know? A little. That there's two of them? No. I love you, Vi. You're a unique individual and I'm happy if you're happy. Do they know about me?"

"Don't be mad, but yeah, they know everything. I trust them the way I trust you. If you're uncomfortable, you don't have to meet them. It's just that Austin's sister was assaulted. She tried to kill herself in the aftermath and almost succeeded. She's upstate now."

"Damn, I'm sorry. I'm glad she wasn't successful."

"Me too. The thing is the perp is walking free. I don't know who it is yet, but they want to end him, and I want to help them do it."

"Gotcha. You know I'm on board with ending all the monsters. Okay, I'll meet them," he answers with conviction, it's a relief.

"Do you want to go to Bugsy's or are you just saying that for my benefit?" he questions.

"It's your call, name a place, day, and time, we'll be there."

"Have they met Randy yet?"

"No. I was planning for a week or two into the future. Why?"

"Why don't we go to Randy's?"

"Dude! I don't know if I'm ready to introduce them to Uncle Randy. He's cool with the poly-thing in theory, but he might have trouble with it when it's kissing his daughter up close and personal."

"I get that, but he'll be all right. He's laid back and if you're happy, he'll be fine with it. Invite his girlfriend too. The more witnesses, the less likely the freakout."

"I suppose. All right, I'll tell him we're all coming. What day and time?"

"Saturday, 4pm. Okay?"

"You got it. I'm pulling up at home now. I've got homework. I'll talk to you later, all right?"

"Cool beans, my Violent Queen. I'm out."

"Later Hood."

Sawyer comes running at me when I make through the door. He rubs against me, and I squat down to scratch all his favorite spots. I bring a glass of water to my computer and pull up the trail-cam footage for today. I multitask and call Uncle Randy too.

"Hey, Violet! What's up?"

"Hey. I was wondering if it would be okay to have dinner at your place Saturday?"

"Of course, what time?"

"We'll come at 4, Okay?"

"By *we* you mean you and...?"

"Colby. And...Jackson and Austin."

"I see. So, may I assume your talk with them went well?"

"We're dating. You should invite Stephanie."

"As a buffer... so I don't grill them?"

"No. Because I like her, and Colby wants to meet her."

"All right. I'll see if she's available. Did you want me to cook anything in particular? Or order out?"

"Colby and I talked about barbecue. Would that be, okay? He likes chicken. Something simple though. I don't want you to have to make a huge meal. Can I bring anything?"

"No. I don't want spaghetti with barbecue," he chuckles at my expense.

"Low blow! I meant; may I bring anything I might purchase at a store?"

"How about I'll text you if I need anything?"

"Okay. Thanks. I really appreciate it, you're the best." A smile seeps into my voice as I appreciate my adoptive father. I'm really thankful to have him. I'm also looking forward to getting to know Stephanie better. I feel so mature and childlike at the same time. I miss my parents in moments like these.

"No, you're the best, I'm just thankful you let me hang around. How was school?"

"So far, so good. I've got projects, but one seems to be especially interesting, and my professors seem nice. I talked to a few people."

"That's great. I look forward to hearing all about your week on Saturday. Call me if anything comes up at school. See you soon!"

"Love you."

"Love you too."

Once I disconnect from our call, I focus on the footage of shiny black cars pulling into the front of Voldemort's lair. I take screenshots of their tags and send them to Colby. He loves research. It soothes his manic side. I zoom in on the men who exit the vehicles and snap more screenshots. I don't recognize any of the men, but that doesn't mean anything. I wasn't always coherent when I was abused, and there was a period of time where I screamed and screamed. The Beast started drugging me to make it stop. Eventually he just hit me, and I learned to keep quiet. Once he had me completely under his control, he could manipulate me by threatening my library visits. After I stopped caring if he hit me, it was very effective.

I send the rest of the screenshots to Colby, and he responds saying that he'll work on it in a few minutes. I also confirm for Saturday, hopefully the guys will be available. I'm thinking since I met their family, they'll be okay with meeting mine. It's going to be interesting.

I still have a little time before I need to order the pizza, so I pull up the riddle from Professor Kunal. Staring at the box that wants eighteen characters, I go over computer terms in my head and their letter counts. I try a few of Babbage's other inventions, but nothing fits. Then it dawns on me, the clue was just his name. It's got to be something personal to him. I don't know much of his biographical information, just his works. He's a fascinating man, and he invented the *cowcatcher*. How cool is that?

I try Google and carefully scan everything that refers to his personal life. My face breaks into a smile when I realize the numbers in the biographical summary are eighteen characters if I line them up. I type his date of birth, date of death, and age at the time of death into the box. Butterflies unfurl in my stomach as I take a deep breath and press enter.

My screen explodes in fireworks with music blaring. The song is Radioactive by Imagine Dragons. As the song plays, a cartoon crosses the screen revealing the next challenge. A video game start page fills my screen, and it makes me laugh out loud. I love old-school video games.

Sawyer comes running and launches himself onto my desk. I silence the music and pet him as he looks me over. He promptly sits on my keyboard and voices his concern, *Meeeow!*

"Sorry, little man, didn't mean to scare you. I promise it's nothing bad. I'm going to get some pizza, your favorite junk food. If you're good, I'll share a bite of crust, okay?"

I swear his response is, *Meh!* Laughing again, I close out my computer and order the pizza. Feeling stale in the clothes I've had on all day, I change into workout clothes and throw on a baggy t-shirt over my yoga pants and sports bra. I'd love to take the bike out to get the pizza, but I don't want to risk dropping it, I'm hungry.

CHAPTER TWENTY-ONE

Craving the fresh air, I hoof it to the little pizza place around the block. I've ordered from here a couple times, but they only do take out. When I get close, the enticing scent of garlic makes my stomach growl. It's the epitome of a hole-in-the-wall pizza shop.

A bell jingles as I open the door and the warm odors of garlic and fresh bread hit me in the face like a chunk of Italy. The owner is in a messy white t-shirt with an apron over it, his back to me as he works quickly on something with lots of sauce. He's using a metal ladle to douse the creation in red. Menus and a half-filled tip jar adorn the short counter next to the ancient cash register. A teenage girl bounces from somewhere in the back, ponytail swaying, and approaches me with a bright smile.

"Hi, welcome to Tony's! How may I help you?"

"Hey, I called in an order for two pizzas."

She spins towards the big metal oven and examines the papers dangling from the pizza boxes resting on top. "Name?"

"Henley."

"Just two pies?" she asks, bringing them to the counter. She sets them in front of me and takes the slip from one. I nod my answer. The girl uses a blue fingernail to type the information into the register. Then she spears it onto a spike with the rest of the slips. She raises the lid of one pizza to show me the contents, then she swaps that one to the bottom in a well-practiced move and opens the second box. I smile with approval.

"Wow, it looks so good. Thanks."

"It's thirty-three-fifty," she continues to smile. It makes me think of Austin's sullen sister, what a difference.

I hand her two twenties, "Keep the change."

"Seriously?"

"Yeah. I'm a waitress. I support my colleagues," I offer her a large grin.

"Wow, thanks. Tony, this is a special one!" she yells over her shoulder.

I have no idea what she's talking about, and I look between them for a hint. Tony stops what he's doing, opens the oven, and pulls out some small circles of bread. Maybe garlic rolls. I can't see them well enough to say for sure. He places them into a small paper lined box and cuts one away from the rest. He scoops that one up with a spatula and closes the lid. He takes a piece of white paper and puts it on top of the box the rests the single ball of bread on top.

He's not a very big man and his dark hair is limp with some grease. Working near a kitchen, I know that happens when you cook over steam. He has a friendly smile that is bright just like the spunky teen. They have matching eyes that crinkle in the same spot on their happy faces.

"My Mona says you're special, you get my secret pizza rolls. Since it's impossible to wait until you get home with them, I saved you one to make it easy for travel and eating, mangia!" He places the box on top of my pizzas.

"Oh. Thank you. Please let me give you something..."

"No!" they both exclaim.

Mona finishes, "Oh no, when you're a special customer Tony gives you his special rolls. You can't pay for them; it ruins the purpose."

"All right. Thanks. I appreciate it, I'm starving."

"You're welcome, miss. Please come again soon."

"I will. Thank you so much." I collect my boxes and heft them to a comfortable angle that won't screw up the cheese.

"Goodnight!" they both say in stereo.

"Goodnight." I push open the door with my ass since my hands are full. When I'm clear of their line of sight, I lean down and take a giant bite out of my traveling roll.

"Homy-uck!" I mumble-exclaim through my mouthful of yum-miness. I've never had anything like it. I taste Italian magic and unicorn sparkles. I keep taking bites the whole way home. I can't stop. My traveling roll doesn't make it to my door. When I look up to plan my moves to unlock the door without dropping anything, the boxes are lifted from my hands. A kiss is placed on my lips, then a warm, moist tongue licks my lips.

"Mmmm, you're delicious. I'm so happy you're a slob right now," Jackson smirks at me.

"It's not my fault, my hands were full. Wait until you taste those things, holy shit are they good."

"Hey baby, will you please open the door? I'm starving and this smells amazing." Austin requests.

We make our way inside and Sawyer is there to greet us. Once Austin places the boxes on the counter, he wraps me up in a hug and kisses me.

"Mmmm, you do taste good. Where do you want to eat?"

"You guys can sit at the table, and I'll hover."

"Hover?"

"You know, stand around." He gives Jackson a look and he carries the boxes to the table. I take three plates from the cabinet and follow him. Jackson brings a few paper towels. Then he sits in one chair, and Austin in the other. When I step close, Austin wraps his arm around my hips and pulls me onto his lap. We all dig into the food and talk about our day between bites.

"What are these round things?" Jackson queries while he exams one in his hand.

"Try it, they're so good. They called it a pizza roll."

"Fuck! You aren't kidding. Damn that's good."

"Tony's is my favorite place. It's a little family-owned pizza shop."

We get back to stuffing our faces and chatting. I'm happy to hear they were able to work out the problem on the jobsite. I explain about my projects and tell them about Wyatt and Aiden. They ask a lot of questions and look at each other a couple times. I can't tell what's up. I suppose they'll tell me if I need to know.

"Do either of you have plans for Saturday?" I ask sheepishly.

"With you, we're hoping," Jackson speaks up.

"I was talking to Colby, and I was able to convince him to meet you. He wants to have dinner at my uncle's house. We made plans to be there at four. Does that work for you?"

Austin squeezes my middle gently, "Of course. We want to meet your family and friends; we want to spend all of our time with you."

I kiss his lips and smile, "Thanks. We're going to have barbecue. Uncle Randy doesn't want any help, but he says he'll text if he needs us to bring anything. Oh, and uh, Colby doesn't drive lately, so we'll have to pick him up, he lives on the way."

Austin says, "No problem."

"I was planning to work out, but I ate so much I don't know if I can move," I groan while I hold my stuffed belly.

"We worked hard enough today that we don't need a workout. I must've sweated off ten pounds, but I wouldn't mind watching you. Maybe I could be enticed to participate," he leers at me with a suggestive grin while his eyebrows hop up and down.

"I need a minute. I think I gained the ten pounds you lost with dinner." I stretch and lean against Austin who is wrapped around me and rests his hands on my thighs.

"Did you tell her what Tori said?" Jackson asks Austin.

"When would I have told her? You've been with me and on our texts." He continues, "Mom and dad were talking about how much they liked you. Mom says you're a sweetheart and dad thinks you're smart and we're lucky you'll have us, because you're too good for us."

"Auz! What the fuck? Don't tell her that, she might believe him!"

"You think he won't tell her himself?"

"You got me there. Babe, please don't listen to dad if he tells you we suck. It's only because he was there during our teen years, but he thinks we're okay now." He looks so earnest, as if I'd let Miguel talk me out of dating them. Besides, Miguel obviously loves them and I'm sure he was only teasing them. I can't help giggling at his pathetic little boy look.

"I promise I won't listen to anything he says," I assure them.

"Anyway, mom asked Kristin what she thought about you, and she agreed with dad. Then without even being asked, Tori said she thinks you're very pretty and cool! Can you believe it? I don't know what you said to her, because she hates everyone. Somehow, she likes you, it's a miracle. Or maybe dad's right and you're way too good for us." We all cracked up.

"What do your parents think about me dating both of you? I was kinda worried they'd have a problem with it, with me." I look between them though I can't see Austin clearly over my shoulder.

"Not at all. They really like you," Jackson reassures.

"I probably need to tell you that Colby knows you're aware of everything. I hope it's okay I told him, but I had to since I told you about his involvement. He needs to know who knows about him."

"Yeah, he does need to know. He's a very important person in your life and if we're all going to be involved moving forward, there can't be any secrets. We have to be on the same page," Austin immediately responds. I hug him. He always says the right things and makes me feel safe. He kisses my head and holds me close.

"We were thinking about staying over. Would that be, okay?" Jackson asks abruptly.

"Yeah. You guys can stay any time you want." My chest feels hot and zingy. My nipples tighten and there's a twinge in my girlie bits. I feel wetness gather between my legs. Thinking about being curled up with them has me hot and bothered. I wonder if I can last until my birthday, or if I'll have a meltdown when they make a move. Austin's hands rub my thighs, his fingers travel to my waist, and he moves my hair to kiss my neck.

My eyes fall closed, "Mmmm, that feels nice." His hands continue to explore, and he lifts my shirt enough for them to glide up my abdomen to my bra. It's too tight for him to get beneath it, he doesn't bother trying and rubs my peaked nipples through it. I shiver and my skin breaks into goosebumps.

"You're gorgeous when you're turned on... your cheeks are flushed, and your lips are full and red. You're my fantasy come true," Jackson's voice is low and rough. It makes my eyes open enough to see his handsome face. His eyes are focused on Austin's hands, and he's on the edge of his seat and appears ready to pounce. I want to be his prey.

Feeling hot, I rip off my t-shirt, Austin moves instinctively to avoid me accidentally hitting him in the face. His hands surround my breasts and squeeze while he gently pinches my nipples, and it makes me writhe in his lap. I grind against his hard length through our pants, and it shoots delicious sensations straight to my clit, making me moan out loud.

Jackson lunges to me and he presses a hard kiss on my mouth, his tongue begs for access. I let him in, and he devours me. I'm his willing meal. His fingers push into my hair as he maneuvers my face the way he wants, and it's the perfect mix of force and tenderness. I'm so aroused my panties are positively soaked now. I arch my back pressing my breasts into Austin's large, firm palms while his fingers continue their assault of pleasure. I want his hands on my skin. I tug at my sports bra until I'm able to pry it from my body. Freeing my full breasts and allowing me to inhale a deep breath, I take the moment to admire Jackson's perfect lips and half-lidded eyes. His close-trimmed beard is sexy as hell and the brown color of it accents the amber shade of his eyes.

I grab his hands and guide them to my waistband. I lift my hips to allow him to remove my pants, I want him to touch me. He rips them down my thighs and off completely, I'm left in only my purple cotton boy shorts. Austin is kissing my neck and shoulder while he explores my hard nipples with his rough fingertips.

Jackson has his lips barely an inch from mine, his eyes focused on me, his fingers toying with the elastic band of my panties. He watches me intently as he maneuvers his hardworking fingertips beneath my last remaining piece of clothing. I nod in a barely perceptible affirmation of consent. He kisses me and removes my underwear. A breeze meets my damp center and my nipples become impossibly tighter.

"Baby, do you want Jackson to put his mouth on you? To taste you, and make you feel good?"

Still kissing Jackson I respond with incoherent rambling, "Mmmmhmm! Mmm, ah, hmmmm...yeah."

Jackson watches me carefully as he slides his hand between my legs. I can't speak, so I nod again. The corner of his lip curves up in a mischievous grin. His fingers press my thighs apart and I adjust myself in Austin's lap causing him to groan. Jackson maneuvers me so that he can access exactly what he wants, his fingertip explores my technically virginal middle and dips into the arousal he finds there. He continues to watch my face while he feels my slick, slippery pussy.

He wears a joyous smile, and his eyes sparkle with excitement which makes me hotter. I grind down on his hand and Austin's manhood with my ass and womanly treasures. Without a word Jackson questions if he can go further. I believe we've reached the moment of truth. This is my line. Will I allow him to insert his finger where no one has ever been with my permission?

Austin pushes his groin upwards against my ass, I want to see the large, stiff member I can feel there. I want to touch him. I swallow hard and my mouth is watering with thoughts of tasting him, them. Jackson waits patiently for my decision; he swirls his finger in circles like a plane waiting for clearance from the tower.

Unable to think of anything else, I signal him in for a landing. "Touch me, Jackson. I need you inside me, please," I beg surprising myself. Not one to need directions, he circles his finger at my entrance, then he slides the digit inside. I realize I'm holding my breath waiting for my reaction. There's nothing but pleasure. Sensing my needs and my inability to express them, he stretches me with his large finger and adds another. I feel so full and ready to implode.

He kisses my lips and works his way down my neck nibbling along my collar bone, my body sings with electricity. He continues his way down my front pushing Austin's hand out of his path as he goes. Austin bites gently across the skin where my neck meets my shoulder, and I shiver again renewing my goosebumps. Jackson lifts my knee with his free hand, exposing me to his gaze.

"So, fucking perfect." He slides me forward so that my ass rests directly on Austin's hard cock and I'm tilted at an angle. He rests my knee over the arm of the chair, I remain comfortably where he wants me. Austin grips my breasts, holding onto me while still squeezing them. Now that I've moved forward, Austin can see over my shoulder and watch what Jackson is doing to me.

I can't watch because my eyes have closed with pleasure. I feel as though I'm being worshiped, and it's amazing. Jackson kisses down my stomach and the top of my bare pubic bone. His kisses draw closer and closer to where I need them most, the thrill of excitement is as heavenly as the sensation of his wet tongue teasing my intimate skin.

"Damn, I'm going to come in my pants, she's so fucking incredible. How does she taste brother?"

Jackson moves his fingers to hold me open for his tongue, he licks my clit and sucks on it. Then pushes his warm tongue inside me. His fingers find their way back into my drenched pussy, curving to hit the most responsive spot, while his tongue assaults my trigger, and I explode! My back arches involuntarily while I writhe blissfully. He twists and pumps his fingers in and out of me while lapping at my cum. My pussy clamps down and convulses with waves of ecstasy while he struggles to keep my thighs from snapping closed on his head.

"Holy fuck!" Austin exclaims. I make loud incoherent sounds, Jackson groans, and my head falls back as I continue to shake. Austin teases my nipples, and it sends jolts of rapture through my soul.

"She tastes like the sweetest treat was touched by angels!" Jackson says in awe.

My eyes flutter open and I'm not sure if I'm supposed to be embarrassed with my business exposed like this or just bask in the bliss and admiration of my guys. The embarrassment doesn't develop I take it as it is and enjoy the moment with the two guys I'm beginning to fall for, hard.

Austin softly rubs my shoulders and Jackson carefully unhooks my leg, running his hands over my thighs as he closes my legs. He places soft kisses on my belly and then looks into my eyes.

"You're the most beautiful creature I've ever seen, Violet. I want to watch you orgasm all day, forever. Austin, brother, you've got to taste her, you won't believe how much she tastes like sweet honey candy. I'll never get enough." His eyes are alight with affection and my heart beats wildly in my chest. Austin's hand moves to my breastbone, and he holds it over my fluttering heart.

"I think she feels the same... her heart is pounding. What do you say baby? Do you want me and Jackson to make you come every day?"

I shifted enough to catch a glimpse of him, he looks like Jackson. Content and filled with affection, if possible, I think my heart just sped up even more. I can't keep a smile from taking over my whole face.

"Yeah. But when will you let me return the pleasure?"

"Not yet babe. Remember, we're taking it slow. It's not that long until your birthday; just a few weeks," Jackson replies.

I turn back to him, and I can feel my brow crinkle in frustration, "You mean like five weeks, that's almost an eternity," I pout.

"It'll be here soon enough. In the meantime, we'll get to know each other better and we'll learn how to master your body, so you'll be ready."

"I think you already own my body," I blurt without thinking.

My eyes shift between them, and I see only happiness. I guess I keep thinking I'm going to scare them off, especially if I express how much I like them. But they aren't like the guys I read about or remember; they don't just want one thing from me. They actually like me and want to know me, they don't want to use my body, fracture my mind, and throw me away, they care. It's a new experience for me, accepting affection at face value. I don't need to brace for the blows that have followed acts disguised as affection in my past. Of course, my friends don't fall into that category, they've proven over the years they truly care, and it includes Max. Having adult romantic feelings is completely new and adult men have never been worthy of my trust or love. But these men, they just might be, and I need to get a hold of that and embrace it, because the last thing I want to do is lose them.

A look of pride overtakes their handsome faces, and it makes me laugh. Austin helps me into my t-shirt and Jackson has me step into my panties. I notice Sawyer perched on top of his cat tree watching us. Should I feel bad he had to see that? I shrug, maybe someday he'll get a girlfriend and he could learn something from these two.

We clean up our dinner and moved to my bedroom. I'm going to have to give in and buy some furniture. My bed is the only place we can cuddle together, and it doesn't suck but it would be nice if we had another option. I'd love to curl up on the sofa and watch a movie with them.

Once we're settled, I ask their thoughts. "I'm thinking about getting a sofa so we can have another place to sit, maybe watch a movie. What do you think?"

"I'd love to cuddle and watch a movie with you. But the question should be, what type of movie?" Austin ponders.

"That's a good question, what type of movies do you like?"

"Horror. Action. Suspense. What about you?" he elaborates.

"I love horror movies, especially the creepy ones from the eighties, maybe even the seventies. My parents used to watch them with me on movie nights. Like *Amityville Horror, Jaws, Poltergeist, The Exorcist*...that one scared me so bad I slept with them for a week. It wouldn't be so embarrassing, but I was fifteen!"

They both chuckled at my admission. Jackson looks thoughtful, so, I asked him.

"What about you? What's your favorite?"

"I love Christmas movies."

"Seriously?" I'm shocked, I've always thought of him as the least sentimental of the two.

"Yeah, *Die Hard, Die Hard two, The Ref, Gremlins.* All the classics."

Austin cracks up while I flounder in confusion, "I've seen *Die Hard*... it's a Christmas Movie?"

"Yeah, it takes place at a Christmas party. *Yippee ki-yay, mother fucker!* Classic," He smiles like he's perfectly normal. Austin has his hand over his mouth, for some reason he thinks it's way funnier than it actually is.

"All right. I guess that means *Donnie Darko* is an Easter movie?"

When they stop laughing at me, Jackson answers, "Exactly."

"Don't let him fool you baby, he likes chick flicks too. He used to watch them with Megan. Me and Piers would be looking all over for him, and we'd find him in my sister's room watching *Clueless* or *Pretty Woman!* If anyone should be embarrassed it's him." Jackson punches him in the arm, the way guys do to each other that obviously hurts like a bitch.

"Fuck dude! You know it's true, don't take it out on me that you're secretly sensitive and like romantic movies and shit. Damn this hurts, asshole!"

"Fuck you! You and Piers would stay and watch them too, so don't act like you don't like you didn't!"

I start laughing hysterically and they both break into laughter. This is hilarious, I have something good to tease them with now. I can't say I don't like romantic movies; I never watched any. I've heard of the ones they mentioned but I've never seen them. I think my parents were afraid anything romantic or intimate between a man and a woman would trigger me or something. You would think Harmony would've made me watch a few, but she only likes romance if there's vampires involved.

She's a horror chick like me. I have seen Bram Stokers *Dracula* and it's a love story. But it's got enough blood to satisfy my horror needs.

"Well, this certainly is an interesting turn of events. Your girl has never watched any of those romance movies. While you guys have apparently seen them all. What should we do about that?"

"What do you mean you've never watched any? Like, never ever? Not even *Pretty Woman?* What about something more recent? Like *Crazy, Stupid, Love?* Or *La La Land?*" Austin grills.

"Nope."

Jackson tries, *"Titanic?"*

"No."

"Babe, how is it possible you haven't seen any of the movies everyone has seen? You said you like eighties movies, what about *Sixteen Candles?* Or Tom Hanks', *You've Got Mail?*"

"Nope."

"When Harry Met Sally?" Austin tries.

"No! I'm telling you; I haven't seen any. My friends were into horror or superheroes. We never watched any of those Rom Com movies or whatever. I watched horror or action movies with my parents, that's it. I mean I've seen memes with some clips but never any of the movies, like the one where a girl's taking a selfie with the Titanic sinking in the background."

"That's Rose with Jack drowning next to her. I'm so sad you don't know that" Jackson says with exaggerated theatrical sniffles and outrage.

"I'm kinda sad that you do," I deadpan. Austin cracks up again.

Our night continues in this same vein, each of us questioning the others and then teasing each other about the answers. Eventually, Sawyer hops onto the foot of the bed and bides his time waiting for the perfect neck to heat.

When I wake up in the morning, I don't recall falling asleep. I'm happy to find my neck wasn't chosen by Sawyer and both guys are still tangled with me. I'm content to just lie awake and enjoy their soft breaths. I don't know how much time has passed when Austin stirs. When he opens one eye, he finds me staring at him and smiles a sleepy grin. He pulls me in closer to him and throws his leg over mine, kicking Jackson in the process.

"Ow! What the fuck?"

"Sorry, man."

"Where do you think you're going?" Jackson's arm around my waist pulls me closer to him, prompting Austin to snuggle closer from his side. I'm smooshed between them and I'm okay with it.

Somebody's loud as shit foghorn alarm goes off and if they weren't on top of me, I would've been startled right off the bed. I feel Jackson move, then I can hear him fumbling with the phone trying to shut it off. Ahhh, silence. We are once again in blessed quiet.

"Sorry babe, we gotta go. We shouldn't be late tonight, we'll bring dinner, okay?"

"Yeah. I just don't want to move yet."

"I know, but we've got to be on the site early after all the problems yesterday. We have to make sure nothing else goes wrong. I don't want to let go of you, but you've got school too."

That did it. I forgot I have to be at school this morning. I kiss Austin, then Jackson, and bolt over them rushing to the bathroom first. When I exit with my toothbrush in my mouth, Jackson is leaning against the wall in front of me on one leg, with his foot pressed behind him, reading something on his phone.

"No fair, beautiful, next time I'm calling dibs before you make it in there."

"Sorry," I mumble trying not to spit toothpaste on him. I rush back in and spit in the basin. He steps behind me and aims for the toilet, he's unconcerned that I'm standing there and I'm too fascinated to move. He said I can't touch it until my birthday, but maybe I can catch a glimpse.

"Babe, if you stand there looking at it, I won't be able to go."

"Are you shy?"

"No. But just thinking about your eyes touching it is making me hard and then I can't go."

"Oh! I'm sorry!" I run from the bathroom with my cheeks in flames.

"Whoa! Who's after you?" Austin asks as I almost slam into him.

"Oh, nobody, I, uh, I was disrupting Jackson in the bathroom." He looks at me confused then towards the bathroom and back to me. He examines my face, and I can tell when it dawns on him what happened.

He pulls me in for a hug and rubs my back, "Don't be embarrassed, it happens. If you're going to have two boyfriends and let us sleep over, you're going to get to know way more guy stuff than you ever wanted to know. You remember our talk about morning wood, right?"

"Oh my God! Yes, but I don't want to talk about it again." Chuckling at my naivete, he pulls me against him in a tighter hug.

"You're so adorable baby, it's one of the things I love most about you." I freeze. He doesn't seem to notice what he said, and I don't want to draw any attention to it. Do I dare to think he loves me? Or was it only a figure of speech? I suppose I'll have to wait and see, I'm patient. You have to be when you're surveilling your target for hours on end waiting for the perfect opportunity to strike.

CHAPTER TWENTY-TWO

After a sweet goodbye with my guys, I take a quick shower and ride the motorbike to school. My backpack has a special helmet compartment, but it's heavy with it and my laptop in there. It's balanced a little lower than a normal backpack, helping to counterbalance the heavier load. When you don't have a helmet in it, you can zip that compartment out of sight. It was expensive, but worth it. Helmet storage on the go is the only downside of riding a bike, and rain. I'd leave it with my motorcycle if there weren't signs every ten feet warning students not to leave valuables in their cars and the school's lack of responsibility since they warned us.

When I enter the building, a voice calls out, "Violet! Over here!"

I spot Wyatt waving me towards him.

"Hey Wyatt, Aiden." I nod in greeting.

"Hey. This is our frat brother, Bug," Wyatt points to a thin guy with dark hair and brown eyes, next to him.

"I'm sorry. I heard, *Bug.*"

Cracking a smile, Wyatt nods, "Yep. He's studying entomology. We call him Bug. He's in our Digital Logic class."

"Okay then. Hi Bug, nice to meet you. I'm Violet."

"I know. Our whole frat knows who you are, these guys wouldn't stop talking about you. Ouch!" Aiden's elbow retreats from Bug's ribs. I smirk at them.

"We wanted to invite you to our first official frat party Friday night. It should be fun, help get rid of the first week of school crap, what do you think?" Wyatt asks.

"Um, I might have plans," I stall, not sure if I should attend something like that or not. I'm underage, by a lot and I'm not supposed to drink, but being at a party like that, if anything happens, I could be in the wrong place at the wrong time.

"You can invite your boyfriend; we just really wanted you to come," he adds. I guess he thinks my hesitation is relationship related.

"Okay. Let me check over my schedule and confirm some things, and I'll let you know. Thanks for the invite."

My first class of the day is a little boring, Professor Gallagher is the epitome of a computer nerd. She drones on and on while I, and my fellow students, struggle to stay awake. She plans to lecture us all semester, how can she possibly have that much to say?

We don't have much of a break before Computer Programming Fundamentals 1, with Dr. Sabodowski, which is followed by the lab. Aiden is in this class with me, while Bug and Wyatt head off to their next classes.

"Holy shit, I thought that class would never end. I'm going to have to start drinking coffee before class to stay awake," I remark.

"I know, she's the most uninteresting person I've ever encountered. My mind wandered after the first, *let me tell you a story...* I have no clue what she said. Do we have any assignments? Papers due? Hopefully she'll email the syllabus sooner rather than later."

"Right? She knew class started this week, why isn't she prepared? I have a theory she lives in her car and doesn't even own a computer."

"She teaches at the University, so she has access to free computers and showers," he adds to my story. We made our way down the hall to our next class, and he holds the door for me. We choose seats in the middle row, on the aisle nearest the wall.

Dr. Sabodowski enters with a TA in tow. He directs the TA who stacks some papers along the front of the desk. He dons a headset and tests the sound. When the class is full and he's ready to begin, he lowers the big screen from the ceiling and his laptop is projected onto it.

He moves swiftly through the syllabus and describes our projects and papers simply without a single yawn in the room. He launches into a programming lesson and has us follow along on our laptops. No one asks a question, but there's no need because he's thorough. He gives us all of his contact info and offers to respond 24/7. Unheard of for a college professor, since they usually shrug off students to their TA. I like him. He's passionate and an excellent speaker. When class is over, I'm surprised it flew by. We collect a packet from his desk and return to our seats, for the lab.

Each packet has a different project topic. When I open mine, I'm surprised to see Adoption as the headline. I know I didn't get this packet on purpose; it was totally random.

"What did you get?" Aiden asks.

"Adoption," I read the description, "Early adopters and the programming challenges they face. How about you?"

"2050. The future of programming for the average user. Hmmm, not sure if I'm good with it or not. Gonna have to think about it, he said we could make one swap. Maybe I should get a different packet."

"Think it over first, if you hate it, then trade. If you can work with it, at least you know you won't get stuck with something worse."

"Good point. Are you going to work on stuff for this class or something else?"

"It feels wrong to use this lab time for a different class. I've never taken a lab before. Do you usually use the time to do other stuff?" I asked him.

"Yeah. All the time. I only passed statistics because I had extra time in my Student Culture Lab, last term," he grins mischievously.

"I think I'm going to stick with CPF1 for today."

"Can I ask you a question?"

"Shoot."

"Please don't get mad, but we were wondering how old you are, and I can't decide if you're super young and very mature or if you're older and just look really young."

"Wow. I'm not sure if I'm offended because it's rude to ask, or if you're just completely clueless and I should feel sorry for you," I offer him a sarcastic smile, and his embarrassment shifts into a laugh.

"Okay, point taken. You don't want to answer, and I'll respect that."

"It's not like you have any other choice."

He laughs, "Do you know any other cool girls like you, but single?"

"Sorry. My only girl friends are attached or worse."

"What's worse?"

"Single motherhood with an asshole, deadbeat-dad ex."

"Okay. That's definitely worse," he replies while his face checks out as he thinks it over.

By the end of class, I've made substantial progress on an outline for my CPF1 project, and I feel pretty good about it. I have no idea what Aiden decided to work on, but he didn't exchange his packet. We decided to walk to the Student Hub, which I've been informed is interchangeable with Student Center, together to meet Wyatt for some lunch. I notice some canopies around the courtyard, they have lines of students in front of them. I wonder what that's about.

"What's with the tents?" I ask Aiden.

"Most of them are companies trying to get students to sign up for stuff or buy something. They offer free food and swag, if they have something cool to hand out, they'll get a line around the building. I don't recommend them, one of the guys in my frat is in debt for twenty-thousand-dollars from a credit card they gave him. It's like a bait and switch deal."

His words make me think fondly about my BASIL at home. I'm getting closer to springing my trap and capturing Voldemort. I really want to get my blades on him before my birthday. Sort of a birthday gift to myself. I need to visit the trail cams soon and replace the batteries. They only last a few weeks. Maybe I'll have a chance this weekend.

"Earth to Violet. Did I lose you?"

"Oh. Sorry. I was just thinking about some stuff I need to take care of this weekend."

"I asked what you want for lunch."

"Probably a burger. What about you?"

"Depends on what has the shortest line," he deadpans.

Giggling, I follow him into the food court area. The burger place has a long line, so we opt for Chinese. When we get our food, we search for Wyatt and spot him with Bug and a couple other guys at a large table. Aiden leads me to a seat across from Wyatt and sits next to me.

Wyatt and Bug greet me, then Wyatt announces, "Hey guys, this is Violet, she's a CS major and we have a couple classes with her." Looking at me he adds, "That's Riley with the cap, Durango is next to him, and Ahab is across from him." They each wave as he says their names.

"Hey," I reply.

"You didn't lie," the one called Ahab states. I don't know what that means, so I ignore it and dig into my food.

"So, Violet, did these guys invite you to our frat Friday, for our first party this term?" Riley asks.

My mouth is full of General Tso's Chicken, and I cover it instinctually. I chew as fast as I can without letting any food escape my mouth. My cheeks must be pink, they feel hot. Of course, it could be the spicy food.

"They did. I don't know if I can go yet. I need to check my schedule; I have a job."

"Where do you work?" Durango questions.

"Mystic Cove Cantina. I'm a server."

"That's cool. They have good food," Wyatt speaks up.

"Yeah."

Aiden asks, "When do you usually work?"

"I fill in a lot, and now with my school schedule, I wasn't sure how many hours I could handle. I work tomorrow and we're going to sort it out then. They gave me a couple days off for the beginning of classes."

"That's good. You're kind of like a superhero," Wyatt says.

"Because I work at a bar and grill?"

The guy's titter with laughter.

"No, because you're so unassuming when really, you do all this cool stuff."

"I do? Like what?" I ask, fascinated by his assertion.

"You already have your AA, but you look so young. You're going to school full-time, and you work as a server. *And* you ride a motorcycle... you're a bad ass," Wyatt finishes. I ponder how he knows that. Five sets of eyes snap to my face and lock on, instantly making me the center of attention and very embarrassed.

"You ride a motorcycle?" Durango asks.

"Yeah. It was my dad's."

"What is it?"

"An Indian Scout."

"Sweet, my dad's got an Indian. I ride a Harley."

"Cool." I take another bite of rice and chicken hoping they don't keep the questions going. After a minute, everyone returns to what they were doing and I'm able to finish my meal in peace.

Eventually, Bug and Wyatt get into a heated discussion about the grossest insects. I'm thankful I'm done eating because they're trying to outgross each other.

"It's gotta be the Dung Beetle. I watched an entire special about them and they love shit! What's more disgusting than that?" Wyatt asks.

Bug replies, "Actually, we have some Bot Flies in the entomology lab, they're worse than Dung Beetles. They lay eggs in an open wound on a mammal, then those eggs grow into larvae. They feast on the blood and tissue of their host carving out a space to live in their flesh, while they keep a breathing hole open in the host's skin. They create an abscess of puss and infection while they grow larger and larger. They become these huge, hairy, caterpillar type creatures that writhe around under the host's skin until the day they emerge as an adult and fly away. It's by far the most disgusting thing I've ever seen," Bug retorts.

"Dude! What have I told you about that? Not while people are eating. Look at Riley! He's going to puke, he's turning green," Ahab scolds. He looks at me and I believe he notes my lack of green gills, he inspects my face, and his brows lift as if surprised. I wonder about his name. Is he so monikered for Captain Ahab unsuccessfully chasing a white whale? Or King Ahab, flaunting his riches and blasphemy against God.

"Are you finished?" Aiden asks.

"Yeah, thanks." He collects my trash with the other garbage he picked up from the table. He takes everything to the bin and disposes of it. My last class for the day begins in fifteen minutes and like yesterday, I'm looking forward to seeing my gorgeous boyfriends as soon as my school day is finished.

I take a minute to send them a quick message.

Me: Hey. I hope your day is going better than yesterday. I'm looking forward to seeing you tonight.

JAX, AUZ: Hey babe! So far so good. We should be on time tonight. How's your day going?

Me: Good. My first class is boring as fuck, but the next two are good. One more to go.

JAX, AUZ: Hi baby. My day has been too slow, I can't wait to see you. Glad you had some good classes.

Me: Hopefully this last one will be quick so I can get home. The guys I told you about last night invited us to a frat party Friday night. Do you want to go?

JAX, AUZ: Can we talk about it later?

Me: of course, just didn't want to forget to tell you.

JAX, AUZ: Ok. See you soon! Can't wait to taste you.

Me: Austin! Not when I'm at school, I won't be able to concentrate.

JAX, AUZ: Sorry baby. Think about something gross to keep your mind off of my tongue.

Me: Lucky for you, that's not a problem.

JAX, AUZ: you're going to need to explain that one.

*Me: tonight. Gotta go *smiley face emoji**

*JAX, AUZ: *tongue emoji**

*Me: *eye roll emoji**

My final class is uneventful. Actually, the rest of the week goes by without a hitch. Work and school are both going well. The guys have slept over every night, and I can't imagine my bed without them.

When my last hour of my shift finishes, I'm excited to rush home. The guys are picking me up and we're going to the frat party. I'm looking forward to an evening out with them and I've had a fun week with Wyatt, Aiden, and even Bug. I want my friends to meet my boyfriends. I hope they get along; I think they will. I'm also a little excited to shock them with my two boyfriends. I wonder if Wyatt will add that to my list of superhero traits or if he'll decide I'm more anti-hero.

CHAPTER TWENTY-THREE

Finally! The last hour of my shift dragged on and on, when it's over, I'm in the parking lot in a flash. The guys are hoping to get off work early and take me to dinner before the party and make a date of it. Technically, it'll be our first date as a *throuple*. A new word I learned this week, it fits but feels wrong in my mouth.

Even though I'm in a rush, I still take the scenic route. Riding dad's bike relieves stress and the scenery this way is so soothing. Trying to fit school and work into my week was a challenge. I'm so happy it's the weekend even though I have work; half a day tomorrow, and a full shift on Sunday, not having to be in class is a relief. I'm not a fan of being cooped up indoors for so many hours in a day.

They aren't here when I get home, and after greeting Sawyer I jump into the shower. My phone chimes while I'm shampooing my hair, and rather than break my neck trying to get it, I opt to finish and make whomever it is wait a few minutes. My dad used to tease that when he was a kid you actually had to go knock on your friend's door to find out if they were home. It's so hard to imagine just showing up unannounced in our current reality.

AUZ: Hi baby, I'm just waiting for Jackson. He had to go to Lois' house on his way. We shouldn't be too long.

Me: No worries. I just got out of the shower. I'll be ready when you get here. I'm wearing jeans, that's okay for dinner, right?

AUZ: Yep, nothing too fancy tonight. What time do you work tomorrow?

Me:10-2 just lunch. We should have plenty of time to pick up Colby and get to Randy's.

AUZ: perfect!

Me: Are you guys going to hang out here while I work?

AUZ: Yeah, we wanted to work on your BASIL room. The permit should be ready next week, we want to get started on the improvements.

Me: I'm so excited, I want to have it finished in time for my birthday.

AUZ: shouldn't be any problem. We'll pick up the materials next week and as long as the inspections don't take too long, they should be finished well before your birthday.

Me: thank you! It would've taken forever for me to have this done on my own, plus triple the cost. Free labor is gonna save me a fortune.

AUZ: Who said it was free?

Me: I can pay you, no matter what having someone I trust vs. strangers, is worth it.

AUZ: We don't want any money.

Me: what then?

AUZ: how well do you dance?

Me: WTF?

AUZ: I think I'd like my payment in lap dances

*Me: funny *smiley face emoji**

AUZ: I never joke about lap dances!
Me: Okay, whatever you want.
AUZ: now you're talking. Jackson's here. See you soon!
Me: See you

He's so ridiculous, I finish getting ready then seek out Sawyer to give him some pets and his dinner before I go. I wonder where we're going to eat, I'm starving, and lunch was hours ago. Sawyer follows me to the kitchen for his meal. Once he begins chomping on his kitty food, I absently scratch his rear while I look at my bare living room.

I'm going to need to find something soon, but I hate new stuff. Maybe Austin or Jackson will want to help me find a gently used sofa and a coffee table. I know where there's a thrift shop near the beach. A knock on my door releases me from my musings.

"Bye Sawyer, be good." I lock the upstairs behind me. When I open the warehouse door, Austin is there, looking F.I.N.E. in his darker wash jeans and charcoal button down. He matches me with a pair of Martin's on his feet. While I'm ogling him his gaze slides up and down my skin like a caress.

His hair is golden brown with a spark of auburn when the sun hits it just right. His dark blue-green eyes follow me when he thinks I'm not looking. He has the most perfect dimples, and he's perfect everywhere I've seen. One of his features that I like most is the small gap between his front teeth.

He says he refused to wear his retainer. I like it because without it he would look too perfect to be real. That tiny little flaw makes him human and endearing. When our eyes meet after traveling each other's bodies, one side of his lip's lifts into a movie star worthy smile. The corners of his eyes crinkle and I can't contain myself. I leap at him wrapping my arms around his neck and my legs around his hips. He catches me and holds my hips to keep me from falling. Before he can say anything, I ravage his mouth with a hot kiss.

"Hi, I missed you."

"You don't say? Damn baby that was some welcome. Let's go, I'm hungry."

"Me too. Where are we going?"

"Mexican place, over by Wellington Law, okay?"

"Yes! I love Mexican food. Do they have tamales?"

"I think so, seems like I've seen a sign for them on special. Are they your favorite?"

"Yeah, but it's all good. What's your favorite?" He opens the front door of the truck, and I climb in between them, you gotta love a bench seat option. I climb right onto Jackson and throw my arms around his neck. I avoid squishing in front of the steering wheel with an awkward twist of my body. Our lips meet and he pulls my face closer so he can fill my mouth with his tongue. He tastes like mint.

When I pull back enough to look at him, he's wearing a brilliant smile. I kiss the corner of his mouth a few times, until Austin clears his throat. A twinge of hunger rumbles in my stomach and I remember we're hungry. Situating my ass on the middle of the bench, I wink at Jackson and hook my seatbelt. Austin climbs inside and we're off.

"Hi Violet. You look beautiful this evening," Jackson proclaims.

"You too. I mean *handsome*, I like that color blue."

"Thanks. I wore it just for you, I heard Auz ask your favorite color."

"I see. Anything else you do because I like it?" I realize my mistake the moment the words leave my mouth.

"Yeah babe, I lick your pussy right where it makes you scream the loudest." My cheeks must be flaming red, they're on fire.

"I do that too," Austin adds with a serious face that begins to crack into a goofy grin.

"Oh my God! I can't say anything without you two making it sexual. I need to be more careful about what I say," I pinch Austin on his ribs in retaliation and he yelps. I can't pinch the driver.

"No fair!"

"Sorry, it was a reaction to the overwhelming cheesiness."

His grin crinkles into an exaggerated mock look of shock. We all laugh, they're so much fun, teasing each other is our favorite game, well that, three questions, and sex games. Last night they took turns touching and licking me, it was amazing. I kept coming, and I lost count after seven times. They're learning exactly how to make my body sing. I wish they'd let me touch them at least with my hands. I'm going to be so far behind them in learning about each other, especially in the how to make them come the way they like, department.

Maybe when my birthday's closer I'll be able to convince them to let me touch them. It's really just a few weeks away. I was born on Friday the 13th of October. Growing up I always wanted to have a spooky birthday party on Friday the 13th. Of course, me and my friends in high school had to watch every picture in the franchise. Even though Jason is a slicer like me, they aren't my favorite movies.

"What're you thinking about so hard baby?" Austin questions.

"Just wishing my birthday would hurry up and get here."

"Yeah? Why's that?" Austin continues.

"Why do you think?" I asked, staring at him hard.

"I don't...oh. It'll be here soon enough, you can wait."

"I don't want to wait, I mean we can wait, I just want to be able to touch you. I want to feel you and make you come too." Adjusting his pants he puts his other arm around my shoulders and squeezes me tight.

"I understand, but I promise, we can wait a few weeks. It'll make it even better once we can do everything. Plus, we wouldn't be able to forgive ourselves if we did anything to harm you in any way."

"Maybe I just don't understand how a few weeks-time will make a difference." I whine.

"Despite what you think, and how mature you are, you're in reality, not an adult yet. You will feel differently, and you'll be happy we got to know each other better because we'll have a solid foundation for our relationship. We want to build a long-lasting team that will stand strong against any hurdles we encounter." He kisses my cheek and temple. I can't argue against them wanting a solid, long-term bond, I want the same. I tilt my head up and kiss his cheek. Jackson rubs my thigh in a soothing way. They're both so sweet to me.

When we get to the restaurant there's no parking on the street in front of it and we have to park behind the building. There's a well-lit alley that lets us cut through to the entrance. When we step up to the front door some guys are leaving and they recognize Jackson.

"Hey! Jackson! How's it going man?" The taller one asks.

"Hey Rick! I'm great, you?"

"Really good. Austin? Wow! I haven't seen you in forever. Who's this?" he asks, looking at our intertwined hands.

"Violet. Nice to meet you." I smile and hope I cut-off any awkward questions in case these guys don't need to know our business.

"Likewise, nice catch, Auz." He turns back to Austin. I want to blatantly ignore the douche canoe, but my phone isn't in my pocket. I must've dropped it in the truck when I was aggressively kissing Jackson. I release Austin's hand and signal Jackson for the keys. He's now catching up with the shorter one, his name is Paul.

Jackson gives me the keys and I whisper into his ear about my phone. He nods and I walk with my head down hoping to spot my phone if it fell out of my pocket on the walk in. It's not on the ground, but when I climb into the truck, I spy it on the floor barely peeking out from under the seat. While I'm leaning to reach the phone, I hear a low whistle not far behind me.

When I right myself, I find an older man who looks some-what familiar. He's probably in his sixties, even so, he looks like he's got some muscle. He's blocking my escape because I'm stand-ing in the open door of the truck now. Assessing the situation, I decide to act oblivious to the very negative energy pouring out of him. The last time I felt like this was when that creepy guy delivered groceries to me and Uncle Randy right after my parents died. Damn. That's exactly who I'm looking at right now. I figure it won't hurt to startle him a little bit.

"I know you. You deliver groceries, right?" He jolts. His eyes flutter rapidly looking between mine, like he just got caught with his hand in the cookie jar.

He fights to compose himself, "Don't know what you're talking about."

"I remember your car, you drive a big dark sedan, dark tinted windows, tag number DII 88K, right?"

"Who the fuck are you? How do you know that?"

"Told you, I remember you."

"Fucking bitch!" He swings at me with his left hand which gets a complete arc because of the angle of the open door.

I'm able to dodge the full force of his strike, but he still catches my shoulder. I don't want to waste time waiting for another blow, I kick him as hard as I can from this ungainly position. My foot connects with his crotch, I'm pretty sure it's not a direct hit because my shin flares with pain. He steps back just enough that I'm able to squeeze past him with barely a touch and I haul ass back towards the restaurant entrance. Jackson is running towards me when I look up.

He inspects me and then questions, "What happened? Are you all, right?"

"Fine, that asshole," I point to the old man. "Grocery delivery guy tried to attack me. I kicked him and ran."

"Good job. Please wait here," he gently requests. I stop and let him take care of it, my solution was effective based on size and muscle mass, but Jackson can handle it a different way. I text Austin.

Me: Please come outside. We're fine, but there's a situation by the truck.

AUZ: On it.

I watch Jackson grab the guy by the back of his hair and neck area, Jackson towers over him and shoves him to the ground. He stomps on his back and holds him down with his foot. The guy is fighting to get up, to no avail.

Austin arrives and wraps his arm around me, then he looks at my face and into my eyes, "You sure you're, okay?"

"I promise. He tried to attack me, but I kicked him and ran. Jackson came and I texted you."

"Are you sure he didn't touch you?"

"He swung at me, and I was in the doorway of the truck so I couldn't maneuver out of the way, he caught my shoulder. It's fine."

"Let me see." I lean towards him and pull my shirt away from my neck. He pulls it out further and examines me carefully, his face distorts into a scowl. His hand forms into a fist and looks ready to deliver a blow.

"Please wait here." I nod. I don't want his anger aimed my way.

Austin approaches the asshole and kicks him hard in the hip. The man yells out in pain, and it's a satisfying sound. Austin and Jackson speak quietly, and Jackson kicks the asshole in the temple, he stops moving. I take a few steps closer to the unconscious piece of shit. My mind is analyzing all of our options in a fast and calculated effort to resolve this situation.

"I think we should call the cops and take off. What do you guys think?"

"Yeah, you're probably right. Damn, I really wanted a burrito." Jackson drags the creep's limp body away from our truck. I check the buildings for security cameras. I spy one on the third story but it's not pointing this direction. I scanned the lot for a dark sedan.

"Gotcha!"

"What?" Austin asks.

"That's his vehicle. Let's take him there."

"How do you know? Did you see him coming?"

"Nope, he delivered groceries to me at home before I moved out. Didn't like him then, and I hate him now."

"All righty, I'm going to need more input on that one."

"I know, but let's dump him and get out of here first, yeah?"

Jackson takes his legs and Austin gets his arms; I pick up his keys from the ground. Moving ahead of them I open his back door, for a dirt bag, his car is surprisingly clean. Austin drops him and he falls slumped over against his car. Then Austin makes his way to the far door and crawls across, to pull the asshole in. Jackson shoves his feet, and they get him clear of the doors before they slam them closed.

I place his keys on his windshield wiper. He's going to enjoy searching for them with a pounding headache and I can't help but smile. We're quiet until we're back on the road.

"Okay baby, explain please."

"After my parents died, Uncle Randy stayed with me while we figured out what to do. Trying to do too many things at once, Uncle

Randy ordered groceries to save time. That cretin was the delivery guy. He kept sneaking up behind me, silently, and I got bad vibes from him. I told Uncle Randy how I felt about the guy, and I'm pretty sure he filed a complaint of some sort. We didn't order groceries anymore after that. The guy didn't seem to remember me. I tried intimidating him by recognizing him and describing his car and license plate. He freaked out and got mad, then he tried to punch me. I kicked him in the crotch and ran."

"Damn babe, you're such a badass. You did exactly the right thing. I'm glad you're safe. You aren't hurt, are you?" Jackson asks.

"No. He grazed my shoulder, but it didn't really connect."

"There's a mark on her shoulder, but it's not bad," Austin adds. I hear an angry squeaking sound as Jackson's hands tighten and twist on the steering wheel. His knuckles turn white as he moves them like he's wringing some asshole's neck. Time for a subject change.

"Where do you want to eat now?"

"I still want a burrito, but that was the good Mexican place. What about that Texmex place on Route 19, it's not bad?"

"Lulu's?" Jackson clarifies.

"Yeah, that's it. Okay with you baby?"

"Sure. I'm really not picky, I'll eat almost anything if I'm hungry." Uh-oh, I said something I shouldn't have, I can tell by Jackson's mischievous grin.

"Really? What about frog legs?" he asks.

"Never had them, but I would try them. I've had alligator and venison. Technically, I even ate crow once."

"What?" Austin asks.

"I'm serious, not in the metaphorical way. I was camping with my parents, and they were teaching me to shoot and hunt, they were always training me to defend myself and survive, even when we were having fun. They wanted me to be safe and self-sufficient. Anyway, I was practicing, and I screwed up and shot a crow. The rule was, if you shoot it, you have to eat it. A great deterrent to target practice on live animals, but I accidentally squeezed the trigger. They made me clean it, cook it, and eat it. I cried the whole time. I felt bad for killing it and I really felt bad eating it, but it was a valuable lesson. I've been extremely careful ever since and would never kill an innocent animal unless it was for survival."

"Wish we could've met your parents; they must've been amazing. Their influence has made you the incredible person that you are today," Jackson rubs my thigh in a soothing stroke.

"They were the best, I'll never stop missing them, but I hope I can live up to being a person that would make them proud."

"Baby, I know they're proud of you. How could they not be? You're very special," Austin kisses my cheek and then holds his hand there for a moment until we pull into the restaurant.

Chapter Twenty-Four

We have to park in a lot at my school and walk down the block to Greek Row. The frat house for Beta Chi Theta is three stories tall with a large front porch. It's a dark blue Victorian house with white shutters and trim. It looks well kept, even with some people scattered on the steps and lawn.

One of the guys on the porch greets us. "The bars in the kitchen, the keg is out back next to the beer pong, wet t-shirt contest is at eleven." He looks at me pointedly, and I can't tell if he's joking.

Jackson pats him on the back, hard. "Thanks man, our girl-friend will keep it in mind." His mouth falls open and his eyes go wide. He inspects Jackson and Austin, then smiles politely at me.

"My apologies, miss," he states with his eyes deftly downturned.

Holding in a giggle I accept, "No worries."

We make our way into the house, and I don't see anyone I recognize. They follow as I continue through and out to the back patio. I scan the yard and spot Wyatt at one of the pong tables. There's some loud music playing from a speaker on a stand, a few people are sitting around in a circle laughing. There're three pong tables, two kegs, and a large, oval, above-ground pool filled with sickly green water. *Ick!*

I guided us towards Wyatt and found Aiden before we reach him. He's in an intense discussion with Ahab and Durango. They're waving their arms around and look very animated. They each hold a red cup like the ones stacked near the kegs. As we get closer, I can hear a few words of their conversation and it sounds sports related. My only sports are MMA and dirt bikes. I watched football because dad liked it and he and Uncle Randy always watched the games, but I've never played. They had to teach me the rules so I could enjoy it.

I stop next to Aiden and wait for a break in their conversation. Durango notices me. He smiles and nods, then pokes Aiden in the ribs and points at me. Aiden and Ahab stopped talking and look at me, their faces break into smiles. Then they both look immediately behind me, and their smiles look uncertain. I look where their eyes are locked and see both of my guys standing like my bodyguards with their arms crossed. They're both sporting intense looks filled with intimidating vibes. I shake my head at them. Grins fill their faces, and they smirk at me, always full of the devil.

"Hey, Aiden. These are my boyfriends, Austin and Jackson," I point to each one.

Looking at my boyfriends, I introduce them to my school friends, "This is Aiden, Ahab, and Durango." They all greet each other with that manly chin lift. Wyatt, Riley, and Bug join us, and I introduce them too.

Once Austin and Jackson go to the keg Aiden leans in, "Did you say, *boyfriends?*"

Trying not to laugh I nod, "I did."

He looks thoughtful for a moment then says, "I think Wyatt's right."

"About what?"

"You are like a superhero. Kind of like Ironman, Batman, and Deadpool mixed with a cross between Wonder Woman and Bat Girl." I bust out in laughter, Austin and Jackson are trying to figure out what's so funny when they get back to my side. Aiden just looks embarrassed that I'm laughing at him. It's not so much at him but what he said is ridiculous, because you can't ever mix DC and Marvel.

"I'm most definitely no hero. Did you make any progress on the game for Kunal's class yet?" I asked Aiden, seeking a change of subject.

"A little, but now I'm stuck in a basement, or a dungeon and I can't figure out how to get out. Do you know how?"

"Sorry, I haven't been in a dungeon or basement yet," I admit.

"Maybe we can work on it together next week? Like a study group?"

"Yeah, we can try it. Maybe if we work on it together, we can figure it out. Honestly, I haven't played it much. Getting used to my new schedule has been a little hectic."

"You work at the restaurant in town, right?" Bug asks.

"Yeah, why?" I ask with suspicion.

"I have a project for one of my entomology classes. I need to conduct an experiment in one of those walk-in freezers that restaurants have, the food court at school is privately owned and they said no. I was thinking if you wouldn't mind asking, maybe I could use the one where you work," he gives me a puppy-dog-eyed look and eagerly waits for my reply.

"Are you going to bring bugs into the restaurant for this experiment?"

"Yes. But they'll be sealed in a container the entire time. I personally guarantee they won't escape. Maybe you could just introduce me to your boss and put in a good word for me?"

His head tilts to the side with his eyebrows raised in a pleading expression, it's very hard to say no.

Calculating a plan, I reply, "Okay, I'll ask for you, but I want something in return."

"Name it! You have no idea how much this will help me out. The restaurants I've called to ask, well let's just say they didn't like the idea and hung up at the word *insects.* Having someone speak on my behalf will be a huge help, thank you."

"My request will come later, but you owe me a no questions asked favor. Deal?"

"Yes! Thank you. I really appreciate it," he gushes with appreciation. I smile at him thinking about how his help will make my birthday extra, so very extra.

"You guys wanna play pong?" Wyatt asks when the table becomes free.

"Yeah, but I need a designated drinker. I don't drink," I state without a bit of self-consciousness. I hate pointing out my age because people treat me differently when they find out how young I am, but there's no shame in choosing sobriety.

Durango of all people steps up to be my pinch-drinker. Austin and Jackson join my team and we play against Wyatt, Aiden, and Ahab. We wipe the floor with them. Almost literally when Ahab ends up on the ground, wasted. Apparently, he had an early start warming up for the party and he ends up being the designated passed out guy. Looking for the rest of our group I spot Bug making out with some girl on a lounge chair and Riley speaking way too close to the face of a cute redhead.

I'm pleased to see my boyfriends getting along with my friends, there's some unspoken challenge to merge your romantic connection with your friend group. It's especially complicated when they're all male. I feel satisfied that all the guys in my life seem to be okay with each other. Just a few more to go, arguably the two most important ones, my uncle/father and my closest friend. I hope tomorrow goes as well as tonight.

My guys switch to water after the game of pong, I think they've had a total of three beers between them. Still, I appreciate their efforts to be responsible and make sure I make it home safely. Their actions reinforce their words that they care about me, it keeps surprising me. My chest feels warm and content. It's a feeling I'm having more and more, and it feels good.

"How long do you want to stay babe?" Jackson whispers.

"Not too much longer, I have the morning shift and I need some sleep. Are you ready to go?"

"I'm happy to stay as long as you want, I was just thinking about having some food. But if you're ready to go soon, I'll wait until we get home." His words make me smile. It's just a phrase, an expression, but him calling my house, *home* tickles my insides.

"Go ahead and eat something, we won't leave in the next twenty minutes." He kisses my lips and takes off towards the food tables by the door with a smile.

"So, Violet, I'm cur-mi-ous how it works with two boyfriends," Wyatt slurs a little.

"How so?" I ask.

"Did you meet them together?"

"No." He continues to stare at me, and I give in, elaborating. "I met Jackson first. They're cousins and we all three started hanging out. We realized we had some feelings and decided to try it."

"Do you sleep with them both at the same time?" His eyes sparkle, betraying his thoughts.

"I sleep between them most nights," I answer with a smirk, daring him to be more specific.

"No, no, no-no-no...I mean..."

"I know what you mean, and I'm not answering that. I'm not punching you in the throat because you're obviously drunk, and I'm choosing to forgive your rude interrogation. I can't guarantee they'll forgive you however, if they hear what you're asking," I say with a stern expression.

His brows shoot up comically and his eyes shift as they scan our surroundings for my large boyfriends. "I'm sorry. I didn't mean to be a dick. I swear. It's just, I was wondering and we're friends, so I thought it was okay. I was cur-mi-nus, not trying to perv on you. I plom-niss."

"Sweetie, I think you may need to head upstairs to bed. You're slurring a lot and swaying. Do you need help?"

His face lights up with a big grin, "That sounds awesplumb!"

I chuckle and call out, "Hey Austin, will you please help Wyatt make it upstairs to his bed? He's pretty wasted."

"Sure baby. Come on man, which floor are you on?" I watch as Austin leads a confused Wyatt towards the house.

Grinning to myself I make my way towards Jackson who has a plate of little sandwiches and some cheese cubes. I wasn't hungry but the sight of the food makes my mouth water.

"I got you some cheese and a turkey sandwich. Sorry it has white bread, there wasn't any wheat," he offers the plate to me.

"Thanks. You're the best." I stand on tiptoe and plant a kiss on his cheek before I liberate a sandwich and two cubes of cheese from his dish. He smiles with pride. I've read that men's nature makes them want to provide and protect, it's so cute how his face lights up when I praise his efforts in providing, or protection for that matter.

"Austin went to take Wyatt upstairs, but when he comes back, we can go if you're ready."

"Did you have fun?"

"I did. Pong was fun. I've never played before. But my main reason for coming was to introduce you and Austin to my friends from school. I wanted you to know who I'm talking about when I mention them, and if I need to study with them or whatever, you'll know who I mean."

"I see. Did it go how you hoped?"

"It did. Nobody yelled, nobody got punched. Everyone seemed to get along pretty well, I'm happy."

"Were you expecting us to punch someone?" Jackson tilts his head and squints a little as he looks into my eyes.

"No. I just wasn't sure if the guys from school would be annoying or dicks, and if anyone acted like an ass, I thought maybe you might punch them. The only boyfriend I've ever had before was already a part of my friend group, so I wasn't sure how it would go. Sometimes I don't understand why people act the way they do, and I don't want you and Austin to be uncomfortable when I'm with people at school. I figured if you met them, it eliminates the discomfort of the unknown. Does that make sense?"

He nods, "I get it. I'm glad we didn't need to punch anyone. You don't need to worry about us getting mad at you for being you. But we understand with your history you might worry about consequences for living your life. I promise we'll never do anything like that to you. As time goes on, you'll know it, right down to your gorgeous soul." He shoves the last bite of his food into his mouth, while I watch him with awe. He's so much smarter, sweeter, and observant, than he lets on. He tosses his trash in a bin ten feet away, *swoosh!*

"So, what do you think of them? I'm in the most classes with Aiden and Wyatt, but their frat brothers join us at lunch sometimes."

"They're cool. The only one that's a little bit of an asshole is the Ahab dude, who passed out. Is he a jackass when he's not drunk?"

"I haven't spent much time around him. He seems a bit outspoken, but he's okay. I had a great talk with Bug. I have an idea for something, but I'll tell you later, at home." I watch him closely to see if he notices I said home. He smiles and then leans down placing a sweet kiss on my lips. I have no idea if it's due to my comment, but it's nice either way. I reach out and hug him, pulling him close. He's solid and warm, and his muscles are strong beneath his clothes. My hands rub up and down on his back and I press my body into his, squishing my breasts between us. He feels so good, I'm having the strongest urge to strip off my clothes and rub my naked body against his skin. Austin returns and puts his arm around my shoulders.

"Are you ready to go? Remember you have work in the morning."

I offer him an appreciative smile and nod, "Yeah, let's go."

"Do you want to say bye to anyone?" he asks.

"Nah, it's getting late, I don't want to start a whole new conversation, let's just head out through the gate."

"Your wish is our command," Jackson announces with a twirl of his hand, indicating I should go first.

After an uneventful shift at the restaurant, I'm excited to head home and see what type of progress the guys have made with the upgrades to BASIL.

Once I'm parked, I make my way immediately to BASIL with excitement spinning in my gut. When I stick my head through the doorway, Austin is on a ladder attaching a two-by-four to some other pieces of wood. Jackson is on his knees screwing an electrical box to a post. The room is empty except for their tools and some materials. The new wall is in the corner and will eventually house a bathroom. It'll have a small shower, toilet, and single sink. Just enough to allow someone to keep clean if they stayed in this room. There's an orange X glowing in the middle of the concrete floor and a few more marks with arrows and numbers surrounding it. Things are shaping up nicely. I think they're right, it'll be finished quickly, and definitely before my birthday.

"Hi Baby! How was your day?" Austin asks as Jackson looks over his shoulder and lets his eyes roam me from head to toe.

"Hi. It was good, they said Bug can conduct his experiment when the place is closed. If any insects escape, he's responsible for finding them though. How's everything going here? It looks like you got a lot done."

Jackson answers, "Yeah, everything went smooth today. We'll have it finished in no time."

"What time do we need to leave to pick up Colby?"

Checking my phone and calculating in my head, "We need to leave in about an hour. I need a shower. I feel slimy."

"Me too, I've got sawdust in my hair. Jax thought it would be funny to sweep it onto my head when we were cutting the supports for the walls." He glares at Jackson's back, which I see moving with his laughter.

"You got me back! I've got concrete dust in my hair from when you screwed them into the wall above me, ass wipe."

"Yeah. That was just karma. But I guess we all need a shower, do you wanna go first while we clean up here?"

"All right, how's Sawyer? He's not used to anything loud besides my workout music."

Jackson stands and begins collecting some tools from the ground as he answers, "He's okay. When I was up there to get lunch, he followed me around."

"Great, see you upstairs."

Sawyer greets me with some meows and aggressive rubs on my legs. I scoop him up and scratch him while I carry him to the bedroom. I collect my clothes for after my shower and leave him on the bed. Once I get the water running hot, I strip down and step into the heat. It feels soothing and I let it course over me for a moment, just enjoying the massaging effects of the streams of water. I startle when I open my eyes and find two shirtless men staring at me through the glass enclosure. They chortle like demons, and I let out an exasperated sound.

"You guys can't scare me like that! One day you're going to sneak up on me and my firearm or blade will react first," I scold.

They both plead with the eyes of a Disney kitten and beg my forgiveness, "We didn't mean to scare you. We just wanted to stalk you," Jackson tries.

"We're sorry. Can we watch you, pleeease?" Austin begs. I can't help rolling my eyes, but they're so cute it's impossible stay annoyed with them.

An idea forms in my head, and I try my own form of imploring eyes, "No. But I'd love for you to join me..." My finger traces my lip in my attempt to seduce them.

They communicate between themselves in their silent way, and Austin is the designated speaker. "Okay." I gasp, shocked and excited in equal measure. "With rules." I freeze as the caveat sinks in.

"Awww, man. All right, what rules?" I ask with a twinkle in my eye, and a fake pout on my lips. Testing their commitment to the rules, I firmly squeeze the bottle until shampoo oozes suggestively onto my hand and raise my arms, massaging my scalp slowly, as if caressing a lover.

Like a flock of birds in perfect synchronization, their eyes focus on my breasts carefully following the movement of my nipples as they jiggle. I turn slightly, giggling as they lean in that direction to keep my chest in their line of sight, their necks on swivel, as precise as a NASA gyroscope. "No touching. Will you agree to follow the rule?"

"Yes?" I can barely contain myself, are they going to let me see them finally? My heart pounds with excitement. My nipples tighten into peaks and my center tingles with arousal. I can even feel my cheeks growing flush in the hot water, they must be so red. Their eyes get brighter and their lids droop slightly, mouths growing slack. Austin licks his luscious lips and Jackson slides his lower lip between his teeth.

"Was that a question, baby?"

"No?"

Austin rips his gaze from my hard nipples and meets my eyes, "That still sounded like a question. Will you follow the rules for real or not?"

"I will." I answer with confidence. He looks me over and must decide I pass his test, because he removes his jeans. Jackson removes everything in one swift movement, he opens the door, and steps into the shower with me.

I'm frozen in place with my eyes roving his perfect form. He has a bit of a farmer's tan; most construction workers do. His muscles in his arms, his shoulders, and across his sparsely hairy chest are well defined. The tattoos decorating his skin accentuate the cut of his muscles and my mouth waters. I follow the lines of his chest to his carved abs, and I find it difficult to swallow. The center line of his six-pack abs has a thin trail of hair leading from it that makes its way to his pubic bone and is the crowning glory of his very erect manhood. I gulp for air and I'm finally able to gasp a breath. He's perfectly proportional and his hard dick is straight and beautiful, it looks delicious. For some reason I desperately want to fall to my knees and put my mouth on him.

"Babe, you've got some drool right here." He swipes at my mouth with a smirk painted across his lips.

Before I can recover from the heavenly sight of Jackson in front of me, Austin steps into the shower and flexes his muscles for me like a goof, a very hot goof. It doesn't make his physique any less gorgeous.

His hair is lighter than Jackson's more golden brown or dark blonde. His body hair is golden, until I spy a more distinct line and follow it to the promised land, which is surrounded with well groomed, barely there, dark hair. His muscles are defined and he's a bit longer and leaner than Jackson, still he makes my girlie bits light up like the fourth of July, just as much. They're both stunning in different ways, and I want them desperately. I want to touch and lick them all over. I want to rub against them and climb them like a tree. I'm panting and trying to keep from touching them, but it's so fucking hard, literally.

"Are you all, right?" Austin questions with a more serious tone.

"Yeah. Fine. Just, um, it's really difficult not to touch you."

Jackson reaches out and cups my waist, he places his other hand on my other hip and gazes at my face. He looks into my eyes and smiles, he must be happy with whatever he sees there because his smile grows into a huge, glowing grin that lights up his eyes.

"Babe, you're blushing so much. Your face is flushed, even your chest is red. Are you sure you're, okay?"

"I'm good. I just have the strongest urge to lick you."

"Holy fuck," Austin mutters behind me.

Jackson's hard member twitches and I'm fascinated. Clear liquid sparkles on the tip and I want to taste it, lick it, and suck it. I desperately press my legs together in an attempt to soothe the need I feel between them. I hear movement behind me and then I can smell my green apple conditioner as Austin's large and gentle hands work it into my hair. He places a kiss on my shoulder before rinsing his hands under the water.

Austin and Jackson both fill their hands with body wash. They each rub the berry scented soap on my skin from opposing angles. Jackson works on my back while Austin washes my front. I may have died and gone to the hereafter. Jackson's firm hands massage my back and then work their way to my ass where he squeezes as much as he washes. Austin has been washing my breasts with a circular motion for much longer than necessary to ensure their cleanliness. He rubs his rough palms over my pebbled nipples repeatedly and I'm enjoying his attention. My head falls back against his shoulder, and I feel his thick length graze my ass cheek.

Jackson steps back and lets his eyes roam my form, he watches Austin's hands kneading my straining breasts. His hands slide from my hips to my chest, he usurps Austin's grip on my flesh and feels my hard nipples for himself. Austin doesn't lose a beat and moves his palms to my now abandoned and aching waist. He continues his trek along my muscled ass and sets up camp there.

Jackson moves one hand deftly down my abdomen and gently presses his fingers between my thighs. He expertly finds my clit and rubs it in a circular motion that heats me up even more sending sparks of pleasure through me. He lifts my leg and uses his other hand to hold it up leaving my chest available for Austin to swoop back in. He supports me while Jackson assaults my throbbing pussy. When I begin to moan loudly, Austin tilts us both so he can swallow my cries with an all-consuming kiss.

Jackson moves to his knees and maneuvers my thigh over his shoulder exposing me to his tongue, working it on my clit, leaving his hand free to insert a finger inside me. He curves his digit to ignite the spot that makes my cries rise in pitch. He gently sucks on my clitoris and presses a second finger into my tight pussy. He stretches me with an expertise that makes me scream out my release. Just as I reach my climax, Austin cries out behind me, and I feel his hot cum hit my ass and it makes me shudder with pleasure.

Jackson continues to carefully suck on me while his fingers slowly pump until the intensity wanes. Austin groans as a few more spurts of his release land on me and slide off onto the shower floor. When I'm quiet, Jackson carefully puts my leg beneath me and holds onto me until I'm steady. His hand strokes his length and his eyes close. Austin supports me from behind and places soft kisses along my neck and shoulder. His lips cause shivers to travel through me and I touch Jackson's hard cock with my hip as I shudder. The touch of my skin to the head of his cock sends a shiver through him igniting his climax. He makes a growling sound and throws his head back as his cum explodes from him and lands on my belly. His eyes open and he watches as more of his release bursts from him and onto me.

"Holy hell, you're so fucking beautiful, babe. You look amazing with me marking you. I see the most stunning woman in front of me. I see that you're mine...that you're ours...you are perfection."

He leans into me and presses a sweet kiss on my mouth. His hands squeeze my shoulders, the shower has washed away their release from my skin, and they both hold me close between them. My heart beats with warmth and contentment. I feel safe and loved, not something I've ever felt from men before, who weren't my dad or uncle. I don't want to let them go, I have the most magical feeling inside of me and I struggle to label it. Whatever I'm feeling, these two amazing men are responsible for it, and I don't ever want to lose it.

CHAPTER TWENTY-FIVE

"**D**epending on his mood, Colby can be a little off. He's super smart, lots of fun, and my best friend in the world. He's always had my back, and I trust him implicitly, he's a vault."

"So, what you're saying is, he knows all your secrets and if we want answers, we need to ask him?" Austin clarifies.

"He's a vault, he won't spill my secrets."

"Does he take bribes?" Jackson asks.

I smack his arm playfully, "No. Don't you dare." Our laughter dies down when we pull up to the guard stationed at the gate. Jackson rolls down his window and explains we're here for Colby.

The guard leans to look at me and Austin, "Hello, Miss Henley."

"Hey Julio, how's Marguerite doing?"

"She's much better, thanks. Haven't seen you in a while, how are you?"

"I'm good. Started college, got my own place, started dating Jackson and Austin," I point to each of my guys.

"That's terrific Miss Henley, I'm glad you're well." He presses his finger to his ear, then looks at us.

"Mr. Colby would like you to collect him from the pool house. Nice seeing you, take care of yourself. Sirs," he nods, and the large decorative gate swing open.

"Thanks Julio, give Marguerite my love," I call out to him as we pull away. I ignore the large structure to our right; Colby's parents live there and if they're in town they won't bother acknowledging me anyway. They don't hate me, they just don't understand me, or their son.

As we round the back landscaping, Colby's pool house comes into view. It's nothing to sneeze at, with four-bedrooms, three bathrooms, and probably four thousand square feet in its own right. The main house is closer to twenty-eight thousand, a true mansion by all accounts. Colby's family has more money than some countries, and beyond the pool house are some cottages further back on the property for the staff. My parents did okay, and we have a nice house, but nothing like how Colby grew up.

Ugh, I hate thinking about my house sitting empty, locked in a court battle thanks to Grandmother. That reminds me I haven't spoken to Krewe, and I probably need to call him to check in. Living in my warehouse affords me blissful isolation from my difficulties with that woman. Growing up and being the adult I am, despite my impending birthday, I need to act like it and not avoid my problems.

When we park, Colby's door flings open and he exits dressed in black and white. He almost looks like a crossword puzzle. I don't know where he shops, but he's always the most interesting of my friends. Austin chuckles under his breath and I elbow him in the gut.

"Hey!"

"Open the door and let me out, please."

"All right, no elbows needed baby."

"You deserved it, and you know it," I scold. He opens the door, and I scramble out and rush to Colby. I throw my arms around him and squeeze tight. It's been a long time since I've seen him in person. He came to the funeral for a quick minute, and I haven't seen him since.

"Geez, Vi! You're crushing me!" I release him.

"Sorry. I've missed you."

"You talk to me almost every day."

"Yeah, but I don't see you enough. Come meet my guys," I'm beaming with pride and notice both of them are standing tall as if waiting for inspection.

Colby stands before them and he's noticeably shorter and pale. He doesn't look intimidated though and that makes me feel good. I was a little worried he'd feel uncomfortable, I'm relieved to see him looking confident.

"Colby, this is Jackson and Austin, my boyfriends."

Jackson reaches out to shake Colby's hand, "Nice to meet you, man."

Austin smiles wide and holds his hand out as well, "Pleasure to meet Violet's best friend. She's told us a lot about you."

Colby smiles as he shakes each hand offered, "Thanks. You too. She's told me about you guys as well. She seems pretty happy so, I'm cool with you. But if you hurt her in any way, I'll destroy you both." His smile never falters. Austin and Jackson look a bit confused for a moment before their faces break into large smiles. First hurdle conquered.

Completely serious, Colby doesn't waver. He may not be able to physically harm them, but electronically, it's no joke, he would obliterate them both. I decide to ride in the back seat with Colby, I don't want him to feel left out or alone. One of his diagnoses is agoraphobia, which goes hand in hand with his claustrophobia, and OCD. When he's doing well, he can go out and not get stuck flicking the door lock thirty-seven times. He's always claustrophobic, and he gets panic attacks in uncomfortable situations. I'm honored that he trusts me enough to go out with me sometimes. He knows I will protect him and get him to a safe space at the drop of a hat. He's been to Uncle Randy's place before and likes and trusts him also.

"You're okay riding with me in back?" I ask Colby, confirming he feels safe in the truck with Jackson driving.

"Yes. I'm willing to start with trust and they'll lose it if they fuck up. Besides, there's no evidence of any past collisions." With Colby that could mean he surveyed the truck's exterior for repairs and damage, or it could mean he did a background check, motor vehicle check, driver's license check, and probably a complete comprehensive level four or higher, background history check. Knowing him as I do, I'm certain he completed all of the above.

"Good plan. Thanks for trusting me." I squeeze his hand in gratitude.

"Is Stephanie going to join us?"

"Yeah, Randy said she wouldn't miss it. Apparently, she wants to meet you and my boyfriends as soon as possible."

"Does that mean she's going to grill us?" Austin asks innocently.

"I have no idea. I've only met her once. She knows much more about me than I know about her. Although I do know more than I should," I look down with my admission.

"You know about her history in Washington?" My eyes snap to Colby. I don't know why I'm surprised, of course he looked into her background, just like me. He won't let anyone enter my life without his scrutiny.

"Yeah. What a load of BS, huh?"

"What are we talking about?" Jackson asks.

"Stephanie had some trouble at her previous job. She's a whistle blower and had to deal with harassment until the asshole went to jail. She decided to start over because of it and moved here."

"It's much worse than that. I think I know why she moved. The person who was committing the sexual assaults on patients was her boss and it took a long time for anyone to do anything about his activities even after she reported him. He attacked her and threatened to kill her before he went to jail. I found the police reports," Colby elaborates.

"Damn. That's crazy," Austin announces.

"Yeah, but I'm more impressed with her the more I learn. Plus, Uncle Randy is smitten, and I want him to be happy."

"Does she know about us?" Jackson asks.

"I told him to tell her. Don't worry, she's down to earth, I'm sure she'll like all of you," I smile at Colby.

"Of course she'll like me, it's them you need to worry about," Colby laughs.

"Hey!"

"I'm just kidding Austin. Even though I don't look like I have a sense of humor, I'm hilarious."

"Oh my God! You're the only one who thinks you're hilarious. Most of the time nobody gets your jokes," I state through giggles.

"I can't help it if people aren't smart enough to know what's funny," Colby folds his arms with a pout. I can hear Austin and Jackson chuckling in the front seat.

"If nothing else, this is going to be an interesting evening. Is there anything new in the Voldemort camp?" I ask Colby.

"Yeah. Is it cool if I update you now?" His eyes shift to the front seat.

"It's cool."

"The guys in the big cars were from out of town. They're businessmen from Orlando... in public. In private, they're criminals with ties to the mob. I'm still digging but I think one of their main areas of business is human trafficking, one of them is Russian. I'm not sure what his name is yet, but face recognition has brought up some images of him with known Russian mobsters from Pennsylvania. The camera didn't get a clear enough shot to identify him. But his side profile pulled up three other images, so far."

"I need to swing by there tonight or tomorrow and swap the batteries for the trail cams. It's going to run out in a couple days."

"Who are you talking about?" Austin asks.

"Voldemort. We have a few cameras watching his lair and I need to change out the batteries, so we don't miss any surveillance. I'm trying to map out his schedule so I can plan when to grab him."

"Who is Voldemort, really?" Before I can answer we're, all flung forward hard against our seatbelts as Jackson locks up the breaks, barely missing a red Honda that just pulled out in front of him.

"Fucking hell lady! You have to look before you pull out! Are you all, right? Violet?" Jackson yells at everyone.

"Yeah, fine."

"All good."

"Mother fucker." Jackson shakes his head from side to side and angrily gestures at the oblivious older woman. She can barely see over the steering wheel; she's got to be pushing ninety. She continues on her way at a turtle's pace.

"I hate snowbirds!" Jackson grumbles.

"It's not snowbird season, it's been over for months," Austin prods.

"Fine. I hate retirees. She shouldn't be driving if she can't see a fucking truck."

"You know how it is; she probably got her license renewed for twenty years fifteen years ago, when she could still see."

"Shut up, Auz."

The navigation on Jackson's phone guides him through the last couple of turns and we pull into Randy's driveway. Stephanie's SUV is already parked near the front porch. My stomach flutters with a few nervous butterflies as I climb out. I take a deep breath and let it out slowly.

Austin takes my hand, "Don't be nervous baby, it'll be fine." He gently squeezes my fingers and places a kiss on my knuckles.

"Thanks. I know. It's just, I've never brought anyone home to meet him before. He knew Max for a long time before we tried dating. This is new and I'm not sure how I feel."

Using his other hand, he pulls me in for a hug and places a kiss on my cheek. I smile with gratitude and kiss his lips. Jackson waits patiently by the door watching us. When we approach him, he takes my other hand and pulls me in for a kiss while I continue to hold onto Austin.

"Wow. Watching you with two guys is as lame as one," Colby observes. He turns to the front door and rings the bell.

"You don't have to knock, it's basically my home."

"But it's not mine."

"You could've waited one second for me to open the door."

"Nope."

I roll my eyes, "Is this some of your hilarious humor?" The door opens and Uncle Randy looks at Colby, then me, then he stalls on my guys.

A smile breaks across his face, "Colby! Good to see you, come in. Hi Sweetheart, come here." He hugs me.

"Hi, Uncle Randy, this is Austin Matthews and Jackson Hunter. Guys, this is Dr. Randall Nercy, my uncle." They all shake hands. I'm relieved, not sure why, I just feel some tension draining out of my shoulders like I pulled a plug.

"Come in, and you can call me Randy. We're in the kitchen finishing up."

"Thank you," Austin says.

"Thank you, sir," Jackson adds.

We follow Uncle Randy to the kitchen and find Colby seated at the bar while Stephanie mixes vegetables in a bowl on the other side. She's laughing, and Colby looks smug as he gives me a pointed smirk with his eyebrow raised. I lift my hands in surrender.

"Fine. You're funny. Get over it, dude. Hi Stephanie, how are you?"

"Hi Violet! I'm good, just getting to know Colby. Hello..." she looks at my guys.

"This is Jackson Hunter and Austin Matthews. Guys this is Dr. Stephanie St. James," I say pointing at each of them in turn.

"Please, call me Stephanie. It's nice to meet you." They shake hands.

Uncle Randy claps his hands, "I'm going to check the grill, but it shouldn't be long. Why don't you all get something to drink and head into the dining room."

"Do you need any help?" Austin offers.

"Sure, will you grab that platter?" Uncle Randy says with his hands full.

"Got it," Austin hefts the large plate and follows Uncle Randy outside.

Jackson asks, "Do you want me to get the drinks?"

"I got it. Do you want tea, soda, or water?" I ask.

"Tea for me," Colby answers.

We get everyone's drinks and make our way to the table. As we're ready to sit down Austin and Uncle Randy join us with a platter of chicken shish kabobs on one plate and steak kabobs on another. Jackson carries in a bowl of salad for Stephanie, and she has a dish with rolls and a bowl of green beans. Everything looks delicious and I'm hungry, I skipped lunch.

Things start quietly, mostly Stephanie and Uncle Randy ask a few questions about the guy's work, which they explain in detail. Colby asks a few questions of his own, he's one of those people who truly wants to know all the specifics of everyone's career.

"How did you three meet?" Stephanie asks. I told her how we became friends and then they talked me into dating them.

"Hey, not fair. We all agreed to try dating when we realized we liked each other. We didn't have to convince you of anything," Jackson admonishes playfully.

"Yeah, okay. I didn't need convincing, they're pretty sweet. Stephanie, I was wondering about what we talked about before.

You said you had some trouble at work, and you decided to start fresh by moving here. Would you mind elaborating a little?"

She looks at Uncle Randy and clears her throat, "The hospital where I worked in the Seattle area was fairly large and we often had homeless, mentally ill, and minor criminals like addicts and prostitutes who were all vulnerable patients. I accidentally discovered my boss was taking advantage of them by drugging and abusing them. I reported him to the hospital, and they talked to him, then they made us have a mediation conference to resolve our differences. They acted like I did something wrong, and equal to him assaulting patients, as if we could fix it with a conversation. I told them if they didn't call the authorities, I would. He followed me home, attacked me, and threatened my life. I reported the assault and his activities as well. He was arrested. I had to testify at his trial. The hospital got in trouble and a few people were fired. He got sentenced to only eight years with the possibility of parole after five."

"Holy shit. Sorry, but that's ridiculous. They punish a pot dealer longer than that!" Austin exclaims.

"They didn't have enough evidence for all of the assaults, just mine and one other. The victims were afraid of the system and the detectives, they wouldn't cooperate, or they weren't stable enough to be located. The one other victim was a prostitute who got pregnant from his attack and got her life turned around for the baby."

Colby listens intently with wide eyes, mesmerized, "Stranger than fiction."

"The only hope is some of the others will change their minds and testify. The statute of limitations for violent crimes doesn't keep them from coming back later and adding to his sentence with more convictions."

"At least that's something. I'm sorry that happened to you, he sounds like a real monster."

"He is, it's one of the main reasons I moved away. I didn't want his job in a hospital where I didn't feel safe, but I also wanted to be as far away as possible."

"We're glad you're here," Uncle Randy takes her hand and smiles warmly at her.

"Definitely," I chime in.

"All right let's get this stuff cleaned up and we can put the game on and chat some more," Uncle Randy says.

Austin offers to help with the dishes and Colby joins him. Jackson and Stephanie begin clearing the table. Uncle Randy winks at me and jerks head towards the family room asking me to join him. He puts on the UM game and mutes it. Then he pulls an extra chair over and has a seat patting the spot next to him for me.

"How are you?"

"I'm great. I love school, and things are going well with Jackson and Austin. How are you?"

"Also, great. I like them, they're smart and polite. I especially like that they watch you, checking on you. It tells me they care about your well-being. Is everything going okay navigating a three-sided relationship?"

"It's been amazing. They're with me most of the time when we aren't at work or school. They're as close as brothers and best friends, and they definitely both like me as much as I l-like them. They found out my age, not that I was concealing it, I just didn't tell them. They won't sleep with me until after my birthday. So, we've spent a lot of time talking and hanging out getting to know each other, building our relationship."

"That's wonderful. I think I respect them even more for that choice. I noticed you stuttered a bit, anything you want to tell me?"

"How do you always know how I'm feeling? I don't even know half the time. Fine, yeah, I'm feeling things, and maybe I more than like them. How do you know if you're in love with someone?"

"It's a very individual thing, and you don't need to rush into anything. For me, I can't stop thinking of her from the moment I wake up, she's always on my mind. If something good happens, I want to call her and share it. If something bad happens, I want to call her and commiserate. I worry about her safety and if she's had lunch or skipped it. She makes my insides tingle with excitement, and I want to spend every minute with her. Being with her makes me happy."

"That was a fairly specific explanation, anything you want to tell me?" I can't keep the smile from my face, talk about happiness, I'm thrilled for him and Stephanie.

"Okay, I admit it, we're in love. I'm asking her to move in with me. Are you good with that?"

"Are you kidding? I'm beyond good, I'm so happy for both of you!" I hug him and it startles him, he jolts, then hugs me back.

Everyone else trickles into the room and Uncle Randy pulls Stephanie onto his lap in the recliner, Colby sits in the armchair, and Austin and Jackson sit on each side of me on the sofa. We spend the next two hours talking and laughing while we keep tabs on the football game. By the time UM scores the winning goal, we're all well acquainted and pleasantly closer. I have another early shift in the morning, it's cleaning day at the Cantina.

"We need to think about heading out soon, I have to get some sleep before I have to scrub the restaurant in the morning." As I finish my sentence, an advertisement for the news comes on the TV. I watch as Voldemort talks to a reporter. The sound is off, but the headline confirms it's him. My sole focus is on his hideous face, and everything else fades away.

"Okay, Violet? What's wrong?" Austin asks quietly, keeping the conversation between us, and his gaze follows mine to the television.

"Mother fucker..." he gushes under his breath.

Jackson looks for what has the two of us frozen. He looks from the screen to Austin, then from the screen to me. His face scrunches up in confusion, his mouth falls open as if he has dropped what he was going to say onto the floor. The three of us watch until Voldemort leaves our sight.

Jackson asks, "What's wrong, babe?"

"Voldemort. That was him."

"From Harry Potter?"

"No. Yes, but he's the one, I just named him that after the evil villain in Harry Potter."

"He's the one what?" Austin whisper growls.

"My target."

"Hey, sorry to cut everything short but we need to get going. Violet has an early shift in the morning. We really can't thank you enough for having us, it was so nice to meet both of you," Jackson tells Uncle Randy and Stephanie, while he stands and helps me up by taking my elbow and encouraging me to stand. Austin follows his lead and leaves with our cups, presumably to the kitchen. Colby stands, Stephanie and Uncle Randy follow suit.

"Okay. It was great meeting you both," Randy tells Jackson shaking his hand. Stephanie steps forward and hugs Jackson, then me. When Austin returns the ritual continues. When we make it back to the truck Austin offers Colby the front seat, then climbs into the back with me. He keeps looking at my face, and I'm not sure what he sees or what he's looking for, but it's making me anxious.

Once we're underway, Austin asks, "Who is Voldemort, baby?"

"He's my target, the one I want to grab. He's the worst of my nightmares, the coldest, cruelest, most evil monster of all." His fists clench tight in his lap, his face glows red, his jaw is tense, all of his muscles seem taut and ready to pounce.

"Did he hurt you?" I can't prevent the tears that fall from my eyes and I can't look him in the eye either. Focusing on the yellow piece of string twisted into a figure eight on the floor mat by my feet, I relent and utter the truth.

"Yes. He hurt me when I was a little girl."

Jackson pulls over, slams on the brakes, and exits the truck in what feels like one motion as Austin pulls me into his lap. Jackson rips open the door and jumps in next to me and Austin, he pulls me onto his lap and kisses the tears from my face. Austin continues to hold my waist and rubs my arm in circles. Jackson continues to wipe the tears from my face with his thumbs as he holds my cheeks with his hands. He looks into my eyes forcing me to look into his. My lip trembles and the tears refill my eyes.

"Babe, you're safe. Say it with me."

"I-I'm safe. I'm free. I'm safe. He can't hurt me anymore. I'm strong, I'm a warrior, I'm a badass, he can't hurt me anymore." He kisses my lips, while Austin squeezes my middle and pulls me onto his lap holding me close between them.

"You're safe. You're a beautiful badass. A warrior. Right?" Jackson questions.

"Right. I'm okay. I just don't like talking about Voldemort."

"Baby, if you don't want to talk about him, that's okay. But I need to tell you something." Austin says with trepidation.

"What?" I lift my watery eyes to meet his in expectation. Jackson takes my hands and Austin holds me tight, around my waist.

"Voldemort, the asshole bishop?" He confirms.

"Yeah?"

"He's the bastard that raped Megan." The floor drops out from beneath me and I'm falling. Austin holds me and rubs my skin anywhere he can reach it. Jackson holds my cheeks and looks into my eyes.

"Babe, you're safe. He can't hurt you." He places soft kisses on my face accentuating each word.

Eventually Colby reminds us of the fact he's still here, "Ahem. If we hurry, we can get the batteries swapped out of the trail cams, before it gets any later."

Chapter Twenty-Six

"Colby likes you both."

"Good. He's a nice guy. It makes me feel better knowing he's always with you when you hunt," Jackson reveals.

"Uncle Randy likes you too. Stephanie basically asked me how you are in the sack." Both of them turn to me and wait for me to elaborate.

"What did you tell her?" Austin questions.

"Nothing. I don't really know because we haven't had sex. But I may have hinted that everything we've done so far has been spectacular," I smirk at Jackson who pounces and tickles me.

"No fair! Not fair! S-stop! You're cheating!" I squeal between laughs. Austin holds me still while Jackson tickles my ribs and thighs. I try to wiggle free, then kick at them to escape, nothing works until Austin lets go. I take off running and when I step into the kitchen I slip across the floor and fall on my ass with a bang.

"Baby! Are you okay?"

"No, I broke my ass. Owww." I roll to the side and rub the affected area while giggles continue to trickle out of me. When Austin squats down, I scoot back away from him and get ready to run.

"Let me see," he offers.

"No. It's too embarrassing."

"You realize I've seen it before."

"Yeah, but you weren't inspecting it up close."

"Ha! That's what you think." I roll my eyes and huff at him in mock disgust.

"You're being such a *man.*"

"Lucky you, I *am* a man. Now come on, let me make sure you're all right."

"Fine." I slowly stand and stretch a little then turn my butt towards Austin.

He peeks into my waist band and exclaims, "Oh no!"

"What!?!" I spin like an idiot trying to look at my ass. Even Sawyer isn't that ridiculous, it's more of a dog trick.

He sadly delivers his medical diagnosis, "I'm sorry baby, it's definitely broken, it's got a crack right down the middle."

"Har-har! Jackass," I give him a disgusted glare and yank up my shorts.

"Why're you a jackass, Auz?" Jackson asks as he enters the kitchen.

"Just teasing our beautiful, badass warrior. She didn't appreciate my witty commentary."

Jackson looks me over a question on his face, "You, okay?"

"Yeah, just a slightly bruised ego and a cracked ass, apparently."

Austin and Jackson bust out in fresh laughter. I fight my urge to chuckle along. As we hang out in my tiny little kitchen and they tease me, I notice that feeling in my chest again. It's sorta warm and buzzing. It feels electric and I'm getting little shocks radiating outward that tingle in the best way, it doesn't hurt at all. I only feel pleasure, it feels almost like the waves of thrills I feel when they make me come between them. Like I'm cresting the highest peak on a rollercoaster, teetering precariously anticipating the fall over the top.

They watch me with sparkles in their eyes and wide grins on their faces. I'm happy. I wondered if I would ever be happy again after I lost my parents, but having these two in my life has spackled over the holes in my heart. It's forever changed and still darker than most, but my black heart is capable of love again and I'm a little freaked out about it.

I dodge past Jackson and rush to the stairs, "Bet you can't catch me!" I slide down the stairs without really ever touching a tread. When I reach the floor, I run for my workout space. I hear a metal scrape behind me and lunge for the bar of the weight machine. I use it to swing up to the beam that supports my apartment. I hoist myself onto the short beam end and then hop to the next one.

"Playing hardball, huh babe?"

"Nope, just playing."

"Hmmmm," he growls behind me.

From the corner of my eye, I spot Austin sneaking around the workout area to get ahead of me. Crap! I don't have anywhere to go to avoid him that won't let Jackson catch me. Hopping to another beam, I look over the space above me. It's far, but if I can make it to the edge of the framing for the storage room, I think I can get past Austin and surprise him. No time like the present. I edge over to the closest beam, then I swing onto the support overhead like a monkey. I arc through the air and land almost silently on the frame of the storage room. I skip from beam to beam, and when I reach the far edge, I scale the wall to the floor and land without a sound. I crouch and stay close to the wall, hiding in the shadows. I work my way into the garage and then crawl under Jackson's truck to come out in front of Austin.

"Ah-ha!!" Shit. Where the heck is he?

"Gotcha!" He grabs me from behind and lifts me up as I scream. *"Mother-puss-bucket!"*

Jackson cracks up, "What? Where do you get this stuff?"

"It's from *Ghostbusters*. How did you get past me?" I glare at Austin.

"I'll never tell." He loosens his grip on me and kisses my cheek before I can react.

"Awww, don't be mad, babe. He got you fair and square."

"No ganging up on me."

"We aren't. We didn't. We're just trying to help you see clearly now, you should know we'll always catch you," Jackson defends.

"All right. Let's make a new game."

"What do you have in mind," Austin asks.

"Let's each hide something and whoever finds the item gets a prize."

"I like it. What's the prize?" Jackson questions.

"What would be worth it for you?"

"Naked time," Austin answers.

"Dude, what if you find my item? I'm not having naked time with you. Violet has to be there."

"Okay, okay. I've got it. Since you guys aren't going to look for each other's hidden item, the two of you hide one together. Then the winner who locates the item first gets to pick our next date and gets an hour of naked time." I can't help my huge grin. I can tell by their faces they're imagining me naked, and they've forgotten what we're doing.

"Yeah. Okay, that works. What items are we hiding?" Austin comes around first, which surprises me. He's such a perv.

"Let's get our item and meet here, same time tomorrow. What do you think?"

"Deal." Austin shakes my hand.

"Okay," Jackson holds his hand out and we shake on it. We get ready for bed and get snuggled in for a restful night.

Working the early shift on Sunday is the hardest day of the week. Everyone goes out for breakfast on Sunday morning. Then the after-church crowd shows up closely followed by the brunch people. I don't mind, and I like the place busy. My shift goes faster the busier it is. During the after-church hour I serve a young family of six and mom is expecting. No surprise for the religious followers. They're really nice and polite, the kids are adorable, and they all look exactly like their Asian father. Not a one has mom's blonde hair or light eyes.

One of the boys is around two and he's the sweetest two-year-old I've ever met. Aren't they supposed to be terrible? He wants me to play cars with him, so we race them across his highchair tray. Every time I walk by, we have another match. I let him win mostly. He laughs with the sweetest giggle; his parents are amazed he's sitting for so long without complaint. It makes me want to keep him happy so the family can enjoy their meal out.

When the family is ready to go the little boy yells for me. When I rub his little arm, he hands me a black motorcycle. I try to hand it back thinking this is our new game. He won't take it.

His mom interprets his little voice, "He wants you to have it."

"Oh, sweetie, I don't want to take your motorcycle. Don't you want to keep it?"

"No. No moto-cycle! Viwet, keep it!"

"You better keep it. It's just a dollar store toy. I recognize his tone, and you won't change his mind," his mom explains.

"Okay. Thank you for sharing. I love it!" I hold it close to my heart and smile at him. His little face lights up and he lays his head onto his father's shoulder, the smile never leaves his face as they all wave goodbye.

I pocket the toy and get back to work. Later when my shift is over, I find the motorcycle in my pocket and look it over. It looks just like my bike. How did that little kid know what I ride? My bio mother used to say children had a direct connection to the devil and they learn secrets from him. I think it was just another way for her to say she hated me, but it makes me wonder.

I put the toy in my backpack and shove my hair under my helmet before I hop on my full-size bike and take off for home.

Enjoying the short ride, I decided to stretch it out and take a pass by Voldemort's lair. He's probably not there since it's Sunday, and religious leaders like to hang out in church on Sunday's. He probably uses the time to spot future victims.

His enormous house on the hill looks empty when I ride by, and the windows look lonely, dark, and sad. The evil seeps from its bricks, I can feel a change in the air as I pass his ornate wrought iron gate.

On Sunday's he goes to the services at Our Lady Queen of Sorrow, his home turf. He sits on an elaborately adorned throne that even the King of England would find garish. His image in that golden chair is plastered all over their website. He sits through two masses and then, for the right price, he'll oversee baptisms or other ceremonies. He rarely presides over mass or delivers a homily. He likes people to kiss his ring and bow in deference to his position in the church. All I can think about is how many children has he harmed? Does he harm women too? Boys? Girls?

When I drive by his lair, I swear my blade heats against my waist ready to slice into his repulsive flesh. My birthday is coming fast, and I want him in my BASIL for the anniversary of my birth. Purging the world of his vile countenance will be a rebirth of sorts. Once I'm past the ungodly property, I hit the gas hard and race home. The guys had to go home for a while today, but they'll be back later. It's a good time to check in with Colby and see where we stand on *Project Voldemort.*

Settled behind my laptop with string cheese to munch, I connect with RobN and see where we are with the logistics and our timetable. He's sent me some encrypted updates. I look over the results and the reports on the men from the big black cars. Next, I open a folder and the floor plan of his lair opens on my screen. I shrink it so I can see the whole thing at once. Wow, this is great. I wonder where he found the plans, but he probably won't tell me. After I look everything over, I call him.

"Hey Vi, I'm going to the parents for dinner, everything okay?"

"Yeah, just checking in."

"I'll hit you up when I get back."

"10-4" With some free time on my hands, I pull up the game for Professor Kunal's class. I haven't made much effort to beat it yet, and I may as well kill time with it now.

After twenty minutes I beat the game. When I capture the prize, my screen falls black. Next a skull and crossbones fills the screen and begins laughing. I watch as it plays a pirate tune from the Caribbean and the bones transform into dancing skeletons. They find an X on the ground and dig until they find a treasure chest. They find bottles of rum, drink them, and stumble off the screen carrying their chest. Before they completely vanish, a coin falls from the chest.

My avatar appears on the screen, and I maneuver to pick up the coin. When I lift it, a trap door falls open beneath my character and I land in a cave. When my avatar rotates her view, I can see a single torch on the wall emitting the only light in the stone chamber. Before moving on, I circle the room. A glimmer catches my eye along the back wall. I collect the torch and bring it to the wall. There's a map, it has a dotted line tracing a path which ends in an X.

I look over the cartograph carefully looking for hidden markings. It dawns on me this is a map of my school. If I'm looking at it correctly, the X appears to be in the Student Center. I mull over the possibilities. My little avatar wanders the cave, there's no escape and no other markings. I try touching the map and walls, but nothing happens. I think I need to find a clue in the Student Center to move on. I wonder how my classmates are faring in the game.

Checking the time, I have about twenty minutes before the guys are due. I take a quick shower, and when I pull on my clothes, I hear them come in. Yep, I gave them keys. I really hope that wasn't a mistake. It seemed like a good idea when they started spending the night working on my remodeling project. I trust them. I have to believe it's not the huge step it feels like.

"Babe? Where are you?"

"I'm coming down!" I bring my item to hide with me, anticipation filling my veins with excitement. I love fooling around with them in every sense of the word.

"Hi, how was work?"

"Busy. It went quickly. How was your day?" I ask them both, peering between them.

"I did some laundry, cleaned a little. Then went to mom and dads for a visit," Jackson answers.

"I did laundry, washed my car, mowed the grass, and met up with Jackson at my parents. The inspector should be here tomorrow morning to look at your remodel and then we'll be able to do more work on your project."

"What time will he come? I have class."

"We're gonna stay here until he leaves. If you have to go it's fine, we'll take care of everything."

"Thanks." Austin's closer so I hug and kiss him first, then Jackson.

He watches me, "Did you bring your item to hide for our game?"

"Of course. What'd you bring?"

"You first, baby." Austin smirks.

"Okay. I got this today," I hold up the black motorcycle the little boy gave me.

"Did you buy it?" Jackson tilts his head.

"Nope, a young man gave it to me at work."

"What young man?" They both ask in unison.

It tickles me, "A two-year-old, *misters I'm not jealous!*" I tease them with a poor imitation.

They both puff out their chests, "Ahem, we're not jealous. Just curious who's giving you a gift, that's all. It's normal curiosity, not jealousy."

"Uh huh. So, spill, what's your item?"

"We found it at our parent's house. It's something we got as kids, and they saved it. We thought it would be perfect for our game," Austin explains.

"Yeah. We wanted something small and easy to hide," Jackson adds.

"Okaay..."

Austin raises his fist and opens it. There, in his palm, is a gold coin. He holds it towards me so I can see it better. I move closer and examine the carved image on the side of the coin facing me. It's a pirate's Jolly Roger flag. I release a small gasp, and my hand covers my mouth.

"What?"

"Sorry. It's...hmmm, I literally just got to the next level on that computer project, the one for class? It gave me a flag just like that, then a pirate's treasure map, and I found a coin in the game. Isn't that a weird coincidence?"

"That is weird," Jackson answers and Austin nods in agreement. He flips over the coin and that side is carved with a galleon, a pirate ship flying the same flag.

"Where did you get your coin?"

"It's a souvenir from a trip to The Keys. There's a treasure museum from a sunken ship. They had replicas of the actual coins found on the ship with real gold plating, but we wanted a pirate coin instead. It's still gold-plated, just not a replica of a real coin. It was a good trip... before Megan changed. The girls were little, and Pierson was with us. We had a blast looking for shark teeth and treasure. We went snorkeling and fishing, and we stayed in a house right on the water. It belonged to a friend of Miguel's, and he let us stay there for free; it was like camping out in a house."

I think back to the photographs hanging on the walls of his parent's home. I remember a picture of the three boys on a beach with huge grins on their faces, masks pushed up on their heads, shirtless and covered with sand. It gives me that familiar warm feeling in my chest, it's becoming a common sensation when they're around.

"What's that look mean?" Jackson asks, a sweet grin on his face.

"What look?"

"Sometimes you get this look, it's like you're watching your favorite movie and you're struggling to contain the happiness it makes you feel. Like you want to laugh out loud or jump for joy, but you're at the library so you have to hold it in."

Austin contrasts with, "I think she looks like she's watching a puppy video, and she's allowed to keep whichever one she wants as long as she doesn't scream with joy about it... like she wants to."

"I have no idea. I wasn't thinking about movies or puppies." I shrug.

Jackson asks, "What were you thinking about?" My cheeks heat instantly, and I can't maintain eye contact.

"Wow, look at those red cheeks, was it dirty?"

"No!" I smack Austin playfully on the chest.

"Awww, come on Violet, you can admit it. I mean, it's kinda hot if that's what you were thinking about."

"I wasn't. It was...just thinking about how much I like you. Both of you." I stick my chin out and dare them to make fun of me.

"That's sweet, baby. I really like you too." He pulls me into his perfectly carved chest and kisses me. Holding me close for a moment.

When Jackson takes me from him, he lets me go. Jackson wraps me in his big, strong arms pressing his body against mine. He kisses my cheek and my temple. After a few seconds, Austin wraps me up to, he pulls me close and presses his body into mine, so I'm sandwiched between them, and it feels exactly like it's where I'm supposed to be. My right arm reaches back to hug Austin's middle and my left squeezes Jackson tight.

"All right, what are the rules for our treasure hunt?" Austin asks, reminding us of what we were doing.

"I say we have to hide it somewhere inside this building. We have a time limit to find it, or we lose."

Jackson looks thoughtful before he says, "How about after twenty-four hours we get a clue, but the prize is cut to half an hour?"

"Okay, then after the clue how long do we have before we lose?" Austin asks.

"Another twenty-four hours?" I offer.

"Yeah. But there needs to be a punishment if we lose," Jackson decides.

"Spanking?" Austin suggests with a serious look he can't quite maintain.

"No." Jackson and I answer together. Austin manifests a manufactured look of disappointment.

"Ooh, how about the losers do the winner's chores for a week? Like laundry and cleaning the bathroom? Washing their car?"

"That works for me, Auz?"

"Yeah, okay. I still think spanking is a good idea though, just for the record," he maintains.

"Noted. Shake on it?" Jackson asks.

"Wait. How long do we get to hide our item?" I submit.

"Good catch, how 'bout twenty-four hours?" Austin suggests.

"Sounds good."

"I'm in."

"Okay, let's shake." We each shake with the other two. Although in all reality this is a game between them and me. But I like the illusion that I'm against each of them separately.

"Time starts now. Let's just say seven. Your item needs to be hidden by 7pm tomorrow. Then the game starts, and you have until 7pm, Tuesday night to find it, or you get a clue. Okay?" He gives my hand another shake and I shake with Austin again for good measure. I know exactly where I'm going to hide the little motorcycle, and I wonder where they'll hide the coin.

"Do you want to walk down the block and get some food?" I ask since I didn't have anything for dinner yet.

"Sure," Jackson agrees, Austin nods.

Sawyer is watching us from the top step, and he looks worried I forgot about him. I climb the stairs with my boyfriends in tow and make sure Sawyer has a meal fit for a king, before we leave for dinner.

CHAPTER TWENTY-SEVEN

After a long day at school and a short shift at work, I was prepared with my item hidden when we passed the witching hour of 7pm. I was less successful locating a clue at school for Kunal's project. Aiden and Wyatt are still stuck in the game, and I gave in and gave them a good hint so we can work on the next clue together.

The remodel in my BASIL passed inspection and the guys can get the bulk of the work done now, including the boring beneath the floor for the drain and plumbing. Colby broke down the floorplans for the lair and he wants me to study them carefully. He says the chart of Voldemort's routines is about seventy percent done and will be complete before my birthday, yet another thing I need to learn inside and out.

Despite my best efforts, I have no luck finding the coin the guys hid in the first twenty-four hours. My only solace is they didn't find the motorcycle either. When the first twenty-four hours comes to an end, we each have to give a clue.

Since they were already here, we discuss it in the dining area of my little kitchen. I brought home chicken from the Cantina for dinner, so I pulled together some mac and cheese and opened a can of rolls to bake in the oven. Now that we're seated and dinner is ready, time is up, and we're all needing a clue. I realize this has been another long day for all of us. But I still feel that warm electric feeling in my chest, that little thrill of excitement in my stomach, and a twinge of arousal in my panties. The feelings I refuse to name despite their constant presence.

Smiling I ask the question, "I give up, what's the clue?" Austin shoves a big bite of food in his mouth and Jackson takes a sip of his sweet tea. I wait patiently.

"It's in a place you won't want to search. How about yours?"

I chew on my lip, "It's in a place you won't want to search." Their eyes instantly snap to mine, squinting while they examine me.

"I'm going to die laughing if we hid both of our items in the same place," Austin states skeptically.

"I can't imagine we did. I feel like we would've found the other item while hiding ours, right?"

"Seems like. I guess we'll find out when we meet tomorrow."

"What happens if we both find the items?" I ask.

"If you find it, text us right away so we know the exact time. Whoever finds it first wins. Does that work?"

"Yeah. Okay."

"Sounds right." Jackson adds.

"I'm glad I don't have work tomorrow maybe I'll be able to find it. Of course, I need to search campus for the next clue in my project too."

"We have a short day tomorrow; we're planning to get here after lunch and work on the BASIL. We're going to bring the auger so we can get the drain and plumbing runs installed," Jackson explains.

"Do you care if we pull the trailer inside when we're finished? We can't leave it on the street, somebody will steal it," Austin states.

"I don't care, will it fit?"

"Yeah. I'll back it in and disconnect it. The truck can stay in the alley."

"Oh, that should work. Have I told you how much I appreciate your work on my warehouse?"

"You have, but we don't mind extra appreciation," he raises his eyebrows a few times suggestively, its more comical than sexy.

"Especially if it's the naked kind," my pervy boyfriend adds. He's lucky it comes off as cute and endearing, not lewd and creepy.

Changing the subject, I fill them in on Colby's progress. I know they have questions that they haven't asked. I can only assume they don't want to seem overbearing. As long as they don't try to talk me out of it, I'm fine with constructive discussion.

"What do you want to ask?"

"Who says we want to ask anything?" Jackson counters.

"I can tell, the looks on your faces when I talk about my plans. You're trying not to ask a question. Please ask me. I'm okay with helpful input." I watch as they silently communicate and decide to ask me a question. Pretty soon I might be capable of interpreting all of their conversations.

"You haven't said how you plan to catch him, just that you're going to do it. Do you have a step-by-step plan for the capture of Voldemort?" Jackson inquires.

"I don't have all of the details yet. I won't until I know exactly where he'll be when I'm ready to collect him."

"What's the general plan? Are you entering his house?" Austin goes next.

"Yes. His staff is off on Sunday's. He has a routine he follows most Sunday's. We're working on nailing down every minute of his day. I plan to get into his lair and lure him as close to an exit as possible, before I... render him unconscious." I watch their faces carefully, looking for anything negative.

"So, you plan to enter his, lair, alone and use yourself as some sort of bait in hopes you can get him in a position to render him unconscious? Then what? How does he get here and into your killer room?" Jackson asks.

"I plan to render him unconscious in a way that I can get him into a vehicle. Once we're here, I can get him onto a cart or other transport device, and wheel him into my BASIL. I guess I'll be bait technically, but my plan doesn't involve any skimpy clothing or seduction. More like, I'm a new parishioner and I need advice or assistance with something urgently. I haven't come up with the exact scenario yet."

"Maybe, a better way to ask is, what can we do to help you collect him?" Austin suggests.

"Yeah, that is better. What he said," Jackson concurs.

"Are you sure you want to be involved? I don't want you at risk."

"We don't want you at risk. Especially your safety. If we can help, we'll be able to have your back, just in case. Don't forget we have our own vengeance to deliver," Jackson states.

Thinking out loud, I run through it, "It would help if you guys could be there to help keep watch and load him up. Maybe we could get a van, you guys could hide in there, and come out when I need you. If I had some muscle to get his fat ass into the van, that would be faster than me struggling to load him into a trunk. You could help me clean up the scene too. Okay. You can help."

"That's it? No argument? No questions for us? You just trust us?" Austin asks incredulously.

"Yeah." I shrug, confused by his shock.

"You're amazing. Do you realize how incredible you are? How perfect?" Austin leaves his seat and pulls me up into a hug.

"Baby, you're the most, the best, ahhh! I can't even come up with words! You're just...I love you." He takes my face in his hands and kisses me, his tongue pushes into my mouth and his hands return to my waist as he kisses me like I'm the answer to his prayers. I'm instantly filled with bright fireworks that spark from my heart through all of my veins. The familiar warmth in my chest blossoms into an electrical current that travels across all of my nerve endings, filling each one with a tingle that raises goosebumps on my skin. I want to shout with joy. I can feel myself trembling with excitement and happiness. I've never felt like this before and suddenly, I want to lock my arms around him and never let him go. Fuck that, I want to lock my arms around his neck and my legs around his waist and I never want to stop kissing him. We're clawing at each other, kissing so hard and fast. His hands squeeze me tight, find my ass and lift me. I don't even hesitate to wrap myself around him exactly the way I want.

My hands trace his face, his neck, shoulders, and I squeeze him as close as I can get. It's not enough. I let go and tear my shirt over my head. I want to feel his skin with mine. He carries me away and when I notice where we are, it's my bedroom.

He places me onto the bed, and I take the opportunity to lift his shirt. Grabbing the back of his collar, he rips it over his head. Then kisses my face, my neck. I'm desperate for him to touch me everywhere. He figures out my bra and tosses it behind him. Then he lays me back on my bed and kisses my chest. His hands squeeze my breasts, and he gently pinches my firm nipples. A jolt of energy goes directly into my center, and I can feel the arousal building there.

Still needing more, I pull him on top of me and grind my pussy against his tented jeans. I can feel his very hard cock pressing against me and it sends shivers of pleasure through me. He's happily lost in my bosom, but something isn't right.

I search for the missing piece and find him watching from the doorway. His lips are clenched between his teeth and his arms are crossed in a way that makes me think he's holding himself back. I need him. I want him as much as I want Austin. I love him as much as I love Austin. Facing facts at last, I know in my heart of hearts, the feelings that have been growing inside me are love for these two men. I can't be without the other half of my heart for a moment longer.

"Jackson, please..."

Austin shifts us so he's on the bed and I'm on his lap. Somehow his hands are still squeezing my breasts and my hips, I think he's part octopus. I watch Jackson remove his shirt, exposing his cut pecs and defined abs making my mouth water. My eyes lick his nipples and his tattoos while he approaches. When he's close enough, I pull him towards me with his beltloops. He lifts my face to look into my eyes with gentle hands under my jaw. His thumb traces over my bottom lip while his amber eyes peer into my blackened essence. Somehow, he finds the barest sliver of a glowing ember left there and draws it out. I feel his glimmering soul intertwine with my tainted one. It lifts mine into the light just enough to allow a deep purple hue to overtake the darkness. He makes me a better person, redeemable.

"I love you, Violet," Jackson proclaims in a gruff whisper before he presses a kiss to my mouth that sends a surge of lightning down my throat rendering me speechless. But his tongue in my mouth would prevent me from speaking anyway. I close my eyes and ride the flood of adrenaline and the rush of emotion that fills me to bursting.

My pants disappear and strong fingers find my needy places. Lips suck on my pinkest skin, driving me closer and closer to the edge of a cliff. I need to touch them. I want to kiss them, everywhere.

"Please!" I whine. Filled with a blinding need.

"Please what, baby? What do you need?"

"You. I need my mouth on you, please!"

"Okay, baby. Okay. Come here."

His strong hands lift me and shift me around so I'm facing the opposite way. He pulls my pussy down over his mouth and he uses his tongue in the most amazing way. I grind down on his mouth and lift myself up so I can use my hands.

I unhook Jackson's pants and pull at them until his very hard cock springs into my face. He watches me carefully as I reach out to touch him. They haven't let me touch them before and I want to savor the moment. I run my finger through the clear liquid that leaks from the tip. I swirl it around the head and enjoy the slick feeling. I want to taste it and I lean forward and let my tongue connect with its swollen end. He sucks in a breath between his teeth. His eyes fall half closed and he bites his lip again.

I circle my tongue around his tip and his erection jerks against it. I use my hands to unbuckle Austin's jeans, I yank on them, and he lifts his hips to help me move them down his thighs. He adds a second finger inside me and moves it to stretch me while he rubs the pad of a finger along the spot that makes me squirm.

I begin to fall over the cliff, and I scream, as a rush of liquid spills from me while my eyes close and shooting stars make their way across the inside of my lids. I take a penis in each hand and stroke them while I writhe on Austin's tongue. He gently rubs every last sensation from my walls while they throb in pleasure.

When I'm able to breathe again, I slide my lips over Austin's engorged head and move my tongue around the ridge of his sensitive end. I continue to stroke Jackson and Austin with my hands. When I begin to come down from the climax Austin so easily orchestrated, he softly licks at me. I alternate between them both, kissing, licking, sucking, and stroking. Austin makes a sound that I think means he's reaching his release, so I concentrate my focus on his happy ending. I'm rewarded for my efforts when his balls tighten and he swells even larger, exploding into my mouth. I press his cock as far as I can down my throat, swallowing everything he gives me.

When Austin is finished, I turn my attention to Jackson. I use both hands stroking his shaft and softly squeezing his balls while I move my tongue around his head and try my best to swallow his cock. He puts his hands on my head and holds me where he needs me while he fucks my mouth. In a few more thrusts he hits the back of my throat and his come bursts from him, flooding down as I swallow it all.

My own release is building again and as I finish swallowing Jackson's hot cum, I begin to grind on Austin's mouth. His fingers and tongue work their magic and I scream out as another orgasm leaves me breathless. I think I collapse as I finish, the next thing I'm aware of is Jackson softly kissing my shoulder on one side of me while Austin gently rubs my chest and places soft kisses on my cheek and temple.

We're all naked on my bed and I feel fantastic. Like all is right in the world. I can't keep my eyes open and it's difficult to find words that make any sense. I want to thank them. I want to shout from the rooftop.

"I love you," leaves me in a rasp.

CHAPTER TWENTY-EIGHT

Meooow!

One eye pries open in search of Sawyer. His face is about five inches from mine, when he sees me move, he presses his face into my neck and starts purring. My hands stretch above me, and Sawyer takes full advantage, curling further into my neck. Reaching out my hand I find the bed empty next to me. Lifting my head to survey the mattress I find nobody but me and Sawyer. My heart sinks. I hate it when they're not here.

After a few more kitty butt scratches I climb from my warm sheets and look around. I found an insulated cup on the nightstand with a note leaned against it.

Babe- We had to be at work early so we could get back early. We didn't want to wake you. See you later beautiful. I love you, Jax.

I love you too-Austin

PS- don't forget to look for the coin! -Austen

A smile stretches across my face as I recall the events from last night. I can still feel their kisses on my lips and their touches on my skin. That sweet feeling of joy surges through me, and I know it's going to be a good day.

"Come on cutie, let's get some breakfast before we look for the coin."

Sawyer and I both wolf down a quick meal. Even after taking a shower, I still have a good forty-five minutes before I need to leave for class. All through my time in the bathroom and eating breakfast, I think about where the coin could be. A place I wouldn't want to search covers lots of great hiding spots. I check inside the toilet tank, the garbage cans, the thing in the fridge that's been there since I first moved in... I don't even remember what it was anymore. No coin, but it's been thrown away now, so I'm still a winner.

I check all the shoes in my closet and then every cabinet in the kitchen. I spot my bookshelves and have a terrible thought. What if they put it in a book? I don't want to search every single book, dammit that's what they said isn't it? I won't want to search there. I'm almost out of time, but I can't leave without checking. I start pulling books two at a time and shaking them before I put them right back on the shelf.

Ten minutes late, and still no coin. I rush off to class. After barely staying awake through Digital Logic, I'm happy to have CPF1 with Aiden.

"We finally finished the game!" Aiden announces.

"Thank God! I'm stuck on the next clue. What do you think it means?"

"We think it means the clue is on campus. What do you think?" Aiden offers.

"I think it's in the Student Center, but I haven't found anything. I think it's going to be one of those things where it's right in front of your face and when you figure it out, you're going to face palm, hard."

"Sounds right. Let's try to look around at lunch, okay?" Aiden adds.

"Yeah. Maybe we can split up or something?" I posit.

"Sure, we'll figure it out." By the time we finish up our lab, I'm hungry and looking forward to a gooey slice of pizza.

Wyatt and Bug join us at our table. We all opted for pizza, so we have two pies to share. I'm not sure why they got so much, I only plan to eat two slices. I scan the room while I chew, looking for anything that shouldn't be there or seems out of place. Nothing catches my eye.

"I'm going to be ready for that experiment this weekend, do you think that'll be okay with your boss?" Bug asks.

"Probably, give me your number. I'll ask tomorrow and let you know."

"Thanks, I appreciate it."

"Don't worry, I'll be cashing in that favor," I reply gracing him with a sinister smile. In our strategy discussion about Kunal's project, we decided to split up and each search a separate section of the Student Hub. My assignment includes the ladies rest room, conveniently. I don't discover any long-lost clues, but I read a few choice limericks.

As part of my section, I need to check the Campus Spirit shop. It's an open front little store that doesn't carry much selection. Mostly mugs and t-shirts, with the school's name or mascot emblazoned across them. The bookstore has everything, this shop is geared towards impulse buys of candy and gifts.

"Hi, this may sound dumb, but is there a clue in this shop?"

"What?" The skinny, man-bunned, pot head, clerk asks.

"I need to find a clue for a computer class and the map shows the Student Center as the location of the next clue, so I'm checking everything in here. Anything around that might be a clue?"

"Nah, bro. But you can check whatever you want."

"Thanks, bro." He nods and goes back to whatever he's doing on his phone without noticing my sarcasm.

I stand in the middle of the room and look carefully at the walls, shelves, floor, even the ceiling. Almost ready to give up, I spot a large letter "R" above the lighted exit sign over the back door. Moving in to get a closer look, I can see it's been stuck there with tape or something. It's not painted there. It doesn't seem connected to anything else in the room. I took a picture of it and finish scanning the rest of the walls. There's nothing else in the shop, but when I step out of the store, I notice an "8" over another exit sign. I took a picture of it too and I'm getting excited now. It feels like it might actually be something.

"Hey, did you find anything?" Aiden asks.

"Maybe, what do you think?" I show him my phone and swipe between the photos.

"Looks like something. I'll text Wyatt, maybe we can take a quick look around for more before we have to get to our next class."

His phone chimes, "He's on his way."

"Guys! I think you're right. Look after your text I looked around and found this one," Wyatt holds out his phone to show us a picture of the letter "S".

"Let's split up, Violet got the spirit shop and the wall outside the store. Where did you get yours," Aiden asks Wyatt.

"In the hallway right outside the men's bathroom. I'll go this way, Aiden you go that way, and Violet, check the ladies' room and the kitchen. We'll meet back here in a few minutes, okay?" Wyatt points out our assignments.

"Okay." I agree.

"Yup." Aiden confirms.

We take off to our assigned areas, I lose sight of them as I focus on the walls, particularly near any exit signs. When I find the rest room I'm encouraged to spot the letter, "T" in the hallway. I enter the restroom to check there as well, nothing. I make my way to the kitchen door. When I knock a tall thin girl opens it, her hair is a rainbow of colors and she has a pierced nose, eyebrow, and I don't know how many earrings.

"Hey, what's up?"

"Hi. I'm Violet, I'm a computer sciences major, and I have a project that has me looking for clues. Would it be possible for me to take a quick pass through the kitchen? Just to see if there's anything in there?"

She looks over her shoulder, then back at me, "Yeah, okay. Just act like you belong and don't touch anything. There's another door on the far side where you can exit. If anyone asks, you never talked to me, cool?"

"Thanks! Yeah, I've got it. You might be helping me pass my final." I offer her a grateful smile.

She nods and steps aside, allowing me entry. After a few steps I realized I need to check above the door I just walked through. When I spin around, I'm rewarded with a "2" over the door. I snap a quick photo and move on. I never realized all the different food vendors shared this huge common space. From here I could enter the small kitchen area of any of the food court restaurants. There's an exit that goes directly outside, my guess is that's where the dumpsters are located, and lucky me, a "4" is taped above the double doors. I don't find another clue until I reach the door the pierced girl described. Once again, my luck holds, and I spy a "G" taped above the lighted sign. I snap one last photo and make my way to our meeting spot. Wyatt waves at me excitedly from across the room. Aiden gets there at the same time as me. We're all smiling like idiots, it's a good sign.

"I found U, O, G, L," Wyatt offers.

"I got A, C, E. How about you?" They both look at me.

"T, 2, 4, S, G, 8, 4, and the R, I found originally. Oh, there's two G's. Hang on...okay. I think I've got it. GO 2 STARG8 4 CLUE. Does that seem right?" I ask looking between them. Both of their mouths are hanging open and their eyes are wide. They're just staring at me and it's creeping me out.

"What?"

Wyatt recovers first, "How the fuck did you do that?"

"Do what?" I asked, perplexed.

"How did you solve the puzzle so fast? It took you like thirty seconds. I figured we'd be on the phone all night trying to decipher it, and you just, like magically pulled it out of your ass."

"Damn, Violet, I knew you were smart, but you're like genius smart," Aiden adds. They both continue to stare at me like I'm a purple unicorn. I shrug.

"We need to get to class, can we finish this chat later?"

I begin walking in the direction of the computer sciences building. They follow after me and I don't slow down. I don't want to talk about my intelligence, and I don't want them to look at me like I'm a freak. If I had thought about it, I might have waited to figure it out, I was just excited to finally have a clue.

When I sit down in class, my phone vibrates with a text.

Aiden: Will you please text us the clue?

Me: GO 2 STARG8 4 CLUE

Aiden: Thx

Wyatt: Thx we still need to figure out what to do next.

Me: Yeah, I'll try to work on it tonight, but I have plans

Wyatt: Work or boyfriends?

Me: Mind your business plz

*Wyatt: *lol emoji* that means boyfriends.*

Me: dick!

Wyatt: that's what I'm saying.

Me: grow up or I'm blocking you

*Wyatt: *smirk emoji**

*Me: *eye roll emoji**

After class they walked me to the parking lot and thankfully don't say anything about the clue except that we need to figure out what to do with it. I have an idea, but I don't say anything. I've got to keep from showing my cards again. People treat me differently when they find out I'm smart, my history of abuse, and when they find out I've been in a mental health facility. Usually, I carefully guard all of my secrets.

On the ride home I relax and the tension from the events at school flies away in the breeze flowing over my skin. The sun is shining and it's one of those perfectly sunny days, even though it's technically fall, the seasons never quite make it to Florida. If I wasn't moving, I'd be sweating in the heat, at sixty miles per hour the heat can't catch me.

When I turn onto my street, I can see Austin's work truck parked on the sidewalk. They must be using the equipment to bore under the BASIL. I've never seen a machine do that before and I'm interested to see it in action. I pull down the alley and park my bike inside. I run upstairs to drop off my backpack and check on Sawyer. He's happily playing with a new toy. Awww, the guys must've brought it for him. They're the best, and my heart pounds with that familiar feeling.

I make a pit stop in the restroom and find kitty litter flung out of his litter box and across the floor. I make quick work of cleaning it up and decide I may as well empty his litter box while I'm at it. When I scoop out a particularly large clump of litter, I spot something shiny in the bottom of the box. Using the scooper, I dig down and find a plastic bag. Inside is the golden coin I've been looking for. Of course! Now their clue makes perfect sense. How funny we both hid our items in the bathroom.

I decide to go downstairs and tell them I found it, instead of texting them. I pull on a pair of nylon gloves and remove the bag, I empty it into the sink and toss the baggie with the used litter. I refill the box with fresh litter and dispose of the old litter. I carry the kitchen trash out to the dumpster in the alley as well.

Once I get washed up and clean the coin, yeah it was in a baggie, but gross, I place it in my pocket and go searching for the guys. They're not inside when I search BASIL. I follow the sounds to the front of the building. They're wearing hardhats, reflective vests, hearing protection, and safety glasses. They look like real construction workers and it's making my insides flutter. They're so incredibly handsome on any given day, but the ruggedness of their work clothes is doing something for me and my mouth waters. I lean against the wall and watch them work, feeling their strong hands on me from last night. When they move their arms to lift the equipment, their muscles bulge and ripple beneath their tan and tattooed skin. Mmmm, it makes my nipples perk up into hard points. I distantly feel my teeth chew on my lip and my tongue aches to lick the sweat from their chests.

Austin notices me and he smiles and waves, the boring machine is too loud to communicate verbally. He points to his wrist and holds up five fingers, I think he means they'll be done in five minutes. I nod my understanding. He taps Jackson's elbow and uses his head to point towards me. Jackson meets my eyes and a smile breaks across his strong jaw. His straight white teeth gleam in my direction. I wave like an excited contestant on a game show. I can tell he's laughing at my antics. I sigh, they're so fucking hot it's causing arousal to flood my panties, and I'm not embarrassed about it. Anyone would have the same reaction.

I don't take my eyes off them the whole time I wait for them to finish. When they have the machine put back to its starting position, they finally shut it down. The sudden quiet is loud, and the street noise comes rushing back to my ears. I can hear a distant siren and the breeze blowing through the trees along the street. I approach them and Jackson wraps me in his embrace planting a firm kiss on my lips.

"Hey babe! We got your boring work done. We'll get the drain installed out here first and then get the plumbing connected. Look in this box, see right there? That's where your drain will connect with the sewer pipes that go under the street right here." He points to the landscaping just beyond the sidewalk. I'm so impressed. Not that I doubted they know what they're doing but seeing them do the work is very cool.

"Hi baby, did you have a good day?" Austin asks as he places a soft kiss on my mouth and hugs my waist then releases me.

"Yeah, we finally found those clues and now I'll be able to move to the next section of my project. It looks like you guys are getting a lot done here. I'm very impressed."

"Yeah, we're experts. It's no problem little lady, we'll take care of all your needs," he gives me a cheesy grin, shifting his eyebrows up and down, I can't help laughing.

"I hope so. Sawyer showed me the toy you brought for him. Thank you, he's very happy."

"We just saw it at the store and thought he'd like it. We're gonna get the drain hooked up, then we'll be inside."

"Can I do anything to help?"

"Would it be inappropriate to ask you to bring us something to drink?" Austin asks.

"I don't get offended by stuff like that, and you can always ask me for what you want," I try for a seductive smile hoping he'll catch my flirtation. He catches it and reels me in, he squeezes me tight and puts his lips against my ear.

"Baby, you're going to make me not want to finish working. You can't say stuff like that when we're not in a place where I can rip off your clothes."

I gasp, I might be panting at the thought of him ripping off my clothes and pressing me against the wall while he ravages me. He squeezes my ass and sends me in the direction of the door presumably so I can get a cool drink for them. I happily hum while I pour them each a big Stanley cup of iced sweet tea. The cups were a gift from Harmony, and it dawns on me I haven't spoken to her in a while. I need to make it a point to check in with her. I wonder how Max is doing. I hope he's very happy, especially since his father disappeared. Nobody knows what happened to the guy, wink-wink, but rumors abound that he stole something from someone and skipped town, or they found him.

I deliver cold drinks to my hot guys and hang around watching them work. Once they finish with the drain connection, Austin drives the trailer into the warehouse and disconnects the hitch from the truck. Jackson closes the big door and pounces on me. He lifts me up by my ass and holds me close while he kisses me like he means it.

"We brought dinner too. It just needs to go in the oven. Mom sent it with Austin; it's her famous meatloaf and potatoes."

"That sounds amazing. I'll have to call and thank her."

"She'll love that." He releases me and we climb the stairs. I preheat the oven, and he exits for a quick shower. Austin comes in and is pleased to find the oven heating.

"Mom said to tell you hello. She wants us to come over this weekend."

"Okay. We can definitely do that, I'm off on Saturday."

"Great. What's up man?" I turn to find Jackson wearing only a towel. Tilting my head, I try to figure out what's wrong, his face is twisted in confusion.

"Did you change the litter box?" he asks me. Ah, I understand now.

"Yeah. Why?" I keep my composure like a Broadway star.

"Did you throw out the old litter?"

"Of course, why would I keep it?"

"Where is it?"

"Ummm, the dumpster. Why? What's wrong?" I feign innocence. He and Austin have a silent conference, and I wait, maintaining my poker face, for just the right moment to reveal my prize.

Austin turns to me, "Do you know which bag it was in? Where you put it exactly?"

"No, I chucked it into the dumpster, I didn't stick around to see where it landed. Why? What's the problem?"

He looks at the ceiling, "We may have hidden our coin in the litter box."

"You mean this coin?" I whip it out of my pocket and hold it up between two fingers so they can see it clearly.

"Thank fuck!" Jackson exclaims. He approaches and Austin takes the coin, while Jackson hugs me.

"Wait a minute, why didn't you tell us you found it?" Jackson holds me at arms-length and scans my face.

"I went outside to tell you, but it was too loud. Then I kind of forgot about it," I shrug with feigned virtue, and look around the room at everything but him.

"Because you were busy drooling?"

"You noticed that, huh?"

"You may not realize it, but when you're turned on, your cheeks get red. Your eyes get kinda glassy, and your nipples look like they're gonna rip out of your shirt," Austin explains.

"Yeah, and you chew on your lip and rub your legs together. We'd have to be blind not to notice, babe."

"I see, well I'm not sorry. I'm not embarrassed either. I'm very attracted to you both and you're hot as shit in your work clothes." I shrug, and I'm out of words.

"No need to apologize for that. Plus, I think you're sexy as hell when you're turned on," Austin adds.

"It's sexy as fuck, babe," Jackson nods in agreement.

"So, I guess I win, huh?" They look at each other.

Then Austin answers, "Yeah. You didn't hide the motorcycle in the litter box?"

"No. I think you should keep looking, though. Do you want a hint?"

"Okay. What happens if we find it before the deadline?"

"You have sixty-four minutes, and if you find it, I'll increase naked time back to an hour. Does that work?"

"Sounds good to me. Jax, hurry up with your shower. We need to search high and low." While Jackson takes a quick shower, I swear he's back in about six minutes, Austin and I get dinner in the oven and make a Cesar salad.

Once Jackson returns, I give them a hint, "It's below the knee, and applies only to me."

"Well, that narrows it down, everything in here is yours."

"True but knowing it's below the knee is a big help. Plus, don't forget the other hint."

"Yeah, it's where we won't want to search. Which was our hint for the litter box. Hmmm." They glance around the room in thought. Jackson rubs his beard; he looks like that thinking statue. Austin starts looking through the bottom cabinets. Jackson goes down the hall and I see him turn into my bedroom. This is funny but I want them to find it, maybe I should apply the hot or cold method to help them out.

When Austin makes his way into the bathroom, I hold my breath hoping he'll check the right place. I hear him dump out the dirty clothes hamper.

"Dammit!"

I hear the cabinet open, and I get excited thinking he has to find it, unfortunately the cabinet closes a minute later. He exits the bathroom and joins Jackson in my room. I sneak to my door to see if I can spy on them. Austin is on the floor taking things from under the bed. I have some plastic boxes with my sparse winter wardrobe in them under there, and he's opening each one. This is brutal, I'm going to have to give them some direction. Jackson is on the floor in front of the closet now, he's shaking out every shoe. Thankfully I don't have that many, but this is going to take forever.

I tiptoe back to the living room and call out, "Forty minutes left! It's not in my room!"

Austin runs out to me, "Don't cheat and tell us baby." He holds my shoulders and kisses me before he runs off to the kitchen. I face palm.

Jackson goes into the bathroom and my hope resurfaces. I hear things being moved around in the bathroom cabinet, Austin starts making too much noise in the kitchen and I can't hear anything more from my bathroom.

"I got it!!" Jackson shouts.

Stopping to ask, "What did he say?" Austin waits for my answer.

"He said he found it; you're done."

"Man, I wanted to find it. Oh well, next best thing, right?"

"Most definitely."

"So... where was it?"

Jackson joins us with a tampon box in his hand. He lifts it up while he looks into my eyes. His brows lift as if in question. I offer him a smile; I'm relieved he found it. But I know my time is limited, they'll want their reward right away. Austin takes the tampon box from Jackson; he holds it up spilling the contents onto the kitchen counter. Among the colorful plastic packages is one small black motorcycle.

Austin smiles salaciously, "What time is it?"

"Time for you to get an hour of naked. After we eat though, I'm starving."

The timer sounds and it couldn't be better timing. We collect our meal and make our way to the table. Jackson pulls me onto his lap, and we eat the delicious dinner they brought from Angie, and all is well in my little apartment. We talk about plans for our date that I get to decide for my win. Then we agree to a new game, a scavenger hunt of sorts. We're each going to come up with some clues, some things the others need to find, and a reward. Even though they'll technically be a team, and not searching for each other's clues, I'll make some clues solely for each of them and some for them together. I'll come up with ten total and they'll come up with five for me.

I'm not sure why it fills me with excitement to play games with them. I love the hunt, and I love them; it just seems perfect to combine the two. They seem just as interested in the game as me, in fact, I think it was Jackson who suggested this new adventure. There's no time limit for this scavenger hunt. It's just a race, whoever collects all of their clues and items first, wins. The prize? A trip! The winner gets to choose where the three of us will take a vacation. I have a week off school at the end of the semester, and Austin and Jackson are both owed two weeks of paid vacation. We're all going to put in for time off tomorrow. It's great timing because it'll be a few weeks after my birthday and the Voldemort situation should be resolved by then. Anticipation forms a smile across my face.

CHAPTER TWENTY-NINE

"I'm not saying it doesn't qualify, I'm just saying it's not what I had in mind."

"I don't see how it's a problem. The clue said I had to find a dog statue, and this is a dog statue. Not to mention, it was in the thrift shop. I followed exactly what my scroll said."

Shaking his head, Austin argues, "Dude, come on, that's a piece from a Monopoly game, it's not a statue."

"Auz, you're not the judge, Violet is, and she already said it's a dog statue. That means I've got four of my clues finished!"

I can't help laughing, "He's right. Sorry, he's in the lead. We're just going to have to try harder and catch up to him."

"But you guys didn't accept my first dinosaur, I had to find another one! It's not fair to say a tiny metal piece from Monopoly passes as a dog statue when my dinosaur picture didn't count as a dinosaur."

"Austin, sweetie, you drew a dinosaur with a red crayon on a piece of notebook paper. Your clue said you had to find a fossil from a real dinosaur, it's hardly the same thing. Now quit whining and get dressed." He pouts and stomps off mumbling under his breath. I can't help chuckling at his antics, he's very entertaining. Jackson is pleased as pie with his first place find. I need to spend some time thinking in depth about my clue, but right now we're all focused on catching a monster.

It's finally time to spring our trap for Voldemort. Over the last few weeks, I've been attending mass right under his pointy nose. I've worn a disguise, not that he would recognize me, but just to be safe. I've acted like an innocent young lady seeking spiritual guidance. I've cried at emotional sermons and behaved as if I'm having a crisis of some sort. Last week, he showed interest. Today, he offered to counsel me, privately. Tonight, I'm going to accept. He gave me his private number; I'm going to call hysterically and in need of urgent counseling.

We've gone over the plan again and again, we all know our rolls, our placement, and even the contingency plans inside and out. Colby is ready, and he's broken into Voldemort's security system and has control of the alarms and cameras. We'll each be wearing a camera and communication devices Colby was able to put together for us. If everything goes right, we'll have Voldemort in my freshly remodeled BASIL by midnight.

I feel my face spread into a large and evil grin, so much so the Joker would be envious. I wonder if I'm capable of an evil laugh. I would try it out if I was alone. We're at Austin's house, it's our first staging area, and from here we'll go to the warehouse in the van we bought. It looks like a thousand other work vans on the road at any given moment. I'll leave my SUV here so the van will easily fit inside the warehouse, making it perfect for loading and unloading without any unwanted cameras or eyes watching us.

When Austin returns, he's wearing black tactical pants and a long sleeve moisture wicking shirt with extra pockets. Jackson is dressed the same with a cap on his head. I haven't put on my disguise yet, but I'll be in a sweet and innocent looking dress that has special hidden pockets to contain my blades. I have a special sheath for *David Bowie.* He'll be strapped to my thigh. My dark wig will hide my blonde and blue hair, and my shoes will be simple white sneakers, especially designed for climbing, just in case.

When we're all ready, and the van is loaded, we climb in and make our way to my warehouse. I'm excited, not nervous, but I wonder if they're doing all right.

"Are you nervous?"

They both say, "No."

Austin's driving so I focus on Jackson, "Are you worried about anything? Any part of the plan bothering you?"

"No, I think it's solid. The only possible snag would be if someone unexpected is there. As long as he follows his regular routine, and nobody but you surprises him, I think we're golden."

"Good. Are you okay with the new nine? Does it feel comfortable now?"

"Babe, I promise, I'm good. It felt great at the range yesterday, it's just barely lighter than my other one and I think it's more accurate. Everything is set, we're going to be in and out in no time."

"Okay. I'm excited, but a little nervous. At least the time I've spent near him at church has helped keep me from gagging in his presence. I just worry I'll freeze or something."

"You won't. You're all grown up now. He has no power over you. You're a badass warrior, remember?"

"Yeah, it's just that tiny *what if* that pokes the back of your brain, you know?"

"I know, that's why you'll have us right outside and Colby with us in your ear. You're gonna be great."

"I love you," I kiss him on the cheek because my seatbelt won't allow me any closer.

"I love you too, beautiful."

"I love you too!" Austin adds from up front.

"I love you too Austin."

When we get to the warehouse, I use the remote to open the door and we pulled inside. They go to the BASIL, and I go upstairs to get dressed. Sawyer follows me into the bedroom and perches on the bed to watch me. I pull on some shorts just to feel slightly less vulnerable. Then my dress; it's blue with little pink flowers. I carefully strap *David Bowie* to my thigh and double check he's not visible in the mirror.

My throwing knives go into their special pockets, the dress hugs my body until the skirt flares a little. The blades aren't heavy enough to impede the flow of the fabric. But the pockets are designed to keep them from bunching or shifting, you would never know they're there. I wish I could bring my sword, but since I have to see him first, without looking like I'm there to attack him, that won't work.

I apply a small amount of natural makeup, just enough to look feminine and virtuous. My wig goes on last; it hangs past my shoulders, so it covers the earpiece easily. I check myself in the mirror from every angle. I can't spot anything amiss with my weapons or the little bud in my ear. We'll do a comms check before I place the call to Voldemort.

When I'm ready, I feed Sawyer who meows appreciatively, then I take a seat on my new sofa. I finally caved in and bought one. It's a nice sectional that curves into an L shape against the wall. It's a shade of dark gray that matches Sawyer almost perfectly. I figure it's the best way to avoid it looking like it's covered in cat hair all the time. It's some type of hybrid between leather and faux leather. It was affordable, my favorite feature.

Until my grandmother Joyce decides to drop her lawsuit, I still need to be thrifty with my finances. The court was able to release funds for school, but that's it for now. There's a possibility when I turn eighteen, she'll lose her rights to sue me. But of course, the court has to decide that as well, and our next court date is sometime at the end of October. It's time to check in with Colby.

Me: Hey RobN, how's everything?

Colby: Perfect, everything is a go. How's your side?

Me: We're at the second staging area and I'm dressed. When they finish setting up, we'll do a comms check.

Colby: Perfect. You good VioleNt1?

Me: 10-4

Colby: Ok

"Baby, do you have any tape?" Austin asks as he enters.

I hop up and check the kitchen drawer, "I think so, will clear tape work?"

"Yeah, I just need to tape down the lid on the little toolbox. It doesn't want to stay closed. Hey, you look great."

"Thanks. Here you go." I hand him a roll in its own plastic dispenser.

"I'll be right back; Jackson is loading the last thing and then we can do our check with Colby."

"Sounds good." As soon as he exits Jackson enters. He steps towards the kitchen, then he spots me and stops in his tracks.

Staring at me he says, "Wow, you look amazing. Stand up and spin. Perfect, I can't see any blades, not even *David Bowie.*"

"Good. Are you ready to check everything with Colby?"

"Yep, just want to grab some water. Do you want anything?"

"Water sounds good, thanks."

Austin comes back and puts the tape away. Jackson hands me a cup of ice water and sits next to me. Austin joins us with his own cup of water. "Are we ready?"

Austin nods and Jackson answers, "Yeah." I press send on my phone.

"Hi, VioleNt1, are you all ready?" Colby greets.

"Ready as we can be. Should we turn them on?"

"Yeah. Put your phone down and I'll talk to you through your ear."

"Testing, can you hear me?"

"We hear you. Now the guys?"

"Yeah, put the phone down again and everyone go into another room, so you can each talk," Colby instructs. I walk into my bedroom and wait to find out if I can hear anyone.

"Can you hear me?" Austin asks. I holler from my room, "I can hear you!"

"How about me?" Jackson tries next.

"Yes! I hear you!"

"Do you want me to talk dirty baby?"

"No. Please don't, and don't call me baby," Colby responds to Austin's question. Me and Jackson laugh, I can imagine Austin's face, he's probably pouting.

"Your turn, Vi. Turn on your mic."

"Can you hear me, Colby?"

"Yep."

"Jackson?"

"Yes, ma'am."

"Austin?"

"Yeah baby, do you wanna talk dirty?"

"Sure, wash my car."

"You're no fun."

"That's not what you said last night..."

"All right, that's enough! I'm calling the comms test successful. Vi, call Voldemort and let's get this party started," Colby cuts in.

I walk back to the living room and shoot Austin a wink, then I pick up my phone, "Okay. I'm calling. I guess you'll be able to hear the call through our comms, right?"

"Yeah, as long as you guys keep everything on, I'll hear it. Good luck. You're going to be great, just be careful and remember help will be right outside."

"I know. Thanks, love you."

"You too, now go get that bastard!"

I hang up with Colby and pick up the burner phone. Voldemort is the only number in the phone. I pace back and forth for a minute and try to work myself up to sound emotional. I tap into my grief over my parents, and I avoid anything before that. I don't want to examine my past with Voldemort, even though I've been through tons of therapy, and I consider myself past the trauma, thinking about his particular brand of torture is still too difficult. He was the worst one of all the men who hurt me. He's the one who broke me. When I killed my stepfather, it was to stop Voldemort from hurting me again. I wanted the Beast to stop too, but the dark thing inside me that thrust the knife into the Beast was spurred on by Voldemort.

When I feel like I'm ready, I open the burner flip phone. Three sets of eyes follow the motion. Sawyer is on the arm of the sofa next to Austin. I think all three of them are holding their breath. I don't want to act like a desperate damsel in distress with them staring at me, so I turn my back to them and dial.

"Bishop Thorne, how may I help you?" His slimy voice answers.

"Oh, thank goodness. Hi, um…it's me, Rose, Rose Danvers, from mass? You said I should call, if I needed help?"

"Yes. Of course. How can I help you, my child?"

"I um, I need someone to talk to. I think my parents are getting a divorce. I-I heard them arguing. My f-father said I'm not his kid. Then my mom came into my room and she, she, blamed me for their argument. She said she wishes I was never born. She slapped me when I said I wish that too. She made my lip bleed. I just feel so alone. I mean, maybe it would be better if I wasn't around. You know?"

"I'm very glad you called. I think we need to discuss this in person. I can counsel you better if we're face to face about such serious matters. Do you drive, my dear?"

"Yeah. My uncle, he's in jail, he left his van here and my parents let me drive it to school. I can sneak out. Where should I meet you?" I make a sniffling sound.

"Do you have a pen?"

"No, but I can type it into my phone, hang on while I put you speaker."

"Okay, go ahead."

"Come to St. Andrew's Hall, 122 Pinewood Acres Drive."

"Got it. Can I come now? I need to get out of here."

"Yes, of course. Pull all the way up the drive, park by the entry door. I'll make certain the gate is open and the light is on for you. I'm glad you called Rose; it was the right thing to do. I believe the Lord has sent you to me and I can help you."

"Thank you so much Bishop Thorne, I'll see you soon."

"Drive safely, my dear. Goodbye."

"Goodbye."

Woosh, a large breath leaves me in a rush and I flop onto the sofa.

"Damn Babe, that was impressive. You may need to look into acting classes. I mean, shit, that was flawless."

"Yeah. That was, wow. I felt bad for poor Rose. You nailed it. What about the bloody lip though?"

"No worries," I whip out one of my throwing knives and poke my lip in a quick move, it doesn't even hurt. My blades are clean and sharp.

"Whoa! What the fuck are you doing? Why would you cut yourself?" Jackson shouts. Austin's frozen with his mouth hanging open.

I meet Jackson's frantic gaze and in my calm tone explain, "I needed a cut on my lip, I have a sharp knife, and I took care of it. Don't freak out, it was painless."

"Please promise me you'll never do that again," he pleads. Austin closes his mouth, but his eyes are wide as he watches us.

"No. If it needs to be done, I'll do it again. I can promise I won't ever wound myself fatally. I promise I'm not suicidal and I don't make a practice of self-harm. But if I need to have an injury to catch a monster, I'm going to have an injury."

"Baby, I think it just startled us, you did it so quick and without any warning. Right Jax?"

"It fucking pisses me off to see your blood dripping from a cut whether you did it yourself or not. I don't like it and I don't want you to do it again. At least let's talk about it first if it seems like something that needs to happen in the future."

"I'll agree to that," I say with a huff.

"Here," Austin hands me a tissue.

"Thanks." I dab my lip and get it to stop bleeding. It's really no big deal. Jackson grabs me and pulls me into his lap. He sits me up so I'm straddling him. He holds my hips and stares into my eyes.

"I don't want to fight with you babe, I love you. I wasn't expecting you to cut your lip with a knife like it was nothing. I don't want anyone to hurt you, even you. I'm sorry I got mad and thank you for agreeing to talk to us in the future."

"I'm sorry I didn't talk to you first. I love you too. I honestly didn't think it was anything that needed to be discussed. I promise I won't do it again without talking to you both first." I lean down and kiss him on the lips. It stings my lip a little but I kind of like it. He smacks my ass and helps me stand up. Austin hugs me and kisses my lips gently. He looks into my eyes and then kisses me again.

"I love you baby. Let's get going."

"I love you too." I give him a squeeze before letting him go. I scratch Sawyer under the chin before I follow them out the door.

We're quiet on our way to Voldemort's lair. I don't know what they're thinking about, but I'm imagining getting that fucker back to BASIL. I can't wait for him to be strapped to my shiny new metal table. It's an autopsy table with a drain. All the fluid stays on the table because of the lip around the edge and then it goes out the drain and right into my new floor drain. I can slice him any way I want, and it won't make a mess, as long as I avoid the arteries. I can feel the evil smile pulling on the fresh cut in my lip.

"How are you doing baby?"

"I'm excited, I can't wait to get that mother fucker strapped down."

"Do you have any questions? Last minute things you want us to know?"

"Nope. I feel confident in our plan. I'm going to get him comfortable with me, drug him, and call you guys in to help me get him out."

"What's your panic phrase?"

"My brother Tony."

"Don't forget to describe anything important that we can't see."

"I know. Don't worry, I've gone over all the blueprints, his habits, everything. I know every square inch of his mansion by heart. We've got this."

"Don't drink or eat anything, no matter what."

"I know." I nod as I tell them, "We're here, stay down. I love you both."

"I love you baby, you're gonna be great."

"I love you too, be careful. Don't turn your back on him." Jackson warns.

"I won't. Okay, shhh."

As I pull through the open gate, a feeling of dread comes over me. The house is on a hill and the front is brightly lit, but the darkness within seeps out of every brick. There's a palpable feeling of pure misery. I take a few deep breaths and repeat my mantra in my head a few times.

Through clenched teeth I give them one last thought, *"Are you guys ready? Let's roll!"* I read somewhere, it's what the heroes of U.S. Airways flight 93 said before they stormed the cockpit on nine-eleven. Seems appropriate for our situation.

We turned off the cab lights so the interior remains dark when I open the door. I smooth my skirt as I climb down. I take a deep breath and steel myself for the face-to-face interaction to come. I unconsciously touch the blade in my right pocket for reassurance.

Feeling as ready as I'll ever be, I make my way to the large wooden door.

I press the doorbell and roll my eyes as church bells play out inside the giant residence. I can hear footsteps echo as they approach the door. A lock clicks and the door opens inward. Voldemort smiles at me and then his eyes caress my skin while he moves them slowly over my body. I suppress a shiver of revulsion and check the gag in the back of my throat.

"Good evening, Miss Rose, please come in. Normally I would conduct this type of counseling in my office here," he gestures at a dark doorway. He continues past that room, and I follow him deeper into his lair. The air is oppressive and stale, the way I picture a dungeon. I'm surprised I can't smell any sulfur since he's the devil.

"But I thought it might be more comfortable for you if we meet in the den. It's much less formal and since it's after hours and I'm no longer in my cassock, I thought it would be more relaxed. Is that all right with you?"

"Yes, of course bishop." I note he's dressed in black with a white collar, just like a priest. He wore the same thing when I was a child, and I wonder idlily if it's his *raping outfit.* My skin breaks out in goosebumps at that thought. I touch the blade in my pocket again for reassurance.

"Here we are, please have a seat anywhere you like. May I get you a glass of something cool to drink?"

"That's so kind of you, but it's not necessary."

"Nonsense, I'll be just a moment. Please relax and make yourself comfortable." When he leaves the room, I quickly lean out the door to see which way he goes. Left, then right, he's heading to the kitchen. I quickly searched the room for hidden cameras. I don't find anything, but I can't trust it, Colby will be searching.

I whisper towards my pin containing the microphone, "No visible cameras in here. He went to the kitchen. There's two sofas and two chairs in this room. I'm going to sit in a chair. There are two walls filled with books; anything could be hidden in them. I'm going to take a closer look at them." I start at one end of the closest bookcase and look for anything suspicious while I scan the titles. Most of them are written by priests and popes, religious tomes, or examinations of religion and the bible. I don't spot any hidden cameras tucked between the books.

"Do you like to read?" I startle even though I heard him returning, I want him to think I'm vulnerable, easy prey.

"I do, but I usually read young adult fantasy books. I've only read a little of the bible, none of these other books. Have you read them all?"

"Not all, but most. Why don't you have a seat, here you are, it's my famous lemonade."

"Thank you." I sit on one of the chairs and place my drink on a coaster. I give him my full attention, but I'm looking at his shoulder, not his face. I hate his hideous face, it's the stuff of nightmares.

"Why don't you tell me about what happened today."

"My parents have been fighting since we moved here, they think I can't hear them when they're in their room. But I can hear everything when they yell. Today they didn't even try to be quiet. My dad was accusing my mom of being a tramp. But he said much worse words. He said I'm not even his kid. They had me really young. After their fight my mom was crying, and she came into my room. I tried to comfort her because she was so upset. She yelled at me that it's all my fault, that she wishes I was never born."

"My child, I'm so sorry. But I'm certain your mother doesn't actually wish that. She was upset and said something unfortunate, how could she possibly think such a thing about a lovely young lady like yourself? Go on dear." I swear the creep is rubbing his hands together like a cartoon villain. He's so disgusting.

"Well, when she said she wished I was never born, I felt so bad I yelled at her that I wish I was never born too, and maybe I should just kill myself to make her happy. She slapped me and my lip split open," I stick out my lip to emphasize the story.

"Oh my. Do you need something to clean it up? First aid?"

"No, it's fine. I already put some peroxide on it."

"How do you feel now? Do you want to harm yourself?"

"No. I never wanted to hurt myself, I just wanted to scream something hurtful back at her after what she said. I think that's why she slapped me. I think she knew I was just really angry and hurt. The thing is, I do want to run away. If it's my fault they're fighting, if I'm not his kid, if my mom wishes I was never born, why should I stay here? I want to take off and start over somewhere new."

"Let me play devil's advocate for a moment. Do you have any money?"

"Yeah, I've had a job for six months and before that I used to babysit all the time. I've got two-thousand Twenty-eight dollars."

"That is a hefty sum. Do you have transportation?"

"No. But I was thinking I could take the bus to Tennessee. My old best friend lives there and she said I could stay with her for a little while 'til I can find a job and a place."

"I see. Do your friend's parents agree with this plan?"

I look embarrassed with some effort, "They don't know yet, but they always liked me."

"How do you plan to get to and from the job you'll find?"

"Bus? Bicycle? I don't know yet. They live in town, so I think there'll be buses."

"What if your parents track you down and demand you return home?"

"I would argue that I'm not welcome. She wishes I was never born, I don't belong to dad, and she split my lip, so I don't feel safe."

"Do you want to find out if you're not your father's child?"

"I don't know. Should I?"

"It's your decision, but I would want to know."

"It's hard to decide because right now he might still be my dad, if I get a test, he might be nobody to me. I don't want to lose my father. I've always been close to him, until they started fighting." Here I use my recent grief and push tears from my eyes, and I shiver for good measure.

"You look cold, I'm so sorry this room is always cold. Why don't you sit next to me here on the sofa and maybe it'll help you stay warm." He pats the sofa next to him. Ick climbs the back of my throat and I swallow it back down. I force a small smile and move to the sofa.

"Thank you, this is warmer."

"Wonderful. Tell me Rose, have you snuck out of your house before?" I do my best to appear caught and embarrassed by it. I force my eyes down while trying to heat my cheeks, what a weird feat to attempt. I keep my face turned away from him hoping he believes I'm feeling ashamed.

"I...um, yeah. I snuck out to hang out with some friends after my curfew, and once to meet a boy. But nothing happened, we just talked for a little while. We were just on the sidewalk in front of my house."

"He didn't try to kiss you?"

Still keeping my face turned away, "N-no. We just talked."

"He didn't hold your hand?"

"He might've touched my hand, but he didn't hold it."

"Show me what you mean."

"Baby, he's starting to make a move. This is grooming behavior. Be alert, try to drug him soon." Austin's voice warns in my ear. I nod on reflex and thankfully Voldemort thinks I'm nodding at him. I use my own hands to show him how the imaginary boy touched my hand. He's not impressed.

"Did he maybe hold it like this?" He reaches out and takes my hand in his. I swear it's as if a slimy toad has taken hold of my hand and I want to jerk away from him. I fight my instincts and let him touch me, all while I repeat my mantra in my head and take a deep breath. Vomit tries to make an entrance and I close my eyes. I'm safe, I'm going to cut this bitch from limb to limb, I'm a badass warrior! Repeats in my head, it's a modified version but I like it.

"I'm not sure, Bishop. May I use the restroom?"

"Certainly, come this way," he won't let go of my hand. It's so difficult not to pull it out of his grasp. I'm going to scrub it raw in the rest room.

"Here you are my dear. Are you hungry?" He says as he opens the door for me and finally releases my poor contaminated hand.

"A little bit, if it's not too much trouble."

"No trouble at all, I'll meet you back in the den in a few moments. All right?"

"Thank you so much for being so kind."

"It's my pleasure dear." Finally, I'm out of his sight. I scrub my hands first. Once they feel somewhat less disgusting, I reach out to my guys.

"Hey, I'm okay. Just needed a break and I'm hoping to drug his drink before he returns. I can't stay here long. I love you."

"You're doing great babe. Stay strong, you got him. We love you too. Now hurry before he comes back."

"Okay, I'm out."

I leave the bathroom and listen from the hallway in the direction of the kitchen. I can hear some movement out there. I quickly remove the vial of liquid Ketamine from one of my hidden pockets. I dump the whole thing into his cup. It's clear and shouldn't alter the taste in any noticeable way. I put the empty vial in my pocket and dumped some of my own glass behind the sofa. The carpet catches it silently and I keep the cup in my hand.

"Here we go, just some cheese and crackers with fruit. I don't usually entertain without a caterer, but I had a few edible items in the kitchen." He places the tray on the table, and I lower the cup from my lips and lick them, as if I swallowed some lemonade.

"Thank you. It looks delicious. I love grapes, they're my favorite." I take a couple and try to figure out how to fake eating them on the fly. Thankfully he looks away when he reaches for his glass of drugged lemonade. I stuff the two grapes in my pocket and act like I'm chewing. I even poke my cheek with my tongue a little hoping it looks like there's a round grape in my mouth. I almost bite my tongue in the process and decide to fake swallow before I hurt myself.

"Tell me more about your relationship with your mother. Do you normally get along with her? Or have you always struggled?"

I imagine my birth mother to exude the emotion I want, "We've never gotten along. I've always been a daddy's girl, but if he's really not my father, I don't know what I'll do. Since my mother hit me, I don't want to go back there, ever. Maybe I can sleep in the van tonight while I figure out what I want to do."

"Don't be silly, I have plenty of rooms here, you're welcome to stay as long as you like. I wouldn't forgive myself if you slept in a van."

"I don't want to cause any trouble for you Bishop, you've been so, kind."

He takes another drink from his glass, and I try not to smile. He reaches out to me and places his hand on my knee, and I freeze. Every nerve ending in my body is screaming for me to run. I take a breath and try to keep my fight or flight reflex in check.

"Rose, you're a lovely girl, I'm happy to have you as my charge until you can work things out with your situation. You know, I've taken many young people under my wing and helped them reach their goals. It is my job, after all."

"I wasn't aware you helped kids in this way," I state with a hard edge and my eyes glued to his filthy hand. He squeezes my knee and my fists clench, my jaw tightens, I'm ready to rip his hand off of me and punch him until he's a bloody mess.

"Yes. I've taught many children the ways of the world, guided them, and helped them move successfully into adulthood. I'd love to teach you, Rose. I'd love to be your mentor."

"That's a very kind offer, Bishop. But I really don't want to take up your time. Perhaps I should go," I let my unease seep into my voice, and it trembles obviously. For a moment I wonder if he'll back off and let me go. I've never had this much freedom in his presence before. But I don't want to revisit those memories right now, I need to be focused and in the moment.

"No! I mean, don't be silly, it's no inconvenience. I truly want to help you. Will you let me help you, Rose?"

"I don't know what you mean."

His hand moves up my leg and then he rubs it up and down my thigh to my knee, "I want to teach you how to be a grown up so you can be successful on your own. I want to help you with spiritual counseling as well. Would you like to share a prayer now? It'll help you relax."

"Yes," I pull away from him and fall to my knees pulling my hands together in prayer.

He startles, with a delay. Hopefully the drug is taking effect. He slides closer to me while he remains on the sofa. I turn my back on him and lean on the coffee table to pray. Unfortunately, he decides it's a good time to put his hands on my shoulders. Ick! My skin crawls.

"My dear, why don't you begin the Lord's Prayer? I'll join you."

"All right. *Our Father, who art in heaven, hallowed be Thy name. Thy kingdom come...* "I zone out and recite the well-known prayer on autopilot. His hands begin to massage my shoulders and his thumb rubs against my neck. I can't control a shiver of revulsion. I've had enough of his hands on me. He needs to drink the rest of his lemonade.

When I finish, he is reciting it with me and he takes over to add, "Oh, heavenly Father, please watch over this child and guide her so that she will make the right decisions and one day she can repair her relationship with her parents. Thank you, Lord, God in heaven for all of your blessings, amen."

"Amen." I move away from his grasp and sit back on the sofa out of his reach, I hope.

He takes a drink, and I pray some more that he'll finish the glass. Thank you, God! He finishes it and I breathe out in relief. I watch him and he looks a bit disoriented and uncoordinated. He has trouble getting his glass back on the table without knocking it over and I smile.

"Where were you thinking I should sleep Bishop?" I want to see if he can string a sentence together.

"S-sleep? Oh, yes. You can sleep with me. I think you'll make a good little t-toy." He tries to focus on my face, but his eyes are mirky, and he sways, in his seat.

"You think so, huh? What if I told you I'd like to take you home to my place? I'd love to have you stay with me for a few days. My parents aren't there."

"But you don't have my toys, you're just a toy. I n-need to get you in there so I can play with you."

"In where?"

"My s-special sant-sank-ah-wary. Santavery! Dammit! Sanku-very! You'll see."

"Do you mean sanctuary?"

"Yes! Praise God! I'll show you...it's s-special."

"Where is it?"

"It's a secret. But I'll show you, we can p-play."

"Why don't you tell me where it is, and I'll go there and wait for you?" He's leaned back on the sofa now, slumped to the side. His eyes are slowly blinking, and they stick a bit longer each time they close.

"Omay. But you need my key, it's in my pocket by my cock. If you touch it, you'll get a surprise," his eyes close.

"I'll touch your key, but where is the sanctuary? The special one where we can play?"

"My p-prayer woom...the key is magic. My Lord is g-good for s-secrets...I wanna play wiff you doll..."

"Baby, we're coming in, we'll help you find it and get him in the van. Is the door locked?"

"I don't know, I'm coming to let you in. Colby, turn off all the cameras."

"Already did. You're clear."

I rush to the front door and unlock it. My guys have their hoods up and balaclavas around their necks in case there's a reason to hide their faces. They both look me over and concentrate on my face.

"I'm fine, I promise. Come on, we have to find his secret room. I've got a bad feeling."

Austin takes my hand and looks into my eyes, "Are you really, okay? He said some fucked up shit to you."

I stop and meet his gaze, "I'm really okay, I promise. I just want to get him out of here and back to BASIL. I have bad vibes about his secret room. The last secret room I was in was a torture chamber." He kisses me and nods. Jackson hugs me and checks my face for himself. I smile at him, and he grins in return, our own silent communication. He kisses me and we all make our way back to the den. The bishop is out cold, and I don't want to touch him for the key.

"I'll get it. I better not touch anything else or I'm punching him," Austin volunteers.

"I think we should punch him anyway. Just for the fucked-up shit he said to Violet, he deserves an ass whipping. He's a sick fucker."

"We already knew that. How's it going, Austin?"

"I'm trying to concentrate so I don't touch anything but a key." I can't help laughing at his panic. Bless him, he's braver than me. He reaches around in Voldemort's pocket and eventually his eyes go wide, and I cringe thinking he touched something gross.

"Got it!" He holds up a gold key, relief floods me. His sanctuary is located next to his office around the corner and down the hall. I can picture the blueprints of the house clearly in my mind.

"It's this way, come on," I pass the doorway.

"Wait. I think we should tie him up in case he wakes up, at least his hands and make sure he doesn't have his phone on him."

"I'm not sticking my hands back in his pockets," Austin argues.

"It's okay, his phone is on the table next to him. Turn it off and take it with you. Here's the plastic restraints," I hand Jackson the zip-tie handcuffs I got from Dozer. He also provided the Ketamine. He's been an invaluable resource. I'm glad Colby found him.

Jackson secures Voldemort's hands, and he makes the cuffs tighter than they need to be. The plastic cuts into his skin and it soothes something inside me. I make my way to the sanctuary and I'm feeling a little lighter. When I open the door, it takes a minute to find the light switch.

It's a beautiful room with dark wood panels on the walls, a stained-glass window, and pews. There's also a few cushioned wood benches and an ornate chair is raised on a dais. A pulpit holds a large bible and a massive carved wooden crucified Jesus hangs on the wall behind it. I don't see a door that would use a key anywhere. There's a bookcase on one wall and an alcove in the corner. I approach the bookcase and start pushing against it.

"What're you doing?"

"Trying to find the secret room. Do you see a door?"

Austin looks around before he answers, "No. But it's got to be here, right?"

"Maybe behind those curtains?" Jackson moves them, with no luck.

I close my eyes and picture the blueprints of the house. I think about what's behind each wall as I spin in the room. When I get to the wall with the huge crucifix, I realize I don't know what's behind that wall.

"I'm pretty sure it's got to be behind Jesus. I don't know what's behind that wall, the blueprints didn't show anything there, but it's not an exterior wall either."

"I think you're right," Jackson uses his fingers to trace the edges of the wooden panel behind the iconic image of our lord and savior.

I join him and press on Jesus' abs; I say a silent prayer asking forgiveness in case it's blasphemous. But I don't think it can be worse than whatever we're about to find in this room. The whole cross gives and then clicks open. Jackson opens the panel by swinging it out like a large door. Behind the holy panel is a large black door, with a keyhole above the door handle. It looks like a door that belongs in a castle, maybe a dungeon. It's foreboding and I get goosebumps across my skin as Austin wiggles the key in the lock.

He shoulders the door open and we're looking into a black abyss. Jackson clicks on a flashlight and aims it inside the room. The odor emanating from the space is musty, it smells of leather, fear, and bleach. None of those smells evoke pleasant memories. My stomach lurches and I don't think I can enter the room.

"Babe, you can wait here, we'll check it out. Okay?"

"Yeah. Thanks." He kisses my cheek.

"Of course."

They disappear into the darkness, and I look away from the room I can only imagine is filled with shattered innocence and broken dreams. I picture *David Bowie* slicing into Voldemort's chest, blood flowing freely from the wound, and it calms my anxiety about this evil place.

A light turns on in the room and I lift my eyes in reflex. I'm assaulted by the items within this hell hole of purgatory. I wonder if Dante visited this despicable den of horrors before he wrote his poem.

From my vantage point, I can see a wall of black things that look like whips. A bed with restraints, there are chains hanging from the ceiling, leather straps are attached to the headboard and footboard. I can see the edge of what looks like some sort of cage, and I can't take it anymore. I flee and make it to the bathroom just as the vomit leaves my mouth. Grateful I made it in time, I kneel before the toilet and empty my guts. Tears stream from my eyes and I don't know if they're from the force of my projectile regurgitation or emotional distress.

Austin hands me a cup of water. I gargle with it and spit it out. He helps me up and I rifle through the drawers and cabinet until I find a travel size mouthwash that's sealed. I rinse my mouth with it and feeling minty fresh, I wipe my eyes with a tissue.

Austin's hand rests on my lower back, he watches me in the mirror, he looks worried. I lean into him and give him a small grin in my reflection.

"Are you all, right?"

"Yeah. Thanks. Did you find anything in there?"

His eyes shift away from mine, and he fidgets, "There's a huge trunk of videos and some cameras and computers. Jackson's loading it in the van so Colby can hunt down whatever or whomever is on the recordings. Baby, do you think he has video of you?" His eyes meet mine laced with shock and fear, I'm not sure if he scared himself or he's just that scared for me. I don't want to think about that possibility.

"I don't know. I don't think you or Jackson should look at any of it just in case. My stepfather did take pictures and videos regularly. I don't know if Voldemort would have any of it. Unfortunately, there's probably a good chance there's something with me in it." Shame tries to lift its ugly head and I banish it with my mantra.

He takes my face in his hands and his eyes search mine, "Baby, I don't know what's happening in that beautiful head of yours right now, but don't let it sink its teeth into you. You're safe, you're free, you're a beautiful badass warrior. You aren't there anymore, and you won't ever be again. I love you; Jackson loves you. You're never going to be alone or vulnerable again." He hugs me and I hug him back. We hold each other until Jackson finds us. He wraps his arms around me while Austin holds on. Jackson hugs me from behind and they both squeeze me tight between them, I feel safe and loved. The light they project fills me and my black soul eases back towards purple once again. They keep me sane and protected. Jackson kisses my ear through my wig, and I idly wonder if Colby can hear it.

When I feel recharged, we exit the restroom. I catch Jackson and Austin sharing a silent communication, and I know he's telling Jackson about the videos. He needs to know, but I don't want to think about it.

"I think we should stage vague evidence of suicide. If we leave that dungeon open, they'll be able to make their own conclusions about why he'd kill himself. Let's check his desk for anything we can use."

"Yeah, it's this way," I guided them to his office. We check his desktop and drawers. There are several notes in his handwriting; it looks like they're quotes for sermons. I don't know why, but he never performs them unless it's a special occasion. Maybe he's getting a jump on the holidays.

"How about this one? *John 1:9, If we confess our sins, He is faithful and just to forgive us our sins and to cleanse us from all unrighteousness.*"

"That's great. Vague but about begging forgiveness. Let's put it on the kitchen counter and one of his bibles."

"Here, what should I open it to?"

"*Luke 17:2 It would be better for him if a millstone were hung around his neck and he were cast into the sea than he should cause one of these little ones to sin,*" Austin recites.

"That's perfect, how do you know that?" I asked.

"I'm mostly Irish Catholic," he confirms.

"Hopefully, whoever finds this will put two and two together and believe he jumped off a bridge or something. It makes as good a story as any."

Chapter Thirty

We unload him directly into BASIL and I'm satisfied it's finally being used for its true purpose. They heft him onto my shiny new table and strap him down. After we get him situated, Jackson drives Voldemort's phone and the trunk of evidence to Colby. None of us want it here. Colby has a unique ability to step outside the pain and suffering of others and only focus on information gathering. He'd make an ideal FBI investigator. He doesn't let personal stories affect him the way most people would. I wish I could do that, but despite my dark soul, I still feel too much for those innocents who are harmed by evil.

My detachment skills come into play when I'm carving up the monsters who harm those victims. Nah, victims aren't right, they're *survivors,* and I make sure nobody else has to survive the despicable acts the monsters like to commit. I can slice and dice any part of a monstrous creature without batting an eye. But show me his prey and I freeze, vomit, cry, or all of the above. I don't understand it, but I'm grateful to be able to meet justice where it's due. Especially when the courts fail.

I haven't told the guys about my deal with Bug. He conducted his experiment and was able to complete his project. He said he didn't want to know my plans, which is for the best. He handed over what I asked for and we're even. I hope it works the way I have planned. The thought makes me want to chuckle with an evil laugh.

"What do you want to do now?" Austin asks as he watches me carefully.

"I'm tired. It took all of my energy to keep from throat punching Voldemort. Can we take a nap?"

"Sure."

He follows me and I remember the disgusting asshole touched me. I enter my little bathroom, and he follows me. He lifts my dress over my head and starts the shower. I pulled off my wig in the van, but the pins are still in my hair holding on the net to keep any of my blonde and blue spikes from poking out from under the fake dark hair. He carefully removes the pins and then brushes my hair.

The steam from the hot water begins to fog over the mirror, and he flips the switch turning on the exhaust fan. Then he unhooks my bra and slides my shorts and panties down my legs. My blades are secured in a case I left on the island in the kitchen on my way past. He uses the back of his collar to lift his own shirt off. He then removes his pants and matching black boxer briefs.

He guides me into the shower and allows me to soak under the stream of glorious hot water. Without a word, he conveys his love with his eyes and my heart pounds in my chest, the familiar warmth spreads from my middle and out to my extremities. He works shampoo into my hair and then rinses it carefully avoiding getting any in my eyes.

Next, he conditions my hair and massages my muscles with body wash on his hands. I want to wash him too and I reach up with shampoo scrubbing it into his hair and scalp. After he rinses it out, I wash him with a handful of green apple bodywash. There's nothing sexual in our actions, just love and care.

When we're clean, he steps out and turns off the shower. He wraps me in a towel and dries himself with another. We make our way to my bedroom, and he dries my back and my hair, leaving no water on my skin. He pulls a big t-shirt over my head and slides clean boxer briefs on himself. We climb under the covers and cuddle together. His skin smells warm and clean, and a little like apples.

His body pressed against mine leaves me feeling safe and I'm able to fade into sleep almost immediately. Sometime later another clean and warm body moves behind me and my world is complete. When I open my eyes again, the room is completely black. I can feel Austin behind me now and Jackson in front of me. My hand is on his chest and his breathing is soft and steady. Austin's hand is curled around my waist and his chest moves against my back as he inhales and exhales, his warm breath against my neck.

Slowly, the evening's events come back to me, and I recall Voldemort is strapped to my table. A jolt of excitement zings through my stomach and I'm wide awake. I shift and think about getting up to check on the bastard. He's not suffering yet, and I need to change that right away.

"Are you getting up baby?" Austin whispers.

I nod, "Yeah. I want to check on Voldemort."

"I checked on him when I got back. He's still out."

"I want to inflict some pain. Want to come with me?"

"Yeah," Austin answers.

"Okay," Jackson adds.

"You gotta move then," I order. Jackson rolls onto his back and stretches. His chiseled chest muscles flex and I'm distracted by the movement.

"Come on, beautiful," he brings me back from the fantasy involving my tongue, that's playing out in my mind.

I follow him, and even though the room is dark, I can see enough to avoid stubbing my toe or tripping. Austin joins us and turns on the light. I've already got panties on and I'm pulling on yoga pants. He and Jackson get dressed as well. I put on socks and sneakers just in case.

I stopped in the kitchen for some orange juice. Jackson pours himself a glass as well and Austin drinks from the jug, finishing it off. I open my knife case and remove *David Bowie.* He feels good in my hands... solid, sharp, and as cold hearted as me towards Voldemort. I make my way to BASIL, and they follow me. I'm not sure I want them to see me carving into the monster on my table. Will they still love me? Or will they think I'm unhinged and run?

I don't want to lose them, but I can't change what I am. Either they'll love me enough to stay or they won't. My breath hitches at the thought, I feel the vibration of a trembling shiver work its way down my spine. I steel myself and open the door. The vacuum of the sealed room releases when I break the suction. They did a fantastic job on the remodel.

We left the light off and Jackson did turn it on when he checked on him earlier. He's asleep, or unconscious, but I suspect sleep based on the snoring coming from his open mouth.

Jackson tore off his priest collar in the van. He thought it was offensive to every good Catholic, or maybe every Christian, he didn't specify. I can see a gold chain around his neck, and I pull on it. A large gold cross flops onto his chest. I pull the chain over Voldemort's head; he doesn't deserve the implied protection of God. I let the chain pool on the nearby counter and place the crucifix on top.

"Baby? Do you want us to remove any of his clothes?"

"No. I don't want to look at his disgusting pale skin. But if you want to search him and remove anything in his pockets, that's fine. His shoes should probably come off, I don't want him to kick us."

"You got it, babe." Jackson removes his shoes and sets them out of the way on the floor. Austin, ever the brave soul, feels his pockets. He removes a few prayer cards and a handkerchief, gross. He doesn't find anything else.

"Jackson, will you please crack the smelling salts under his nose for me?"

"Sure," he holds the white capsule under the monster's too large nose.

I held the tip of *David Bowie* to his thigh. He jolts awake and looks at us wide eyed and mouth slack with fear. Exactly how I want him. I press the tip into his skin until I get his full attention.

"Hey there, bishop. Do you remember me?"

"I...uh...no?"

"Let me remind you. Keep in mind I have a very large knife next to your artery and if you move, you could sever it and bleed out." He nods hard and too many times. He's shaking and I love it.

"You might remember an old friend of yours, Jerry Raider?"

"Y-yeah, I remember Jerry. Isn't he dead?"

"Yes. I killed him." His eyes open impossibly wide, and he shakes his head in denial. He fights his wrist restraints, while trying to hold his legs still. He's not successful and I can feel the tip of my blade pierce his skin as he moves.

"I'm guessing you remember me now, and maybe you're thinking about how Jerry died. Maybe you're realizing that you're strapped to a table defenseless while I hold a very sharp and very large knife to your skin. I bet you're thinking about what you did to me and what I might be planning as revenge."

"Mmmaaah!" Voldemort expresses a sound I can only call terror.

"Please, p-please, I have money. I can give you anything you want. Please, don't hurt me," he tries the usual bargaining that doesn't sway me in the least.

"I don't recall you ever caring about hurting me. If I remember correctly, you said my fear and my pain made you harder than anything else ever did." Jackson punches him in the gut.

"Ooof!" Tears begin to fill his eyes, and he shakes his head again.

"Sorry, babe."

"It's okay handsome. He deserves it."

"Please. I'm a very important man now, people will look for me. You'll never get away with this. They're going to find you and you'll go to prison. Please, let me go and I won't tell anyone what you've done. I'll give you some money and you can leave the country, so they can't find you. There's no extradition from Bolivia or Columbia, if you like colder climate there's always Angola."

"I don't need your money. I want absolutely nothing from you but your screams."

"Please, what can I offer you to spare me?"

"Maybe if you apologize, I'll forgive you," I say with all the sarcasm I can muster.

He doesn't grasp the sarcastic remark in the spirit it was intended, "I'm so sorry. I'm a sick man. I've made terrible mistakes. Please! Have mercy."

"Ha! No."

"But I'm sorry. I shouldn't have done what I did, I made a mistake. Please, I deserve forgiveness!" He struggles against his restraints again.

"Wow. That's your idea of an apology? I don't accept and I don't forgive you. But you do deserve something special."

"W-what?"

Looking at my guys I warn them, "I'm sorry for this. Guys, if you want to step out, I understand. I need to cut him in a sensitive place." I use my head to indicate Voldemort's crotch.

"No, we're good. We'll even hold him still for you baby."

"Awww, thanks, sweetie. You're the best."

"What the fuck is happening? You are NOT cutting anything!! You, stupid bitch if you cut me, I'm going to...to..."

"Oh, are you gonna report me? To whom? The police? Go ahead I'll wait." He struggles again while I laugh at him.

"Go ahead and get it out of your system. You're not going to like what I have planned at all. You can scream if you want, I don't mind. Remember how you loved to make me scream? You owe me your screams, and I want them all." I stab at what I hope is his ball sack and it gives easily when my favorite blade slices right through his pants and whatever else he has on.

"Noooooo!! Oh my God!!! You're insane!! You cut my balls!!"

"Perfect." I collected the small container I got from Bug.

He said they just need the scent of blood, and they'll do the rest. I open the lid and dump the disgusting little creatures into the hole in Voldemort's clothing. The small and slimy beasts squirm towards the blood and out of sight.

"Was that what I think?" Jackson asks.

"Yep. Bot Fly larvae. If you remember correctly, they feed on blood and tissue while they become engorged. Then they leave a hole in the skin so they can breathe air. Bot flies grow and grow hollowing out a large cavity in their host that becomes infected usually and fills with pus and goo. When they grow big enough, they molt into flies and the cycle starts again. They lay their eggs on the delicate skin of a vulnerable creature, if it already has a wound, all the better."

"What the fuck is wrong with you? Why would you do something like that to me? I'm a man of the cloth! They're going to track me down and catch you!"

"Not if they think you killed yourself by jumping into the sea with a millstone around your neck." Again, his eyes grew wide with shock. He violently shakes his head and fights against his restraints. This time my blade isn't pressed to his thigh, and I enjoy his struggle. Maybe he'll wear himself out.

"Baby, I'm completely grossed out and so turned on. You're such a badass." I wink at Austin. Jackson has a huge grin on his face, he's a bit like me, he enjoys punishing the monsters.

"I think we're going to let you get acquainted with your new guests. If you need anything, feel free to scream, we won't hear you. Come on guys, let's leave him to contemplate his life choices for a few hours." I turn for the door and the guys join me.

When I reach out for the light switch, he screams, "WAIT! I have something you're going to want."

Turning back, I ask, "Yeah? What makes you think I would want anything from you?"

"You'll want this. There's some men bringing me something special. If you let me go, I'll give it to you."

I turn away again, "Not interested."

"It's three children." I stop. I take a calming breath and look at him. He smiles, he knows he has something I want.

"They're bringing me three little girls tomorrow. I can choose whichever one I want or for a price, I can have all three. They're some men I've been working with to make a deal. I use my connections, and they provide me with the objects I desire. We finally came to an agreement."

"What time tomorrow?" I ask trying not to display how eager I am.

"I'll tell you when you let me go."

"I don't think so. You're not trustworthy. If you want me to let you go, you'll have to give me the information first. We'll need the children in hand before I let you go. My word is good. I'm not a child abusing liar." Both of my guys watch me carefully. They watch for any signals I don't say out loud. I hope they can read me as well as I think they can.

"How do I know I can trust you?" He asks, rightfully suspicious.

"You'll just have to take a leap of faith."

He studies my face, "I don't have much choice, but neither do you. If they don't hear from me, they'll take the children elsewhere and you'll never get them."

"I see. Let me think it over, meanwhile you can enjoy your guests."

"NO!!! No! Don't leave me in the dark! No!!" I turn out the light and we locked the door behind us. As soon as the door is closed, we can't hear his pleas. They really did a marvelous job on my remodel.

"Babe, just to be sure, you're not really going to let him go, are you?"

"Of course not. He doesn't need to know that. We need to call Colby. We may not need him at all, we just need to see how much Colby can get from his phone and those computers. If we don't need him, we'll stay on schedule. If we do need him, we'll wait until we don't. I want those kids and I want those assholes. I know it's those guys I saw at his house a few weeks ago. They were some bad guys, mob guys."

"That sounds fun. We might need some help. I wish Pierson was here," Austin muses.

"We can get Dozer to help us, he's very reliable."

"What if he works for the guys, we want him to help with?" Jackson asks.

"I guess we'll need to find out in advance. Let's see if Colby knows."

I dial him and put it on speaker, "Hey VioleNt1! How's it going in your new BASIL?"

"You're on speaker, the guys are both here. Everything here is good, but we have another issue."

"Hey, Auz, Jax, what's the problem?"

"Hey Colby, the asshole says he's got three kids being delivered to him tomorrow... I mean later today. Do you think you can impersonate him and get them delivered so we can intercept them?" Jackson explains.

"Shit! That's a problem, all right. Let me start on his phone now. I was gonna do it tomorrow."

"He says they're traffickers, I'm pretty sure it's those mob guys I saw at his house a few weeks ago. We're gonna need everything you have on them."

"Hey Colby, we also need to know if Dozer has any allegiance to said mobsters or if we can get his help," Austin adds.

"No, Dozer doesn't work with those mobsters. He only works with the Irish, they're his family, by marriage, I think. He's done some work with a few MCs, and there's one here that's been trying to clean up the drugs and trafficking. He helps them out and I know he's done a few undercover projects for some paramilitary outfits."

"RobN, I don't know what any of that means, is it cool to have him help us or not?"

"Yeah, he's down for anything that rescues trafficking victims, especially kids. I don't know much of his history; he's a ghost. But he has a definite thing against trafficking. I'll message him now. I can have him come for planning in the morning. Okay?"

"Perfect. Now what about Voldemort's phone? Can you impersonate him?"

"Dozer will be at your warehouse at nine. Looks like Voldemort is a moron. I have all of his messages with the traffickers. He calls them, the children, dolls. Otherwise, he didn't cover his tracks at all. They're supposed to be at his house at eight pm. You have until then to get the plan in place. I just turned the cameras back on at Voldemort's lair, so I can watch who comes and goes."

"Thanks Colby. We'll call you for the planning meeting in the morning."

"All righty. Goodnight, everyone."

"Goodnight."

"See ya."

"Later."

CHAPTER THIRTY-ONE

When I reach into the tampon box, I feel something weird. I drop the box and hope it's not a rat or a bug. I peer into the box, and I see something shiny. I lift the box so I can examine it more closely. There in my tampon box is a small trophy. I lift it out and it's one of those little novelty trophies. It's got a cup on top, and the stand has an engraved plate. I read the plate and laugh out loud.

It says: *Congratulations! Because we love you, this one's free, you solved your fourth clue.*

They're so sweet. I am the luckiest girl ever. I finish up and head to the kitchen where I find them working on breakfast. I watch them for a minute before they notice me. Jackson is mixing something in a bowl and Austin is frying something on the stove. It smells like bacon which is always the best. While I watch, Jackson dips a piece of bread into the bowl and then puts it in a hot pan.

"Will the bacon be ready when everything else is done?"

"Yeah, it should work out perfectly, that's why I put it in the oven first. Your pan is too hot."

"Worry about your eggs, I've got this."

"Just trying to help... if you burn it, she won't eat it."

"No shit. I'm not gonna burn it. Ah, dammit! Shut up. The first one's always a throw away." Jackson adjusts the temperature on the stove. He dumps the burnt French toast in the trash. Then he dips a fresh piece of toast and sets it in the pan.

"Good morning beautiful, how did you sleep?"

"Great. Look what I found," I hold up my trophy.

"Congratulations! Does that mean it's shark attack time?" Austin asks.

"It's Shark *Week*, dumbass. Congratulations babe!"

"Thanks. Yeah, Shark Week. I appreciate the easy win."

"Well, we figured it sucks to have Shark Week. So, we wanted to give you an easy one while you have to deal with that," Austin explains.

"Thanks. But now you're in last place. Jackson and I only have one more to go."

"Yeah, but I'll catch up. I just need to figure out my clue. I'm sure it'll be easy as soon as I have a minute to focus. *What do Sam, Butch, and Woody have in common? Buy the item(s) and wear it.* Not hard at all." Jackson smirks at the French toast. I wonder if he knows the answer. Now I need to find my final clue. Has Jackson found his yet? I really want to choose our trip.

It's not even eight when we sit down for breakfast. I'm calm and relaxed. Knowing Voldemort is trapped alone in the dark with some disturbing parasites makes me happy. The darkness inside me is smiling at the thought of Voldemort's suffering. It's a good morning, I hope the rest of our day goes this well.

"Mmm... Jackson this is the best French toast I've ever had, and Austin! These eggs are perfect. Thank you both for making breakfast. I love you so much, you're the best." I can't keep the joy from my face.

"I love you. You're the only woman I've ever cooked for, and the only one I ever wanted to cook for," Jackson replies. He squeezes my hand before encouraging me to eat up.

"I love you too, baby. You're so amazing, I can't get enough of you," he leans over and kisses my shoulder.

"Well pretty soon you'll have all of me. My birthday's only a few days away." I can't help the ridiculous grin that covers my face. I'm like a kid who can't wait for their birthday party.

"That's right," his brows shift suggestively. "We're gonna be having extra special naked time soon." He makes me laugh.

"Be still my heart. You always have such a way with words."

"I can't wait either, it's been so hard to stop. Pun intended." A giggle escapes me at Jackson's joke. The happiness in my heart sings in my body, and it makes me feel light and so lucky. As we finish up our breakfast the buzzer from downstairs sounds. It must be Dozer; I hop up to let him in.

"I've got it." I rushed down the stairs and let him in. He's bigger than I remember. He greets me with a nod.

"Hey. Thanks for coming. I know it's short notice, but it was sprung on us after midnight, and we could really use your help."

"You've got it. Let's figure out what needs to be done."

"Follow me, my boyfriends are upstairs. They'll be boots on the ground with us and Colby will be remote." He nods again. He's still a man of few words.

Jackson and Austin stand when we enter, and Sawyer looks up from his food, decides nothing important is occurring, and goes back to eating his breakfast. I'm pretty sure a hurricane wouldn't keep him from his food.

I point to each of them as I introduce them. "Austin and Jackson, this is Dozer."

Jackson sticks his hand out to shake with Dozer, "Hey man, good to meet you."

"Same. Violet has told me you're both joining us in the field."

"Yeah, we'll be with you. Nice to meet you," Austin adds.

"Let's sit in the living room and go over what we know. I'll call Colby." The guys and I sit on the sofa, Dozer pulls a chair closer. I place my phone on the coffee table on speaker, it rings.

"Go for RobNdaHood!" I roll my eyes. Colby has a flair for drama.

"Hey RobN! We're all here and you're on speaker."

"Gentlemen, and Lady, welcome to the Matrix. Just kidding," he chuckles and the rest of us wait for him to get past his weird sense of humor.

"Ahem, okay, here's what I know. I've identified the three little pigs from Voldemort's lair in the big black cars. The taller one? He's Misha Grigorovich, definitely a mobster. He's a full-fledged member of the Russian mob. The guy from the second car, he's Diego Rojas. He's a car salesman in Orlando, as in he owns ten dealerships and donates to the mayor's political campaigns. He's Colombian, rumor has it he's hooked up with his family cartel. Also, he's known for selling drugs and people, not just cars. The third guy, Julio Alvarez, is a congressman in Orlando. He's the *It Kid* everyone wants to endorse their bill or project. He's never been accused or caught doing anything illegal. He's Cuban and comes from a wealthy family. But his father has been accused of government contract misdeeds. Nothing has come of it yet, but he's being closely watched."

"Who is supposed to meet with Voldemort tonight?"

"The Russian, but I think the car dealer may show as well. He's into the same merchandise and wants to benefit from Voldemort's influence. I think the car dealer plans to pay for all three and then hang around to party with Voldemort. The Russian is just a business guy. He brings the merchandise, gets paid with cash or promises for deals and takes off. He doesn't party with the product."

"Can we stop calling the victims, *child* victims, products and merchandise?" I ask.

"No. It helps me not to dwell on the reality of the circumstances. I can focus on the work if I don't have to think about that. Believe me, I never really forget, it just helps me conduct the business of what I need to do. Okay?"

"I understand. Are they both scheduled to arrive at 8pm?"

"Yeah, but they're coming separately. The Russian implied he's coming in some sort of truck to transport the product. The car dealer said something about taking his new car for a drive. I got the impression he plans to use the car as part of the payment. He sells high end sports cars at three of his dealerships."

I get up and pace the end of the room. "Let's assume then, the Russian will have at least one other person with him to watch the product and drive the truck after they leave the merchandise. Ugh! I hate calling three little kids that. So, depending on the type of truck, he may have two people with him."

"That's a reasonable assumption. If it was my operation, I would have a box truck with a driver, and the boss in the front, with a second flunky to ride in back with the product," Dozer offers his thoughts.

"What about the car dealer?" Jackson asks.

"If he plans to pay with a fancy sportscar, he's got no ride home. But he plans to hang out and party. So maybe he doesn't need a ride until morning."

"Again, if it were my operation, I would assume the car dealer arrives in his fancy payment. Followed by his big car and a driver who arrive shortly thereafter so he has a ride whenever he wants it. I wouldn't let them arrive more than thirty minutes after the car dealer." Dozer adds.

Colby tacks on, "In our video of their previous visit to Voldemort's lair, the Russian had a driver and a bodyguard. The car dealer had the same. Only the It Kid had a driver and two bodyguards."

"Okay, if the It Kid shows, we have approximately ten bodies. If not, we've got six?" Austin questions.

"That's how my math adds up," I confirm.

"We need to go to Voldemort's and decide where we want to wait, where's a good sniper spot, ambush location, and how to lure the bodyguards," Jackson throws out.

"We need to check the location," Dozer agrees.

"There's been no activity today. His staff isn't there. I'm thinking he gave them today off to party in private."

"Great. When do you want to go?" I ask.

"We should check on him. Maybe he'll be in a more talkative mood today?" Austin suggests.

Dozer surprises me when he says, "I would like to see him."

"All right. Colby we're going to check on our prisoner. I'll call you back later, okay?"

"You got it my Violent Queen, I'm out."

"He actually thinks he's funny?" Austin asks as he leans in conspiratorially.

"He does."

"We may need to stage an intervention."

"I think he's funny sometimes. Like you."

His mouth falls open in outrage, "That wasn't nice, beautiful. I'm funny, you told me I was funny, at least once."

"I meant your looks." I run when he tickles me, then he chases me down the stairs and across the gym. Before I can enter the hallway to BASIL, he corners me and grabs my waist and tickles me until I'm ready to pee my pants.

"Okay! Okay! You're funny! Quit it before I pee!" He immediately holds his hands up in the air like I have him at gunpoint. I gasp for breath and try to calm my giggles.

"If you make her pee her pants, you're cleaning it up," Jackson says as he passes with a wink at me.

"I'm done. I'm sorry, please don't pee."

"Don't tickle me and I won't."

"Deal. Now kiss me, so I know you're not mad at me."

"I'm not-" He pulls me close and cuts me off with a kiss. His tongue pushes into my mouth and I completely forget what I was saying. Electricity travels my veins, and my nipples harden. I kiss him back with enthusiasm until someone clears their throat and I recall we aren't alone. Sheepishly I break our kiss and smile apologetically at Dozer.

"Which room is he in?" He asks.

I point to the door for BASIL. "There. I already began the torture. Have you ever heard of Bot Flies?"

He smiles a decidedly evil grin, "I have, and I like the way you think. May I have a moment alone with him?"

"Sure. Just, don't do anything to unalive him. That's all mine."

"Certainly." I'm not sure if he agrees it's my kill or if he was agreeing he won't do anything. Both my guys are looking at me confused. I guess they couldn't tell either. I shrugged.

When Dozer opens the door, a weak voice calls out, "Pleeease..." He switches on the light and closes the door behind him. I wonder what he's going to do, but I kinda hope he tortures him.

"Have you figured out your clue yet?" I asked Austin. I collect *David Bowie* from his resting place. I hold him in his sheath, his presence always excites me a little. I can feel the thrill of that excitement in my chest.

"I think so. I've got to go shopping to fulfill it though. Then I'll be caught up with you guys."

"No, you won't," Jackson states.

"You found your clue already?"

"Yep. I just need to figure it out, then I win."

"Baby, you can't let that happen. If he wins our vacation is going to be spent sweating in line at Disney World." My mouth falls open as my eyes snap to Jackson.

"No. You can't be serious."

"What's wrong with Disney?"

"Nothing, when it's not a thousand degrees outside and not everyone in the world is lined up for Space Mountain."

"I've never been able to take someone I'm dating before. It would be amazing to share some Disney Magic with the woman I love." He reaches out to me, and his fingers touch my cheek as he gazes into my eyes with his sexy amber orbs.

Aww, how can I be mad about that? My head tilts and my eyes water a little. "That's so sweet. Okay, if you win, I'll go to Disney."

"Dammit," Austin gripes. "I'm gonna need to leave for a little while before we go on our mission."

I hug Jackson, and he kisses me. It's so adorable when he's sweet. He's a big tough guy most of the time, so it catches me off guard when he says and does sweet things. It's one of the traits I love about him.

The door to BASIL opens and I'm fairly sure I hear sobbing coming from the slicing room. Dozer approaches, unfazed. I look him over and see some marks on his knuckles that I didn't notice before. He nods a greeting, and steps aside so we can make our way into the room. I decided not to ask him any questions about his visit with Voldemort.

I open the door not sure what to expect. The light's still on and Voldemort has his face turned away, he looks as if he's trying to roll over, but his restraints won't allow the movement. He's sniffling and his chest is heaving. My smile is instant.

The tip of *David Bowie*, now clean, scratches its way along the edge of the metal table creating an excruciating screeching sound that resonates in the soundproof room.

"No-oo! Pleeease...please, you need my help. Don't you? Please help me. I'm sorry. Please don't hurt me."

"Ah, the pleas of the wicked, such a pleasant sound, don't you think?" I taunt.

"Please tell me what I can do. What do you want from me?"

"That's an interesting question considering each of us want something different. I want you to suffer. I want to hear your screams and watch as your spirit breaks. I want your vile soul to spill onto my floor." He looks at me and I see his eye is puffy and red around his eye socket. His lip is bleeding, and it looks like he's going to have a black eye sooner than later.

"These two want revenge, an eye for an eye, so to speak. It seems you hurt their sister in such a profound way that she is forever changed. Can you turn back time and not rape her? Or abuse me?"

"I don't know their sister! I didn't know what I was doing when I hurt you. I'm a sick man! I need help. Please. I'll go to jail, I'll turn myself in, anything you want! Please just let me go."

"Our sister trusted you, asshole. She went with you because you're supposed to be a man of God. She wanted to volunteer at the church, you were supposed to help her get signed up and trained to help with the soup kitchen. You manipulated her and you raped her. She almost died, because of you!" Austin growls at Voldemort through angry clenched teeth. He suddenly lunges at the monster on my table and wraps his hands around Voldemort's neck. He can't fight back; his restraints won't let him lift his hands enough to fight off the angry brother crushing his esophagus. As much as I want him to have a slow and painful death, I can't bring myself to ask Austin to stop. The anguish on Austin's face and the fear on Voldemort's leave me entranced.

"Auz! Stop! He's Violet's. Let go, brother. Come on!" Jackson steps in and pulls gently on Austin's biceps. Austin seems to snap out of his blind rage, he lets go of Voldemort and steps away. He looks chagrined and pleads forgiveness from me with his eyes. I rush into his arms, careful not to stab him, and hug him. My love and forgiveness flows out of me and into him in a gush of emotions.

"I'm sorry baby."

"No, don't apologize for your feelings. I'm not upset. If you ended him, I wouldn't have been angry with you. Your hurt and need for revenge are just as valid as mine. We're in this together."

"I love you so much."

"I love you too." I swipe a tear from his cheek and give him a soft smile.

Returning my attention to the evil creature waiting for justice, I find him coughing and gagging. His hand moves in the air desperately reaching for his throat, forever unable to break free and meet that goal. Needing to release my aggravation with his sniveling and begging, I lash out with *David Bowie* and pierce his shoulder. I'm careful to avoid his arteries, not wishing for a quick demise.

He squeals like a stuck pig. I enjoy his screams, but I hate his voice. He tricked me too. Like Megan, I trusted him. I fell for his costume and thought he would help me. I believed he was a priest, a man of God, a righteous man. I had no way to suspect he was a demon in priest's clothing. I was a little girl, no longer sweet and innocent by the time he showed up, but worthy of saving.

When he hurt me, it broke my mind and damaged my soul beyond repair. He manipulated me again and again. I kept trusting him, he offered me hope. Then he extinguished it. When hope left me, my soul cracked open, it filled with darkness, and I became a murderer. I lost all hope and faith. The void left behind was filled with an inky black hatred.

Somehow, my uncle, friends, and my parents, were able to reach inside me and let in some light. Just enough that I wasn't completely gone. My parents were the ones who truly filled my soul with love and, over time, rebuilt my ability to trust. Uncle Randy, too. He never doubted me, never gave up on me, loved me no matter what. Sensing I'm falling into the rabbit hole, Jackson wraps his arm around my waist. He rubs his fingers on my hip.

He mumbles softly in my ear, "Babe, you're safe. He can't hurt you anymore. You're a badass. A warrior. I love you more than anything."

I turn in his arms and look at his gorgeous face. His words sink in, his love shines in his eyes. That sliver of light in my black heart shines with a blinding fierceness. My chest warms and I can feel the beating of my heart; it feels strong and steady.

"Thank you. I love you too." I let my face show the emotions in my heart and he watches me, he reflects my love, and I feel strong, safe, and happy. I stab Voldemort's hip, and *David Bowie* hits bone and stops. I twist him a little as I pull him free.

"Please! No more! Please! I can't... I can't do this, please!"

"Do you remember how I begged you to stop hurting me? Do you remember how I cried? I was a little girl! I couldn't fight you; I couldn't escape. Does that seem familiar?"

"I'm SORRY!! Please! Ple-e-e-ase! I'm begging you! No more..." he sobs, and I wipe his blood from my blade on his stomach. He flinches and I giggle. He doesn't seem to grasp that his suffering makes me happy.

"There was a time I thought you might be an angel God sent to rescue me. How ridiculous is that? You weren't anything close to God at all were you? You still aren't. You tried to drug me just last night when you thought I was poor, vulnerable Rose. DIDN'T you!?!"

"I-I-I'm sorry!"

"But you're not really sorry, are you? If I let you go right now, you'd go home and assault those kids tonight, wouldn't you?"

He sobs harder, he shakes his head from side to side, perhaps trying to come to terms with his circumstances. I think he might be ready to answer some questions.

First, I want to test his honesty. "Who's bringing the children to you? I want a name." I point at him with *David Bowie* and his eyes follow his every move.

"I don't know his name."

"BZZZZTT! Wrong answer! Try again!"

"I don't know! He didn't tell me his name!"

"Austin, what do we have as a consolation prize for this contestant?"

"Well, Violet, we have a special prize... he gets to lose a tip of a finger!" Voldemort fists his hands and tries to pull them beneath his body to hide them. Jackson and Dozer step up and grab his hands. Austin picks out his little finger and holds it up for me. I nod. He and Dozer hold his wrist and finger to the table, so I'll have enough leverage. I don't hesitate.

Thwack! I chop off the top piece of his pinky finger.

He screams louder than ever, and blood gushes from the wound. I pick up the tip of his finger and hold it up for him to see. He squeals and faints. I burst out laughing.

"What a chicken shit! For someone who has no problem raping children he sure is squeamish. Dozer, will you grab that little torch and cauterize his wound please?" He nods and does as I ask without a word.

The smell of burning flesh is disgusting, but we all brave it.

"Auz, sweetie, will you please get the smelling salts?"

"Of course, baby." He waits ready for my signal with the little capsule. Jackson releases his hand, and Dozer turns off the torch. They all watch me.

"Okay, wake him up, please." He coughs and gasps. He lifts his head and looks at me, then around at the guys. Then he looks down at his finger, tears overflow his eyes and run down his face. He doesn't plead or cry out.

"Ready for round two?" He nods and his wide eyes show nothing but fear.

"Tell me the name of the person bringing the children."

"Please. He'll kill me."

"Haven't you been paying attention? What do you think I'm going to do to you?" I lift his former fingertip and roll it between my own fingers. The tears gush from his eyes.

"Misha. Misha Grigorovich. Please, I told you what you wanted. Please let me go."

"Oh no, not yet. I need to know who else is coming."

Over the next hour or so, he spills his guts, figuratively. He tells us the truth as far as we know it. He names the car dealer and the It Kid. Though, the It Kid isn't expected to show tonight. He tells us about his torture chamber and the videos. He admits to raping girls and boys as young as four. It's the most disgusting thing I've ever heard.

He tries to bribe us with the hundreds of thousands of dollars he claims is hidden in his secret safe. With any luck it's really there and he gave us the correct combination. Colby's going to do his best to track down the victims and hand out the money to all of them. We're also going to take the jewels from his secret safe and sell them off for more cash for the victims. Dozer knows a guy who can get us cash for the gems.

We decided to rest while Austin runs his errand. Dozer takes the sofa and Jackson, and I cuddle in my bed. Interestingly, Sawyer chooses to nap with Dozer. He liked him instantly. I hope that means Dozer is as trustworthy as I believe. I liked him instantly too.

Austin bursts into the bedroom wearing a cowboy hat and boots. I bolted upright wide awake, startled from my nap. When I realize what he's wearing, I can't help laughing.

"Oh my God! You look hilarious!"

"It's my clue. I'm caught up to you guys, right?"

"You're caught up to Violet, but I found my final clue, remember?"

"Yeah, okay. But I'm even with Violet and we'll catch up to you."

"Okay. I believe you. We were asleep before you busted in here. So shut up and lie down or get out."

"Did someone wake up on the wrong side of the bed?"

"You woke us up! Of course we did. I love you dude, but you need to be quiet, please?" I yell. Then I roll over and Jackson cuddles back around me. Austin grumbles as I hear him stomp his boots out of the bedroom.

Sometime later I wake up and open my eyes. Austin is wrapped around my front and Jackson is at my back. Mmmm, perfection. My eyes snap open when I remember what we need to do. We need to go to Voldemort's lair before everyone shows up. we need time to position ourselves in the best locations for our assault. When I check the time it's only half past noon. We're not late, but we need to get moving, we have firearms to load and ammo to count.

I stretch and my bladder decides it's time to visit the restroom. I try to extricate myself from the guys and they both wake up. It never works.

"Sorry, I need the bathroom. It's also time we got up and started packing up."

"Okay babe. Here, climb over me, I'll help you." Jackson helps me until I'm above him, then he pulls me down on top of his body.

"Hey! Full bladder!"

"You gotta pay the toll." He steals a kiss, and I kiss him a few more times.

"Keep the change."

"Cute. Go on," He helps me until I'm steady on my feet.

I brush my teeth while I'm in the bathroom and I decide to wash my face while I'm there. I run the water until it heats up. The steam from the sink begins to fog the mirror and, in the fog, I see a word at the bottom of the glass... *bench*.

I turn on the shower and leave the exhaust fan off. I let the room become filled with steam and the message on the mirror becomes clear.

Barracuda Beach under the tiki bench.

I'm not sure where the tiki bench is located, but I know where Barracuda Beach is, I've been there. I don't have time to check it out now, so I file it away for later. I'm so happy I found my clue. Poor Austin, I hope he finds his, maybe I can give him a nudge.

Chapter Thirty-Two

"Let me know what you find. I've got ears and eyes on you, but no cameras inside. Remember we can all hear you, if any of you have a problem, call it out and help will come. I'm hanging up."

"Okay, thanks Colby."

Using our key, we entered the house. Following Voldemort's instructions, we find his master bedroom, check the closet, and locate the safe. It's hidden behind a shelf that lifts out of the way on a stay lift hinge support that keeps it open. Austin bends down to try the combination. He twists the dial left and right until it clicks and he's able to pull the door open.

I hold my breath waiting for him to check the contents. Relief floods me when he pulls out a few stacks of cash. We brought a duffle bag for whatever is in the secret safe. He loads it up with stack after stack of hundred-dollar bills. If I had to guess, I'd say there's upwards of eight hundred thousand dollars in the deep safe.

After he's removed all of the cash, he pulls out jewelry boxes of various sizes. I choose one and open it up. There's black velvet inside of the square box. A men's, large, ruby ring in a gold setting, glints brightly nestled in the soft fabric. It contrasts with the darkness of the owner. He doesn't deserve something this good. It looks promising, and I know it's bound to fetch a decent price. Maybe we can ease the tiniest bit of struggle for Voldemort's victims.

Once everything is shoved into the huge duffle, Jackson locks it in the trunk of Dozer's car. He's the only one with a trunk to lock the bag out of sight. We explore the rooms and windows where we can watch the approach to the house. We check out trees, the stairwells, closets, anyplace we can ambush them from and rescue the children while we take down the bad men.

I'm already formulating a plan where they double cross each other, and both die in a gun battle. It's plausible and leaves no loose ends for anyone to hunt down. My way also lends itself to our suicide scenario for Voldemort, since his body won't be found. While we come up with our hiding spots and roles in the transaction and take down, I sharpen my blades.

When I finish, *David Bowie* is strapped to my lower leg, hidden by my boot cut jeans, my trusty sword in her scabbard is hanging at my back, beneath my hoodie. I have my favorite throwing knives at my waist and my 9mm in a holster in the back of my pants. We all have plastic restraints that Dozer handed out. I'm going to lure them into the house and then hide the children in a locked room.

I made the guys stop for stuffed animals in anticipation of scared children. We also got them each a flashlight in case the hiding spot will be dark. I know it's not ideal, but I want them to feel like someone cares. Hopefully they haven't been manipulated with toys. God how I hate evil monsters who prey on children. I placed the items in the safe room so they're ready. I plan to let them keep the lights on but I'm glad we're prepared if that's not an option.

As the witching hour, or maybe it's the *monster* hour, approaches we watch the driveway and Voldemort's phone. The car dealer is very excited, and Colby thinks he'll be here early. Despite the way we want things to go, Colby is prepared to call in the authorities if necessary. I don't trust them, but Colby and Dozer know of some FBI guys that are more interested in stomping out traffickers, than the people who catch or harm them. If we end up needing help, I suppose they'll be our best option.

Colby has handed them a few evil rings in the past and they've kept their word and prosecuted the traffickers, leaving Colby anonymous as promised. Hopefully everything will go as planned and we won't need any outside assistance. We're all decked out in our best gear, and we have communication earbuds and mics. We've conducted a few tests and now that we're in our assigned hiding spots, we're communicating through the tiny devices.

"Hey, baby?"

"Yeah?"

"Please be careful. We don't know much about these guys, and they might be smart, skilled, or worse than we think."

"I know. Don't worry, I'm assuming they're the worst level of evil possible. I promise I'll be careful. You guys be careful too. I love you. Dozer, I don't know you well enough to love you yet, but I like you a hell of a lot and I don't want anything to happen to you either."

"Thanks. Same." Always a man of few words.

"Babe, I love you too. Don't hesitate to stab or shoot first and ask questions later, alright?"

"You got it, same to all of you. We're likely to be outnumbered but we have surprise on our side."

Colby speaks up, "I've got headlights incoming. Looks like a sports car. I'm guessing the dealer has arrived. Definitely a fancy sports car... looks like an Aston Martin convertible. Just one ass-hole getting out. He's heading to the door. You're up Vi."

"Ten-four," I can't help playing with codes when I'm on this type of communication device. The doorbell chimes and I take a moment before I answer.

I pull open the door, "Yes?"

"Well, hello there beautiful, and who might you be?" He's not ugly, probably mid-forties, in dress pants and a dress shirt, no tie. His hair is wind-blown and dyed too black, probably covering gray. I'm dressed like the teenager I am. I figured it would be enticing to a pedophile. Seems like I was right, he leers at me his eyes tracing my form from top to bottom and back again. Yuck. I don't see any weapons on him, but he may have one tucked into the back of his pants like me.

"Hi. I'm Rose. I'm a houseguest of the bishop. He's expecting you. He asked me to show you into the den. Would you like anything to drink?" I offer.

"Nice to meet you, Rose. I'm Diego, I'd love a whiskey."

"All right. This way," I point with my hand and follow him. I don't want him behind me. He finds his way into the den. I've already put Ketamine into the glasses. It's coating each one so anyone who drinks anything from one of the glasses will be drugged. It was a gamble that they might want alcohol, and I'm glad it's paying off. The fewer men we have to fight the better.

"I've got incoming headlights," Colby announces. Without turn-ing my back to him, I pour some bourbon into a glass. He didn't ask for ice or a mixer, so I left it neat.

He smiles at me and asks, "How long have you been a guest here, Rose?"

"Only a couple days, I had some issues at home and the bishop is counseling me and helping me figure out what I'm going to do now," I flash a bright smile, trying to seem friendly.

"I see. Are you in school?"

"I'm supposed to be in my sophomore year, but I'm not going right now, while I figure things out."

"In college?" His dark brows raise higher than what seems comfortable.

I giggle like an idiot and say, "No, silly! I wish. I'm in high school."

Now he dons a bright smile, "I'm so glad the bishop is able to help you out. Where is he?" He looks around with his question.

"He said he needed to get some things ready for his other house guests that are arriving soon. Are you staying here too?"

"I'm just staying overnight. I came a long way and it's too far to drive back tonight."

"Oh. That's good. The bishop has been really nice, I've enjoyed staying here. The cook makes a great breakfast." I'm rambling like an idiot.

"So, um, what are you studying? What do you want to do when you grow up?"

"I'm not sure. I like computers, but I like music and dance too," I say, trying to keep him focused on me and imagining me dancing. I don't want him to look for the bishop or get distracted and leave this room.

"It's a big black car. Two guys got out: they're leaning on the car smoking. I think they're the dealer's security and ride home," Colby relays what he sees happening outside.

"What type of music do you like?"

"Hip-hop, it's what I like to dance to. Do you like hip-hop dancing?" I say with another big smile like he's the most interesting person ever.

"Never tried, but I go to the clubs. I can dance fairly well to Latin music... you know like salsa dancing. Have you ever tried dirty dancing?" I let my cheeks heat, I'm truly embarrassed by his behavior, could he be more obvious? Ick! Dirty dancing, really dude?

Jackson pipes up in my ear, "Please punch him, babe!"

"No, I've seen that movie though, it was really good. I didn't know people still danced like that," I try not to laugh in his face.

"I've got Austin and Dozer coming behind the guys in the driveway. They have them at gunpoint. They're directing them to the garage side entrance. They're out of view. Audio only."

"Sure, they do. Do you have Wi-Fi in here?"

"Yeah, the password is *amen2000*, no spaces or caps," I recite, more info Voldemort kindly shared while he watched me grind his fingertip in a coffee grinder during our discussion. He fiddles with his phone and in no time, he has music playing from his phone's speaker. Ugh! He better not try to touch me. He gulps the remainder of his glass and stands. Then he holds his hand out to me. I shake my head feigning embarrassment.

"Aww, come on beautiful, I'll show you. It's fun!"

"You first, let me see what you expect before I completely embarrass myself," I giggle again like I'm having fun.

"All right. See first, you swing your hips to the beat like this," he demonstrates. He looks ridiculous. I nod like I'm interested.

"Then you move with your partner, kind of like this," he thrusts his hips and holds his hands out like he's holding another dancer. He starts grinding on the imaginary woman and I feel sorry for her even though she isn't real. He loses his balance and stumbles.

I stand and sway a little to the music trying to distract him. He teeters again like he's on a ship while the ocean is tossing the boat on rough seas. I move my hips a bit more in hopes he'll focus on me and not his deteriorating condition.

"How's this?" I ask.

He steps closer, unsteady on his feet. He staggers towards me and lumbers into me, his outstretched hands land low on my hips. I don't think... I react. Before either of us can take a breath, I grab his hand and pull it towards me while I place my foot behind his leg, then I use his off-balance position to push him backwards, he falls over my leg. I twist his arm as he falls. When he lands on his side, I use my knee and my body weight to shove him over and I pin his arm behind his back. Both of my knees and all of my weight hold him down. I hook a cuff around his wrist and grab his other wrist and cuff it before he can fight me off.

"Heey?! What the fuck? W-whad you doin' me?" He bucks against me, but I ride him like a rodeo cowboy. I need Austin's new hat.

"I've got him cuffed, Jackson, can you give me a hand?"

"On my way, babe." He wriggles a bit more and then he stops moving. I climb off him as Jackson arrives. He rolls him over and punches the dealer right in the face. He's already unconscious but his head jerks to the side in reaction to the hit.

"Feel better?"

"Not really, I want to kick the shit out of him, but I want him awake for it. Are you okay?" He looks me over and I place a kiss on the corner of his mouth.

"I'm fine. Let's get him moved." We decided beforehand that we'd put prisoners into the big pantry in the kitchen. It's far away from the den and oddly has a locking latch on the outside of the door.

"I've got a truck pulling in, followed by two cars. Everybody on deck!" Colby reports with audible panic lacing his voice.

"Shit let's move. Get his feet, babe."

I lift his feet and Jackson lifts most of his weight as we carry the dealer to the pantry. We drop him in there and latch the door. I'm sweating now and I'd love to take off my hoodie, but I can't with my weapons.

CHAPTER THIRTY-THREE

"Go! I've got the door," I urge Jackson.

"Be careful. I love you," he kisses me and hustles out of sight.

"Auz? Are you and Dozer set?"

"We're watching the driveway. All set. Be careful, I can't see how many there are, but there's more than we planned for. I love you."

"You be careful. I love you, too."

"Truck driver door opening. I think the Russian is the passenger. Both of them are heading to the front door. Nobody else is moving, I can't tell how many there are, Violet, please, please be ready for anything."

"I'm good, don't worry. There's the bell." I give it a minute and then casually open the door.

"Hello, may I help you?"

The taller man scowls at me while the thicker man behind him remains impassive. He doesn't move or have any expression on his face. The Russian grumbles something under his breath, in what I assume is Russian.

"Where is the bishop?" He asks, obviously impatient.

"He's getting ready for guests, is he expecting you?"

"Yes. Go get him."

"Oh, are you Mr. Grigor-uh-vich?"

"I am Mr. *Grigorovich.* I'm here to deliver something to the bishop. He is expecting me, go get him."

"Hi! I'm Rose. He asked me to show you into the den, he'll be with you shortly." He looks me over and he seems to determine I'm no threat, and he enters, his friend follows. I point with my hand which way I want them to go.

"This way please." They go the way I want and stop in the den.

"Please, have a seat. May I offer you a drink?" I use my spokesmodel hand gesture again and indicate the alcohol on the small bar.

"No. Go tell the bishop I'm here." He stands with his arms folded, steadfast and angry. He's not going to be easy. I need him to get the kids inside before anything goes down. I'm not sure what to do to make that happen. His phone chimes. He pulls it from his pocket and reads the screen.

Mumbling something under his breath again he types a message back to whomever texted him. He looks at me, then he types some more. He says something to the other man in Russian again and that man nods.

"I will be back, stay here." He seems to be speaking to me; I can't tell for certain because he's not really looking at me. He stomps off towards the front door.

I turn to the other guy and ask him, "Where's he going? Is he going outside? The bishop wanted him to wait here, he'll be right out."

The guy just stares at me. I'm hoping at least my guys are warned that the Russian is heading outside. I watch the man carefully and move over to the bar, I stay to the side, so I don't turn my back on him.

"Would you like a drink? I didn't catch your name, I'm sorry," I smile at him like this is all perfectly normal. He approaches me and I prepare to draw a weapon.

"Yes, please. I am Dimitri." He speaks slowly, carefully, as if he's trying to speak a foreign language. I suppose he mostly speaks Russian, he does okay with English. He smiles at me, and I quickly pour him some of the vodka he pointed to. If I can at least drug him, that's one down.

I smile in return. "I like that name, Dimitri. I'm Rose, it's nice to meet you. Is that guy, like your boss or something?"

"Yes, boss. Thank you." He chugs the whole drink and smacks the glass down on the bar. Okay, I guess he likes shots or maybe he's in a rush, so his boss doesn't see.

"Would you like more?" I ask.

"Yes, thank you, Rose." He smiles, and I refill his glass. He drinks it down as quick as the first. I'm still holding the bottle; I bring it close to his cup and lift my brows in question.

"No more, thank you, Rose. You are kind."

"You're welcome. I'm just polite." I smile unsure what to say next.

"The Russian is yelling at the guys in the first car, there's two of them. They're running around opening the back of the truck. They're getting the kids out. I texted him as the bishop and told him to bring the merchandise inside. He can inspect his payment while the bishop inspects the product. I didn't know how else to get the kids inside. Violet, when they come in, you immediately take them to the safe room and lock them in... they look to be around age ten. Hopefully they can easily follow instructions. Oh man, the kids are crying, the guys are dragging them to the door. Be ready Violet." The bell rings and then the door opens, I can hear kids crying, and a man telling them to be quiet. Dimitri and I make our way to meet them in the foyer.

The men are pushing the crying children, who stumble with the shove, in through the doorway. I rush to them, trying not to look overly concerned. I bend down to speak to the closest little girl. She's a beautiful little thing with long blonde hair and big blue eyes, tears track through the dirt on her face. She's not the youngest and I'm guessing about eight or nine years old.

"Hi. I'm Rose. Come with me," I hold out my hand and plead for her to give me her hand. When she reaches out to me the man who was pushing them grabs her arm and pulls her back.

"No. The bishop needs to approve them."

"I'm going to take them to him. Don't do that again." He startles at my threat; his eyes widen, and his mouth flops open in shock. I stick out my chin and puff up my chest. He chuckles. I guess I'm not very intimidating, but that's okay, I like it when they don't see me coming.

He lets go of the girl's arm. "Go," he directs her with a stern face that causes her tears to flow faster.

"Come on sweetie, come with me." I reach out for her again. She carefully reaches back to me, chewing on her lip as she cowers, waiting for the man to stop her again. Dimitri says something to the men in Russian and they heartily agree and follow him back to the den.

I finally get a hold of the little girl and I quietly tell the three of them, "Please come with me quickly and quietly. We're going to a safe room. Come on." I hold the girl's hand and lead her away; the others stay right with her. I thank my lucky stars they're cooperating.

"The Russian is sitting in the sports car. He's touching everything, but this won't last long without the keys."

"I've got the girls, we're going to the safe room," I report. I focus on the kids, and I do my best to exude safety and confidence. We arrive at the safe room, and when I open the door and go inside, they come with me. Their eyes are wide as they look around.

The littlest one, with mussed darker hair and eyes, focuses on the brown teddy bear.

I hand it to her. Her little eyes light up and I kneel in front of them. "I'm Rose. What are your names?"

"Isabel," the one holding the bear speaks barely above a whisper. "Hi Isabel, how about you sweetie?" I ask the blonde, whose hand I held.

"Tiffany Thompson, I'm nine, almost ten. Are you going to hurt us?"

"No. I'm going to rescue you and make sure you go home to your family." Little Isabel's face falls and as she squeezes the bear tight, as her tears return.

"What's wrong Isabel?"

"I don't have any family. My mama was the only one and she gave me to a bad man. He gave her drugs." Oh my, the poor child! I hate that she knows this and has to live with it.

"You know what Isabel? My mom gave me away too and a wonderful family adopted me. I grew up loved and happy with my adoptive parents. I promise you I will search to the ends of the earth to find you a mom and dad who will love you. But first we need to get out of here. So, I'm going to need you to stay locked in this room and be very quiet until it's safe to come out. Can you do that, Isabel? Tiffany? And...I don't know your name, who are you honey?" I ask the last girl who hasn't said a word, but whose eyes have been wide, and her ears have certainly been listening.

"Tameka Johnson. I have a mama and a nana, and I want to go home."

"Good. I'm going to make sure you get home. I put these pillows and blankets in here for you. I also got the stuffed animals for you, they're yours to keep, and I got each of you a flashlight. I'm going to leave the light on, but if you get scared by any sounds you hear, you turn off the light and use the flashlights. Okay?"

"I need to pee," Isabel speaks up.

"I'm thirsty," Tameka adds.

"I understand. I can't give you anything to drink right now, it'll just make you pee. But I promise as soon as we're safe you can have anything you want. Isabel, do you think you can hold it?"

"No," she shakes her head.

"All right. I'm going to lock you two in here. Don't make a sound, and if you need to talk to each other, you whisper quietly. Don't open the door for anyone but me. The secret word is *Violet*. If anybody tries to come in, you don't let them unless they know the secret word, okay?" All three girls nod.

"Tameka, what's the secret word?"

"Violet."

"Good girl." She smiles with my praise.

"I'm going to lock the door, but I can't open it from the outside. When I say the secret word, you open the door. Got it, Tiffany?"

"Yes, you say Violet, we open the door."

"Perfect. Come on Isabel, we have to go fast, and be very quiet."

I don't feel good about taking Isabel out of the safe room. But what choice do I have, the poor thing needs to go. When you gotta go, you gotta go. I hold her hand and she walks along with me. She's silent and thoughtful about making noise as she moves. I take her to the closest restroom, it's a half bath, which is fine, it has the half we need. She rushes in and doesn't hesitate to relieve herself. I decided to go while we're here, too.

"The Russian is going back into the house."

I speak softly to her, "I'm going to explain something to you Isabel. See this little thing in my ear?"

She looks intently, "Yes."

"It's an earpiece that lets me hear what's happening with my friends and they can listen to what happens to me through this." I hold up the tiny Mic that looks like jewelry. She checks it out and nods.

"Okay."

"My friends are here, in this house with me. They're going to help us get to safety. Do you remember the secret word?"

"Violet."

"Good job, Isabel. Now we're going to sneak back to the safe room so you can hide with the other girls. Same rules... be quick and quiet. You did a great job getting here. I know you've got this."

She nods, "Got it." When we leave the bathroom, I can hear shouting in another part of the house. *Shit.*

"Talk to me someone, what's with the yelling?"

"Hey babe, I can't understand what they're saying. But I think Dimitri might be unconscious and the Russian is pissed at the other two who were definitely drinking. I'm hoping they drank enough and from the right glasses to knock them out. You need to get the girls into the safe room."

"I'm working on it, two are there, but I've got one with me." I speak very softly while I hold the microphone to my lips.

The shouting is getting louder, and I pull Isabel to go faster. When we round a corner, I can hear footsteps coming towards us. I don't have any options; I yank her into a room and pull her behind the door. The Russian passes us, and my stomach falls to the floor. Please, if anyone is listening, don't let this monster catch us, or at least Isabel.

I peek through the door jamb; I can't see anyone. I listen carefully and hear nothing. I hold my finger to my lips and implore Isabel with my eyes to be very quiet. She nods and follows my lead shadowing my every move. We make our way towards the safe room. I keep checking behind us. I'm terrified of the Russian finding Isabel and taking her.

"The last car doors are opening, four guys just got out. I repeat four more guys are outside." When we reach the door, I hold my breath and knock softly. There's a faint rustle on the other side of the door.

I lean in close and whisper, "Girls, it's me. Violet."

The door clicks and opens a crack. Tameka peers at me through a thin strip of the opening. I grasp Isabel by the arm and guide her into the room. I look at each of them, loathing to leave them.

I mime with my hands as I whisper to them, "Lock the door, don't open it without the password, keep quiet." The three of them nod like little bobble head dolls. I don't have time to ponder how adorable it is. I wait while they lock the door, and I hear the lock click. Once it makes the noise I expect, I move on. I need to find the Russian.

I walk as silently as I'm capable of and I wish that grocery guy could teach me his stealthy trick. Too bad he was a jackass. I stop at a doorway and listen. I don't hear anything, not even the men arguing in the den. I quietly pass the open door. Next, I come to a corner. I stop to see if there's any noise to betray another person. I hear a faint scuff from behind me. I lean back and look down the hall and at the open doorway, but I don't see anyone. I step past the corner and continue on, hoping to locate the Russian.

Another room is up ahead, and I wait once more and stretch my senses to their limits. When I detect nothing, I quickly make my way further down the hallway. When I reach the dining room, I check the room carefully for anyone. I find a cup on the wood table without a coaster, but no other signs of life. I work my way around the table and peek around the column than frames the large opening into the formal living room.

"They're approaching the house, Austin and Dozer are right behind them. They're trying to hold them at gunpoint, but they aren't stopping. Two just ran in opposite directions, two went inside. Violet and Jackson, you have two more inside. Austin and Dozer are chasing the two outside."

Not wanting to wait in one spot too long I rush across to the formal living room. There's a butler's pantry off the back of this room. I need to check it. I feel like I need to draw my gun but then my hands won't be free for my blades. I keep moving while I decide to keep my hands free. Once I'm outside the door, I stop and listen again. I can hear fast footsteps; someone is running outside this room.

Ducking behind a chair I hold my breath and try to hear where they go. Their lumbering footfalls fade as they move further away, and I release the air caught in my lungs. I stay low and listen at the pantry door. I don't hear any sound from within, so I reach up and quietly turn the handle opening the door slowly. I peek around the door and scan the inside of the room. It's empty. Relief floods me and I take a minute to catch my breath and decide where to go from here. Staying low, I make my way into the back hall. The coast is clear, so I move quickly towards the kitchen. From there I should be able to see some of the den, the back patio and yard, TV room, and breakfast area, I hate large houses. Why does one old guy need so many rooms?

The main pantry is still locked, and I'm hoping the dealer is still inside and knocked out. We don't need any more assholes wandering around here. I crouch behind the island and use all of my senses to check for others. The den is just up the hall, and if I was standing, I would see a portion of the room. Is Dimitri knocked out? Did the other two have a drink and are they drugged? Curiosity is making my skin feel tight, my tense insides want me to rise and seek out the answers.

The granite countertops are gleaming with a bright shine, the wooden cabinets are warm, and if I wasn't hiding and trying to stay alive, I would appreciate the décor. I crab walk to the edge of the well stationed island. I place my hands on the rich walnut floor and stretch to see the rooms beyond. I'm leaning as far as possible without falling on my face, when I notice a pair of shoes in the den. I can just barely make out the black leather dress shoes, which most certainly don't belong to any of the guys I brought. With a quick glance in every direction, I bolt to the outer edge of the den entrance and press myself against the wall.

Waiting to hear who's in there and their state of consciousness, I attempt to be silent. I made myself as still as physically possible and slowed my breathing. I wish I could suppress the pounding of my heart in my ears.

"*Skol'ko?*"

"*Ya ne znayu.*"

With no idea what they're saying, the conversation tells me there's two of them. The second one sounded out of it, and he must be drugged, perhaps he's one of the men with Dimitri. If the first voice is the Russian, maybe I can distract him long enough to capture him. I slap a friendly smile on my face and hope I pass for sweet and innocent.

"There you are! I was looking for you, the bishop is ready to see you in his office. Will you kindly walk this way with me?" I gesture towards the office. I have a shadow of a plan forming.

"What have you done to my men?" he asks, pointing a .45 handgun at me. I guess he's not buying my innocent act.

I raise my hands in surrender, "What do you mean?"

He waves his gun at the rest of the room. Dimitri is unconscious on the sofa, beside him is one of the men who brought the children, he appears to be out as well. In the chair next to them is the third man, he still has a glass in his hand and he's staring at the painting on the wall with his jaw hanging slack, a bit of drool escaping his lips.

"I have no idea what's wrong with them. I didn't do anything. Should I call nine-one-one? They must be sick."

"No. You lead the way to the office, *now.*" His stern demand makes my guts clench. He's going to see my sword, unless I can keep him distracted.

"Okay. Sure. Please, don't shoot me. I'm doing what you ask, I'm only fifteen. Please, don't hurt me."

"Move." Keeping my palms in the air, I bring my elbows in close, pressing them together, and hope I'm making my hoodie looser in the back, so the sword is hidden better in the bulk of fabric.

Wanting to keep him distracted and unable to focus, I ramble, "I think the bishop is really nice. He's been so good to me for the last couple days I've been here. Do you know him well? Please don't hurt him either, he's waiting for you, he doesn't have any weapons. You're making me nervous. I don't understand why you have a gun. Are you going to shoot me? Here's the office," I announce as we stop at the closed door.

"Open it." Doing as he asks; I turn the knob and then step away as I push it open. He waits to the side, expecting to be shot on sight I suppose. Of course no one shoots, because no one is in the room.

"Enter."

I step over the threshold and immediately next to the door so I can move behind it if necessary. He enters just a single stride into the room. I'm next to him now and able to reach for one of my throwing blades without him seeing. I use my body to shield my movement. It happens within the blink of an eye. I remove the blade on my right and hold it beside my leg. He takes another step scanning the room and concentrating on the large desk.

When he's in front of me, I lash out with my blade and thrust it into the center of his spine. In a reflex of movement and shock, he twists and swings his gun towards me. I dive away from the barrel, but not quite quick enough. He fires, and I feel a hot burning pain slam into my side above my hip as I hit the ground and roll away. He falls the opposite way and begins dragging himself from the room. I crawl behind the desk.

"Violet!! Are you okay!?! Please be okay!"

Speaking softly, I answer, "I'm okay. I'm hit in the side. I don't think it's too bad but I'm pinned in the office. The Russian is injured, he can't walk, but he has a gun and use of his hands. Please don't come running blind. Three are incapacitated in the den."

"Dozer and Austin neutralized the outside two. By my count, there's two more and the Russian loose in the house."

"Make that one in the house, I caught the other one. He's unconscious. I dragged him into the weird pantry in the dining room. I'm coming to you babe. Put pressure on your wound," Jackson interjects.

"We're coming inside, we'll hunt down the last guy. Jax, get our girl. I love you, Violet," Austin adds.

Tears puddle in my eyes. It's an emotion I'm not used to feeling, having people care is something that always surprises me. I'm grateful. My side is throbbing now with a pain like I've been stabbed with a hot poker. It radiates out and my back and ribs are aching. I gently pull the hoodie off over my head, my sword goes next, but I keep it close.

I swipe at my eyes with the back of my palm. My bunched-up hoodie becomes a compress for my injury. It hurts when I put pressure on it, then quickly settles into an unpleasant pulsing pain. I can't hear any sound from the Russian, I don't know where he is now.

Slumped against the intricately carved wood of the desk I want to lie down, fear of bleeding out with movement keeps me in place. Despite the artistic beauty of the behemoth of a desk, it's not comfortable as a resting place. I take a deep breath and attempt to see past the carved gargoyle-like corner of the furniture. Finding I'm able to move without too much discomfort, I wiggle my way around the desk and to the door. Listening before sticking my head through the opening, I don't hear any movement. For all I know, the Russian is right outside passed out. Footsteps reach my ears, and they're deliberate and cautious. Pressing myself against the door, I wait with my sword at the ready in my free hand. It's not long before a voice reaches me, in person, not through my earpiece.

"Violet? Can you hear me?"

"Yeah. I'm right inside the office. I don't know where the Russian is, he crawled off." I hear some movements and scuffling sounds. Then my Jackson enters. He falls to his knees when he sees me.

"Damn, babe. Let me see."

"It's not as painful as it looks. But it won't stop bleeding if I don't press on it. Did you find him?" Gunshots ring out from somewhere in the house, not close to us.

A moment later, "Violet! We're okay... we found the guy. He's toast," Austin announces in my ear.

"Great. Is that all of them accounted for?"

"Yeah. They're all dead or captured. Except the Russian."

Jackson adds, "The Russian is...toast."

He looks at me a small grin lifts his lips, "Great job. He was paralyzed, then bled out. We need medical care for you, though."

"Not yet. I want to see the captures."

"Where are you baby?" Austin asks in my ear.

"The office. Three doors down from the den, on the right." Austin bursts into the room and Jackson and I were startled even though we heard him coming. He falls to his knees next to me and carefully kisses my cheek. His eyes fill with emotion, sadness, and fear. He plants one last soft kiss on my lips.

"Can you stand?"

"I don't know. Here, take my hand and lift when I push. Grrrah!" I'm standing. Sweat breaks out across my brow. I hold the hoodie in place as tight as I can.

"Come on, I'll take you to the others." He holds my elbow in support.

"Thank you. Jackson, please grab my sword."

"Got it."

Dozer waits outside the office acting as guard. We all make our way to the garage, it's where they bring the three men from the den. Dimitri is in and out, barely walking with help from Austin. Jackson and Dozer dragged the others. Dozer is going back for the dealer, since he's the only major criminal left alive in the house. I size up the men before me. They're all just flunkies doing as they're told, but none of them have made an effort to stop it. They escorted those sweet little girls here and had no issues handing them off to the monster.

Dozer returns and drops a still unconscious car dealer on the ground. My side aches and I need to act quickly. With my decision made, I hold out my hand to Jackson.

He takes my sheathed sword from his shoulder and holds the handle out to me. I remove it from its case, and in one swift movement, slice the dealer's throat. A liquid gurgle escapes him and within seconds most of his blood is pooled above his head and streaming towards the overhead door. I step closer and wipe his blood from my blade onto his dress pants. My verdict for the rest of the men is for the authorities to determine their jail time.

"Colby, please help Dozer with whatever he needs. He's going to take the sports car, and he can keep it as payment or sell it and donate to the fund and we'll pay him, his choice. His associates are going to load up the living bodies in the box truck and hand them to the authorities. Then they'll dispose of the dead bodies and clean the house. Any questions?"

"When are you going to the doctor? It's been a minute since you were shot. Please get going, my Violent Queen."

"On my way. Thank you. Dozer, ask Colby for anything you need. Boys, let's get those little girls and get me to the doctor." Jackson insists on carrying me to the safe room where they're hidden. I know they won't open the door for anyone but me. When we get to the door, I'm happy to find it still locked.

I knock softly, "Girls, it's me. You can open the door."

I recognize Tameka's voice, "What's the password?"

"Violet. Don't be scared, my two boyfriends are with me, they're good guys." The lock clicks and her small face peers out. When she sees me, she smiles. All three girls come out and stop short.

"You're hurt!" Tiffany exclaims.

"Yeah, a little bit. My uncle is a doctor and we're going to see him to fix me up, let's get moving, okay?" All three of them hold their stuffed animals. Isabel has her flashlight as well. They nod, their eyes are wide, and their sweet faces are a little pale.

Pointing at Jackson, I tell them, "This is Jax or Jackson, and this other guy is Austin. You can trust them just like you can trust me." They nod and look over both of my guys.

I remember something important and ask, "Who needs the restroom before we go?"

"Me."

"I do."

"I need to go." We take the girls to the bathroom and let them take care of business before we leave. They climb into the back seat without argument, and let Jackson strap them in.

CHAPTER THIRTY-FOUR

"Violet? What's wrong?" Uncle Randy answers with a sleepy voice.

"I have a small medical situation. I'm on my way over."

"How big is small?" he asks sounding much more alert.

"A hole in my side, set up for stitches. I'll explain when I get there." I can hear Stephanie asking what's wrong in the background.

"Okay, I'll be ready. Maybe we should meet at the ER?"

"Can't. I'll be there in about ten minutes. Thank you." I hang up.

There's no point in explaining on the phone. Austin's driving us. He's holding so tightly to the wheel his fingers are white. Jackson is holding me in his lap and pressing his own jacket to my wound. His face is tense, and his jaw is clenched, while his eyes keep searching my face for any changes in pain level or consciousness.

I feel a constant ache in my side, which isn't surprising thanks to being shot, but I'm getting used to it and it doesn't hurt as much as it did at first. I want to reassure them, but I don't know what to say. When we pulled up at our destination, Uncle Randy rushes to the car and opens the door. He's in doctor mode and Stephanie is behind him. They're both wearing gloves.

"Carry her into the dining room. I have a sterile cloth on the table... put her there."

"Okay, come on babe. Let me carry you."

Not wanting to argue, I allow him to lift me from the car and carry me inside. Austin holds the front door open, then goes back for our little passengers. Every light in the house is on and there's some medical tools and supplies on the end of the table. All of the chairs have been pulled away. Jackson sets me on the table, and I scoot to the middle and lie down. Uncle Randy lifts the jacket from the wound. It spikes with a sharp pain.

"Is this a bullet wound?" Uncle Randy asks with astonishment.

"Yes."

"We need to go to the ER."

"You know if we do that, they'll call the police."

"Dammit, Violet."

"Please don't make me talk to them. I'll explain, I just don't want to talk to the cops, you know they're crooked. Remember what happened to me. Please..." I plead. He nods and his face scrunches up with tension.

"Stephanie, please start cleaning this up, I need to poke inside and make sure I sew up anything that's been hit. I don't have any anesthesia, just some lidocaine. You're going to feel some of this."

"It's okay, do whatever you need to do."

Stephanie uses a liquid on a gauze cloth to wipe at the hole in my side, the front is fairly small, like a quarter around. The back is bigger, about twice the size. She cleans the front and then... she has me turn over. The room spins a little and the edges of my vision cloud for a moment. Once I settle on my stomach it stops. She works silently and I take deep breaths to counter the pain of her touch and the sting of the cleaning solution.

"It passed through which is good, I couldn't do surgery to re-trieve a bullet in my dining room. I'm administering the lidocaine now, it burns, I'm sorry."

"*Hisssss,* yowza! Yeah, it burns." I suck in breath through grit-ted teeth with each injection.

"I need to give it a minute to work, *explain.*"

"I was abused by the bishop, when I was a little girl. He's the one we talked about, remember? I've never been able to get him into trouble, the police did nothing even though I told them. He was a priest back then, and they ignored me. I wanted to stop him from hurting anyone else, so I decided to capture him and torture him. Then kill him. During this mission he revealed that he was expecting three small children from a Russian mobster to be delivered for him to abuse." I point behind Uncle Randy and Stephanie.

They turn and look. "Oh my God!" Stephanie gasps.

"Holy fuck! Shit. Sorry," Uncle Randy adds. They both turn back to me with huge eyes and mouths hanging open.

"We had to rescue them." Uncle Randy takes a deep breath and closes his eyes for a minute. When he opens them again his face is softer, his eyes seem understanding and open to my side of events.

"This is Tiffany, Tameka, and Isabel. Isabel was given away in exchange for drugs while the other two were taken, by the Russian mob, thanks to a human trafficking ring. We stopped the head guy who was there, and his team is being turned over to the authorities. I promised these girls they would be returned to their families, except Isabel. She's going to find a new family. A good one. Do you understand?"

"Austin, please take the girls into the other room and find some cartoons on TV for them. Also get them some food and water, have them wash their hands first," Stephanie instructs.

"Yes ma'am. Come on girls, are you hungry?" His voice fades as they follow him to the kitchen. I have to smile. He handles girls of all ages without a blink. I love him so much.

"Randy, she's right. We can't involve the authorities; we have to help her and those little girls."

"I know. I'm just struggling with my morals and the urge to dial nine-one-one under these circumstances. I love you Violet, and I would never want anything to happen to you, whether it's a gunshot or jail. I'll do everything in my power to protect you, even from yourself."

"I love you too. Thank you. I think it's numb now." He looks at my side and seems to remember he was meant to be sewing me up.

"This might hurt a little, I'm sorry."

Over the next hour or so he digs into the wound in my side and sews up the damage caused by the bullet. It nicked my small intestine which can be problematic, but he thinks it wasn't bad enough to leak much if anything, into my abdominal cavity. He stitches muscle and flesh until I'm whole. He gives me a steroid injection, antibiotics, and Xanax. Jackson carries me to bed and lies down with me while I drift. Austin climbs next to me at some point, his kisses are sweet on my face.

The next time I wake, my side is throbbing painfully, and I reach out to find I'm alone. I open my eyes trying to remember where I am and what happened. Staring back at me are two little curious eyes, attached to a clean face surrounded by wet locks, and she's holding her teddy bear close to her chest.

"Hi." I croak.

"Is your name Violet?"

"Yes."

"Why did you lie?"

"When we were in the bad house, I didn't want the bad men to know my real name. I told them my name was Rose, so I had to tell you the same thing while we were there. I meant to tell you the truth right away, but since I was hurt, I forgot. I'm sorry."

She scrutinizes my face carefully, "I forgive you, Violet. But no more lies."

"I promise. Did you take a bath?"

"Yes. Stephanie helped me, and she's really nice. I like her a lot."

"Me too. Is there breakfast?"

"Randy made us eggs and bacons. It was so good. I think he saved you some, come on."

"Okay. Oh, ouch. I need a minute. How about I'll meet you out there?"

"Okay," she says, and bounces out of the room. She's adorable. Owww. Damn my side hurts. Taking a deep breath, I roll to the edge of the bed and use my legs instead of my stomach muscles to sit up. I sound like I'm in labor as I huff in and out trying to ease the pain. The room shifts as I stand. I grab onto the dresser and take a few more deep breaths until it straightens out again.

Following the aroma of bacon, I make my way to the kitchen. I'm not sure where he came from, but Jackson is suddenly there and helping me walk. As he takes my hand, I realize I was holding onto the wall for balance.

"Thanks."

"I was going to bring you breakfast in bed."

"Isabel asked me to come out. She said you guys saved me some."

"We did, but it's hard to say no to Isabel. That one's gonna be running the house in no time. Here, sit at the table." He helps me into a seat, and I groan when I bend.

"Here baby, take some pain reliever," Austin hands me a glass of water and some pills. I swallow them down and pray for relief.

"Thanks. What have you been up to?" Jackson takes off, I assume to get my breakfast. Austin looks very happy, giddy.

"I've been helping with the kids. We played tea party, and we read some books, then when they got baths, I helped pick out the smallest t-shirts in the house. Randy wanted the girls in them until their clothes are dry. It's been nonstop fun."

"Have you heard from Colby?"

"I think Jackson spoke to him; I heard him telling Randy something about the girl's parents."

"Where is everyone?"

"They're out back. The girls haven't been outside in a while, and they wanted play out there. I came in when Isabel said you were awake."

"Here you go. I heated everything up. I made fresh toast, because there's not a good way to heat up old toast." Jackson explains.

"Thank you. Did you talk to Colby?"

"I did. He found Tiffany's family; her parents are on their way here. They're in southern Alabama and it was faster to drive. Tameka's family is in Louisiana, they're flying in this afternoon. Both families agreed not to ask any questions. Colby's FBI guy... or maybe he's Dozer's connection...? Anyway, he vouched for us and the safety of the girls. They were happy the girls are staying with two doctors and have been checked out."

"Randy and Stephanie are going to meet the parents in a safe location and hand them over. The FBI guy is helping with all that. Is there anymore bacon, Jax?"

"Sorry, Violet's got the last of it."

"You can have a piece of mine," I offer, holding a slice out for Austin. I chew for a few minutes, and I'm relieved the pain meds are kicking in, because my side isn't throbbing so much now. I can enjoy my breakfast, or almost lunch, now that I'm in less discomfort.

"What's the plan for Isabel?" I ask no one in particular.

"I think Randy and Stephanie are going to let her stay here for a while," Jackson states. He watches me for my reaction.

"That's great. She's adorable and her parental situation might be, difficult."

"He said he's calling your lawyer, Krewe, for help. Why do you have a lawyer?"

"I told you about my childhood, my stepfather, my adoption. All situations that require legal help. Now he's helping with my parents' estate. My adoptive grandmother is contesting their will, and he's trying to manage the trouble she's causing."

"She sounds like a real bi-witch. Stephanie asked me to watch my language in front of the girls. They sneak up on you, so I'm trying to keep it G-rated," Austin explains.

"Good job. I need to get home. I want a shower, fresh clothes, and Sawyer's probably having a fit. Do you think we can go soon?"

"Sure babe, whatever you want. Let's just check with Randy to see how you can shower safely."

"Let's make sure they don't need us for anything either. We can come back later. I just need to get cleaned up and take care of my little guy. I don't want to leave them without help if they need it."

After a talk with Randy and Stephanie, Austin decides to stay behind and help them. He's going to shower when we get back with clothes for him. Jackson is going to drive and help me shower, and we'll be back in a couple hours, before any of the parents arrive to collect the girls.

When we get to the warehouse, Sawyer meows his head off. He's definitely angry with me. A can of his favorite food makes him as forgiving as a nun. Jackson and I shower together, but he won't let me fool around, at all because of my injury. As we're packing up to head back to Uncle Randy's I decide to retrieve Austin's final clue and I hide it in his overnight night bag in the pocket of his clean jeans. I want him to have a fighting chance to win our game. I don't care how he's doing but curiosity forces me to check on Voldemort before we go. He barely lifts his head when I turn on the light. His eyes, are the barest slits. The stench in the room is putrid. It smells like a rotting corpse. I convince Jackson to peek into his ripped pants and see how his little friends are making out while they eat him from the inside out.

"Oh fuck, that's nasty. Babe, it's got green shit coming out and his nuts sack is swollen huge, looks like it might burst. Holy, fuck, I might puke. Damn!"

"Awesome. So, bishop, how does it feel to suffer? How does it feel when you beg and plead, and nobody cares? How does it feel when they break their promises to save you?"

"I'm sorry. You're right, I'm evil. A sick man. Please, just kill me. Please, have mercy," his voice is barely a rasp. His throat must be raw from dehydration and screaming.

"You don't deserve my mercy. But I was able to save those little girls from you and the car dealer. Plus, the Russian won't be trafficking anyone else. I suppose that was due to you ratting them out. All right, I'll kill you."

His sunken eyes grow wide, "No! Please, let me go!"

"That's not gonna happen. I'm willing to end your suffering, but I won't let you be set loose on the world again. For all the sins you've committed, I sentence you to death. May God have mercy on your soul, because I never will." I pull on a paper suit used in hospitals for biohazard situations. I just don't want to get blood on my clean clothes or skin. Once I'm in all the gear, Jackson hands me my freshly cleaned and sharpened sword. I lift it above Voldemort and my side pulls a little, it's tolerable, and I swiftly strike down without another word.

Voldemort screams, until his head and his cries are cut off, literally, as my blade slices into his throat. When my blade hits the table, I feel satisfaction and relief. His blood sprays in an upward arc and decorates my stylish protective gear making it a one-of-a-kind work of art. I remove my darkened blade from the evil remnants of a monster. I wipe his poisoned blood from my sword and place it into the metal sink. I'll trust Dozer's crew to clean it when they dispose of the carcass.

I strip off my decorated outfit and leave it on the floor, they'll burn it with everything else. I noticed the red liquid trailing from the drain on the table and down to the drain in the floor.

"Hey, look, the drain works perfectly. Good job!" I smile at Jackson, and we collect our things, kiss Sawyer goodbye and head back to Uncle Randy's.

After his shower, Austin shows us the clue he found in his jeans and Jackson gives me a sideways glance. He knows what I did. I shrug, I just wanted us to be even. He shakes his head at me with a stunning grin and I burst out laughing, then both of my gorgeous guy's hug and kiss me. I think it's finally sinking in that we made it out of that evil house, only slightly worse for wear, in my case anyway.

The rest of the day is spent with the girls until they each leave to be reunited with their families. They hug and thank each of us, and I'll never forget the feeling of a little girl who doesn't even understand everything she's been saved from, hugging me in gratitude. It fuels me to continue the fight.

Uncle Randy wants me to call in sick for a minimum of three weeks at work. I decided to resign. I tell Javier I've been in an accident, and I have a long recovery ahead at Uncle Randy's suggestion. He's going to write a note for school asking them to allow me to attend classes virtually for a couple weeks. Which sucks because we're getting close to finals. I'll be okay though, since I'm ahead in all of my classes.

My birthday comes without much fanfare, and because of my injury the guys refuse to touch me until I have medical clearance. I'm healing quickly and I definitely want to be physically fit for our first time, however my patience is wearing thin. I even got an implant, so I'd be ready for today, but at least I'll be prepared whenever it does happen.

We celebrated at Uncle Randy's with BBQ and a cake. Isabel is thrilled to help me blow out my candles and open my presents. She confiscates the gray kitten stuffed animal I receive from

Colby. She lets me keep the engraved necklace from Jackson and Austin. It's a beautiful little heart with blue opal, my birthstone, and the back is engraved with: *You make our hearts one.*

"I love it! It's beautiful, thank you both so much." I kiss Jackson first since he's closer, he lets me guide our kiss and I'm loving it until Uncle Randy clears his throat reminding us that Isabel is here. I take Austin by the hand and kiss him out of sight. He doesn't let me get carried away.

"Trust me baby, it's just as difficult for us, but we can't do anything until you're healed. It'll happen soon, and you're healing fast. I love you," he gives me one more quick kiss and pulls me back into the room with everyone else.

Uncle Randy and Stephanie gave me an airline voucher good for travel anywhere in the US, for three. I'm so excited, I jump up and throw myself at him, he yells but I feel my side pull before he can stop me. Thankfully I didn't do any damage, and I finish thanking them like a civilized adult, instead of a crazy teenager.

"We heard you're planning a trip soon, but it doesn't expire so you can use it any time," Stephanie explains.

"It's perfect, thank you both so much."

"We have some other news," Uncle Randy hesitates. "We're officially fostering to adopt Isabel."

"That's amazing!!" I jump up again but stop myself before I can do anything dumb.

"Congratulations! We need to celebrate your news!" Austin adds.

"I'm really happy for all three of you. Congratulations," Jackson says.

"Yeah, congrats! Fantastic news," Colby piles on. We all hug and shake hands as needed.

Isabel whispers in her little girl voice, loudly in my ear, "Are you going to be my sister now?" My heart stutters in my chest, this girl, she's amazing.

"You know what, I think I am. Is that okay with you?"

She wraps her little arms around my neck and carefully climbs into my lap. "Yeah. I always wanted a big sister, and you're the best. I love you, Violet."

"I love you too, little sis," My voice cracks and tears fill my eyes. Jackson notices and looks concerned.

I shake my head at him and grin through my tears, "Happy tears." He and Austin both have huge smiles on their faces.

Stephanie wipes her eyes, and Uncle Randy sniffles and asks, "Who needs another glass of lemonade?" Before leaving the room. When I look at Colby, he wipes his eyes and suddenly finds the painting over the sofa fascinating. Despite the lack of sex, it's still a great day. How many people get a new little sister for their eighteenth birthday?

My final gift is a solo ride on my motorcycle. I wouldn't mind if the guys wanted to join me, usually, but I have a secret mission. This is the first time they're letting me out of their sight since I got shot. I have a feeling they know what I'm planning, and they're okay with it.

The wind in my hair, despite the helmet, and the setting sun on my face fill me with joy. I've missed riding, even though it hasn't been that long. I'm different now. Having looked down the barrel of a gun while a bullet exited it and entered my body gave me a new appreciation for the little pleasures in my life. Riding will always be important to me.

When I pull into the park past the Barracuda Beach sign, I check the map. The arrow points right, for the tiki bench. I follow the winding road and enjoy the overhanging trees above. When I reach the end of the road it has a few parking spaces in the cul-de-sac. I park and take off my helmet, then walk to the bench near the water. The supports of the bench are carved into totem poles and there are tiki torches on either side of the bench. They aren't lit, though the sun hangs low on the horizon. I look out across the water and observe some islands with mangrove trees and white sandy beaches. A sailboat moves through the waves and pelicans fly ahead of it. Probably headed to their roosts for the coming nightfall.

Pulling my gaze from the perfect scenery, I look over the bench. I take a seat and decide I don't want to put my hands under there without looking, who knows what could be stuck there. I lie down and lean my head over the seat so I can see what's beneath the bench. I kind of expect something to be taped there. But written in block letters, it says:

Violets are blue and roses are red, the treasure you seek is under your bed.

For some reason this makes me laugh hysterically. I lie on the bench and laugh and laugh until my eyes water. A guy fishing a little way down the sea wall looks at me like I've lost my mind, and maybe I have. I'm delirious. Deliriously happy, I love them so much. I can just picture them here together, one writing this under the bench and the other watching his back. I stay and enjoy the sunset. It's the perfect birthday. The only way it could be better is if mom and dad were here.

The guys followed me to the cemetery earlier. I wanted them to meet my parents, as odd as that sounds, but it felt right. I get off the bench and head home. When I get there, I'm supposed to text them so they can join me. I think they planned it so I'd have time to look under the bed. I smiled the whole way back.

I get down onto my hands and knees, careful not to hurt the side with my bullet wound. It's still crazy to think I was shot. I lean down and put my face on the rug. I can't see anything it's too dark under the bed. I sit up and turn on the flashlight app on my phone. Sawyer comes in to investigate. He rubs against me, though he probably thinks it's weird that I'm on the floor. I take a minute to scratch his butt and cheeks. Then I lean down again and search under the bed. I forgot I stuffed a few boxes under here.

I keep my winter sweaters under the bed. I don't have too many occasions to wear them, but even in Florida the stores sell beautiful winter clothes every year. We can't resist, despite how we end up stripped down to our tank tops by lunch. I pull out a box and then another one when I don't see anything. Once the boxes are gone it's empty under there except for a bit of dust. I need to vacuum better next time.

I open the first box and find my sweaters neatly folded and undisturbed. The next box looks like someone rifled through it. Excitement coils in my chest as I look through the garments. Inside the only blue sweater I own is a small, gift-wrapped box.

"Look Sawyer, I found it! I win!" I hold up the box for him so he can celebrate with me, but he doesn't care and jumps onto my bed. I refolded my sweaters, all of them, because I need them to be folded correctly. I twist the wrapped box and shake it gently, but the sound doesn't reveal the contents. I have no idea what it could be.

I place it on my nightstand and text the guys. Then I take a quick shower before they get here. I clean my wound the way Uncle Randy showed me and pat it dry like he explained. I'm on antibiotics for about ten more days, and if I don't move wrong, I actually feel pretty normal. I dress in a tank and boy short panties, ready for bed. I'm hoping I can entice them into something even if we don't have sex, just some fooling around and orgasms would be awesome.

I pick up the wrapped box again and turn it over in my hands, it has a heft to it, but the contents aren't moving around. I want to open it, but I want to wait for them. I'm not sure why, maybe so they can celebrate my win with me. When I hear the door open, I lie down in what I hope is a seductive pose, on my unwounded side, my ass aimed at the door.

I call out to them, "I'm in the bedroom!"

Chapter Thirty-Five

"So, you are...my lovely Rose." I freeze, and my skin crawls.

I turn slowly towards the door. Standing there, free and healthy, is none other than Dimitri. The Russian's helper who was nice to me in Voldemort's lair.

I think hard about where all of my blades are at this moment. Unfortunately, not even *David Bowie* is here. I cleaned them all, sharpened them, and stored them in a new custom cabinet made especially for my precious blades, downstairs, in my new weapons room. It has a biometric lock, steel reinforced door, and the custom cabinet has a combination lock of its own. I really wish I was at least dressed and wearing shoes.

"Dimitri. How did you get in here?"

"The door was unlocked. I just walked in." He's partially right. The warehouse outside door was definitely locked, it locks automatically. But I did leave the door to the apartment unlocked for my guys. They have keys but I often leave the door unlocked for them.

"What do you want?" I try engaging him.

"Well, *Violet*, we didn't get enough of a chance to chat when we met. I didn't even get to introduce myself properly. I'm Dimitri Grigorovich and I am in charge of our family business. Perhaps you were confused because my brother enjoyed yelling and bossing everyone around. I'm much more laid back, as you Americans like to say." His English flows well and it's clear he was playing me at Voldemort's lair.

I sit up and pull my legs beneath me. I'm going to need to move fast if an opportunity arises. I'm so glad I loaded up on pain relievers in anticipation of fooling around with my guys. They should be here soon. I hope Dimitri came alone.

"I see. So now you're here for revenge?"

"Not exactly. My brother was a huge pain in my ass, I couldn't get rid of him because he was family. But you, my lovely flower, did it for me. I would like to thank you for that, however, you also put a huge dent in my business. You killed some of my best customers, arrested my men, took my product, and even sent me to jail."

"Why aren't you still there?"

"That's the thing about you Americans with all your rights and sympathy for everyone. Anyone who can afford a good lawyer can be out in no time at all. The ink was barely dry on my fingerprints before I was free. It took me a little while to track you down but imagine my surprise to find you are so young and living alone. With only your boyfriends and your uncle in your life, right?" Good, he doesn't seem to know about Colby. I need to get Dimitri away from the door so I can get out. Thankfully Sawyer took off, he doesn't like strangers.

"Yeah, the courts let out all the worst people and lock up the mentally ill and addicts for years. If you're not here for revenge, why exactly are you here?"

"I lost a lot that night...I think you owe me. Since you don't have enough money to pay me all that you cost me, I'm going to let you work it off in trade. I like you better with your real hair by the way. I want you to be my companion until I tire of you, then you'll work with the rest of the girls until you've repaid your debt. Lucky for you, I don't see the value in an eye for an eye revenge."

"When you say companion, what exactly do you mean?"

"I mean you're going to suck my cock and fuck me whenever I say, without complaints. When I grow tired of you, and I will, you'll go to work with the rest of the whores until you've repaid your debt. I'm going to use you up and take your youth, just like you took my customers, my men, and my merchandise. You're going to pay with your pussy until it's so worn out nobody wants it anymore. Now let's work on your first payment. Come here and get on your knees for me."

"Dude, I don't know how you found out my name or where I live, but you definitely didn't find out who I am. I don't get on my knees for anyone."

"This is going to be fun. I had hoped to play with you the other night, but you drugged me. It won't happen again." He takes a step into my room. Logic would dictate I should put my bed between us, but I want to get out of this room. I stand on the side of my bed closest to the door. He steps closer. I step away from the bed to my right, not any closer to him. I inventory the contents of my dresser and the nightstand in my head and I can't think of anything that would work as a weapon. The only thing is the gift-wrapped box I just found. It'll have to do; I hope it's not breakable. I reach behind me and close my fingers around it.

He takes another step closer, "If you're trying to get your phone to call for help, there's no point. I'll get it away from you before you can dial. Why not make it easy on yourself, just get on your knees. Come on, you might enjoy it." He tilts his head and bites his lip, like I'm going to find him attractive while he assaults me.

"I can promise neither of us would enjoy any such thing. I think you need to leave." I fist the package. He comes for me, and I chuck it as hard as I can at his face, hoping I hit an eye. I don't wait around to find out. When he bends forward grabbing his face and yelling, I take off and push past him. Unfortunately, it makes him really mad which appears to override his pain because he comes after me much quicker than I hoped. Opening the front door slows me just enough that if I had long hair, he would be able to grab it. Thankfully I don't.

When I get through the door and make it to the landing, he's almost on me, and there's no way I can make it down the stairs without him catching me. With not enough time to think, I leap for the beam above me. I extend my fingers as far as I can and ignore the pulling pain in my side. My fingers catch the edge, and I hold on to it with all I've got. My life depends on it. Swinging my legs, I'm able to grasp the beam with my feet. I pull myself up and I don't slow for a minute, I move along the beam and when I get to a vertical support I climb around it. The movement uses my abdominal muscles, and it hurts like a bitch. I'm panting hard from the pain, but I still don't slow down.

KABOOM! A shot rings out and I swear it ricochets off of the vertical support I just climbed over. It must have missed me by inches.

"Come on Violet, please don't make me kill you. I really think we could have fun together. Look, I'll make a deal with you, if you come down right now, I won't make you suck my dick."

"Seriously?"

"Sure. Seriously, you never have to suck my dick. Now come down, please." I keep moving along the beam, slower now, but still as quickly as I can. I have a goal. If I can get to the cross beam, I can make my way into the hallway where my weapons are, or possibly out the door that goes out to the main street.

"Why should I trust you? How do I know you're not lying?" I call out as I continue on my way.

"Why would I lie?"

"Why wouldn't you lie? If I climb down, you'll have me at gunpoint and you'll be able to make me do anything you want. As long as you have a gun and I have nothing, it's not safe for me."

"What do you propose we do then?"

"Why don't you unload the gun, discharge all the rounds and toss it on top of that roof section? It'll be out of both of our reach, then I'll come down."

"Okay."

I turn so suddenly I almost fall, "What?"

"I said, okay." He begins unloading the gun by removing the clip. He tosses it on the ground, then he racks the slide, ejecting the chambered round, he racks it a few more times clearing any rounds remaining. When the firearm is empty, he tosses it on top of the roof of my storage rooms across from my BASIL.

Well shit, I didn't expect him to actually do it. He must have another weapon. I move to the next support beam, carefully climbing around it, then I'm within reach of the cross beam. I stay there and hold onto the support.

"I'm waiting... I did what you asked."

"I know, but how can I trust you? How do I know you don't have another weapon?"

"What can I do to prove it?"

"Take off your jacket. Lift your shirt so I can see your waist and turn around so I can see your entire waistband." He removes his jacket and lifts his shirt, twirls around in a circle and shows me there's no weapon there. He watches me and when I don't move, he lifts his hands in a big shrug.

"Well?"

"Lift each pant leg and show me there's nothing there either."

"You know Violet, I seem to be doing everything you ask, and you haven't done anything but try to blind me. How about you climb part of the way down, and then I'll show you my ankles?"

"All right. I'll climb over to where I can get down." I make my way onto the cross beam and then traverse it towards the roof of the storage rooms. It's where he threw the gun, but I don't have any ammo so he shouldn't complain.

He lifts his right pant leg and shows me the ankle, "You get the other one after you climb down to the roof."

I get an idea, "Okay, I'll climb to the roof and then you show me the other ankle, right?"

"Absolutely."

Following along the beam I wait until I'm over my weapons room. Then I sit on the thick steel and think about the steps to do what I'm planning. I look at him and he's standing completely relaxed watching me. I twist on the metal, and keeping him in my sight, I lean down carefully not pressing on my wound, then I use my arms to swing back and hang there for just a second before I let go and land on the reinforced roofing of my weapons room. I ignore the pang in my middle on impact.

He bends down to lift his other pant leg. I take advantage of his lack of focus on me and hop down into the hallway. I stick my hand on the biometric lock for the door and the instant it opens, I dodge inside and slam it closed behind me almost catching his hand. He pulls it out of the way just in time. Then he bangs on the door relentlessly. I inhale a few deep breaths to take the edge off my pain.

Moving to my locked cabinet I twist the combination until the lock opens. My beautiful blades are resting in their velvet beds, I hate to disturb them. Being in my panties and tank leaves me with no pockets, I can't attach a holster to my underwear. I decide to strap *David Bowie* to my thigh and hang my sword on my back.

"Violet! I know you can hear me, come on pretty girl, you can't stay in there forever. You saw I don't have any other weapons with your own eyes. Please come out. I'll wait over where I was before, okay?"

"Okay. Just give me a minute, please."

"All right. I'll wait here until you're ready, then I'll move. Why did you run in there? There's no way out, right?"

"Right." I close my weapons cabinet. The last thing I need is for him to get a hold of my weapons. I'm hungry and tired. The antibiotics are pretty strong, and they make me a little fuzzy sometimes. I'm probably really lucky I didn't fall. It makes more sense for me to wait for the guys and hope he really doesn't have another gun. I want to stab him though. I'm so frustrated that he was in charge and I assumed it was his brother. I had him at my mercy and I didn't know he needed to stay there. From now on, *nobody* lives. I'm not doing this again. I sit on the floor and lean against my fancy cabinet.

"Dimitri?"

"Yes, Violet."

"How did you find me?"

"That asshole bishop likes to brag; he told me about his favorite of all time. Told me your name and told me everything about you. I did a little research and found an article about your parents death. I visited your grandmother and charmed her into divulging some information. She doesn't like you. From there it was easy to search the real estate records to find your address. I wasn't sure it was you, at first, the same girl the bishop bragged about. He showed me your film debut and when I watched you yesterday, I could tell by your mannerisms it was you. I staked out your place and waited for you to come home alone."

"Do you have any more brothers? Or sisters?" I ask him.

"Nope, Misha was the only one."

"You said I did you a favor by getting rid of him, why can't we leave it at that, call it even?"

"Interesting. You definitely did me a huge favor getting rid of him. How about a deal, because you disrupted my business by a very large amount as well. What if I agree to keep you as only mine? If I get tired of you, I'll let you go. That's fair, yes?"

"Still doesn't sound right to me. I don't want to belong to any-one. I need to be free."

"You must pay your debt. Do you like to kill?"

"Depends on the circumstances. For me it's usually something I have to do for a reason, in self-defense, or to save someone else. I don't just go out and kill for fun. But when it's the right person for the right reasons, I enjoy it. Why?"

"Perhaps you would like to kill for your debt instead? You would have to kill who I say, with no questions. Would you, do it?"

"I don't know. I wouldn't be willing to kill an innocent person or a child, ever. I think we wouldn't agree very much."

"You're honest, I like that."

"Most of the time."

"If you come out, can I trust you not to hurt me?" he asks.

"No. I can't make that kind of agreement. Not when I don't know what you're going to do to me."

"Oh shit! Hey!" I hear a scuffle outside the door. Scraping sounds and as if someone got the wind knocked out of them.

"Baby? Are you in there?"

I stand and rush to the door. "Austin?"

"Yeah, babe, you can come out. We've got him at gunpoint and cuffed." I press my hand to the mechanism, it turns green, and the door opens. I rush into Austin's arms, he's closest.

"I'm so happy to see you!" He holds me at arms-length and looks me over.

"Are you hurt?"

"No more than I was before he showed up. I might be sore tomorrow, but I don't have any new injuries." He pulls me into his chest and hugs me close kissing my head and face. Then he hands me to Jackson and uses his gun to point at the prisoner. Jackson lifts me into his arms, and I wrap myself around him and plant kisses all over his face.

"I'm so happy to see you, too. Thank you for saving me."

"Don't think we don't know you probably would've had him strapped to your table if we gave you another half an hour," he chuckles.

"I was working on a plan. It turns out he's actually the mastermind of the Russian trafficking ring."

"We know. The FBI guy contacted Colby and told him who he was, and that he was already out on bond. Colby panicked for your safety when he couldn't reach you, so he called us. We were wasting time at your parent's and then we went to Austin's. When Colby called, we hauled ass over here and we heard a gunshot. We had to try to figure out where the asshole was and if he had you, if he was holding his gun on you, or if he shot you. Thankfully Colby was able to see you when you got into the weapons room. He told us you were safe in here and the asshole was outside the door. How did you disarm him?"

"With my brain." They both laugh and shake their heads. Austin pulls me back in for some kisses.

"Baby, you're amazing. You've got to be tired, how about I take you upstairs and then Jackson and I can take care of this asshole?"

"I am tired, and I'm hungry. Did you bring food?"

"Sorry, we didn't have a chance to stop. What would you like?"

His phone chimes, he looks at it and laughs. "Of course. Thank you, Colby. He says he already ordered pizza and it'll be here in five minutes."

Speaking to the camera I add, "Thanks RobN! You're the best."

"You better call Dozer for us." Austin's phone chimes again.

"He says he already called Dozer and he's on his way. Dozer asks that we try to find the asshole's vehicle and leave him the keys. Jax and I will do that."

"Thanks for everything, Colby," I tell the camera again.

"Come on, let's get you upstairs before the pizza comes." I hug Jackson's waist and kiss his cheek. Then Austin and I make our way upstairs. Sawyer comes running the minute we walk through the door. He meows and rubs against me.

"Come on baby boy, I'll share." Austin seats me at the table and brings me a glass of ice water and two Tylenol. He gets my phone from the bedroom and places it in front of me. Glancing at the screen I see missed calls from both guys, Colby, and Uncle Randy.

"Did someone tell Uncle Randy I'm safe?"

"Yeah, Jackson talked to him when Colby told us you were safe. Then Colby agreed to keep him updated from then on."

The doorbell buzzes and Austin returns with two pizzas. He places a slice on a plate and tells me to eat. Then he takes off to help Jackson. I eat two slices, clean up, then brush my teeth. I have to look for a few minutes before I find my wrapped box that I threw at Dimitri. It's a little crumpled and the paper is torn on the corner, but otherwise it seems fine. I decided to wait for the guys to open it. Exhausted, I lie down to rest my eyes.

Chapter Thirty-Six

My neck is too hot, and I slowly become aware of a fuzzy beast curled there. Assessing my surroundings the familiar sheets and sounds comfort me, while my side pinches when I shift slightly.

"I love you buddy, but I need you off my neck, please." As expected, he doesn't move, so I gently scoot him onto my pillow.

Lifting my head I look around and notice the sheets are rumpled like two extra-large bodies had been lying on either side of me at some point, though they're not here now. Checking my phone, I'm surprised to find it's after nine and my winning wrapped box is not where I left it.

"Hmmm, I wonder what they're up to if you're hanging out in here instead of following them around. What's going on out there?" Sawyer tilts his head and squints his eyes at me before twisting his body around and going back to sleep with his head upside down and his belly exposed.

"You're no help. *Hrmfp!*" Exasperated with the lack of explanation from my fluffy housemate, I flip my sheets off and force my stiff body out of bed. I make my way silently down the hall, when I'm close to the kitchen I hear masculine whispers.

"We need to wake her up! She's going to be mad if we let her sleep all day."

"No. She needs to rest so she can heal. Don't you want her to get better?"

"Fuck you! Of course, I do I just think she's going to be pissed if we let her sleep too long."

"Let her be pissed, she needs to rest."

"When did you get a medical degree?"

"You're a dick. How long before we need to wrap up the food?"

"I don't know. We can put it away now; we'll heat it up when she wakes up."

"No! I'm starved, I wanna eat now." Two handsome faces turn towards me in unison.

"Good morning, gorgeous. How're you feeling?" I stop in my tracks, taped on the wall behind the table is a *Congratulations* sign.

"What's that about?" I question pointing to the banner as my eyes shift between them.

"You won! Congratulations!" Austin jumps up and hugs me.

"Yeah, congratulations, babe." Jackson kisses my lips and pulls me in for a hug. Then I noticed the wrapped box on the table.

"But I didn't open the box yet."

"Well open it then," Austin cajoles.

My hand trembles as I tear at the paper, and they're frozen in anticipation. I nervously glance at them and a shaky breath escapes me. I lift the lid of the plain black box; black tissue paper is neatly folded inside. When I move the paper out of the way, the most gorgeous purple and black folding hunting knife is tucked inside. My mouth opens in surprise, and the handle is so smooth and so shiny, I can see myself in it. I click open the blade and engraved along the spine it says: *You're always a winner in love!*

"We didn't know if you'd win. I mean we thought you would, but we wanted a message that would work either way." Austin gives me his goofy grin and I turn into a puddle.

"You're the sweetest. Thank you, it's just beautiful! I love it, and I love you both so much." I kiss Austin.

"I love to too, baby." Then I turn towards Jackson and kiss him.

"I love you so much, babe." He pulls me onto his lap, and Austin hops up, and takes my plate to the kitchen. He microwaves it for just a few seconds. They sit with me and tell me about how they decided on everything for the game, and my imagination was pretty close to how they handled the tiki bench. When I'm finished, my plate is still half full, and I realize my eyes were bigger than my stomach. The guys quickly clear everything away.

Jackson carries me to my bed and Austin brings me a glass of water and my meds. They undress me, carefully removing my bandage and Austin takes me to the shower, then he removes his clothes and joins me. Jackson isn't far behind.

"Are you going to let me touch you?" I ask them both. Jackson nods, his teeth catch his lip as he looks at my body. His eyes stutter on my breasts and heat bursts in my chest and spreads to my cheeks.

"Your uncle had a chat with us last night. He said as long as you're up for it, and we're gentle, he's calling you cleared for intimate relations. Apparently, someone told him we were waiting until your birthday." Austin smiles even though he's trying to act accusatory.

"My uncle and I don't generally keep secrets. It was hard not telling him about my hunting habits. But sex and love, I'm pretty open with him. Remember, he started as my psychiatrist."

"We know. He had a fairly long chat with us. Isabel had her bath, brushed her teeth, and had her bedtime stories, all while we were chatting. He's a good guy and he loves you very much, definitely like a father."

"Like a father plus," Austin adds.

"He gave us some tips on what to do if you have any trouble with intimacy, which was awkward as hell, but much appreciated. He wants you to be happy and threatened our lives if we ever hurt you."

"Yeah, we told him you'd probably kill us yourself if that happened," Austin laughs.

"He didn't exactly like that joke," he admonishes Austin. "But he does want to know more about your hunting. We told him he should speak with you about it, and he agreed. So, he's going to ask, babe."

"He asked about our involvement, and we told him about Megan. He understood. We really like him and Stephanie by the way."

"I do too. She's great, I love seeing her with Isabel. They're going to be wonderful parents for her."

"They are, and for you too. I know Stephanie is fairly new, but I think she loves you already. It's hard not to love you. Jax and I have talked about it a lot, and he's pretty sure he fell in love with you the minute you turned him down. I fell in love with you when you grilled me." There's that sweet goofy grin again.

"Rinse. Anyway, if you're up for it, we're ready to fuck you silly."

"Dude! I thought you were going to be romantic, what the fuck was that?"

I can't help giggling at them, they're perfect. I trace their incredible physiques with my hungry eyes. Their handsome faces stir the emotions in my heart the same way their hot bodies stir arousal in my loins. Holy fuck are they gorgeous and they love me. My heart is pounding like crazy; my nipples are hard as diamonds and my pussy is throbbing with need.

"I'm in. Kiss me, Jackson."

He leans in without hesitation and places a soft kiss on my lips. My hands trace his hard pecs and nipples, while Austin plays with my hair. It sends a shiver through me, and my body is on fire. Jackson kisses along my cheek and his fingers find my pink nipples. He plucks at them like an instrument. His hot breath grazes my neck, and his lips find my ear. If I wasn't in the shower, I'm certain the liquid leaking from me would be obviously dripping down my thighs.

Austin carefully avoids my injured side, slides his hands over my hips, then squeezes my ass and brings his fingers between my legs. His lips press kisses along my shoulder. He moves his hand to the front and rubs my clit gently. I push against his hand, desperate for more. They rinse off and make sure I'm soap free. Austin pulls me against him as we step out of the shower. Jackson pats my wound dry, applies ointment, and a fresh bandage. I can leave the front uncovered, but they prefer it if everything is protected from germs. Since we're planning to rub against one another, I'm okay with it.

"I want to carry you to bed, babe."

"I want to carry her."

"I want to fuck you guys before my next birthday... I'm walking. Close your mouths and follow me." I press their chins up and step around Jackson and away from Austin. They follow me like adorable puppy dogs.

We make our way to the bedroom, and once there I climb into the middle of my bed and pat the sheets on either side of me. I'm oddly not nervous at all. I'm proud of myself. I know it's because of them, and they make me feel safe and loved. Jackson sits next to me, kisses my shoulder, and the electricity of his kiss travels across my chest and into my already hardened nipples. They tingle like a vibration.

Austin joins me on my other side. His hand squeezes above my knee sending electric shocks right to my clit. It pulses and my pussy clenches with a pleasant throb. My body is lighting up like

New York City on New Year's Eve. It's a wonderland of pleasurable sensations. I want them so much. I don't waste any time. I grab their manhood, one in each hand. Their cocks twitch in my grasp and they both make needy sounds, almost like a growl, it's so sexy. I have no idea how to orchestrate a threesome logistically. I'm not sure where to situate myself, and I make a needy and frustrated sound of my own.

"What do you need baby? Show me where you want me."

"Mmmm... I want you both, everywhere. You make me feel so good, and I want to lick you. I want you to lick me. I'm not sure how to make it work, so you're going to have to guide me. All things considered, this is my first time."

"Come here, beautiful," Jackson pulls me onto his lap and shoves his tongue into my mouth while I straddle him grinding on him with purpose. He rubs his hard cock along my wet pussy setting off fireworks in my clit.

"Oh! Yes!" I detonated almost instantly, and I want more. He pulls his lips from mine. His smile is sexy and primal.

"Turn around, gorgeous. There you go, now you're in charge of what happens and how quickly. You lift up when you're ready and I'll help you. You choose when I enter you. You're stunning when you come, and Auz needs to see it too."

I'm facing Austin now, and he's on his knees between Jackson's. I'm straddling Jackson and writhing on him when Austin squeezes my breasts in his firm grip. He presses his tongue into my mouth, and I hold his shoulders. My hand reaches out and grasps his rock-hard dick, I squeeze his length and stroke him. He moans into my mouth, and I return it as Jackson's head rubs my clit.

Needing to be filled, I shift my hips lining up the head of Jackson's perfect cock with my opening and I press against him. He groans behind me and squeezes my ass pressing his genitals upwards into mine. Austin kisses me harder, and I stroke him faster. He shifts his hands to my hips while carefully avoiding my healing wound. He helps me move my hips until Jackson is able to lift his cock at the perfect angle to impale me. I press against him until the head of his cock enters me. My clit sings with joy and my pussy gushes arousal making it easier for him to be enveloped by my vibrating walls.

"Oh! Oh my God! Yes! Please, Jackson, fuck me!" He thrusts upward as I press down. It's a tight fit and it takes some maneuvering until he's able to fill me to the hilt. I hold still with him as my body adjusts to the pleasure invasion. When I can't wait any longer, I begin to move up and down.

"Holy fuck, babe, you're perfection," Jackson growls out.

"Austin, I want you in my mouth, please."

"Okay, baby, let's move positions." He and Jackson help me move forward onto my knees and Jackson gets on his knees behind me. Austin is on his knees in front of me. I reach out for him with my tongue licking the clear fluid from his tip. Jackson thrusts into me from behind and he hits a whole new set of nerve endings.

"Holy shit! This feels amazing!" I exclaim before wrapping my lips around Austin's beautiful cock. He holds my head where he wants me, and I press his dick further into the back of my throat. His manhood fills my mouth, and his head falls back as he groans in pleasure.

I feel my body building to a climax and I move faster and with purpose. I suck harder and try my best to swallow him whole. Jackson hits exactly the perfect spot inside me and another orgasm shoots off like a rocket. I scream with my mouth full and my entire body shudders and goosebumps break out along my skin. My breasts slap my body hard as I fuck them as fast and hard as I can.

As my body begins to come down, Jackson taps my ass. "Babe, we're going to switch. You stay there."

"Mmmhmm..." Austin slips from my lips as Jackson does the same. They swap positions and Jackson is in front of me. Austin rubs my ass, and it makes the remnants of my orgasm tingle and my pussy clenches. He touches my clit and I almost shoot off the bed.

"Is your side, okay?" he asks.

"Yes, but my clit isn't. Fuck me, Austin."

"Babe, kiss me." I don't hesitate to shove my tongue into Jackson's mouth. Austin presses his hardness into my aching pussy and my insides light up again. Holy hell, these men are amazing. I'm never going to stop fucking them. I hope they're up for endless sex with me.

I reach out and grasp Jackson's cock, and it's wet from being inside me. For some reason that turns me on even more. I can't believe all that wetness came from me. When he fumbles our kiss, I press one last kiss on his lips and devour his cock. It tastes like me and I'm okay with it. I suck and lick him. Swirling my tongue around him, he thrusts in and out of my mouth.

Austin fucks me hard, and holding onto my hip bones, he avoids my waist. His thrusts are wild, and he hits all the right places. His balls smack against my clit and at just the right angle. He's moving faster and erratic, my pussy is clenching him tighter, and another climax is building. He suddenly begins fucking me like his life depends on it. My orgasm rushes in and takes over my own movements. I'm almost deep throating Jackson with how hard I'm trying to swallow him, he's thrusting into the back of my throat and I'm in heaven.

"Holy fuck, yes! Baby, yes!" Austin buries himself inside me and I can feel his cum hitting my walls. My orgasm doubles down and my vision sparks with explosions of colorful fireworks. A moment later Jackson thrusts all the way into my mouth, and I swallow and suck as hard as I can.

"Oooh... my fucking God! Yes! Babe, fuck!" His cum shoots into the back of my throat and beyond. I swallow every drop. We all make a few last thrusting movements, which sends fresh electricity shooting across my spent nerve endings. I fall onto my belly and Jackson falls next to me. Austin moves from behind me and falls on my other side. We're all panting and sweating. I start to giggle, and I can't stop. They laugh at me, then I laugh at them. We lie there laughing until we need to catch our breath.

"Oh my God! That was incredible, thank you!"

"You don't need to thank us babe, if we need to thank each other, you're going to end up running out of room in your house."

"What? Why?"

"My go to *thank you* is a flower arrangement. If I need to thank you for incredible sex, you're due like fifty bouquets just for tonight."

He makes me laugh again. "Okay, definitely no need for flowers. But I might still offer a verbal thank you once in a while. Thank you for making my first time amazing. I love you, both."

Austin speaks up, "Thank you for letting us be your firsts. I love you so much and I'm really happy with you." He looks a little embarrassed, I'm not sure why.

"What's wrong?"

He pulls up onto his elbow and looks down at me, "Absolutely nothing. I just, I love you so much. It's really hard for me to explain how much you mean to me. I never want to be away from you, I think about you every minute we're apart. You're my first thought when I wake up and my last thought when I go to bed. Being with you makes me happy. You're an amazing woman. Thank you for letting me stick around." He leans over and kisses me.

"That was really sweet, I think you expressed yourself pretty well. I love you too. I have something I want to ask you both." I look at Jackson and he lifts up onto his elbow too.

He brushes my hair from my eyes, "What is it babe?" I look between them, a little nervous now that I have their intense attention.

"I want you to move in with me." My eyes flit rapidly between them. They look at each other and do their silent communication thing. I'm so nervous I'm afraid that means they're going to say no.

Jackson is elected spokesperson, "We'd love to. But Austin has a house. Maybe we should move there?"

"I love your house. Maybe we can keep the warehouse as a gym and murdering space?"

"Does that mean you're moving in with me?" Austin asks excitedly.

"Is that okay? Sawyer has to come too."

"I love Sawyer. Of course it's okay!" He wraps his arms around me in a happy hug.

"You know I'm coming too, right?" Jackson asks.

"I'll make do. Yeah, dumbass, of course you're coming too." I kiss Jackson too. I'm so excited and happy, I can't wait.

"How soon can you pack?"

"I can be ready tomorrow, my stuff may take a little longer, but no rush to get everything there if we're keeping this place for work."

"True. Randy and Stephanie want us to come over for dinner. Maybe we can stay at the house tonight? Bring Sawyer and your clothes tomorrow?"

"Sounds perfect."

CHAPTER THIRTY-SEVEN

"Congratulations on moving in together. Once you're settled, we'll have to do a housewarming party for you."

"We don't need a party. You don't have to fish for an invitation, Uncle Randy. You're welcome to come over and check it out."

"Thanks. We have some news too. You want to tell them Steph?" She holds out her hand and the lights sparkle and reflect off the huge diamond on her new engagement ring. I gasp.

"Oh my God! Congratulations!" I hug Stephanie and my eyes water. I'm so happy for them.

Isabel wants a hug too since they're going to be her parents, "Violet, you're going to be my sister for real!"

"You better believe it, kiddo." When the guys are finished shaking hands with Uncle Randy, I rush to him and throw my arms around him.

"I'm SO happy for you! Congratulations! You made a fantastic choice."

He drags me from the room, "I'm sorry I didn't talk to you first. I got the ring right before you got shot and I didn't want to bring it up while you were dealing with all that. Then this morning we were talking about Isabel and our adoption, and she was worried about it not going through because we aren't married. So, I asked her. Are you upset?"

"No! I love her, I think it's wonderful. Isabel is a lucky little girl; you're going to be wonderful parents. You've been a great dad to me."

His eyes tear up, "I love you so much Violet. Please be careful. I wouldn't be able to live with myself if anything happened to you."

"I love you too. I'm going to be very careful. I wouldn't ever want to hurt you or anyone in the other room. I love you all very much. But I need to do this... I need to stop the monsters."

"I know. All of the victims are lucky to have you and so are we." He squeezes me again, and we smile at each other.

"Thanks, let's get back in there." Stephanie looks upset when we return. Uncle Randy rushes to her, he takes her hand and searches her face. Austin is playing with Isabel, and he suggests they go get something to drink in the kitchen. He's so sweet and considerate.

"What's wrong sweetheart?" Uncle Randy asks.

"I just got an email. They're letting that piece of shit out of jail! Something about improper evidence collection during his trial, he won an appeal. They're going to have to start the whole trial over again and he's allowed out on bond until the trial is decided. It could be months, years, I don't even know. Since I'm a victim they're required to let me know. Thank God I don't live in Tacoma anymore, but some of his other victims might still live in the Seattle area. He's a monster Randy, how many people is he going to hurt while he's free?"

After a while, chatting with everyone, Stephanie eventually calms down. We spend time outside with Isabel, and with comments from the adorable girl, we're all soon laughing again. That little girl is going to be on stage when she gets older. She commands her audience like a pro.

We have a lovely dinner where we share stories of our pasts. Isabel shocks us when she tells us more about her mother. She's refused to speak about her at all no matter who asks. Even the therapist hit a brick wall. Krewe is working with an investigator to track down her family to sever their claims on Isabel. We're all hoping they'll just accept a payoff and sign the paperwork giving up their rights. If not, they may end up in jail if he sues them for abandonment and criminal neglect. I'm guessing they'll take the payoff.

When we're finishing dessert Stephanie asks, "Where did you all decide to go on your trip?"

Both of my boyfriends look at me. "Oh yeah, we forgot all about that. I won. I get to choose."

"Yeah, Violet won our game, so she gets to pick. We got excited about her win, and we forgot to ask her where she wanted to go. Well, what's it going to be babe?"

"Oh, um, I was thinking about visiting the Seattle area." Our silent communication tells them my plans and they both nod in agreement.

(Not) The End.

Afterword

Violet's story continues with Vile, subscribe to E.N. Chanting's newsletter for updates on the release:
https://www.enchantingauthor.com
If you enjoyed VioleNt, please leave a review! It's so important, especially for an indie author. Thank you!

Stories by E.N. Chanting

Forces of Nature Series:
Book One: Force of Corruption (November 2023)
Book Two: Force Majeure (Summer 2024)
Book Three: Force of Attraction (Spring 2025)

Southern Suns MC Series:
Book One: Ax (2025)
Book Two: Orlando (2025)

Violet's Tales- Duet and a half:
Book .5: Origin of Violet- Novella (October 2024)
Book One: VioleNt (October 2024)
Book Two: Vile (Spring 2025)

Standalones:
Haunted Hunting Camp-A Short Story: Horror (September 2023)
Deadly-Go-Round: Steampunk Urban Horror (Winter 2024-25)
The Devil's Affair-A Short Story: Dark Romance (June 2024)

Please sign up for my author newsletter to keep up with new release updates, cover reveals, and giveaways.

Subscribe here: https://www.enchantingauthor.com